PRAISE FOR

Jen Stephens

"A moving story of a couple in danger of losing their marriage. Jen Stephens has skillfully crafted a novel anyone who's been in love—or grown distant in love—can identify with. Her message of God's gift of forgiveness holds a strong place in the story line."

—Alice J. Wisler, author of *Rain Song*

"*Heart's Hostage* is a compelling and pleasant read. As an author of fiction, I recognize the importance of portraying solid relationships encompassed by the myriad of emotions and struggles resulting from the realities of life. Stephens does just that by taking an everyday struggle in all marriages and showcasing it in a way which leaves you both cheering for and jeering at Ian and Kate. The end leaves you fully satisfied at the resolution of a fight well fought and a battle won."

—Amber Stockton, award-winning author of *Brandywine Brides*

"What a beautiful story of the enduring power of love and grace—for Jane and Ian and for all of us. In this intricately woven tale, Jane and Ian discover that grace can prevail over human frailty when given the chance. I came away with a reminder that the important things in life should be protected and cherished, and that the power of love and mercy stretch beyond the reach of my shortcomings."

—Kinda Wilson, author of *The Echo Factor*

"Once again, the talented Jen Stephens pulls at the heartstrings of her readers, while telling a memorable story of redemption, love, and God's unique plan. The author's deep faith manifests in the book, making forgiveness a central theme that brings her characters together and encourages her readers. A beautiful story from a beautiful author!"

—Shayla Eaton, Curiouser Editing

THE
Heart's
Hostage

JEN STEPHENS

Elkhart, Indiana
46514 USA

MANUFACTURED IN THE UNITED STATES OF AMERICA

Dedication

This book is for my mom, Donna Otto, the one who saw me through the most beautiful times of my life, as well as my darkest days. I can't think of a time when you weren't there for me, encouraging and supporting me, always helping me, even if that meant just being near to hold my hand or wipe my tears. You taught me all of the important things in life like how to make a house a home, how to trust the Lord all the time but especially during a loss, and most of all how to love with all your heart. I'm so sorry I never truly appreciated you until the day I became a mother, but thank you for providing me with the best example of everything a mother should be. I pray my girls look at me with all the respect and admiration that I hold in my heart for you. I love you so much!

Ovarian Cancer National Alliance

I contribute a portion of the income from everything I write to Ovarian Cancer National Alliance in honor of my best friend, Patty Spears Smith (1975–2011). Every sale of this book helps toward finding a cure for ovarian cancer to save our mothers, grandmothers, sisters, daughters, and friends. For more information, go to my website at www.jenstephens.net, and let's work together to find a cure once and for all!

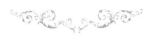

Also by Jen Stephens

THE HEART'S JOURNEY HOME
Book 1, The Harvest Bay Series

THE HEART'S LULLABY
Book 2, The Harvest Bay Series

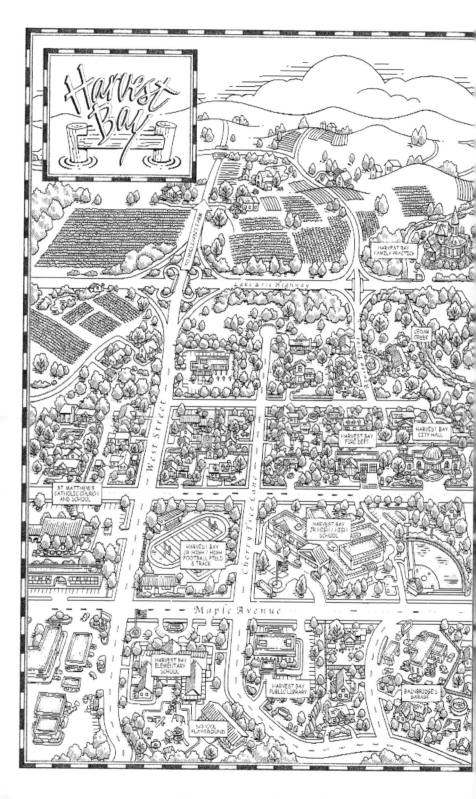

CHAPTER
One

Jane Garner collapsed into the office chair behind her paper-strewn desk in her cheerfully decorated classroom and exhaled heavily. Another school year had just begun, and the first week of kindergarten, which always proved to be quite an adventure, promised to be exceptionally so this year. Closing her eyes, she soaked in the quiet.

"I'm getting too old for this." Reluctant to move but knowing her desk needed attention, she picked up a piece of pink construction paper and looked at it through bleary eyes. A big red heart filled the page, with a blue, green, and purple rainbow stretching from one side to the other inside it. At the very bottom was printed: "From Destiny."

Jane smiled. It had taken the whole week for shy little Destiny Shoals to make even the slightest peep. When the little girl finally managed barely more than a whisper, she didn't make eye contact. But this love note meant Jane must be doing something right, and that made her exhausting week worth every second.

Fishing a thumb tack out of her desk drawer, she pushed to her tired feet and pinned the drawing on the bulletin board behind her desk where she was sure the little girl would see it on display. She vowed to spend time working to make the unsure child comfortable enough in herself and her surroundings to open up. For now, however, Jane was just thankful for the weekend and the reason she wouldn't have to cook supper tonight.

Her mouth watered as she thought of celebrating her anniversary at Bella Notte. She hadn't eaten at her favorite Italian restaurant since her thirty-eighth birthday several months earlier.

It had been a chore to persuade her husband. *Come on, Ian. After twenty years we deserve a night out. At the very least, a quiet meal at nice restaurant, just the two of us.*

Doesn't Bradley have a football game?

Some things truly never changed and rejection always stung, regardless of intention. *Yes, but kick-off isn't until seven o'clock. We can make reservations for five and still make it to the game in time.*

Let me check my work schedule. He'd ended the conversation with a peck on her cheek.

Making the reservations anyway, she found herself wondering now, days later, why he couldn't just say, "Sure, baby. Let's go." How she loathed playing second fiddle to work, to the kids. Sometimes it seemed like she came in second place to just about everything.

Swallowing the leftover bitterness, she picked up a picture book, crossed the colorful carpet to the large bookshelf that housed her classroom library, and stooped to slip the book back into its place.

It doesn't really matter now, anyway. What matters is the time we're going to spend together having dinner . . . maybe a glass of wine . . . maybe a little dancing . . . A smile crept further onto her face with each "maybe."

On a shelf out of reach of her students, sat a collection of picture frames. Reaching for the small wedding photo, she wiped the thin layer of dust off onto her slacks and stared at the young couple in the picture, just out of high school, sights set on their future.

"Now it seems like a lifetime ago."

As on every anniversary before, she recalled the events leading up to their wedding, from prom night going a little too far to the hint of the plus sign appearing on the test. They both knew her very traditional Irish father wouldn't have it any other way, so they had said they were crazy in love, didn't want to be apart a minute longer, and set the date for August twenty-second.

Halfway through July, she had miscarried.

"In some ways it was a lifetime ago." A flood of emotions swept over Jane, and the picture blurred behind unshed tears.

A few had suspected, but no one ever knew the truth. Eighteen-year-old Jane had bottled up her grief, and since they figured postponing the wedding would only make more waves, it went on as planned. She spent her "honeymoon" enrolling in college classes while Ian started working construction to pay for their tiny one-bedroom apartment and put food on the table. Her teaching career began four years later, and Bradley came shortly after that . . . followed a few years later by Emma, then Jessica, and finally Samuel.

It suddenly struck Jane that she'd spent over half her life fulfilling her role as Ian's wife. Shaking her head, she replaced the frame on the shelf. "But there's more to me than being Mrs. Ian Garner. I just need to remember what it is."

Her cell phone, still in silent mode, vibrated wildly on her desk like a wind-up toy, and she rushed to retrieve it. The caller I.D. displayed the words, "Ian Garner," accompanied by his snapshot.

Creases formed on her brow and a small trickle of dread seeped into her heart. Ian rarely called during the day. She was shocked on the few occasions he shot her a text. But today was different. Today was their anniversary. Of course, he'd call her.

"Hey, babe. How's my husband of twenty years doing today?"

"Good. Busy. Trying to get as much done on this project as we can before the front moves in over the weekend and brings three days' worth of rain with it."

"Well, I'm looking forward to our dinner date tonight. It's been a while since we've had time alone together and, after the week I've had, I can use some face time."

"Yeah, about that . . . "

"Oh, Ian." Jane's shoulders drooped under the weight of disappointment. "Please tell me you're not canceling."

"I'm not canceling, just postponing."

Jane didn't respond. The initial letdown quickly compacted into a fiery ball of anger and she knew that if she opened her mouth, it was hard telling what might come out.

"Look, I'll make it up to you, but we're heading into bad weather season and I have to take advantage of every single decent day."

Silence.

"I can't lose any more work. Things are already going to be tight for us this winter. What else do you want me to do?"

"It's our anniversary for goodness sake! I want you to take me out. Don't I deserve that after twenty years?"

"I don't want to argue. You knew when we started this business we'd have to make sacrifices periodically."

"Right."

A deep sigh filled her ear. "I've got to get back to work. Let's finish this discussion at home."

"There's nothing left to say."

Jane ended the call and sank to her chair. It hurt to leave the issue unresolved, but it didn't surprise her. This kind of thing had become the norm. With balancing their work schedules in addition to their four children's various after-school activities, they rarely finished a conversation, and somewhere along the way she'd grown calloused to the emptiness it left inside.

Jane snorted. "So much for not having to make supper."

If she was one hundred percent honest, she wasn't as disappointed about the dinner as she was about postponing the romance. It had already been a long time coming.

Tidying her desk, she gathered her things, while mentally running through quick and easy recipes. Finally, not exactly sure what her pantry was stocked with and not feeling the least bit motivated, she settled on take out from the Bayside Cafe. She slung her purse onto her shoulder and grabbed her keys.

"Burgers and fries it is."

"Sounds good to me."

She snapped her gaze toward the doorway, where Zach Andrews, the new sixth grade teacher stood. She forcefully returned her purse to her desktop with a hard thud and an exasperated breath.

"Please don't tell me you have a problem with my kid because I don't think I can take it right now."

Zach stepped into the classroom. "Actually, I just stopped by to tell you what a great student Jessica is—polite, respectful, hard working. Definitely a testament to good parenting."

"Finally, some decent news." Jane leaned heavily against her desk and crossed her arms. "Well, don't get your hopes up, okay? The school year has only just begun, and Jessica can be quite a handful."

"She takes after her mother then?"

Jane eyed him, unsure of his intentions.

His wholesome laugh filled the air. "Oh, come on, Jane Flanders. You really think I don't remember how spunky you were in high school?"

She arched her eyebrows at the sound of her maiden name, so foreign to her now, then scrunched them together as she searched her mental yearbook. "To be honest, Zach, I don't remember you."

"That's because I was only a freshman and had just moved to town the summer before your senior year."

Amidst the fog in her brain, Jane could barely make out the memory of a scrawny kid, nothing close to this well filled-out man in front of her. "Well, it's Jane Garner now. And that was a long time ago. I'm not the same girl I was back then."

"Sure you are. We grow up and our roles and situations change, but our spirit never really does."

Her gaze met his friendly smile. Somehow, his words, his kindness, his warmth, was just enough to lighten the stress of her hectic week and ease the disappointment of her broken dinner date.

"Right." Pushing away from the desk, she crossed the room. "Well, thanks for the good report, but don't hesitate to let me know if there's ever an issue."

Zach put a hand up in a parting wave. "Will do. Have a good weekend."

"Yeah." Fearing her flat tone revealed a hint of the loneliness she kept buried in the deepest pit of her soul, she put one foot in front of the other until she reached the parking lot and the safety of her Expedition.

Ian stared at his cell phone, Jane's words repeating in his mind like a scratched CD.

There's nothing left to say.

Twenty years ago, he would have shaken his head, maybe even grinned and chalked those words up to her fiery Irish attitude. Now, however, he understood that the real motive behind her response was avoidance.

"It's just like her to shut down when an issue comes up." He twisted his wedding band around his finger as anger started at his toes and slithered its way to his heart. "But, darn it, there are things left to say."

"Like what?"

The voice shook him out of his bitter trance, and his demeanor softened as he turned.. "Hey, sis. It's nothing. What are you doing here?"

Ava Garner, the town's tall and lanky head librarian, leaned against Ian's red F150, shoulder-to-shoulder with him, and pushed her glasses further up on the bridge of her nose. Reaching into her oversized purse, she retrieved a sealed envelope and held it out to him.

"It's your anniversary. Thought I'd save a stamp."

"Gee, thanks." He took the card and tossed it through the open truck window.

"Do I sense trouble in paradise, big brother?"

Wiping his glasses on his T-shirt, he cast his gaze past the roundness of his belly to the hard, dry dirt. He didn't need a mirror to recognize the effect of twenty years on his physique. The fast, fit star running back who swept his high school sweetheart off her feet on prom night had taken a hike. The dashing groom who carried his radiant bride over the threshold of their honeymoon suite twenty years ago was long gone. In his place stood a middle-aged husband and father of four who spent long hours working to keep his construction business afloat in a sinking economy.

He knew he let Jane down over and over by spending so little time at home, and he hated himself for it. But wouldn't he let his whole family down if he couldn't provide for them? He was there for the important things.

There's nothing left to talk about.

Well, most of the important things.

He sighed heavily and shoved his fingers through his thinning hair. "Oh, you know. After a while, things are bound to get a little stale. No big deal."

"No big deal, huh?"

Ian shrugged, crossed one ankle over the other, and stuffed his hands in his pockets, avoiding his sister's gaze.

"You know, there's a book in the library about love languages. Do you know Jane's love language?"

"Of course I do. You can't be married to someone for a fifth of a century and not know her."

"I didn't ask if you knew her. I asked if you knew her love language. What really makes Jane tick?"

Uncrossing his ankles, Ian folded his arms. "Look, sis, I don't mean anything bad by this, but you haven't been in a serious relationship since, what, your freshman year of college over fifteen years ago? I don't think you have any room to give me advice on my marriage."

Ava hung her head. "I was just trying to help. Jane can be stubborn, yes, but you can be down right pig-headed, you know that?" Pushing away from the truck, she stalked off.

He watched her go, guilt replacing the anger that coiled around his heart, squeezing just enough to make him uncomfortable. He reached through the window, picked up the envelope, slid his finger under the flap, and pulled out the card.

On the front, a man and woman danced under a big moon. "Two special people. One special marriage." Inside it read: "A whole lifetime of beautiful memories."

Ian placed the card and envelope back on the seat and returned to work, muttering under his breath, "It sure seems like a lifetime."

Jane sat at the dining room table swirling a spoon around a steaming cup of chamomile tea. The soft glow from a street light filled the large bay window, adding to the faint luminescence of a nightlight in the adjoining kitchen.

The three youngest children had just gone to bed, and Jane was sure Jessica and Samuel were already asleep. Emma was most likely winding down with a book in her bedroom, but she'd be asleep long before Bradley returned from celebrating Harvest Bay High's victory with his friends.

Thankful for the time alone, Jane wondered how she'd get past the hurt this time. How would she be able to face Ian when he got home without turning her disappointment into a big deal?

But it is a big deal. Twenty years of marriage deserves some recognition, and for once I want to be a priority.

Sighing, she set the spoon down and picked up the mug for a cautious sip, weighing whether or not it'd be easier to just not say anything and figure out a way to get over it the way she'd done so many times before rather than start a fight. Should she wave the white flag before the battle even began, pretend as if her self worth and value hadn't been shot down again? The problem was that surrender only ended the battle between them, while the silent war waged on in her heart and she slowly became a casualty.

"We grow up, and our roles and situations change, but our spirit never really does." Zach's words had echoed in her mind all evening.

"Our spirit might not change, but it can die, and mine is fading fast," she whispered.

The reality broke her heart, but what could she do about it? She had commitments, responsibilities, four young people who counted on her to be there every minute of every day. This was her life.

The hum of the garage door opening combined with popping gravel in the driveway outside interrupted her thoughts. It was too early to be Bradley, and besides, he never parked his old Taurus in the garage. Jane's chest tightened. If it were any other day of the year she'd race up the stairs, leap into bed, pull the covers up to her chin, and pretend she was asleep so she wouldn't have to deal with the issue at hand. Instead, she sat in the darkness, calmly sipping her tea with a stony expression while she mentally prepared for battle. No white flag this time.

The door creaked open, and Jane watched her husband's shadowy figure emerge from the adjacent laundry room. He took a step toward the stairs.

"You won't find me up there."

Her voice startled him. Bringing the mug to her lips, she concealed the small grin of satisfaction, but there was no mistaking the spark in her spirit.

"What are you doing sitting down here in the dark?"

"Just enjoying a cup of tea." She nodded toward a Styrofoam container across the table. "Your dinner's cold."

Drawing closer, he thrust a cellophane wrapped bouquet of flowers at her. "It was too much work for you to put it in the microwave?"

"Yeah." She snatched the flowers. "It was about as much work as it took you to stop after the football game for these." Squinting in the dim light, she peeled the price tag off the see-through wrapper, and held it up to him. "Five bucks at the Pit Stop Gas and Grocery? That's what our anniversary means to you?"

Ian heaved a sigh as he slumped into a chair next to her. "Is this about the fact that we didn't go out this evening? Look, I told you I'd make it up to you."

"Twenty years, Ian! And you put no thought into it at all." She stood so abruptly the chair clattered backward. "I deserve more than a five-dollar bouquet from the grocery store."

"At least it's something. What have you done? I haven't even seen a card yet."

"Oh, you mean besides making reservations and finding a sitter so we could have a quiet, intimate evening alone together? Something we haven't done in months? There's a bottle of wine in the fridge, candles in our bedroom, bubble bath next to the tub, and a new negligee hanging in my closet." She carried her tea cup to the kitchen sink, mumbling over her shoulder, "Maybe another time."

Ian stood. "Jane, what do you want from me? You know, I work hard for this family. I always have, and I'm happy to do it, but I'd like to be appreciated, too, instead of just hearing about where I fall short."

"I tell you I appreciate you, but you don't listen. And you don't seem to notice or care when I show you."

"That's exactly what I'm talking about! I can't do anything right around here, and I'm sick of it." Planting his hands on the table, he shook his head and dragged out a long breath. "I can't live like this anymore."

"I can't either." She crossed her arms in an attempt to ease the pain in her heart. "Something's got to change, but at this point I don't know where to even start."

They stood in silence, both unable to bridge the expanse between them.

Finally, Ian took a baby step, his voice low and weary. "I love you. Isn't that a start?"

Swallowing hard against a rising lump of emotion, Jane could only manage a whisper. "Yeah. It's a start."

CHAPTER
Two

*L*ike a giant arm, the morning sun reached through the sheer curtains and dragged Jane from the fog of slumber. Pulling the mauve and sage flowered quilt up to her chin, she willed herself to drift back off. Not that she needed any more than seven hours of sleep. She just wasn't ready quite yet to face another day of being everything to everybody.

She also half-expected her dreams to not make sense, but as she lay perfectly still in her cocoon, it didn't make sense that she no longer recognized herself. That bothered her. Everything she liked about herself had been slowly slipping away, while she morphed into someone she didn't know, someone she wasn't sure she even liked. She'd never been opposed to change, but it hurt to think that when she finally emerged she most definitely would not be a beautiful, vibrant butterfly.

More like the shell it leaves behind. She hugged her knees to her chest, an ineffective shield against the stabbing pain of the emptiness inside.

Cracking one eye open confirmed Jane's suspicion that she was alone. A part of her hoped she'd find Ian still there, especially after she gave in the night before. It was their anniversary, after all. She'd slipped into the pretty, soft, lavender nightie and performed her wifely duty to the best of her ability before they fell asleep on their separate sides of the king-sized bed. But it seemed no amount of satisfaction she gave him could ever compare to the satisfaction he received on the job site. And the part of her believing that breathed a sigh of relief that she didn't have to face him this morning.

Jane listened for signs that the kids were awake. Her teenagers, Bradley and Emma, didn't cause too much of a commotion anymore. Jessica and Samuel, however, were less trustworthy, and the silence meant that they were either still in bed or causing trouble.

Reluctantly she kicked out of her comfortable cocoon, stepped into her slippers, and reached for her terrycloth housecoat. She tied it tightly around her waist, ran her fingers through her short, wild, auburn hair and shuffled to the door.

She and Ian had designed this house together over a decade ago. They'd discussed features they liked and didn't particularly care for. One thing she had wanted was an open walkway upstairs, like a bridge, that looked down on the family room from either side and connected the kids' rooms at one end of the house to the master suite on the other side. Jane thought it would be a romantic and unique feature. Ian insisted that, with small children, an open hallway would be impractical and possibly dangerous. He'd made the choice to leave one side open but put up drywall opposite the staircase and build a bathroom between the two wings.

It was one of many compromises she'd accepted. Now, however, she wished she could cross her own imaginary bridge.

She came to Bradley and Samuel's door first, which stood wide open. Pausing in the doorway, she found the covers on Samuel's empty twin bed strewn about, while Bradley's strapping body spread out across his mattress with his pillow over his head.

Jane watched him for a minute, finding it hard to believe that not so long ago that young man had been her little boy.

One minute he's playing with Thomas the Tank engine and the next he's starting in high school football games. In two years he'll be graduating. She shook her head. *Where has the time gone?*

After one more long look, she pulled the door shut and moved on to Emma and Jessica's room. Peeking through the cracked door, she found Jessica curled up under her purple butterfly bedspread and softly snoring. Emma, propped up on her pillows in her canopy bed and buried in a book, glanced up.

"Morning, Mom."

Jane stepped into the room and whispered, "Good morning. Sleep well?"

Nodding, Emma marked her page and closed her book. "Did you?"

"Sure. Why do you ask?"

"I heard you and Dad fighting."

Jane's shoulders sagged. She worked so hard to hide the ugly truth from her kids. Crossing the room, she sat heavily on the corner of Emma's bed.

"I'm sorry you had to hear that. Your dad and I had a little misunderstanding, but everything's fine now so don't worry, okay?"

Emma eyed her mother uncertainly. "If you say so."

A knot formed in Jane's stomach. She'd have to work harder to dust the cobwebs of negativity from her home. And her heart.

"Do you want something for breakfast?"

Emma shook her head and returned to her book.

"Well, I'll be in my studio if you change your mind." Jane stood and kissed Emma on the forehead. "Do you know where Sam is?"

Not looking up from her book, Emma shrugged. "Probably outside where he always is."

Jane slipped out, pulling the door shut behind her, and descended to the kitchen. Before she reached it, the aroma of fresh-brewed coffee greeted her. She would've appreciated Ian's effort more if he hadn't poured half the pot into his thermos and left the rest for her as usual. Just once she'd like to have the first cup instead of the last. Sighing, she took her favorite mug from the cupboard and filled it three-quarters of the way full.

Hopefully, this pot hasn't been left on too long. My hair doesn't need any help standing on end.

She realized that she was being overly critical and border-line sarcastic. It was the only way she knew to combat those moments of disregard and the ugly emotions that came with it.

She took a cautious sip. *Pretty strong, but nothing a little flavored creamer and sweetener won't fix.* She doctored up the steaming liquid, and carried it out the sliding glass doors to the back patio.

"Sam!"

Her younger son raced around the corner of the house, his strawberry blond hair flapping in the breeze, a stick in one hand, a toy shield in the other. "Yeah, Mom?"

She took another sip of her coffee. "Just checking on you. Stay in our yard. I'll be in my studio if you need me." She turned, and then paused. "Oh, and don't run with sticks."

Listening about as well as usual, he took off again, stick still clutched in his already dirty little hand.

"Sam, did you hear me?" Jane called after him, but he was gone. She shook her head, took a sip of her coffee, and returned to the house.

Her "studio" was an unfinished room in the basement. When they built the house, she'd wanted a small room off the kitchen with big windows to let in as much natural light as possible, which could also serve as a sun room when she wasn't working. But they had to cut the budget.

"We can always add it on later," Ian had said.

Jane hadn't responded. She'd just harbored it in her heart, adding it to the pile of disappointments that weighed down her soul.

So Ian had a practical patio poured where she'd envisioned her studio, and her art was moved to a corner of the basement. He'd had fluorescent ceiling fixtures installed for her in addition to a couple bright spot lights, but it still wasn't the same as natural light. She'd love to be painting in the sun on this exquisite morning instead of stuck in the musty basement. As she stared at her easel and the paints on the stand beside it, her mind resembled the blank piece of canvas. She'd cultivated no inspiration and therefore harvested no ideas.

Creativity couldn't blossom in such a dismal environment. Creativity, like every living thing, needed fresh air and sunlight. That was why she hadn't held a brush in weeks, hadn't even doodled on a piece of paper.

Her passion was dying.

She stayed so busy with the kids, teaching, and chores around the house, she hadn't even noticed it fading away. She'd assumed that she'd always have painting. It was her talent, after all. Her gift. In a way, it was her friend. She'd won a national art contest in high school and had been awarded a scholarship for college. It helped her cope when her mother faded away with cancer just before Bradley was born, so slowly at first Jane didn't even realize she was losing her.

Now, like her mother, her passion was slowly slipping away. The canvas, so full of potential and endless possibilities, blurred behind her hot, angry tears. She wasn't sure if she was still mad at Ian from the night before or if it was years of hurt rolled into one. Maybe she was angry at herself for allowing this to happen. Maybe she was frustrated that her children, who through no fault of their own needed so much from her.

She loved those children ferociously, but most days her spirit resembled the cash in her wallet, completely spent. And there was one missing. How had she been supposed to know that nothing would ever fill the hole in her heart left by her miscarriage? She loved teaching, but it didn't help heal the ache. Instead, it drained her a little more quickly every year.

Jane suddenly realized that she still held onto anger toward her mother for leaving her so soon. *Didn't she know how much I needed her?* She swiped a tear from her lashes. *She never even met my kids. I'll never forgive God for taking her away from me. Never.*

She set her jaw, determination saturating her being. She had to save her passion. She was Ian's wife, her kids' mother, her students' teacher, her father's kid, but painting was the only thing she had that allowed her to just be Jane. If she didn't find a way to breathe new life into the talent that defined her, she feared what would happen to her.

"First things first."

She set the coffee cup down, collapsed the legs on her tripod easel, and heaved the awkward burden up the basement stairs. Setting it up on the cement patio, she returned to the basement for her caddy of supplies. After flipping off all the lights she slammed the door behind her, allowing the sound of finality to echo against the cement walls. Never again would she allow her passion to be kept in the dark.

On the way out the sliding glass door, she grabbed a bar stool. Setting it in front of the easel, she sat down and inhaled the fresh morning air. Eyes closed, she smiled, tipping her face to the warm sunshine.

At last she picked up a paint brush. Chewing on the end of the handle, she remembered the Crayola picture little Destiny had drawn her the day before. An idea slowly emerged from the fog in her brain. She twisted the cap off a tube of blue paint, dabbed her brush in it, and swiped the first hint of color on the blank canvas. She had almost slipped into her zone, the euphoric state where no one or nothing else existed, when a voice pulled her back.

"Mom?"

Jane pressed her eyelids shut. *No, no, no. All I wanted this morning was to lose myself in my painting, and I was almost there.*

"Just a minute, please."

"Mom." Emma's voice demanded Jane's attention.

An exasperated breath escaped her lips. "What is it?"

Standing in the sliding glass doorway, Emma held the cordless telephone pressed against her chest, a worried expression on her face. "It's Dr. Sterling." She held out the phone. "He said it's urgent. Something to do with Granddad."

Jane set the brush down, gave her daughter a nervous smile, and took the receiver. "Good morning, Nathan," she said, knowing her cheerful tone couldn't disguise the worry in her voice from their family doctor and friend.

"Jane your dad was rushed to the hospital early this morning with all the warning signs of a stroke."

She vividly remembered the events surrounding the death of her best friend's grandfather several years earlier, and raw fear filled her chest. "I-is he okay?"

"I'm headed to the hospital now, but the report I received is that he's stable. They're running tests right now. We should know what's going on very soon."

Jane's hands suddenly didn't work right. She fumbled with the caps as she attempted to twist them back on the tubes of paint.

"I can be there in fifteen minutes."

"Do you have someone to drive you? I don't want you to be alone at a time like this."

Jane stifled a snort. *He has no idea how alone I feel with five other people in this house.*

"I appreciate your concern, Nathan, but I'll be fine."

Ending the call, she abandoned her easel and paints and hurried inside. She took the stairs two at a time and ran into her bedroom. In a rush to get changed, she didn't hear the soft tap on the door.

"Mom?" Emma poked her head into the room. "What's going on?"

"Dr. Sterling thinks Granddad might have had a stroke. We won't know anything for sure until they run some tests. I'm going to the hospital. I need you and Bradley to take care of things here until I get back."

"What about Dad?"

Jane snatched her purse off the dresser and dashed to the door, where she paused to gaze down at her daughter. As hard as she worked to shelter her children, Jane had no energy left to keep up her charade.

She shrugged, defeat welling into her eyes. "I don't know, Sweetie. I just don't know."

CHAPTER
Three

The automatic doors whooshed open at Cresthaven Medical Center, and Jane stepped into the sterile-smelling atmosphere. Thankfully, she didn't have to look for Nathan. He'd been watching for her, and as she approached him, the lines of worry creasing his forehead tightened the knot of anxiety in her chest.

"How's Dad? Can I see him?"

"He's having a CT scan and a few other tests run right now. You should be able to see him soon." Nathan scanned the area. "You came alone?"

Pasting on a smile, Jane said, "Yeah, well, Ian has a big project in the works and rain is moving in. I didn't want to bother him before I had any details."

"Jane—"

She put up a quick hand. "It's okay, Nathan. I really don't want to discuss it further."

Nodding, Nathan slipped his arm around her shoulders and led her to a quiet waiting room. "Would you like a cup of coffee or tea?"

"No. I just want to see my dad."

"I understand. Try to relax while I go see what I can find out."

The soft click of the door behind him echoed in her soul. She sank to the over-stuffed sofa, aching for someone to help her shoulder this unbearable weight. Maybe she should have called Ian, but she was afraid that, given the current state of their relationship, having him there would only drain her further.

She stared blankly at the second hand working its way around a clock on the wall. The dull thud of her heart kept pace with the deafening, steady tick, tick, tick as her thoughts raced around inside her brain.

Dad's all I have left . . . He's all I have left . . .

She knew that wasn't true. She still had her husband and children, her friends and her students. But Shaun Flanders was the one person she could count on to be there for her while she was there for everyone else. He was her roots, her history, a big part of her very being.

She felt her world shifting and wondered how she would handle the role reversal of becoming her father's caretaker. *Or worse yet . . .*

She set her chin. "I'll be okay. One way or another everything will be okay. It has to be. There's no other option."

Just as she stood to pace the room, the door swung open. Her heart rate accelerated, and then slammed to a stop as her gaze landed on Ian. At the hurt in his eyes, shame flooded through her.

"Did Nathan call you?"

"No. Emma did. What I want to know is why you didn't."

"Oh, Ian. It wasn't intentional. Nathan called and said Dad had been brought here with a possible stroke. That's all I could think about." It was the truth . . . for the most part.

"Jane, I'm your husband. You didn't think to call me on your way over here?"

A rush of hot anger set her cheeks blazing. "You don't have to remind *me* that you're my husband."

"Is this still about yesterday? Look, I told you I was sorry and I'd make it up to you. You need to get over it."

She narrowed her eyes. "Get over it?" She studied his tanned, unshaven face with the faint creases fanning out from the corners of his chocolate eyes and wondered if it was possible to become too familiar with someone. "I have news for you. I am over it and have been for a long time."

Ian planted his hands on his hips. "And just what is that supposed to mean?"

The sudden clearing of a throat brought them both around. Nathan stood in the doorway.

"Everything okay?"

Glaring at Ian, Jane nodded.

Nathan frowned, but said quietly, "After consulting with Dr. Khalilah, the neurologist on staff here, I have some potentially good news. It appears that your dad had a Transient Ischemic Attack, sometimes referred to as a mini stroke. Basically what happens during a TIA is blood flow to the brain is temporarily blocked by a clot. Typically, the clots dissolve on their own relatively quickly and the patient makes a full recovery with very little permanent damage. However, the likelihood of a recurrence or a full-blown stroke is significantly greater."

Jane pressed her fingertips to her lips. "Just like Grandpa Clayton."

Nathan stepped further into the room and closed the door. "This is a similar situation, yes. However, that doesn't mean it'll turn out the same. Your dad is quite a bit younger than Kate's grandpa was and has an otherwise clean bill of health in his favor. But we still need to view this as a warning sign. He'll be kept here

for observation at least overnight if not for a few days. The specialists will want to discuss his options regarding medication as
well as changes to his diet and exercise. They may even suggest
assisted living or at the very least home health care for a while."

Jane crossed her arms and shook her head. "Dad won't listen
to any of that."

"I know. That's why you'll have to make him listen. He's a
lucky man, Jane, but he's not out of the woods. He may have a
long, hard road ahead of him."

Jane shoved her fingers through her short hair, fighting the
urge to pull some of it out. "I understand, and I'll do my best to
make him understand. When can I see him?"

"They're getting him settled in a room now. It'll be just a few
minutes longer." Nathan glanced at Ian as he turned the door
handle. "I'm going to check on a few other patients. The head
nurse knows to come and get you the minute you can see your
dad, and I'll check back in later this afternoon."

Jane watched Nathan leave, her stomach clenched. She desperately needed a source of comfort and stability, but Ian was
the last person she could trust to guide her through these
uncharted waters.

Alone with him once again, she dragged a long, exhausted
breath out of her throat and pulled further away. "Ian, why don't
you do us both a favor and go back to work. I know that's where
you'd rather be. Emma and Bradley are taking care of things at
home, and I'm going to be staying here with Dad."

"I see." He rubbed his goatee with his thumb and index finger. "Well, if that's how you feel . . ."

Jane set her jaw. "At this point, it is."

Nodding twice, Ian moved to the doorway. "I'm really sorry
you feel that way." He met her gaze briefly, and she saw deep

sorrow in his eyes. Then he stepped into the hallway and disappeared around the corner.

Stopping at home long enough to ditch his truck and fire up his Harley, Ian spent more than an hour flying over Harvest Bay's back roads, unsure exactly where he was going. He suddenly wasn't sure of anything. If the woman he'd devoted his life to couldn't be bothered to call him when her father was rushed to the hospital, and instead told him he wasn't needed there or at home, then he guessed he'd missed something somewhere along the way.

He refused to go back to work, mostly because Jane had told him to, but also because he knew he wasn't thinking clearly and just one mistake on this project could cost his company a bundle.

"I am over it and have been for a long time."

Jane's emotionless tone bothered him more than the words. She never exactly clarified "it," but he had a sinking feeling she was referring to more than the anniversary debacle.

The wind pushed against his body as he drove into it, causing a resistance he enjoyed. He didn't like Jane pushing against him one bit, however. There wasn't supposed to be resistance between a husband and wife.

They used to get along like best friends. He could always count on her being in his corner. Now he didn't know if he could count on her at all, and it infuriated him that she could so easily forget all he'd tried to do for his family.

His whole world revolved around Jane and their kids. Maybe he didn't always show it, but at this point he didn't feel he should have to. Sure, he put in a lot of long hours. Couldn't she see it was only because he wanted the best for them?

That had defined his whole goal and purpose when he started Garner Construction fifteen years earlier, and even in this miserable economy he managed to continually turn a profit. The company he'd built from the ground up provided for all the needs of six people. No, he couldn't afford everything she wanted, but with the big picture in constant focus, a few sacrifices here and there should have been just a drop in the bucket.

It all made perfect sense to him, and he'd thought Jane was on board, on the same page, his teammate through this attempt at reaching his goals.

But maybe he was wrong. It bruised his ego to admit he might have been wrong about a lot of things.

As he coasted into the heart of Harvest Bay, Ian noticed vehicles dotting the high school parking lot, and he instinctively turned in. Revisiting his old stomping grounds, a place where he'd been adored by many, including Jane, sounded like the perfect ointment for his wounded spirit.

Maintaining a close friendship with the head football coach had its advantages, including access to the security code for the weight room. He punched the numbers into the key pad and pulled open the heavy door. He stepped inside, inhaling the familiar scent of hard work and determination.

He followed the hallway that led past the coaches' offices and the locker rooms straight to the gymnasium. The motion sensors activated more than just the lights. They turned on memories from the days when he was valued and respected there.

Grabbing a basketball from the rack by the door, he bounced it a few times. Each time the ball hit the wooden floor, some truths became clear. He had the ability to control where the ball went and how it responded to him.

If he pushed too hard, he'd have to reach for the ball, maybe even chase it down. If he handled the ball gently, with a soft touch and an easy bounce, it'd return to his fingertips every time.

He took a shot. Giving it the right amount of his strength and guiding it with his vision, he told the ball where he wanted it to go and sank it. In his soul, that basket counted for a lot more than two points.

This game was for the championship.

The energy of a packed gym surged through him. He remembered the constant white noise of the crowd, the buzz of excitement. He envisioned everyone in the bleachers on their feet, the cheerleaders chanting "sink that shot," while his coach watched with an expression of hope and high expectations.

And in the sea of faces he found Jane. He always found Jane. She was his center, his rock. She believed in him more than anyone else, including himself. Whether they won or lost, she was proud of him.

"She was proud of me."

With that thought, he faltered. When he took another shot, the ball bounced off the rim and Ian's shoulders sagged. His wife didn't believe in him anymore.

"Where did I go so wrong?"

"I'd say your aim was probably just a little off."

Ian turned at the voice. Adam Sullivan, head football coach and Ian's closest friend since high school, jogged onto the court and snatched up the ball.

"I was watching game film in my office and saw you walk by. I thought maybe you were playing some one on one with Bradley."

Running a shaky hand through his hair, Ian exhaled heavily. "Nope. Not today."

Adam bounce-passed the ball to Ian, who returned it. Adam then faked left and rushed right making an easy layup. Catching the ball as it fell through the net, he lobbed it to Ian.

"So what's up?"

Ian half-heartedly took a shot. Once again, it hit the rim and bounced off. He'd lost his focus.

"Jane's dad is in the hospital. He had a mini stroke."

"Oh, man. I'm sorry to hear that." Adam secured the ball between his arm and his hip and looked pointedly at his friend. "So why aren't you there with her or at home with your kids?"

"It's complicated." Ian batted the ball free and dribbled it to the basket, finally sinking a shot and restoring a fraction of his pride.

"It's complicated? Dude, I know you better than that. We've been friends for like twenty-five years. What's going on?"

Ian shook his head. "I don't know. I honestly don't know. Jane said she didn't want me there." They walked over to the bleachers and sat down. "Something's come between us. I don't know if it was so gradual I didn't notice or if it was out of the blue, but it's like we're living in two different worlds these days."

Compassion filled Adam's eyes. "That's tough."

"Yeah, it is. And since I don't know how it happened, I'm not exactly sure how to fix it."

"You both have to work at it. I remember when Alexandra and I grew apart. I worked hard to keep us together, mostly for Chloe's sake, but Alexandra was too wrapped up in her career to try. So I think the fact that you want to fix it is a big step in the right direction."

Ian cast a defeated glance at Adam. "That's just it. I'm not sure I do anymore."

Crossing his arms, Adam tipped his chin up. "You telling me you're going to quit? That doesn't sound like the Ian Garner I know."

"What if I seem to be the only one whose heart is still in the game? Tell me, Coach, when do you reach the point that it's time to just call it a game and move on?"

Several minutes of silence filled the gym. Finally, Adam placed a firm hand on Ian's shoulder.

"You don't call it a game. You focus on giving one hundred percent of yourself to your team. Some games are over when the clock runs out, and some play on in our hearts forever. But you can never give up. Never."

CHAPTER
Four

By early Monday morning, clouds rolled in dark and heavy, a perfect reflection of Jane's mood. School wouldn't start for another two hours, but she sat at her desk with a strong cup of coffee, scribbling down every minute of the day in great detail, laying out picture books and phonics sheets for her sub.

She hated leaving her class so early in the school year when establishing structure and routine was crucial, and on a Monday morning no less. But her dad was scheduled to be discharged from the hospital sometime that day. She had to help him get somewhat settled into a whole new way of life consisting of a new diet and exercise plan, scheduled medications, and regular appointments with his team of doctors and specialists.

Overwhelmed just thinking about it, Jane inhaled deeply and closed her eyes. "One step at a time."

"That's very ambitious of you."

Jane's eyelids flew open, and her gaze landed on Zach Andrews. Placing a hand over her startled heart did little to settle it into a steady rhythm.

"Sheesh, Zach. Make some noise or something next time. A dark, empty school building is pretty creepy."

Moving further into her classroom, Zach perched on a desk.

"You're telling me. I almost carried a baseball bat down here when I saw the lights come on."

Jane rubbed her tired eyes. "So what are you doing here at six a.m.?"

"I'm working on the student learning objectives for our math curriculum."

Groaning, Jane dropped her forehead to the crook of her arm on her desk. "Are those due soon?"

"You've got a few weeks. Your turn now. Why are you here so early?"

Jane yawned and stretched. Two nights sleeping in a hard hospital lounge chair were catching up with her fast.

"My dad had a mini stroke Saturday morning so I'll be out for a few days. I'm just getting everything ready for my sub."

"I'm sorry to hear that. Is he going to be okay?"

Working the corners of her mouth into a weary smile, she nodded. "There's a chance it could happen again and he's at a higher risk for a full blown stroke, but he's got some great doctors taking care of him. I think he'll be fine."

"And how are you?"

The question caught Jane off guard. It dawned on her that since Saturday morning no one seemed to care about how she was handling this scary situation and the added stress that came with it. Zach's concerned gaze and quiet presence made her feel that she could lay her burdens down for just a second and rest.

"It's been a lot to digest, but I'm okay."

"And Jessica?"

Her shoulders sagged. "To be honest, I haven't seen much of my kids the past two days."

"So Ian's been taking care of them then?"

She blew out an exasperated breath. "Some, yes, but Ian works a lot. Jessica and Sam spent most of the day yesterday at Kate and Adam Sullivan's house. Kate's been my best friend since high school, and you've probably seen how tight Jessica and Maddie are, so they feel right at home there."

"That's right. I remember you two being pretty thick back then." Standing, he slipped his hands in his pockets. "It must help to have someone you can count on."

Sensing Zach's penetrating blue eyes on her, she wanted to run and hide. At the same time, she longed to expose her wounds to someone who cared. Maybe some fresh air would help them heal.

Instead, she stood in a huff and gathered her manipulatives for that day's math lesson. "Look, there'll be a lot of changes taking place in our household over the next few weeks so just keep an eye on Jessica for me. If you notice anything out of the ordinary, let me know right away."

"Yeah, sure. No problem." Zach moved to the door, then hesitated and turned to face her. "And just so you know, I'm here for you too. Whatever you need, just give me a shout."

This time her smile came easily. "Thanks."

He put his hand up in a parting gesture and disappeared down the hallway. But his warmth lingered.

⚜

As forecasted, the rain started by mid morning and came down in buckets. If the amount of green fanning out across the radar was any indication, there wouldn't be a break in the weather all day.

A certain satisfaction filled Ian. He'd been right to work so hard and get ahead of the timeline on this project. Certainly Jane would agree. She'd have to.

He sent his crew home and climbed into his truck. The day wasn't a complete loss, though. A small stack of bills, invoices, and bank statements had piled up on his desk, vying for his attention. Tapping his fingers on the steering wheel to the steady beat of the windshield wipers, Ian decided to get his paperwork done, tackle some odd jobs around the house, and then if there were any hours left in the day he'd go check on his father-in-law.

Ian hadn't spoken to Jane in two days, had only sent a few text messages regarding their kids, so he assumed no news was good news. Surely she'd call if her father took a turn for the worse, wouldn't she?

He wrestled with the fact that he hadn't made a little more effort. He knew his wife needed him, but he needed time. She couldn't possibly know how critically she'd severed his pride when she said she didn't need him there. But he vowed to make the effort now. Maybe between the rain and his support with her dad, she'd forget he hadn't been there for their anniversary.

Feeling good about himself and his accomplishments, he pulled into the driveway and hit the button on the garage door opener. His concern rose with the door as, little by little, it revealed Jane's Expedition parked in its usual spot. He glanced at the clock on his dash, questions starting to form in his mind.

What is she doing home at nine-thirty? If she's not at school, shouldn't she be at the hospital?

Uneasiness settled like an anchor in his buoyant spirit. His intentions had always been good, but it wouldn't matter if he was too late. Sucking in a long breath, he cut the engine and headed inside, hitting the button on the wall to close the garage door.

Through the laundry room and into the kitchen, he saw no sign of Jane. No shoes tipped over on their side on the floor. No purse tossed on the table. Nothing. The coffee pot had been left on from that morning. The house was silent.

Glancing into the living room and finding it empty, Ian started up the stairs. At the top step, he noticed that their bedroom door was partially closed. He stood there staring at it for a moment. It was his bedroom too. He'd built the house, for goodness sake. Technically he should be able to give the door a shove and walk right in. But something told him he should tiptoe on these eggshells under his feet.

He tapped lightly twice and waited for a response.

Nothing.

"Jane?" His voice was just above a whisper as he pushed the door open further and peeked around it. In the peaceful dimness, Jane lay curled up on her side in the middle of their bed, softly snoring.

"Poor thing must be exhausted."

Ian chided himself for not protecting her better, buffering the stress and worry. But what more could he do if she didn't want his help?

Watching her sleep from across the room, he could still see the teenage girl he'd fallen in love with when he was still just a kid. Yet somehow she'd transformed into a completely different person.

He couldn't say when it happened. Maybe when her mom died or when any of their four kids were born. It could have happened after she became a tenured teacher or quite possibly some time since she trained to run a half marathon with Kate. Maybe it was a combination of all of those events and so gradual over the last twenty years it would be impossible to pinpoint the exact moment of her metamorphosis.

Regardless, it hurt to think he didn't know this woman with whom he'd shared his bed for twenty years. He had no idea what made her tick, had grown out of touch with her hopes and dreams, but was fairly certain they didn't include him. He'd always thought they shared the same goals for their future, but as he remembered seeing her easel and paints on their patio, the realization sank in that those were his goals, which she generously supported and encouraged.

But all those dreams were for her, for us. The company has given us everything—this house, nice vehicles, full cupboards and closets, everything the kids need. I always meant well.

It didn't change the fact that she didn't need him like the young girl he'd once known had.

"She doesn't even respect me anymore." He spoke softly enough that he didn't think his words would penetrate Jane's sound sleep, but she stirred, and for a moment he was afraid she'd heard him give voice to his greatest fear.

Jane stretched like a cat in the sun. Her hazel eyes fluttered open and her gaze landed on Ian.

"What are you doing home?"

What kind of greeting is that after we've been apart for two days?

"It's raining." He could have said more, but he bit his tongue. "How's your dad?"

She crawled out from under the covers and stumbled to an already loaded suitcase lying at the end of the bed. "He's coming home today."

"Good."

"And I'm going to be staying with him."

"Wait a minute." His gaze bounced from her to the suitcase and back again. "What?"

She went to the closet and pulled out three blouses. "Dad needs me."

"We need you."

Dropping her clothes in the suitcase, she turned to face him. "Sure you do. To cook your meals, wash your dishes, and fold your laundry. To get the kids to their practices on time and help them with their homework. Should I continue?"

"Jane, I understand that you're exhausted, but you're being irrational."

She stared at him, and he could see the glisten of moisture behind her long thick lashes. "You're right. I am exhausted, but not because of Dad."

Clenching his fists, Ian blew out an exasperated breath. "Okay. Emma and Bradley can take care of themselves, but what about Jessie and Sam? Have you thought about them?"

Instantly he regretted that last question. She set her jaw and her eyes shot daggers at him. He'd pushed too hard, and there was no hope for her to willingly return to his fingertips now. He'd have to chase her down.

"How dare you? Those children have been my first thought every day for the past sixteen years." Returning to the closet, she grabbed two pairs each of jeans and dress slacks. "Jessica and Sam can stay with Dad and me as much as they want. I'll be less than ten minutes away."

Ian's demeanor softened. "How long will you be gone?"

"I don't know, but I think the time apart will do us some good."

"I know I haven't been perfect, but I only wanted to take care of you. I've worked hard so you wouldn't have to."

"But I love teaching."

"You haven't wanted for anything."

"Except for you!" she shouted. Zipping up the suitcase, she hauled it off the bed. "I've tried explaining it every possible way I can imagine. I don't know if you're not listening or you just don't get it, but either way I'm done wasting my breath."

Without another word, she brushed past him, dragging her suitcase behind her. He listened as her footfalls stomped down the stairs and the door to the garage slammed shut. But the only thing he heard was the sound of his heart breaking.

By the time the sun had just begun to set, Jane desired nothing more than to climb into her childhood bedroom and sleep straight through until morning. She didn't want to leave her dad quite yet, however.

The latest novel by her favorite suspense author lay open on her lap, but she couldn't make sense of the words. She found herself rereading the same sentence three times and it still didn't sink in. Annoyed, she snapped the book shut and glanced at her father.

Reclining comfortably in his La-Z-Boy, his newspaper spread open in front of him, Shaun Flanders looked like the same healthy man he was before the weekend. Sweet relief warmed her like a mug of hot cocoa.

"What are you thinking about, lass?" he asked, not looking up from the paper, his words coated in his faint Irish accent.

"Just how glad I am that you're okay. You can't scare me like that anymore."

He folded a corner of the paper down and peered at her over it. "Scared? Not my brave little lassie."

"I'm not always brave." She lowered her voice with her gaze. "Especially when I think about losing you too."

He set the paper aside, lowered the footrest, and leaned forward a little. "Ah, my Janey. You know our days on this earth are numbered, but you will never lose your dear ol' dad."

Nodding, Jane sniffed and blinked back tears. "I know, but I need you here with me."

Shaun pushed to his feet and shuffled to the sofa. Sinking down heavily beside Jane, he slipped an arm around her shoulders and squeezed.

"Come now. What's this all about?"

"I don't know. I guess I struggled so long after Mom died that the thought of something happening to you terrifies me. I'm just not ready."

"No one's ever ready to say goodbye to someone they love."

"True."

"What else is on your mind?"

Jane hesitated.

"C'mon. Out with it."

"The fact that I was ready to say goodbye to Ian."

"Aaah. I wondered if there was more to you staying here than my condition."

Laying her head on his shoulder, she sniffled. "I'm sorry, Dad. I didn't mean to let you down."

"My little lass, you have never disappointed me. I understand that marriage is work."

"You can't understand this. You and Mom had the perfect relationship."

A hearty laugh erupted from deep in his gut. "Did you ever consider there was a reason you didn't come along until your mum and I had been married ten years? That poor woman couldn't get me outta the bars long enough to try. I'd put in a long day's work at the railroad, and then go with my buddies for a drink or two or more." He chuckled again.

"You're joking."

" 'Fraid not. It took her leaving to wake me up."

Jane's jaw went slack. "Mom left you?"

"Indeed she did. Moved in with her mum and dad. Oh, it only lasted a couple weeks, but that was plenty long enough. You came along about ten months later, and I never stepped foot in a bar again."

"Why didn't I hear about this before? Like before Ian and I got married?"

"Would it have made a difference?"

Jane shrugged, considering the circumstances surrounding her hastily planned wedding. "Maybe."

"Ian is a good man. Give him some time to miss you, and he'll try to make things right."

Jane snorted. "You don't know him like I do."

Her dad patted her knee. "But when he does, you'll have to be ready to forgive him and ask his forgiveness in return. It's work, but it's worth it."

Sighing deeply, Jane hugged her knees to her chest. "I'm tired, Dad. I don't want to fight anymore. I don't want to work anymore. I don't want to be taken for granted anymore. I just want peace."

"Hang in there, lassie. We have to go through a storm in order to experience a rainbow, but if we run for shelter after the first drop o' rain, we could completely miss it." He kissed her forehead. "Do you understand what your ol' dad is trying to tell ya? Don't run for cover and miss your rainbow."

CHAPTER
Five

*Y*awning, Jane sifted through the stack of papers on her desk and scanned the note her substitute had left for her. She took a long swallow of her coffee.

"Sometimes it just doesn't pay to miss two days of school."

A sudden tap on her open door caused her to jerk her head up and choke a little on the lukewarm liquid.

"I know. It's tough trying to take care of everyone." Her principal, Margaret Zeller, stepped further into the room. "So how's your dad?"

Cradling the coffee cup in her hands, Jane sagged back in her chair. "Trying to adjust to a new way of life is never easy for a seventy-two-year-old Irish man. Home health care is checking in on him today." Sensing something amiss, she said quickly, "Was everything okay here while I was gone?"

"In your classroom, yes." Mrs. Zeller laid a file folder on Jane's desk. "But an issue has been brought to my attention."

Straightening, Jane set her coffee cup down and picked up the folder. "What's wrong? Has Jessica or Samuel been causing trouble?"

"No. Nothing like that." Mrs. Zeller motioned to the folder in Jane's hand. "That contains legal documents including a restraining order against Destiny Shoals's biological father. He's been arrested multiple times on charges of drug possession and domestic violence. He just made parole after spending eighteen months behind bars, and Destiny's mom is afraid he'll try to take her."

Shifting her attention from Mrs. Zeller to Destiny's Crayola heart and rainbow thumb tacked to her bulletin board, Jane opened the file and skimmed the documents inside, thinking that she would study each piece of paper carefully later. At that moment she could only digest the main details of this situation that now dominated every other trouble on her mind.

"Wow," she breathed.

This quiet little girl with the big brown eyes and black curls could be in very real danger. The thought made her heart sick.

"There's a picture of him in there. Memorize it. If he's seen anywhere near school grounds we'll lock down. I won't take any chances."

"Absolutely, Mrs. Zeller. I'll do my best to keep Destiny safe."

"I know you will, Jane. Just stay alert, always err on the side of caution, and above all else pray that we never have to take action."

Pray? Dread filled Jane. *I promise I'll do everything else but that.*

. . .

"I don't know if you know this or not, but a school-wide memo went out today with a picture of Damion Shoals and strict orders that if he's spotted on school grounds, we're to lock down immediately," Kate Sullivan, Harvest Bay Elementary's fourth grade teacher informed Jane during their after-school four-mile run.

"Yeah. It doesn't seem to be a very good situation." Jane paused, focusing on her rhythm and breathing. "The odd thing is I feel safer having her here. I worry about her being at home with just her mom to protect her."

"I know. I had a similar case when I taught in Tennessee. Sometimes all you can do is give them over to the Lord and trust that He'll keep them safe."

Jane meant to keep the groan inward, but her labored breathing must have pushed it out.

Putting on her brakes, Kate studied Jane. "Are you okay? You haven't seemed like yourself for weeks now."

Jane kept up her pace, calling over her shoulder, "Yeah. Sure. Probably just worried about Dad. You should understand that."

"Jane, wait! I do understand, but you know I'm always here for you if something else is going on. I may not always understand, but I'll always listen."

Jane slowed to a stop and turned back. "You know what? You're right. I haven't been myself. Not just for weeks, but for years. I've been whatever everyone else needed or wanted, and I lost myself in the process. But I'm finally figuring out who I am, and it feels great."

"I remember going through a self-discovery process after Ryan died." The pair took off again on an easy jog. "What do you think led you to this new journey?"

Jane pumped her arms. "I don't know. Running, maybe. I feel good about myself while we're training. I'm strong and confident, almost powerful. But then I go home and it's like my family looks right past me until they need something. Sometimes it feels as if I'm disposable."

"Believe it or not, I understand that, especially during football season. Adam sleeps, eats, and breathes football, but I tolerate it because he loves it and that's what makes him such a good coach. Being a stepmom, however, is a whole different challenge."

Jane's feet pounding on the pavement kept a steady beat for the soundtrack running through her head. "I had to find my own value again. I had to mean something to myself."

"And what does Ian think about your shift of focus?"

Jane faltered, breaking her stride and losing her rhythm. "I don't know. We haven't exactly been seeing eye-to-eye lately. It's definitely a change for him to not be the center of my universe."

"Just because you're taking some time for yourself doesn't mean he's not a priority."

"And just because he's a priority to me doesn't mean I'm at the top of his list."

"What do you mean? Of course you are. Seems like you two have been together forever."

Jane picked up her pace. "How long we've been together doesn't have anything to do with where I'm ranked in importance, Kate." She huffed and puffed and struggled to catch her breath. "Garner Construction is Ian's first love. Then come the kids. I'm third in line. I've learned to accept it."

Turning onto West Street, with Harvest Bay Elementary School in sight, the women began their cool down.

"Have you tried talking to him?"

"On the rare occasion we're actually in the same room long enough to have a meaningful conversation if I even hint at not being his top priority, he automatically takes the defensive, reminds me of how he's provided for us, and shuts me out. That's how it's been for years. So, no, I don't try anymore." Jane shook her head and steadied her breathing. "I don't know, Kate. I moved in with Dad to help him out, but just between you, me, and that tree, I'm enjoying the space."

Kate linked her elbow with Jane's. "I'm sorry you're going through so much. I'm even sorrier that you've been struggling for a while and I wasn't there for you."

Jane bit her lip and squeezed Kate's arm against her side. "You didn't know, and I didn't want you to. It's not something I'm proud of."

"But I've been your best friend since we were thirteen years old. I've seen you in the morning after dozens of sleepovers. Now that's not something to be proud of." Kate playfully bumped hips with her, and Jane burst out laughing. After a brief hesitation, Kate said, "Do you think Ian would consider marriage counseling?"

Jane shrugged.

"Ask him. My pastor has a degree in marriage and family counseling, and I'm sure he'd meet with you."

Jane bristled. "Yeah, sure. We'll see."

"In the meantime, Adam and Kennedy are having a little Labor Day picnic for the elementary and high school faculty and staff on Monday at his parents' farm. Come out and relax. Eat a burger and enjoy yourself. Adam might have already mentioned it to Ian, but just in case, he and the kids are welcome. Maybe he can bring his guitar and you two can entertain us like old times."

Heading up the sidewalk, Jane slid her arm away from Kate and opened the heavy door. "The home health care nurse is supposed to have weekends and holidays off since I'm there, but I'll ask if she can check on Dad. Speaking of which, I've got to pick up Jessie and Sammy from the sitter and get back to him. Thanks for the great run."

Jane turned and made a beeline for her classroom to gather her belongings, thinking that workout hurt in more ways than one.

Ian's mood deteriorated rapidly throughout the week. The more he thought about Jane abandoning him, the angrier he became. By Saturday afternoon he was fuming.

He realized her father needed her help, but not twenty-four/seven. Wasn't that what home health care was for?

"What about my needs?"

As he glanced around the kitchen at the signs of neglect, the fight inside him intensified. Dishes sat in the sink waiting to go into the dishwasher. The countertops were cluttered with mail, the kids' school work, and other odds and ends. It astonished Ian how no one picked up after themselves, but how was he to know when Jane always took care of it?

With his supper consisting of Spaghetti-O's straight from the can and a handful of grapes, he was acutely aware of the empty refrigerator and cupboards. He didn't have to look to know that the rest of the house was suffering too. While cobwebs gathered in the corners, they also gathered in his heart. He missed the woman who took care of him. Lonely tears stung his tired eyes and fueled his anger.

"How could she just leave me like that?" He could hear the selfishness in his words and it bothered him, but he didn't know how else to verbalize the ache in his heart.

At the very moment he needed a distraction from his negative emotions, Emma walked through the door. She dumped a load of books on the dining room table and grabbed a bottle of water from the fridge.

Tossing the empty can in the trash, Ian wiped his mouth and goatee with his palm. "How did your study group go, princess?"

"Pretty good. I should ace the test on Tuesday." She took a swig. "When are you gonna quit calling me those baby names? I'm fourteen, ya know."

"Yeah, I know. And never. You'll always be my baby."

Rolling her eyes, Emma plopped down at the table, propped her feet on an adjacent chair and opened a text book. "What's for supper?"

The knot in Ian's gut tightened, and for a minute he thought his Spaghetti-O's might come back up. "I don't know. Do you want to order pizza? Or we could go to Bayside Café."

Emma slammed the book on the table. "When are you and Mom going to stop acting like kids? You screwed up, she screwed up. Whatever. You both are screwing up our lives. Can't you see how selfish you're being?"

Ian placed a hand over his chest, then checked for the fresh blood this offspring of Jane's had caused with her dagger. "I don't think I'm to blame here. Your mother is the one who moved out."

"Because Granddad is sick. I'd do the same for you."

Ian wondered how a heart could ache and swell at the same time. "Emma, this doesn't concern you."

She pushed to her feet and snatched up her book. "Of course this concerns me. This is my family, but we're not acting very much like one. That hurts. A lot." She turned to storm out of the kitchen, but Ian stopped her.

"Hey, Emma?"

"What."

Struggling to swallow a thick lump of pride, Ian finally forced the words out. "Can you please show me how to do a load of laundry?"

She stared at him for a long moment. "Sure, Dad. Whatever you need."

The disappointment in his daughter's voice finished off his severely crippled self esteem. He was supposed to be her hero, but his little girl had discovered that he was only human.

He trudged into his office and slumped at his desk. "My wife doesn't want me anymore, and now I've failed my daughter too." Anger returning, he jerked the mouse to wake up his computer. "My own home is the one place I shouldn't have to prove myself. I shouldn't have to earn respect here, and yet I'm appreciated more at work." He clicked on a couple icons. "I'm not the one who left. Doesn't that count for anything?"

He clicked on the Google search bar. One of his foremen had mentioned building his young daughter a dollhouse for Christmas, and since he couldn't seem to do anything right for his family, Ian figured he'd browse the Internet for some plans.

When he typed in "doll houses" and hit enter, however, it quickly became apparent that his Hewlett Packard had a different idea of the subject matter. Dozens of images of scantily clad women showed up on the screen.

"What the . . . ? Did I type in something wrong?" His gaze flicked to the address bar. "No. It's right." The connection occurred in his brain. "But I never set the controls to filter out this trash."

He returned the mouse to the address bar, but before he could modify his search, an image of a raven-haired beauty caught his eye. Her tanned skin appeared soft. Her gentle curves captured his attention, and he couldn't help imagining how they would feel under his fingertips. Her exotic eyes taunted him, practically begged him to take a closer look.

"I can't . . . I shouldn't . . . "

Common sense told him this girl wasn't real. The picture had most likely been digitally enhanced until she appeared flawless. But therein lay the problem: She appeared flawless when there was so much wrong with everything else around him. For that reason alone, he thought he deserved a quick peek.

Looking over his shoulder to make sure no one was in sight, he clicked on the image. His pulse quickened as a whole website appeared before him full of beautiful women whom Ian chose to believe were eager to please a man. He had nothing to base that assumption on except for the lack of clothing on their perfect bodies, the provocative way these beauties were posed, and their lustful expressions.

When he found his favorite siren on a beach in nothing but a thong, her thick mane of dark hair cascading over her shoulders, an old familiar fire kindled in the core of his being. This website referred to her as "Felicity." Whether or not it was her real name, he'd never know, but somehow, even knowing full well that dozens of men were ogling these same photos, he easily imagined she was posing just for him.

Suddenly he felt wanted and desired instead of a chore to check off a list or a duty to fulfill. Staring through the computer screen into those hypnotizing eyes, he felt like more of a man. He viewed the next picture and the next, his lustful appetite increasing with each click.

He was so completely absorbed in the fantasy of enjoying Felicity on a beach, under a waterfall, in a meadow, and snowbound in a cabin that he never heard Bradley pull in the driveway or come through the door

"Is anyone home?"

His son's voice almost made Ian jump out of his skin. Frantically he closed all the windows and pulled up a company spreadsheet from eight months ago.

"Yeah, son. In here."

Filling the doorway, Bradley bit into an apple. Ian pretended to focus on the spreadsheet while he waited for his heart rate to return to normal. "How did lifting go?"

"Tough. After losing last night, we maxed out today. What's for supper?"

Ian groaned inwardly. "I'm ordering pizza. What do you want on it?"

"Pepperoni and bacon." Bradley took another big bite of the Red Delicious, but seemed to be chewing on more than fruit. "Dad, Coach Sullivan said we lost because we didn't play together as a team. He said that when you're a team you don't think of yourself first. Instead, you focus on accomplishing the overall goal of the team, and when that goal is met you'll find you've achieved your personal expectations too."

Nodding, Ian clicked on the X in the upper right hand corner and closed his smoke screen. "That sounds about right."

"Well, then you and Mom aren't really working together as a team lately."

Ian slammed the mouse down. "Don't you think I don't know that, Bradley? But what can I do about it? Your mom is the one who quit on me."

Bradley shrugged. "Maybe she didn't quit. Maybe she's just sitting on the bench, waiting for the right time to get back in the game." As he turned to leave, he added, "But you'll never know if you just throw in the towel."

CHAPTER
Six

*I*an spent the rest of the evening and all day on Sunday in a state of confusion.

"I don't remember Bradley becoming so wise . . . or Emma becoming disappointed in me." Shame stabbed him in the gut. "My kids are the grown-ups here."

Thinking back to the conversation he'd had with Adam that day in the gym caused regret to wrap around his heart. "My best friend has been a better role model for my son than I have been lately."

Nothing had ever caused him physical pain like this situation. The emotional ache had grown so intense he couldn't even look at himself in the mirror.

"How could I let my family just fall apart? It can't be too late to make it right, but how? What more does Jane need from me?"

Labor Day dawned with an inkling of an idea. As he recalled bits and pieces of dozens of discussions, more details emerged, and a solid plan formed in Ian's mind. His confidence rose with the sun outside his kitchen window, brightening his spirit and sprouting fresh hope in his heart.

He drained his second cup of coffee and placed the mug in the dishwasher, followed by all the dirty dishes that had been sitting in the sink all week. He added the detergent, turned it on, and started decluttering the counters. Then he swept the floor, took out the trash, and moved to the dining room.

Ian spent all morning picking up the house, vacuuming, tackling a few loads of laundry, and scouring the bathrooms. He even made the bed with fresh sheets in the hope that he wouldn't be sleeping alone anymore.

After taking a quick inventory of the refrigerator and cupboards, which didn't take long, he made a grocery list that included several of Jane's favorite picnic foods and headed to The Pit Stop Gas and Grocery.

On the way back home Ian swung by his father-in-law's. Spotting Jane's Expedition in the driveway caused his heart to skip a beat. His palms became clammy as he tightened his grip on the steering wheel.

"We've been married for twenty years," he chided himself. "It's ridiculous to be so nervous."

Cutting the engine of his truck, he jogged up to the front door, rang the bell, and waited. Each second stretched out to make the longest minute of his life. He considered letting himself in. He was family after all. Deciding to take the plunge, he reached for the knob just as the door swung open.

Ian's breath caught in his throat. It had been a week since he'd last seen his wife, and staring at her now in her yoga pants and paint splattered shirt, he realized just how much he missed her.

He grinned bashfully and stuffed his hands in his pockets. "Hi."

Jane crossed her arms. "Hi."

Ian shifted his weight to his left foot as he frantically searched his brain. There was so much he wanted to say to her, things he probably should have told her a long time ago. But his inadequacies rose up against him, beating him down, and smothering him until he couldn't think, could barely breathe.

"Everything okay, Ian?"

Meeting her gaze, he noticed for the first time how dull and lifeless her green eyes were, and he wondered how long they'd lacked their loving sparkle. His heart sagged in his chest. Had her love for him really died? He honestly didn't know if he wanted to find out.

"Ian?"

"Yeah. Sure. Everything's fine. I just went to the store and picked up a few groceries. Thought maybe we could go on a picnic this evening . . . You know, kind of like old times."

His cheeks blazed as he ran a hand through his hair. It annoyed him that he struggled to find the words to ask his wife on a date, but then again it had been twenty-five years since he'd last stood on her father's front porch trying to persuade her to go out with him. When he asked her to marry him, he thought that was the last time he'd have to fidget and stammer and act like a fool. After she accepted his proposal, he assumed it meant she agreed to be his date for the rest of their lives.

Her demeanor softened and hope flickered in his soul. He knew he'd win her back. He just knew it. She'd come back home and everything would return to normal. Victory was in the bag.

"That sounds nice, but I have plans."

"What do you mean?"

"Adam and Kennedy are having a back-to-school party for faculty and staff at their parents' farm. I figured he told you."

"No." Anger started at his toes and slithered its way to his heart. "No, Jane, he didn't, but why would he? I don't work at the school."

"But you go to every faculty party with me. Look, I'm sorry. I simply thought Adam invited you. He is your best friend after all."

"*You* are my wife, but you don't tell me anything anymore! First, your dad and now this?" Utter frustration raised his voice higher than he intended. He swallowed hard against a rising lump of raw emotion. "You're leaving me out of your life. How is that supposed to make me feel?"

"I don't know." Planting her fists on her hips, Jane glared at him. "How do you think it's supposed to make me feel that I never have your attention long enough to talk to you anymore?"

"You don't have my attention? I just went shopping and bought everything I know you like—chicken salad and cheese from the deli, crackers, strawberries with chocolate dip, and Coke. I'm standing out here making a fool of myself asking my own wife on a date—something I never thought I'd have to do again—and for what?" He shook his head in disbelief and backed up three steps. "I even spent all morning cleaning for you, but you wouldn't know that because you haven't been home for a week."

Stepping out onto the small porch, Jane pointed her finger at him. "Wait a minute. Did you say you cleaned the house for me, like you're doing me a favor to pick up the mess you helped make? Really? And you still don't know what's wrong with this picture?"

Throwing his hands up, he spun on his heel and stalked off toward his truck.

"And, by the way, I don't like Coke," she called after him. "You do."

He maintained his composure as he climbed in behind his steering wheel, but inwardly he couldn't get away fast enough.

His pride, everything that made him a man, had been shot down, and he needed to limp away to lick his wounds.

"Don't look back . . . Don't look back . . . " As he backed out of the driveway and pulled away, the message got lost somewhere between his brain and his eyes, and his gaze flicked to the rearview mirror.

She'd already closed the door.

She was gone. She wasn't watching him drive away with a longing expression, begging him with her eyes to come back so they could work out their issues and become closer than ever. She was done talking, done trying.

If he was one-hundred percent honest with himself, he'd reached that point too. He was tired of not being good enough, tired of not being appreciated for everything he did. He was just plain tired. For the first time in his life, he didn't know what his future held, but he knew neither of them could keep living like this.

He didn't blame her. He realized he hadn't taken into consideration that she might have plans, and he couldn't expect her to change them on a whim. But he wanted her to. He wanted to know he still meant that much to her. At one time she would have dropped everything for him and he took it for granted. Now that he was trying to appreciate her devotion and dedication, it was too late.

Pulling into their driveway, he pushed the button to open the garage door, parked, and carried all the groceries into the house in one trip. When he stepped into the kitchen, he found Bradley standing in front of the refrigerator with the door hanging wide open.

"Hey," Ian said, four full bags dangling from each hand.

Bradley looked up and removed his right earbud. "Oh, hey."

Ian stared at his son in wonder. All the way across the room, he could faintly hear music coming from the tiny speaker.

"What are you doing?"

"It's two o'clock. I'm hungry and there's no food in this house."

Biting his tongue hard, Ian held out the bags. "Here you go. Put away what you don't eat."

Dumping the bags on the floor, he wandered into the quiet living room. Emma was most likely in her room reading or listening to her iPod, and Jessica and Samuel had spent the weekend with Jane.

He snorted. "My kids have probably been planning on going to the party with her, and I never knew about it."

He felt like a complete idiot. And he was alone. Again.

Entering his office, he plopped down in his leather chair and drummed his fingers on his desk. A stack of paperwork vied for his attention. Invoices needed to be mailed out and bills needed to be paid.

But he was a man and he had his own needs. He would have given his right arm to just feel the adoration and respect from Jane that he once had, to see pride shining in her eyes because he was her man. More than anything he longed to feel like a man again instead of an epic failure.

He wiggled the mouse to wake his sleeping computer, giving in to a deep urge for some ego therapy. He had to find a way to feel good about himself again. He searched through his browser history until he found the website where he knew Felicity would be waiting for him.

He found her right away, straddling a four-wheeler wearing a very small camouflage bikini, and a smile crept onto his face. "So she's a country girl. Nice."

He had no idea if that was true. He knew these girls were posing for men, not for themselves. He also knew this make-believe love affair ignited the embers in the core of his being into flame.

When he clicked on the next picture, his eyes widened and his pulse quickened. He threw a quick glance over his shoulder at the empty doorway, then cleaned his glasses on his T-shirt and bent forward for a closer look. Felicity leaned provocatively against a support beam inside the framework of a house, wearing nothing but a tool belt, a hard hat, and work boots.

"I shouldn't be looking at this."

But he couldn't tear his eyes away. This picture was worth more than a thousand words to him and fed his hunger to be understood and appreciated. It spoke to him about his livelihood and how he'd spent the last twenty years of his life building Garner Construction. He'd worked so hard to ensure its success. This picture was a nice reward.

Felicity's passionate expression excited him almost as much as the tool belt strapped across the gentle curve of her hips. He imagined what it would be like to have her on one of his crews, guessing that not much work would get done.

It was a silly thought, he knew. She didn't work construction, probably didn't know how to hammer a nail, but she knew how to rebuild his ego and restore his confidence. She probably couldn't fix much, but she was his fix, his temporary high.

He drank in every intoxicating detail of her body that the camera had captured, and became fully addicted. Nothing could save him now, not when these pictures made him feel young and alive again, like a desirable man instead of a chore to check off a list.

His gaze shifted past Felicity's beautiful body, and he caught a glimpse of his middle-aged reflection in the computer monitor.

Heaving a heavy sigh, he shoved his fingers through his thinning hair.

"What am I doing? This isn't real, and it definitely isn't right. But then why does it feel so good?"

He closed the website. Guilt began to gnaw at his soul, not because of the few moments he'd just spent ogling another woman, but because he knew, as hard as he'd try to fight the urge, he'd be back.

By the time Jane turned onto the long gravel driveway that led to the Sullivans' farm, the party was in full swing. The conversation with Ian had shaken her enough that she almost reconsidered going.

A picnic did sound sweet, and he had gone through a lot of trouble to plan something special for her. If he hadn't given up so quickly, if he'd just asked again or even suggested that they go to the party together and bow out early, maybe this evening would have turned out differently. But then he went and ruined it by flying off the handle.

Besides, the effort is just a little too late. As defeated as it made her to admit it, she couldn't lie to herself anymore. *A picnic doesn't change anything. It doesn't change how alone I've been. It wouldn't magically make things better. But now I'm not afraid of being on my own, and that changes a lot.*

She parked her Expedition in a spot near the cornfield, and Jessica and Samuel wasted no time in climbing down from the back seat and dashing across the yard in search of their friends. Jane, on the other hand, wasn't in a hurry to begin dodging questions. As liberating as being honest with herself was, she didn't plan on broadcasting her struggles.

She knew exactly how it would go when asked about Ian's whereabouts. It was the same scenario she'd been playing out for months. She'd simply say he had a big project that needed his attention at work, and then she'd mechanically smile and nod while her friends commented on her husband's dedication and hard work. They couldn't possibly know the side effect of running a successful business was a lonely spouse and eventually a failing marriage.

Spotting Kate walking toward her, she sucked in a breath, waved, and once again launched Operation Conceal Marital Issues.

"Hey, I was afraid you weren't coming," Kate said, embracing her.

"You should know me better than that. I wouldn't even think of missing this." Afraid her response was a little too over-the-top, she scaled her enthusiasm back a few notches. "I just got held up at Dad's for a few minutes."

Concern creased Kate's brow. "Everything okay?"

Jane smiled weakly. "It will be."

"C'mon." Kate slipped her arm around Jane's shoulders. "The burgers just came off the grill."

"Mmm. Smells great, and I'm starving."

Truthfully, she hadn't had much of an appetite since the anniversary debacle. In that week and a half, she hadn't stepped on the scales, but she noticed her slacks hung a little looser than before.

The farm buzzed with activity to a happy soundtrack of chatter and laughter. Spirits seemed as high as the kites the kids were flying in the field on the glorious end-of-summer holiday. A backyard football game occupied the side lawn, and a heated game of euchre was underway in the Lullaby Ranch arena. Kids scurried here and there, stopping only long enough to grab a sandwich or a handful of chips from the buffet-style food table. Most of the adults filled their plates and sat at a picnic table or on blankets and ate while visiting with each other.

Jane scanned the familiar faces of Harvest Bay's faculty and staff, more like her extended family after all these years, wondering who would be the first to ask about Ian. After filling her plate, she sat at a picnic table with Kate, Kennedy, and a handful of other teachers, who were chatting and laughing. Even though her mind remained preoccupied with her situation, Jane kept up with the conversation in a performance she felt deserved an Emmy.

Am I being selfish? Or does it just seem that way because I've given so much of myself for so long? . . . Shouldn't I take care of myself? . . . Don't I deserve to be happy? . . . Maybe I could try a little harder . . . Ian reached out. Maybe I could reach out, too . . . But what would that change? Nothing. The picnic would be over and everything would go back to the way it's been for years—me reaching, grasping, trying, caring, and Ian working, providing for all our needs, except for my emotional ones . . . Everyone would be taken care of, except for me . . . I hate the thought of my family falling apart, but I'm not strong enough to hold it all together anymore.

The thoughts made her physically sick. Her chest ached from the tug of war taking place inside her heart. She was pretty sure no one, not even Kate, noticed that she barely touched her food. She merely pushed it around her plate until she decided to throw it away.

Gradually her friends vacated their seats at the picnic table to find their families. It didn't bother her until Kate rose from the bench.

"I'll be right back. I'm going to go check on Adam and the girls."

"No problem." It wasn't exactly a slap across the face, but it stung like one, not because she was being left alone, but because she was being left out. "Take your time."

Patting Jane's shoulder, Kate hurried off across the lawn toward where her husband was refereeing the football game.

Jane took a long drink of her lemonade, wishing she had something strong to mix with it. Anything to soften the very sharp edge of reality. It seemed all her friends had perfect relationships, while she had a marriage without a relationship. It was the worst kind of lonely. But she'd reached the point where she'd rather be lonely sitting all by herself than to be lonely next to the man she promised forever to.

Forever. Her stomach turned, and she groaned inwardly. *There was a time I couldn't imagine spending a day without him. Now I can't imagine living the rest of my life like this.*

She swept her gaze across the lawn. Zach Andrews stood off to the side, holding a cup in one hand, the other casually slipped into the pocket of his faded jeans that she couldn't help noticing fit him just right. These family-oriented faculty picnics could be overwhelming for a new teacher, but Zach exuded a contagious type of confidence. She felt a little stronger just watching him.

Meeting her gaze, Zach grinned and raised his Solo cup to her before taking a long drink. Jane felt as if her internal thermostat had gone haywire because her cheeks went from pale to flushed in an instant. Hastily she glanced away.

All Zach had done was acknowledge her. It was nothing. She received attention every day . . . Or did she?

Jane focused on the football game, which Kate had joined after intercepting a pass and being chased across the lawn by Adam. Jane tried to remember the last time she'd had that kind of fun, the last time she'd laughed so joyfully. She was starved for fun and laughter, for affection and happiness.

She sighed heavily. Her gaze traveled back to Zach, and she found his still locked on her.

Well, I can keep sitting here alone like a loser, or I can go make friendly conversation.

It was an easy decision. She recalled how their last conversation left her with a smile on her face. She needed that smile today more than ever.

She pushed to her feet and strolled over to stand shoulder to shoulder with Zach. "Surviving your first faculty picnic?"

He chuckled and nodded. "Just taking it all in."

"Everyone knows each other so well it's like we're family. I imagine it can be overwhelming for the new kid on the block."

Up close his smile, surrounded by a couple days worth of stubble, seemed more genuine than anything in her world lately.

"Are you kidding? This is fun."

"Oh, we are a fun bunch." She eyed him. "But you'd probably have a better time if you were with someone rather than standing over here all alone."

"You're right." Warmth oozed from his blue-gray gaze. "It's much more enjoyable now."

"No, wait . . . I . . . I didn't mean me." She sidestepped to put extra space between them, the color in her cheeks deepening.

His face displayed a smug expression. "Of course, you didn't."

Jane cleared her throat. "How's Jessica doing in class? Is she behaving? She's sharp as a tack, but Lord knows she can be a handful and a half. And Sammy's like a double dose of Jessica, so just wait until you get him in class."

"You want to discuss work right now?"

Jane looked down and kicked at a clod of dirt. "No, not really."

"How's your dad?"

"Making progress. He still has a way to go, but he's getting stronger every day." Her voice came out soft and delicate. Vulnerable. So foreign to her own ears. "Thanks for asking."

He nodded. "That's good to hear."

Just because he asked about Dad doesn't mean anything, Jane told herself. *Except that he must care. At least a little . . . It's been a while since I felt cared about, and it feels kind of nice.*

"Hey, if my memory serves me correctly, you had quite a knack for painting. Didn't you win a couple of awards your senior year?"

It took a minute for Jane to find her voice. "As a matter of fact, I won a national art contest and a scholarship. But how did you remember that when I barely remember you?"

Zach shrugged. "I pay attention to things that interest me. So how's that going? Paint anything new lately?"

"Uh . . . Yeah . . . A little bit. I mean, I took a few years off to focus on work and the kids, but just the other day I got out my brushes and dusted off the cobwebs. I'm a little rusty, but it's coming back to me."

"Good. It'd be a shame for talent like yours to go to waste."

Jane wondered if she'd heard him right. Did he just imply that she had talent? Drinking in just those few words left her feeling intoxicated.

She stared at her feet and focused on steadying her wobbly knees. "Thanks."

"Hey," one of the high school teachers called from the arena entrance, "we need a couple of euchre players. Are you two in?"

Zach glanced at Jane. "Do you play?"

"Sure, but I haven't in years."

"C'mon." He took a few steps toward the arena. "It's like riding a bike. It'll come back to you, and I'll be right there to help you."

"I'm not so sure about that."

Actually, she wasn't sure about a lot of things. But as Jane followed close behind Zach, she'd never been more certain that at that moment she was exactly where she wanted to be.

CHAPTER
Seven

Ian half expected Jane to realize she'd been wrong, come home, and work things out with him instead of going to the faculty picnic. *I've been at every school related function since she started teaching there. Surely she won't go without me.*

But as the minutes turned into hours and the TV shows turned into infomercials, his hope turned into doubt. He began to second guess everything that he'd ever believed to be true, except for the fact that he'd always had the very best of intentions.

I just don't understand where I went so wrong. I'm a good guy and a great dad. I thought I was a pretty decent husband too. What have I been missing? He rubbed his forehead in an attempt to soothe his troubled mind. *I've worked hard to protect my family, but because of something I did, or maybe didn't do, or possibly both, she left and tore this family apart. We used to be teammates. Now it's like we're opponents.*

As he paced the days away, that thought festered, and by the end of the week it seriously infected his mood. Toxic anger seeped through his body.

She's not working with me. She's working against me.

That knowledge caused him debilitating pain. Barely functioning well enough to cook a package of Ramen noodles in the microwave, he went back and forth between thanking Jane for keeping Jessica and Samuel with her since the older two could fend for themselves, and cursing her because he missed his kids. It never had to come to this.

If only that stubborn woman had gone on the picnic with me. Then she'd see how different things could be if we try a little harder.

Yes, he was responsible for part of the problem, but she needed to claim her role too. He wanted to fix it, but he couldn't do it on his own. He needed her to work with him again like she used to.

He glanced at his phone several times every hour. He wanted her to call or at the very least text. He wanted her to want him again.

But she didn't.

Each evening that Jane didn't call or text, Ian turned to someone he could at least pretend wanted him. No, he couldn't hold his computer in his arms or hear it say words that would boost his ego. And he certainly couldn't kiss and caress it. But imagination is a powerful weapon against loneliness, and Felicity's exotic eyes, luscious lips, and beautiful body temporarily soothed his wounded male pride. But each morning, though, when he woke up alone in their bed, regret gnawed at his heart.

By Sunday, dark thoughts threatened to consume him, ideas that went against every moral fiber in his being. He knew he had to gather enough strength to reach out to someone he could trust to not pass judgment on him, to talk him through this, to give him advice and encouragement.

Only one face came to mind. Swallowing his pride, he scrolled through his list of contacts, found the name, and pressed the green button.

After four rings, Adam picked up. "Hey, Ian. How are you?" He sounded preoccupied.

"Umm . . . " Hands trembling, Ian sucked in a deep breath and plunged forward. "Truthfully, I've seen better days, bro. You busy?"

There was a short lull as the background noise died down. "We're getting ready to leave for Sunday school."

"Oh." Ian hated that he sounded pathetic. What must his best friend think? Hearing the faint hum of a garage door rising in the background, he said hastily, "Okay. Give me a call when you get home."

"Why don't you come to church with us?"

Ian hesitated but couldn't think fast enough to come up with an excuse. "What time does it start?"

"Ten-thirty. Don't worry about dressing up. Our late service is more casual. Some people wear jeans."

"So khakis are fine?" He thought he had a clean pair, but he'd have to double check.

"Perfect. See you then."

Ending the call, Ian glanced at the time displayed on his cell phone. A quarter till nine. Grateful for something to occupy his time for a while, he headed to shower and change.

He pulled into the parking lot at Harvest Bay Community Church with twenty minutes to spare. "It's nice to show up early," he muttered to himself as he strolled toward the double doors. "Jane runs late so often I've forgotten what it feels like to not peel into a parking lot on two tires."

When he entered the lobby, he recognized many of his neighbors, coworkers, and parents of his kids' classmates. He greeted them politely as he searched for Adam.

These people are going to know something is going on since I showed up here alone, and then they're all going to start talking. They'll wonder what I did wrong, I'm sure, and probably assume the worst.

He braced himself for the inevitable, but detected neither questioning looks nor gossipy whispers. Instead, he received genuine smiles accompanied with a welcoming handshake or a warm hug. At last he spotted Adam, Kate, Chloe, and Madeline about to enter the sanctuary. Adam had his hand pressed against the small of Kate's back, a chivalrous gesture that magnified the void Ian felt at his side.

He wanted what Adam had, but he questioned whether that kind of relationship was even possible with Jane now. The independent, fiery redhead would shrug off his hand and walk ahead of him. He knew she would.

He picked up his step, reaching Adam and his family as they slipped into their pew. Ian side-stepped into the pew behind them and placed a firm hand on Adam's shoulder.

Adam turned, his face brightening. "Hey, you made it."

"I'm a man of my word, and I told you I'd be here."

Internally Ian cringed, wondering whether his response sounded just a little too defensive. To his relief, Adam didn't give any indication that he noticed.

The small band started to play, filling the atmosphere with a beautiful inspirational song that sounded vaguely familiar to Ian. As he glanced around the sanctuary, he noticed a few older ladies sitting in their pews with their eyes closed, softly singing the words they clearly knew by heart. Part of him wished he'd attended church more often rather than just with his grandmother when he was a kid. Maybe then he wouldn't feel so out of place.

Another worship song, scripture reading, and prayer followed, then another song. As the last few notes faded and the preacher made his way to the front, Ian slouched in the pew, hoping to stay out of his line of sight. Clergy had the innate ability to see right through the people in their congregation, like a holy type of x-ray vision, didn't they?

"Grace and peace to you from God our Father." Placing his Bible on the podium, Pastor Ben Andrews held up a plain sheet of copy paper with a big heart drawn with red marker in the center. "I have in my hand here a piece of paper with a simple drawing on it, as you can see, but something is missing. A heart isn't supposed to be empty."

Ian snorted inwardly. *No, it's not, but lots of things happen that aren't supposed to. It's called life.*

"I need your help filling it up." Pastor Ben laid the drawing on the podium and got out a pen. "Just go ahead and shout out words that describe this sheet of paper."

The congregation was silent for a second or two, then a voice called out, "Smooth."

"Good." Pastor Ben wrote the word. "Keep them coming."

"Clean . . . useful . . . pretty, with the heart on it."

"Very interesting." Pastor Ben finished writing and faced the congregation. "So you think the heart makes the paper pretty. Why?"

A young woman spoke up, "Because a heart represents love and caring and compassion, and to me that's pretty."

It was obvious to Ian that this girl was inexperienced in relationships. She had no idea how ugly love could be.

"Very good insight, Maggie." Pastor Ben scanned the congregation. "Any more thoughts?"

A female voice came from right behind Ian, and he fought the urge to duck when the pastor turned his way. "Well, since the heart represents love, caring, and compassion, can those words describe the paper too? I mean, since the heart is part of the paper."

"Yes! Excellent," Pastor Ben excitedly scribbled the words on the paper. "Give me more."

A man near the front spoke up. "How about eco-friendly? You can recycle it."

Nodding, Pastor Ben wrote down the words.

"It's fun," Kate's daughter, Madeline, offered. "Especially when you fold it into airplanes and cootie catchers."

"Thank you, Maddie." While adding her contribution to the paper, Pastor Ben commented, "For the older generation, like me, who may be out of the loop, a cootie catcher is an origami game that apparently uses a combination of colors and numbers to reveal a hidden message, right Maddie?"

From her seat in the pew, Madeline nodded.

"And if you want to know more than that, I'm sure Maddie would be happy to give you a lesson."

The congregation chuckled, and Ian's nerves settled a bit. He liked how this pastor seemed so personable, relatable.

"Okay. Do we have anything else to add?"

The congregation remained silent.

He held up the paper. "That is a pretty full heart, do you agree?"

Ian found himself nodding right along with the others. He didn't see how another word would fit inside the red outline of the heart.

"Now what if I decided it wasn't as fun as, perhaps, Facebook or Twitter or Instagram or any of the other social media outlets that consume our time and attention?" He took the pen and made a big, ugly scratch mark over the word fun. "And I don't have time to recycle so even if it is eco-friendly, I'm not going to acknowledge that trait." Again, he scribbled over the word. "In fact, this paper is not nearly as high quality as another brand." He crumpled it up in his fist.

Captivated, and slightly alarmed, Ian leaned forward a little in his pew.

"It's not as bright a white." Pastor Ben packed the ball tighter. "It's not as high in poundage." He threw the wad of paper on the floor and stomped on it. "It's just all around not good enough for me."

A baby whimpered. The light and positive mood had evaporated. Ian shifted uncomfortably in his pew. He had a sinking feeling this sermon was about to get deep.

"Wait a minute." Pastor Ben stooped over and picked up the smashed paper. "Maybe I overreacted."

Carefully, slowly he opened it, unfolded it, flattened it. He worked hard at smoothing it out on the podium. Finally he held it up, creased and crinkled.

"I got frustrated for a moment. I said some hurtful things. I didn't mean them. Truthfully, this piece of paper was perfect for me, but I wanted what everyone else had. Now, unfortunately, no matter how hard I try I can't take back what I did. I can apologize until I'm blue in the face, but the creases and wrinkles won't come out. I can smooth and press it against the podium all day, but the marks will still be there. Like scars. I could try to iron out the results of my frustration, but that might actually make it worse. I can't erase the ink that I used to cover up two of my favorite things about this paper. As much as I wish I could return it to the crisp white paper with everything we liked about it written on the heart, I can never undo my words and actions."

Pastor Ben fastened the tattered paper to the podium for the congregation to see. "This is a lesson that began in high schools across the country during the height of the anti-bullying campaign, but this is a lesson we can all use in our daily lives, starting at home."

Ian flinched. Those last three words stung. Had he treated Jane like that crumpled piece of paper? He knew he hadn't been perfect, but neither had she. He assumed that was all a part of the ups and downs of being married.

"We all know the saying, 'Sticks and stones can break your bones, but words will never hurt you,' right?" A murmur rose from the congregation. "It's not exactly a true sentiment, is it? Words can hurt. They can also divide and destroy. They can destroy a person's confidence and self worth. I have seen words divide and alienate family members. I think often we don't even realize the damage we cause until it's too late."

Wedging his Bible under his arm, Pastor Ben stepped away from the podium and into the aisle. "We read in the book of Matthew about a group of Pharisees and scribes, a group that was always trying to discredit Jesus. They came to Jesus and said, 'These guys you're with, they don't wash their hands before they eat. They're unclean, contaminated. That's just not right.' Jesus responded by telling them in so many words that before they criticize they should take a good long, hard look at themselves."

Pastor Ben opened the Bible to a page he had marked with a Post-It. "In chapter 15, verse 11, He turned to His disciples and said to them, 'Not what goes into the mouth defiles a man; but what comes out of the mouth, this defiles a man.' This confused His disciples a little bit so he went on to explain in verse 17, 'Do you not yet understand that whatever enters the mouth goes into the stomach and is eliminated? But those things which proceed out of the mouth come from the heart, and they defile a man.' "

Pausing, he closed the Bible. "The words we say in moments of anger or possibly lust, the lies we tell others and ourselves to make us feel better, those words hurt more than just the ones they're directed at. They affect us too. They make our hearts and spirits filthy. And here's the thing: None of us is exempt from this. We've all said things we don't mean, most likely to the people we love the most. So if we've all done it, what can be done to fix it? Can we ever return that paper to the way it was?"

Ian listened intently as Pastor Ben flipped through his Bible to another marked page.

"If we go back a few chapters in Matthew, Jesus tells us making things right with our loved ones should be our top priority. In chapter 5 starting at verse 23, He says, 'Therefore if you bring your gift to the altar, and there remember that your brother has something against you, leave your gift there before the altar, and go your way. First be reconciled to your brother, and then come and offer your gift.' "

He looked up. "Reconciliation is hard because of one very big three-letter word: ego. We want to be right. We want to win. But if it costs us a relationship with someone we love, is that really winning? When we ask someone to forgive us, we have to humble ourselves, turn away from our pride, from our desire to be right. We have to admit that we hurt someone without excuses or defenses.

"In other words, we can't keep licking our wounds if we're going to use our mouth to say, 'I'm sorry I hurt you. Please forgive me.' It just doesn't work that way. And, at that point, it doesn't matter why we said or did hurtful things. It also doesn't matter what that person did to you. What matters is that you love them enough to put yourself aside and take responsibility for the creases you caused in that paper."

Several members of the congregation shifted in their seats. Ian hoped that meant he wasn't the only one feeling a bit uncomfortable.

That doesn't seem fair. I've been hurt, too. She left me, but I'm the one who has to apologize?

"Hear me when I say I'm not telling you to be a doormat. You don't have to accept hurtful words or behaviors. I'm simply suggesting that you forgive, ask forgiveness, and give God room to work. Which leads me to the next step: Pray for God's forgiveness. 1 John 1:9 promises, 'If we confess our sins, He is faithful and just to forgive us our sins and to cleanse us from all unrighteousness.' He will cleanse us, wash clean our dirty hearts. And over time He can smooth out any crinkle or crease."

Ian turned his wedding band around his finger, noticing how worn and scratched up the metal had become, just like that piece of paper. It seemed appropriate for the current state of their marriage.

No matter how much I polish it, I just don't know if I can make it shine like before. No amount of forgiveness can fix that.

"I know many of you have been hurt by the words or actions of someone you love. God sees that, and He will deal with that person's heart in His time and on His terms. We don't have to understand it. We just have to trust Him. In the meantime, we all need to work on ourselves. No matter what your family dynamics are, no matter what issues you are facing, it's not too late to try. Let's start today by praying for our families. Pray for guarded tongues and quick forgiveness because, as we witnessed, words do hurt. The altar is open and our Father is waiting."

The band began softly playing "Great Is Thy Faithfulness."

It was the one hymn Ian knew. He remembered his grandmother singing it while she cooked in the kitchen or hung clothes out on the line, and it calmed him. As several members of the congregation made their way forward to kneel at the altar, Ian wondered what advice his grandmother would give him about his broken family and his failing marriage.

Adam and Kate rose and walked hand-in-hand to the altar. Kneeling together, they bowed their heads.

Jealous once again of that kind of relationship, Ian couldn't help wondering who they were praying for. Were they thinking of him and Jane? Was it possible that they could be struggling? Or were they praying for families in general?

Ian clasped his hands together and bowed his head, wishing he'd paid more attention when his grandma prayed.

She was always talking to God like He was right there next to her. I used to think she was a little bit off her rocker. Now I wish I knew how to pray like that . . . or even at all. How do you communicate with Someone who isn't there, who can't respond, who I can't feel?

Ian peeked at the individuals sitting nearby. It seemed so natural, so easy for them. Closing his eyes, he sat in silence waiting for inspiration, for a sign or a prompt, something, anything to clue him in.

I don't know how to do this, and I don't know what else to say except that I need help. I'm drowning. I can't keep my head above water, can't breathe, and the more I struggle to keep it together, the more it all falls apart. I just don't understand. I used to love my life and now I don't even recognize it. So how do I fix it? How do I fix me? I'm trying to hold on with both fists, but everything I ever cared about is slipping right through my fingers. God, are you there? Because I need answers. If You're really there, I need Your help right now.

When he lifted his head and opened his eyes, the sanctuary was mostly deserted. "How long have I been sitting here?" His low voice seemed amped up in the silent church.

"Not long." The pastor extended his hand. "I'm Pastor Ben Andrews, by the way. Welcome."

Ian shook the pastor's hand. "Thanks. I'm Ian Garner. Adam Sullivan invited me, but to tell you the truth I'm a fish out of water here. Church isn't really my thing."

"I can understand that." Sitting in the pew in front of Ian, Pastor Ben propped his arm on the back of it. "There was a time when I wouldn't have felt comfortable stepping foot inside those doors."

Ian chortled. "That's kind of an odd thing coming from a pastor."

Pastor Ben shrugged. "What can I say? I'm human, and I was a young man once." He got to his feet and stepped out of the pew. "I hope you found what you were looking for today."

Ian narrowed his eyes suspiciously. "What makes you think I was searching for anything?"

"Everyone knows church is where you come for answers, even if it's not your thing." Giving Ian a parting nod, Pastor Ben turned to leave.

"Wait." Swallowing what pride he had left, Ian stood and lowered his gaze. "I realize I'm not a member here, but I could really use some help working through a few things."

Pastor Ben nodded. "Sure. How about tomorrow morning? Say ten o'clock? We could grab a cup of coffee at the Bayside Cafe."

"Yeah, that works. I'll see you then. Thanks."

As Ian pushed through the church's heavy wooden doors into the warm September sunshine, he felt the faintest flicker of hope. Maybe Pastor Ben could give him the tools to save his marriage. At least it was worth a try.

He climbed into his truck and started the engine. But when he pulled out of the parking lot, he didn't head toward home.

Jane stretched. The double bed in her dad's house wasn't as comfortable as her king-sized bed, and for just an instant she missed her bed, her home, her family. But she quickly reminded herself how and why her life had come to this.

I'm so tired of waking up lonely. Even on mornings when Ian was still at home, he wasn't really there.

Glancing at the half finished painting pinned to her easel, she smiled. The bright morning sunshine streaming through the window made the perfect spotlight, illuminating it in a way florescent lights in the basement never could have.

I want to be me again, not what I feel like I have to be for everyone else.

Her cell phone chimed and she reached to retrieve it. Zach Andrews's name was listed above the text message. Grinning, she opened it.

Good morning, beautiful. Did you sleep well?

Jane reread the words three times, her eyes lingering on the word *beautiful*. She tried to recall the last time someone had called her such a nice name. Maybe on her wedding day? She thought she remembered her dad telling her she looked pretty. Ian rarely even used her name anymore when they talked. That realization stung.

Morning! Yes, once I finally went to bed. She hit send, then as much as she didn't want to, typed out and sent another message. *And you shouldn't call me names like that. It's not appropriate.*

Swinging her legs over the side of the bed, she stretched her arms over her head, slipped her phone into the pocket of her lounge pants, and returned to her easel. As she picked up her brush, her phone chimed again.

Sorry. Just being honest.

Turning her attention to her painting, she decided to ignore both the message and the way it made her heart do cartwheels. She swirled a drop of red paint into a glob of white and spread the light pink hue onto the canvas, first with small careful strokes, and then fanning it out. Each stroke of the paintbrush breathed new life into her deflated spirit, resurrecting her long-buried hopes and dreams.

Her phone chimed again. "I'm not going to pick it up. If it was important, they'd call."

She brushed on a bit more color, but the blinking light on her phone kept taunting her. Sighing, she gave in and retrieved the message.

I know you're painting so I won't bother you. Just had to tell you this past week since the faculty party has been the best I've had in a long time.

She set her palate aside and responded as fast as her thumbs could type. *How did you know I was painting?*

The reply arrived a minute later. *Lucky guess?* Her phone chimed immediately with another message. *JK, lol. You told me when we were texting Thursday evening that you've been painting a lot on the weekends.*

As she reread the message, Jane's heart swelled a little. "He actually paid attention to something I said."

"Hey, Mom." Samuel tore into her room, part of his breakfast smeared across his freckled face. "Dad's here. Can I go home with him?"

"Wait. What?"

Abandoning her easel, Jane stepped into her slippers and headed down the hallway to the living room, where Ian perched on the edge of the sofa shooting the breeze with her dad. She stopped in the doorway, arms crossed, and cleared her throat.

"Oh, hey." He stood. "I know I should have called first."

"It's a little early for a visit. Sammy said he's going home with you. Is that why you're here?"

"I . . . uh . . . " Ian shifted his gaze from Jane's dad to Jessica and Samuel, who were watching the Disney Channel, and back to Jane. He lowered his voice. "Can we go somewhere to talk?"

Truthfully, Jane didn't want to talk. She'd wanted to have a real conversation with him for so long that she'd given up on the notion. Now that they weren't living under the same roof, she didn't see the point, and she kind of liked the space. But she'd invested over twenty years of her life in a relationship with this man, and that was too long to ignore.

"Have you had breakfast yet?"

He shook his head. When she went into the kitchen, he followed her, pulled out a chair at the table, and sat down.

Jane opened the refrigerator and grabbed the eggs and milk. Closing the door with her hip, she glanced in his direction.

"So what's up?"

"Well . . . " He rubbed the back of his neck. "Okay, here's the thing." He sucked in a deep breath. "I realized I need to improve in some areas before we can get back to the way we were, so I'm going to talk to Adam's pastor tomorrow morning. I don't expect it to fix everything, but I figure it's at least a start, and I'd like you to come with me."

Jane concentrated on cracking eggs into a bowl and beating them violently with a whisk. After a long moment she turned to him. "Let me get this straight. You want me to go to counseling with you?"

Ian folded his hands on the table. "Yes I do."

"You mean like how I wanted you to go with me after I miscarried our first pregnancy? Or like when I practically begged you to go after Mom died? It wasn't important enough to you then."

Ian's shoulders fell. "That's not true."

Setting the bowl and whisk aside, she planted her hands on her hips. "You know what? You're right. *I* wasn't important enough to you."

"No, that's not it! You've always been everything to me. I just haven't always known how to show it."

"You didn't try, even when I told you what I needed from you. In twenty years you've never really tried. And now that you are putting forth a little extra effort, you expect me to?"

Unable to see clearly behind her tears, Jane left the bowl of eggs on the counter and headed toward the hallway. "I'm glad you're going to counseling, Ian, but I'm not going with you. And for the record, I don't ever want to get back to the way we were."

CHAPTER
Eight

*J*essica and Samuel had both gone home with Ian for the night, and without the two extra bodies to get ready and out the door Monday morning, Jane found herself running far ahead of schedule.

Good. I'll get my prep work for tomorrow done before school today and be able to stay on top of things all week.

A day in kindergarten was nothing short of managed chaos if she fell behind. Grabbing her purse and duffel bag, she stopped beside her dad who was already comfortable in his recliner with a cup of coffee and the newspaper.

"I'm leaving for school, Dad. Do you need anything before I go?"

"Nope." His hand trembled slightly as he brought his coffee cup to his lips.

Trying not to dwell on the thought that little by little their roles were reversing, she gave him a kiss on the cheek. "I'm going for a run after school today, so I'll be home at about four o'clock. Call if you need anything at all."

"Don't give up on him, lassie."

Her shoulders dropped as she let out an exasperated breath. "I love you, Dad, and I know you mean well, but I don't want to discuss this now."

Nodding once, Shaun went back to his paper. "Top 'o the mornin' to ya."

Jane smoothed her ruffled feathers and hustled out of the house, making it to her classroom as the sky turned back its dark covers and stretched its pale pink arms across the horizon. Putting Ian, her dad, and every other worry out of her mind, she organized her students' activities for the day.

She wished she had time to prepare so thoroughly every morning. Just a few extra minutes would make her entire day run much more smoothly, but she could never seem to get all of her kids out the door on time. It helped some that Bradley drove himself now, but Emma had to apply her makeup perfectly, Jessica changed her outfit three times on average, and Samuel ate his weight in breakfast. The well of Jane's patience was dry before her students ever walked in and hung up their backpacks. It wasn't fair to her class, but she didn't know how to change it.

Until now.

"I'd say it's fair that Ian is in charge of morning duty for a while. Why can't he go to work after he takes the kids to school?" Her strength multiplied just saying the words. "I think I'll talk to him about it tonight." This new independence was a beautiful thing.

Movement at her door caught her eye. She straightened and smiled confidently as her principal entered the classroom.

"Good morning, Mrs. Zeller."

"Morning. How's your dad?"

"Getting a little stronger every day." *We both are.* Jane hesitated and creases of concern lined her forehead. "But somehow I don't think that's the only reason you're here."

"I'm planning our first lockdown drill for after lunch today."

A red flag rose with the hairs on the back of Jane's neck.

"Okay. Did something happen over the weekend that I should be aware of?"

"It's just a drill. I'm letting you know so you can prepare your students. I know the little ones spook easily."

It wasn't lost on Jane that Mrs. Zeller avoided her question. "I will take care of them."

"I know you will. That's why you're one of our best teachers." As Mrs. Zeller turned to leave, Zach appeared in the doorway. "Ah, good. One less classroom I have to go to. Lockdown drill today at twelve-thirty."

"Twelve-thirty. Got it." He shifted his attention to Jane as the click of Mrs. Zeller's heels faded down the hallway. "Everything okay?"

Jane shrugged, both calmed and excited by his presence. "I don't know. She wasn't too generous with her information."

He moved further into the classroom. "No. I meant are you okay? Last night when we were texting you seemed pretty upset."

"Oh." Her cheeks blazed. "I'm fine. A good night's sleep helped."

Her knees suddenly wobbly, she leaned against her desk and cast her gaze to her very ordinary navy pumps. They were comfortable, worn, broken in, and matched everything except her new, vibrant attitude. She decided to toss them into her Goodwill pile as soon as she got home.

Her lips curved into a shy, nervous grin. "So, um, did you sleep well?"

He took a long swig from an insulated travel mug. "Well, it was after midnight when we quit messaging each other, and then I was too worried about you to fall asleep."

She suspected he knew he was tugging on her heart strings, and she kind of liked it. "You aren't blaming me, are you?"

"Of course not. I wouldn't have it any other way."

Now he was downright yanking on them, causing the oddest sensation of satisfaction mixed with ache to resonate through her soul. "For whatever it's worth, I appreciate your being there, not just for me but for Jessie too. It means a lot to know she's in good hands during the day."

Closing the gap between them, he redirected a strand of hair that had fallen close to her left eye and gazed at her so intently she wondered if he could see all the crazy thoughts swirling in her brain.

"She's safe with me. You both are."

Jane's heart thumped so loudly it echoed in her ears. She took a step back, fearful that Zach could hear it too.

"Thanks."

She needed space. She needed room to breathe without inhaling his intoxicating cologne. She needed a moment to gather her thoughts and figure out what exactly was taking place in her erratically beating heart.

Repositioning herself behind her desk, she tried to focus on correlating phonics pages. "But I can take care of myself."

Nodding, Zach retreated to the door. "Yes, you can, but I'm always here if you ever need a friend."

She gave him an appreciative grin as he turned and disappeared down the hallway.

As she stared at the empty doorway, her smile faded. Somewhere between the faculty party and that moment, Zach had gone from being just a coworker to a close confidant, and somehow in her vulnerable state her feelings spiraled out of control. Was it right? Probably not. Was it appropriate? She doubted it, but she also doubted it was okay to go through life invisible.

He sees me. He really sees me. Her heartbeat slowed to a

sluggish crawl and her eyes stung with disappointment. *But he's just a friend. He said it himself.*

Building a swift wall of professionalism, she turned her attention to sweet little Destiny and a few other students just beginning to trickle into the classroom.

I may be safe with him, but I'm not sure my heart is.

Ian sat in his truck outside the Bayside Cafe for ten minutes wrestling with his pride. *I know too many people in this town. Someone I know is bound to be in there. What will they say if I'm seen having coffee with the pastor? What will I say if people start asking questions? I don't have any answers.*

The clock on his dash turned to 10:00, and he sighed. Hating being even a minute late, he grabbed the door handle.

And I'm not going to get any answers by sitting here. It can't be any worse than showing up alone at church.

Thankfully the breakfast crowd had thinned out considerably by the time Ian entered through the set of double doors. Spotting Pastor Ben in a corner booth, he made a beeline for the table and slid into the seat.

Pastor Ben looked up from his newspaper and smiled. "Good morning."

"Morning." Glancing over his shoulder, Ian scanned the dining room. "Sorry if you've been waiting long."

"Just long enough to get caught up on the news." Pastor Ben folded the paper and set it aside. "Your timing is perfect."

Ian drummed his fingers on the table. "I didn't know if I was going to come in."

"I know. I was watching." Pastor Ben nodded toward the window, and Ian turned to see a perfect view of his truck. "What was stopping you?"

Ian shrugged. "My pride, I guess."

A young, Hispanic, raven-haired waitress approached the table. "*Buenos dias*, Ian. How are Jane and the kids?"

"Hi, Maggie. They're well, thanks."

"*Bueno*. Can I get you something to drink?" Retrieving a pen and pad of paper from the pocket of her apron, the waitress offered him a cheerful grin.

"Just coffee for now."

She gave him a friendly nod. "Coming right up."

As she hurried off to the kitchen, Ian returned his attention to Pastor Ben. "That was stopping me."

"Why is that?" Pastor Ben chuckled. "Maggie's easily one of the sweetest, most unassuming young woman in this town."

Ian hung his head. "Yeah, but I didn't want to be asked about my wife by anyone because I honestly don't know how she is."

"I see." Pastor Ben folded his hands around his white coffee cup. "So then what made you come in?"

A hush fell upon them as Maggie returned with a pot of coffee and a small pitcher of cream to fill the white ceramic cup already on the table. "Are you ready for something to eat?"

Pastor Ben put his hand up. "Not right now. Thank you."

"Take your time. I'll check back in a bit."

After Maggie had disappeared behind the kitchen doors, a sigh escaped Ian's lips. "I make a living of building and fixing things, but I can't fix this on my own. I've tried. I don't know what I'm doing wrong, and I need answers."

"Tell me about your wife."

Ian thought a minute. "Well, she teaches kindergarten at the elementary school. She's a great mom. She kept our home running like a machine." Taking a sip of coffee, he washed down a lump of emotion. "I didn't realize how much she did until she left."

"So you're separated?"

Ian wasn't prepared for how much this hurt. "In a matter of speaking, yes. We had a big fight on our anniversary because I had to postpone our dinner plans. The next day her dad was taken to the hospital with symptoms of a stroke. She never called me to let me know. She's been staying with him since his discharge from the hospital and barely speaks to me except to accuse me of never being around."

"Were they false accusations?"

Ian rubbed the back of his neck. "Not entirely, no. I worked a lot, did my best to provide for them and give her the kind of life she deserves. But I made it to most of the kids' games and a lot of practices too. I coached Bradley in little league and the girls in soccer for a while. Doesn't that count for anything? It's like she doesn't even consider that anymore."

Setting his coffee cup down, Pastor Ben held up a finger. "Hang on. I just heard you say you tried to give her what she deserves. Are you sure what you think she deserves and what she really wants are the same thing?"

Ian shrugged. "She never said otherwise." *Or did she?*

"So when did you two start struggling?"

Ian stretched his hands out. "That's just it. I can't pinpoint it, but I don't think my marriage started unraveling just because I postponed our anniversary dinner."

"When was the last time you saw your wife truly happy?"

As Ian considered this question, dread rose in him. "I don't know. I mean there have been many good moments, but I can't remember the last time I saw her truly happy. I guess I've been so busy trying to make a living that I took for granted the things that make a life worth living."

Out of the corner of his eye, Ian caught Maggie clearing off some tables on the other side of the dining room. "Look at her. In a perfect world, Justin would have come home from serving in Afghanistan. He would have married Maggie and been here when little Justin was born. Instead, she's raising her son alone, working here and at the Harvest Bay Family Practice to provide for him. And yet every time I run into her she seems to have a positive attitude. How?"

"Maggie leads our single parent support group. I'm sure she still has her moments like everyone else, but she's experienced quite a bit of healing over the past few years." Pastor Ben shifted his attention back to Ian, his voice gentle while his expression remained firm. "The fact of the matter is that I don't know any-body who hasn't seen their share of hardship. If it's not a rela-tionship issue, it's a problem with finances or health concerns. That doesn't necessarily make it any easier, but when you con-sider all that Maggie's been through, it should give you hope that as long as you keep moving, putting one foot in front of the other—crawling if you must—you'll eventually come out on the other side."

Swallowing a slug of coffee, Ian nodded. "That makes sense. It just doesn't feel that way right now."

"Don't focus on right now. Focus on what God's going to do through you. And remember it may not be what you expect, but it will be perfect."

Ian pondered the words, but before he could ask for clarifi-cation, Pastor Ben continued.

"In my experience, when a marriage falls apart it's not because the marriage itself is broken, but because the people involved are. Now I don't know you. I have no idea what sorts of struggles you've been through, but I do know that everyone carries baggage. No adult is exempt. We're all walking wounded. And just like when a broken bone doesn't heal properly it can cause further damage, if we don't heal from our spiritual wounds properly it can damage any relationship we're in." Pastor Ben paused for a moment to let Ian process this information. "If you try to repair your marriage before you fix yourself, it would be kind of like using a Band-Aid to patch up a gunshot wound. Even with your best effort, it just won't work."

Ian rubbed his forehead. "I understand, and I'll give it a try. At this point, what else do I have to lose?"

"Good. Today was a great first step. Tell you what, let's plan on meeting here for the next couple of weeks, and then we'll reevaluate things."

Ian's lips turned upward into a small grin. "I'd like that. Thank you."

"Between now and next Monday, ask God every day to show you what you can change to be a better husband and father. Make a list. It doesn't have to be anything drastic. Sometimes the smallest adjustments make the biggest difference."

"You're giving me a homework assignment?" The joke left a smirk on his face. "I thought I was done with school."

Pastor Ben's eyes twinkled as he lifted his coffee cup. "Lesson number one: You might be out of school, but you're never done learning."

The men each ordered a sandwich and talked for a half hour longer. When Ian finally climbed into his truck to head off to the job site, he felt better than he had in weeks. Stronger. Hopeful.

Focus on what God's going to do through you. He didn't quite understand it, but it definitely left him in a positive mood.

That evening, though, coming home to a quiet house, the loneliness sneaked back into his spirit like a thief through a window. He longed to share with Jane what he and Pastor Ben had talked about. Instead the only thing he had heard from her was a text message that read, "I need you to start taking E, J, and S to school. I'll have them ready for you in the a.m. Thanks."

Rereading the message, his blood started to boil. "What exactly does she think I am? A servant that she can just order around?"

He stopped himself. Thinking about what he had talked about with Pastor Ben, he reconsidered his quick judgment. "Jane always takes the kids to school without getting much appreciation for it. That is one thing I guess I could change."

Still, the lack of communication with her left him hollow. He wanted to talk to his wife. He wished he could feel the warmth of her body lying next to him in their bed. He ached to share a meal with her at their dining room table. Instead of eating alone, he skipped supper altogether.

He drifted from room to room, clicked on the TV only to click it off again, scanned his empty back yard from his deck, opened and closed the refrigerator, and then the freezer. Climbing the stairs, he stood in the doorways of his kids' bedrooms wishing he could pretend that they were just away at camp. He sat on the corner of his bed, once soft and comfortable, now as cold as the tiles in the shower that still faintly smelled like Jane's shampoo and body wash. He longed to hold her close to him, inhale the scent of her hair, touch her silky skin, taste her sweet lips . . .

"What good is it to work so hard to provide a beautiful home for my family if I have no one to share it with?"

Focus on what God's going to do through you.

Ending up in his den, he sat down behind his desk. After taking a couple hours away from work to meet with Pastor Ben, he needed to get caught up. He glanced at the paperwork waiting for him, and slid his gaze to the dark computer screen.

But someone else might be waiting for me too.

In reality he knew that Felicity didn't even know he existed, let alone pine away the minutes until he came back. But it helped ease his pain to imagine that someone missed him, even a little.

Wiggling the mouse to wake his dosing computer, he found himself awakening too.

"Good night, Dad." Jane kissed her father's cheek and slipped out of his bedroom closing the door behind her.

As she stopped to check on Emma, Jessica, and Samuel all camped out and snoozing in the spare bedroom, her heart sagged a little. Sleepovers at Granddad's a few times a week were fun for the short term, like a mini vacation, but it couldn't be a permanent solution. The lack of stability and consistency would start to have an effect, most likely sooner rather than later. Jane had no other choice than to make some hard decisions fast.

Turning lights off and locking doors through the house, she ended up in the kitchen, where she found Bradley sitting at the table fiddling with his cell phone.

He looked up and smiled at her.

It amazed her how he'd grown seemingly overnight. Did she actually see a hint of a goatee outlining his mouth?

"I thought you were heading out, son. Everything okay?"

"Yeah. I just feel like I haven't seen much of you lately, and I miss you. I thought maybe we could talk for a few minutes."

What am I doing to my kids? Swallowing hard against a rising lump of emotion, Jane reached into the cupboard for a package of Oreos, poured two glasses of milk, and sat next to Bradley.

"Of course, we can. What do you want to talk about?"

Bradley twisted a cookie apart and licked the white filling. "Well, you know homecoming is coming up in a few weeks."

She dunked an Oreo in her milk and popped it into her mouth. "Are you nervous about the game?"

Rolling the cookie back and forth on the table, he shrugged. "Not as nervous as I am about asking Alison to go to the dance with me."

Jane choked on cookie crumbs. Coughing and sputtering, she took a swallow of milk and composed herself. "My baby boy has a crush?"

"Cut it out, Mom." He shoved his fingers through his thick dark hair. "It's not like that. She's different."

Jane propped her chin on the palm of her hand. "Different how?"

"I don't know. We're in a lot of classes together and she's my lab partner, so we kind of got to know each other that way. And then she's on the volleyball team so we run into each other after school on the way to our practices." His cheek bones had a rosy tint to them. "She's a really great friend."

"So what's stopping you?"

Bradley blew out an exasperated breath. "What if she doesn't think of me the way I think of her? Isn't it kind of dangerous to cross over from the friend zone? What if things don't work out? I'll have lost a girlfriend and a good friend."

Jane bit into another Oreo, chewed, and swallowed. "It's definitely a risk, but life's a risk. And who says things won't work out? Some of the best relationships start out in the friend zone."

Bradley met her gaze. "You mean like you and dad?"

She sighed heavily. "Your dad and I were once the best of friends."

"Now look at you." Bradley snorted. "And you wonder why I'm afraid things won't work out?"

"It's not quite so cut and dried."

"Then explain it to me, Mom, because I need to know how two people can go from being so in love to not even speaking to each other."

Jane searched for a way to explain to this young man how it all fell apart. How could she put into words how Ian's dreams grew bigger than hers? Or how his success seemed to grow bigger than her or their children?

A light bulb illuminated her brain. "Stay here. I'll be right back."

Rushing down the dim hallway to her room, she grabbed the quilt off her bed, and hurried back. "This is the quilt my mom made me when your dad and I got married."

She left out the detail that because of the pastel colors she suspected it was meant to be a baby quilt. She and Ian had done their best to keep the unplanned pregnancy under wraps, but her mom was the most intuitive woman she knew. "I used it all the time—when I was sitting on the couch watching TV, when we'd go on picnics. Remember that?"

Giving her a half grin, he nodded.

"I used it, but I didn't take care of it." She turned the blanket over. "I didn't even notice this stitching begin to come out, and now the edges are so frayed it can't be fixed."

Bradley looked thoughtful.

Sorrow welled into Jane's eyes and her voice thickened with emotion. "It's the same with your dad and me. We didn't take care of our marriage. Little by little we drifted apart, and now the tie that's supposed to bind us is so frayed, I just don't think it can be mended."

Bradley reached for the blanket and examined the section that had come undone. "Why can't you sew a patch over it? It might not be exactly the same, but it could be beautiful again."

His quick comeback momentarily stunned her. "I never thought of that."

Bradley set the quilt aside. "Come home. Dad is lost without you. We all are."

"Granddad still needs me here."

"Then I'll stay and help him. Maybe we can all take turns. We'll work it out. We can do anything together as a family, but lately this doesn't feel much like one, and it's taking a toll on everybody."

"I'll think about it."

"Then I'll think about asking Alison to the dance."

Chuckling, Jane ruffled his hair. "What am I going to do with you, boy?"

His handsome grin spread across his face and he shrugged.

"It's getting late, and we both need our rest. You are always welcome to stay here, you know."

Bradley stood and stretched. "I know, but I'm most comfortable in my own bed, and I don't want Dad to be all alone."

Fighting back tears, she embraced him. "I'm sorry."

"Yeah, I know." He kissed her cheek. "I'll see you tomorrow after practice." Turning, he strode toward the door.

"I love you, Bradley."

"Love you, too, Mom." With a wave, he crossed the threshold and pulled the door shut behind him.

As she stood alone in the dark living room, she heard the engine of his car come to life, and then fade as he drove away.

Why can't you sew a patch over it?

Her decision suddenly seemed impossible, and yet quite simple. If her choices were to sacrifice her happiness or her children's, she knew in a heartbeat what she had to do.

Later she lay in her bed, staring at the ceiling with tears sliding down her cheeks and filling her ears. From the minute Bradley was born, she'd been determined to move heaven and earth to protect her children from any preventable pain. She just wasn't prepared for how much it hurt to give up her small taste of freedom.

Glancing at her night stand, she noticed the blinking light on her cell phone. She checked the screen.

Three missed text messages. All from Zach.

Her fingers trembled. She longed to reply, to connect with another human being. With Zach.

Instead, she rolled over and cried herself to a restless sleep.

CHAPTER
Nine

It seemed as though she had just drifted off when the alarm clock screamed at her. When she opened her eyes, she could tell from the gritty reminder of her tears that they were bloodshot and probably swollen. Yes, Visine would be her friend today. That, and an endless cup of coffee.

She checked her phone, sighing heavily when she found three more notifications from Zach. The idea that she might have hurt him by not responding to his messages stabbed her already broken heart, but she couldn't dwell on his feelings. She couldn't dwell on her feelings either.

As excruciating as it was just to get out of bed, she forced herself into motion, certain that if she returned home as Bradley suggested she would just vanish again. As before, she'd feel insignificant and minuscule.

She couldn't spend one second reminiscing about Zach's pretty words that made her feel valued or agonizing over the thought of never hearing them again. Her whole life had revolved around her children's happiness. That hadn't changed. They would always be her first priority, and at least for another ten years, until Samuel flew the nest she'd so meticulously made, she could put her dreams on the shelf. After all, their happiness was her happiness.

"Then why am I so miserable?"

A clap of thunder shook the house and rain pounded the roof. "Figures." Groaning, she plodded to the bathroom. "Well, at least the weather matches my mood."

She maintained a smile and the required level of enthusiasm to teach her class the majority of the day, breaking the facade only once when she sent Ian a message.

We have to talk. When will you be home? She punched in the keys and hit send.

His response came two minutes later. *Don't know. Rain supposed to end by noon so might work late to make up time.*

Jane stared at the words in disbelief. "You've got to be kidding me! He still doesn't get it." She tossed her phone onto her desk and spun her chair around to stare out the window at the dismal day. Tears stung her already irritated eyes.

"I don't want to go back to that."

Taking several deep breaths in between counting the raindrops that landed on the window, she fought to soothe her frayed nerves. Her planning period would be over soon, and she wanted to finish the day with her students on a positive note. When she swiveled around to grade a few papers, however, Zach was standing in her doorway. Her bottom lip quivered, and a few tears escaped over the ledge of her lashes.

"Hi." Her voice sounded puny.

Zach chuckled. "Well, that's more than I got out of you last night."

"I'm sorry I didn't respond to you last night," she sniffled. "I couldn't."

"Hey, it's all right." He came to her side and squatted next to her chair. "I'm not upset. I was just teasing you. I only wanted to make sure you were all right after not hearing from you."

She wiped the dampness from her cheeks with the back of her hand. "I talked with Bradley last night. He likes a girl and I didn't even know about it."

Catching a fresh tear as it was getting ready to fall, he wiped it on his Khakis and covered her hand with his. "Don't beat yourself up about it. He's a teenager, and teens don't readily offer information."

She shook her head. "They need me at home. My kids need their family together. They don't know where they're sleeping from night to night. I'm actually surprised it hasn't affected their performance yet."

Standing, Zach leaned against her desk and crossed his arms. "So then, what's the problem?"

She glanced away, ashamed to admit it and unable to look at him. "I don't want to live with my husband."

"And why is that?"

She heard warning sirens blaring in her brain, but couldn't seem to stop. "Because he doesn't treat me like you do."

She exhaled. There. It was out, and since Zach didn't run away, she continued full speed ahead.

"He doesn't listen to me or make time for me or compliment me. I'd say that we're roommates, but even some roommates get along better than we have been lately."

Silence filled the classroom, and she wished she could stuff all those words back into her mouth. "I'm sorry. We haven't really talked much about my marriage, and I probably shouldn't have said anything now."

"Don't be silly. You know you can tell me anything. And it sounds to me like you aren't the one who needs to be sorry." Grabbing her hand, he gently pulled her out of her chair and closer to him. His voice was soft and so sweet that Jane couldn't help melting into his embrace. "I can't do anything to change him, but I can promise you that I'll always be here for you. That will never change." Kissing the top of her head, he rested his chin there and held her for several minutes.

She knew that one moment in Zach's arms was one too many. Breathing in his scent and absorbing his strength caused an addiction more intense than any drug she'd ever heard about.

When her head finally cleared enough for her to think straight, she took a giant step away from him, her cheeks blazing. "I-I need to go get my class from the art room."

"Yeah, I need to get back too." He moved toward the door. "So I'll talk to you later then?"

Still reeling, Jane crossed her arms over her chest. "I don't think so. At least not like we have been the past few weeks. I just can't."

"Trust me." As he met her gaze, she noticed a new sparkle in his eyes. "It'll all be okay."

He disappeared down the hallway, but his warmth lingered inside her frigid heart, radiating through her body, waking her senses, and reviving her spirit. Against her better judgment, she believed him.

Somehow, someway it really would be okay.

⁕

"Well, Dad, supper dishes are done, your medicine is set out for you to take at bedtime, and I'm all packed up."

Kneeling beside her dad's recliner, Jane patted his knee. She couldn't meet his gaze for fear of breaking down again. Her eyes couldn't take anymore tears.

"I'll stop in every day after school, and if you need anything at all in the meantime, you've got me on speed dial."

"Ah, lassie, you worry too much. I'll be fine."

Sniffing, she swallowed a hard lump of emotion. "I know, but you're all I've got."

"No, my little Janey. That's not true. You've got your husband and children. You've got your teaching and painting. You've got all your friends, and you'll always have your mum right here." He patted the left side of his chest.

She nodded as tears streamed down her cheeks. "But I miss her, Dad. More these days than ever before. And I don't want to miss you too. Not like that."

He held his arms out and she leaned across his lap into them. "I'm not going anywhere any time soon."

She soaked up as much of his embrace as she could. As nice as it had been to be in Zach's arms for that very brief moment, no man could comfort her like her dad. There was just something about a father's hugs.

It hadn't always been that way. Shaun was a very stoic man, and affection didn't come easy to him, but after her mother passed away he'd quickly learned how to help fill the gap. She suspected her daughters felt the same way about Ian. The very short list of things she appreciated about Ian included his generosity in showing affection to their children.

"Well, I better go." She swiped her fingertips under her lashes. "Why does it feel like I'm going off to camp?"

Her dad chuckled. "That's a good thing, right? You always used to love camp."

"But I always hated leaving you and Mom."

"Listen to your dear ol' dad." He gave her hand a squeeze. "It'll all be okay."

She returned the squeeze, remembering that Zach had said exactly the same thing. She released her dad's hand, got to her feet, and picked up her suitcase.

"I believe that too. Whatever happens, it'll all be okay."

Pacing the living room floor like a caged tiger, Ian tossed his gaze back and forth between the window and the clock, which only read half past seven. It seemed much later, but there was still no sign of Jane's Expedition in the driveway.

God, I don't really know how to pray, so I'm just going to talk in my head and You feel free to listen in. If you can help, great, because I messed up big time. Why didn't I think before I responded to Jane's message? I should have just told her I'm available for her whenever she needs me. Instead, I automatically put work first and hit send before I even realized what I did. Now I don't know if she still wants to talk tonight . . . or ever. And to tell you the truth, I don't blame her.

At that moment, the front door swung open, and Jane stepped in, lugging her suitcase behind her.

Her suitcase! He almost shouted the words, but caught himself.

He barely breathed as they stood staring at each other. Studying her expressionless face and demeanor, he found it impossible to determine her emotions. He couldn't sort out his emotions either, but he knew joy and fear were both there.

"You're coming home?" He was afraid of the answer.

She kicked off her shoes, walked into the living room, and perched on the sofa. "That's what I wanted to talk to you about."

"Okay." He walked with cautious steps around the coffee table and sat on the opposite end of the couch, giving her plenty of space. Fear of making one wrong move gripped his heart. "I'm listening."

"This does not change anything between us. The kids need me home. They need both of us under the same roof, functioning as a family."

Nodding, he folded his hands in his lap. "I agree."

"But there need to be some boundaries. Don't think that things can just go right back to the way they were because I can't live like that." Jane's expression softened. "How did your counseling session go?"

"It went well. Pastor Ben gave me some things to work on before the next session."

Jane's eyebrows arched in surprise. "So you're going back?"

Shrugging, he gave her that boyish grin she used to love, but it didn't seem to have the usual effect. "What can I say? I'm a work in progress."

"I'm glad it's helping you." She stood and crossed to her suitcase. "I'm going to unpack. Since we turned the guest bedroom into your den, do you want me to stay there or somewhere else?"

Ian scratched his head. "I'm sorry. I don't understand."

"Did you think I was just going to move back into our bedroom? I told you this changes nothing between us."

Pushing to his feet, he took a step toward her, but stopped. "I get that, but what I don't get is where exactly I stand with you. Just a couple weeks ago we had our twentieth anniversary, but right now you're acting like we're strangers."

"That's what happens when two people drift apart."

"How did we drift so far apart in just a couple weeks?"

"If you paid attention to anything besides work, you'd know it hasn't been just a couple weeks. It's been months, Ian. Maybe even years."

She might as well have socked him in the gut. The comment about work knocked all of the wind out of him. His shoulders sagged in defeat.

"You can stay in our bedroom. I'll stay in the den."

Jane hesitated, sorrow or maybe regret or possibly both welling in her eyes.

He would have given his right arm to hear the words, "I missed you." He would have given anything in his possession to hold her close for one minute, for just sixty seconds, but all too soon the moment passed.

Setting her chin, she grabbed the handle of her suitcase and rolled it toward the staircase. He could hear her struggling to get it up the steps, but he didn't move. He couldn't.

His pride had been mortally wounded and was lying there dying on the living room floor. Besides, she wouldn't have allowed him to help her. He might not know her very well anymore, but he knew that much was true. She didn't need any man, no matter how super, to swoop in and save the day, least of all him.

He gritted his teeth and clenched his fists. *Are You still listening, God? Did You hear all of that? Tell me, what am I supposed to do? I mean, I'm glad she's home, but not like this. It's just not right.*

Shaking his head, he trudged to his den and glanced at the futon that would indefinitely serve as his bed, currently serving as a filing cabinet for paperwork, statements, and bills. *I might as well just sleep on the floor.*

He sat down in front of his computer and pulled up his homework from Pastor Ben. *1. Take the kids to school in the mornings.* He rubbed his goatee. *I'm off to a slow start, but how do I know what to change if I don't know what I'm doing wrong.*

A chat box popped onto his computer screen, and he straightened in his chair. It included a picture of Felicity's beautiful face and the words, "Wanna chat?"

The rhythm of his heart picked up a bit as he glanced over his shoulder. *This is something I probably should change.* Moving the mouse, he directed the arrow to the X that would close the box, but first he took one more look at those red lips, that thick, dark mane, that little tease of cleavage, and he was weak.

What would it harm? It's just fantasy, not much different than those erotic books women read. It doesn't mean anything, and shouldn't I be allowed to enjoy a conversation with someone since my own wife doesn't want to talk to me?

Clicking inside the text box, Ian took a deep breath and began to type.

"Hi. My name is Ian."

CHAPTER
Ten

Jan woke on Sunday morning and stretched his back. After five restless nights of sleeping on the futon, he needed an appointment with his chiropractor as soon as possible. He wondered how much longer he'd be banished from his bedroom. Jane couldn't expect him to be satisfied with this arrangement forever, or even for very much longer. Yawning, he rubbed his lower back, never more sure that they had to fix their marriage soon.

Shuffling to the kitchen, he started a pot of coffee and showered while it brewed. Since no one else was up, he allowed himself a few extra minutes letting the hot water massage his neck and shoulders. Breathing in the steam, he tried to clear his cluttered mind, but when stubborn thoughts wouldn't budge, he resorted to prayer.

"Hey, God. It's me again. It's been almost a week since I tried this last. I don't know if you weren't listening or maybe I wasn't doing it right, but things aren't much better. I knew it would take a miracle, but isn't that your specialty?" He sighed. "Jane's right here, so close but still so far away, and it hurts every bit as much, if not more than when she was gone. So I'm going to go to church again this morning. Please give me the answers I've been looking for."

Turning off the water, he towel dried and dressed in a pair of khakis and a polo shirt he grabbed from a laundry basket that had served as his closet and dresser for the past five days. Smoothing the wrinkles against his body, he once again cursed the situation, but what could he do about it? He resolved to try to make the best of it and hope for a breakthrough soon.

In the kitchen he poured a cup of coffee, took a careful sip, and then took a chance. Reaching for Jane's favorite mug, he poured in the steaming black liquid, stirred in a little flavored creamer and sweetener, and, sucking in a deep breath, carried it up the stairs. He paused at the bedroom door. It was his room too. He should have been able to just walk in, but instead he tapped on the door.

No response.

He knocked again, a little louder this time.

"Come in." The words, wrapped heavily in sleep, were barely audible through the door.

Stepping softly inside, he set the mug on her bedside table. "Good morning. I brought you a cup of coffee."

Jane cracked an eye open. "What time is it?"

"A little after seven, I think."

Groaning, she covered her head with the pillow. "Geez, Ian. I appreciate the gesture but couldn't it wait for a couple hours?"

Ian fought to keep his blood pressure steady. "Actually, no. I'm going to church in an hour, and I was hoping you and the kids would come with me."

"Is this part of your counseling?"

"No. I went last week and I kind of liked it."

Lowering the pillow, she squinted at him. "What's gotten into you?"

Ian shrugged. "I've just done a lot of thinking lately, I guess. I want to start being a better man."

Rolling her eyes, Jane snuggled down into her covers. "Well, you'll have to be a better man on your own today. I'm taking the girls shopping."

He chose to ignore the mockery, reestablished his footing, and crossed his arms. He wouldn't give in that easy. "It's only an hour-long service. Maybe we can all go out to lunch and shopping this afternoon."

Propping herself up on her elbows, she glared at him. "I told you just because we're all living under one roof again doesn't mean we're one big happy family. You do your things—go to church, be a better man, whatever—and I'll do mine."

"It can never work that way."

She closed her eyes. "I'm too tired to discuss it further." On the end table, her cell phone chimed, and she reached for it.

Ian snorted. "But I see you're not too tired for whoever texted you."

He stormed out before she could fire back. It was so hard not to be bitterly angry. He didn't expect all their relationship issues to be solved overnight, but he didn't think he was asking too much for an hour of her time.

Stopping at the boys' door, he poked his head in. "Bradley, Sammy, wake up."

Samuel shot straight up like a rocket, while Bradley only moaned.

"I'm going to church, and I'd like you to come with me. Be downstairs in half an hour."

Stirring, Bradley opened his heavy eyelids. "Is Mom going?"

Disappointment coated Ian's words. "No. Apparently she's taking Emma and Jessie shopping."

Samuel had already climbed out of bed. He began dressing as Ian headed back to the den. When he glanced at his homework on the desk, his shoulders slumped. While he deserved an A for effort, the actual assignment would probably receive an I for incomplete.

He rubbed his chest in an attempt to ease the ache from the tug-of-war going on inside his heart. A big part of him wanted to turn in the assignment as is, just give up and let go. It'd be so easy to just be done, and it seemed to be what Jane wanted. Why waste any more time?

But a small, strong, stubborn part of him still had plenty of fight left. As defeated as she often left him feeling, he was not a quitter. He could go all out, keep pushing, force her to see that they belonged together. Even now. After twenty-plus years. Together they had a history and kids, dreams and plans for a future. He would fight for that until there was no fight left in him, and someday she'd thank him for continuing to believe.

Grabbing a pen, he scribbled something he could change: Attend church regularly. And as he turned off the light and shut the door, he vowed to add more that evening.

Forty minutes later, with plenty of time to spare, Ian, Bradley, and Samuel slid into a pew toward the back of Harvest Bay Community Church.

No sooner had they sat down when Sammy leaned forward. "Dad, I gotta go to the bathroom." His voice could hardly be considered a whisper and seemed even louder in the peaceful sanctuary.

Ian sighed and shook his head. Recently he had begun regretting his dismissal of Jane's suggestion to have their son tested for ADHD at the end of the past school year.

"He's a boy. I was just like him at his age. He'll outgrow his energy soon enough."

"It's more than extra energy, Ian. I'm a teacher. I see the red flags every evening when he does his homework. He works standing up so that he can move around a little bit. Otherwise he can't focus long enough to finish a simple worksheet. And it's going to get worse before he outgrows it."

"I don't care. You're not putting my kid on downers."

"We don't necessarily have to put him on medicine, but if we have a diagnosis we can help him by researching alternative options, like changing his diet or giving him certain herbal supplements."

"That still sounds like medicine."

"Vitamins and minerals? Ian, quit being so close minded. It's not—"

"The answer is no. I'm not comfortable with it. Period."

Remembering the conversation now made him feel like an irrational bully. In reality, he just didn't want to face the truth that there was something not quite right with his youngest son because by association it meant there was something wrong with him. Although he had never been diagnosed, Ian remembered behaving very much like Samuel at the same age.

What if he had genetically caused his son's struggles? He didn't want to face that possibility. Now as he looked at his eight-year-old son holding himself and squirming in the pew, he was so sorry he hadn't listened to Jane.

"I'll take him, Dad," Bradley volunteered. "There's someone I want to talk to anyway."

Following the direction of Bradley's gaze, Ian saw a pretty brunette with sparkling eyes. "Oh. I see. Okay, but be back before the service starts."

The boys side-stepped out of the pew, walked over to the girl, and said a few words. Ian couldn't read lips, but he recognized the word bathroom. The girl smiled sweetly, nodded, and led them out of the sanctuary and out of sight.

Bradley's always cared more about sports than girls. When did that change and how did I miss it?

Ian knew the answer to that question. He'd been so absorbed with his problems lately he hadn't noticed much of anything else. His emotions rose like a flood, threatening to drown him. Not only had he been wrong about Samuel, he'd also completely missed this step in Bradley transitioning from adolescence to manhood. Sure he had a ways to go, but shouldn't a father be there for all of it.

He'd been about Bradley's age when he noticed Jane—her eyes like jade, deep green and sparkling; her smile, warm like a day on the beach; her personality, explosive, but beautiful like fireworks; her body, strong yet slender with curves in all the right places. He remembered the way he felt more like himself around her, the way they talked and laughed for hours, the way she'd sing when he played guitar, not caring that she was slightly off key.

Looking back, he thought the thing that had made him fall madly in love with her was the way she made him believe he could do anything. He struggled at school, thought he was stupid, but she never accepted that notion. She encouraged him to work harder, helped him study. When he wanted to give up altogether, she yelled at him and told him people in this world needed his God-given gifts, including her.

He still remembered how it changed his heart as a young man to think that this amazing girl needed him. Someone actually needed him. For the first time in his young life he was important. He'd promised himself then that he would never let her down.

The memories caused his sight to blur, and his heart sagged in his chest. *I lost sight of everything.* The ironic thing about it was that he never would have even considered the idea of starting his own business without Jane by his side, believing in him. *I wonder if she still believes in me or if it's too late.*

As the first notes of a prelude piped through the organ and into the peaceful atmosphere, a stream of people entered the sanctuary including Adam, Kate, and their girls. They greeted Ian as they passed on their way to their seat. Right behind them, Bradley and Samuel returned to their pew.

"Feel better, son?"

Swinging his legs so that the toe of his shoes grazed the carpet, making a soft scraping sound, Samuel nodded. "Alison told us where to go." He turned around in his seat and pointed. "It's right down that hall and through that door—"

"Okay, son. Okay. Turn around now, and maybe you can show me later."

"Cool."

Facing Bradley, Ian raised his eyebrows. "Alison, huh?"

Cheek bones suddenly turning slightly rosy, Bradley only shrugged. Ian chuckled under his breath.

Following the hymns, scripture reading, and prayer, Pastor Ben made his way to the pulpit carrying his Bible and an antique-looking candlestick.

I wonder what that's for. Ian didn't know of any other pastor who used props, but he liked it. It helped him understand things a little better.

"Grace and peace to you from God our Father."

Ian recognized Pastor Ben's greeting from the week before. Glancing at his boys, he found Samuel on the edge of his seat as if in the front row of a Transformers movie, while Bradley already looked borderline bored until he shifted his attention in Alison's direction.

Whatever it takes, I guess. Ian turned back to Pastor Ben and readied himself to receive the answers he'd asked for.

"Recently my wife and I went to an estate sale. I was surprised to find the owner of the estate there during the sale, a dear, little eighty-eight year old woman. While my wife studied the antiques, I studied this lady."

Pastor Ben set the candlestick on the edge of the podium where the congregation could admire it and stepped down into the aisle of the sanctuary.

"She sat there watching strangers come with nothing but their pocketbooks and leave with their arms full of her treasures. I finally got around to asking her how she felt about that. The lady shrugged and said, 'It's just stuff.' She went on to tell me, 'I enjoyed my belongings for a while, but I can't take them with me when I go. So I'm glad they'll make someone else happy.'

"In our materialistic world, I was so humbled by her words. I asked her to tell me about some of her favorite pieces so I could pick out the perfect one. Her face lit up at my request. Lesson number one: Giving someone your time and meaningful conversation is more valuable than material things."

Pastor Ben meandered from one side of the sanctuary to the other, engaging the captivated congregation. "So this lady took hold of my arm, and I assisted her in strolling around the property. I listened as she told me stories about her belongings. Before too long I began to notice that her stories were less about the details of the items and more about the relationship she had with the person who gave it to her. She didn't see value like the world did. A piece of inexpensive costume jewelry that her great-grandson gave her meant every bit as much to her as a set of fine china that had been a wedding present. The relationships gave her stuff its worth."

Pastor Ben returned to the podium, picked up the candlestick, and carried it into the aisle.

"Then we came upon this silver candlestick." He held it up. "As you can see, it's pretty but fairly ordinary, and it wasn't part of a matching set. Truthfully, I wasn't expecting much when she began telling me about it. Imagine my surprise when she said it was her most prized possession."

Enthralled, Ian leaned forward slightly.

"She told me that one summer many years ago she had learned about the art of refining silver. She learned the silversmith constantly controls the temperature of the fire. If it's too hot, the silver would be destroyed. If it's not hot enough, he can't remove the silver's impurities. Either situation would keep it from becoming the valuable material it was made to be. Even more important than temperature is the attentiveness of the refiner. He not only holds the piece of silver, he watches it carefully the entire time it's in the fire and knows the process is complete when it's so shiny he can see himself in it."

Ian scrunched his brow.

"And that was why this piece was her most precious treasure. It defined her relationship with Jesus. She knew she'd experience pain in her life, but she trusted that it would not destroy her, and that when the trial had passed, she'd be a little more like Him. I asked her why she chose a candlestick. She said, 'Pastor, when you baptize new Christians, what do you instruct them to do?'"

From somewhere in the congregation, Ian heard a voice. "Let your light so shine before men that they may see your good works and glorify your Father in heaven."

"Exactly." Pastor Ben retraced his steps to the podium, deposited the candlestick, and picked up his Bible. "In the third chapter of Malachi we read what my wise friend already believed. It says, 'He will sit as a refiner and a purifier of silver; He will purify the sons of Levi, and purge them as gold and silver, that they may offer to the Lord an offering in righteousness.' God loves you as you are but sees all you can become if you trust Him to hold you in the fire. Psalm 66 starting at verse 10 says, 'For You, O God, have tested us; You have refined us as silver is refined . . . We went through fire and through water; But You brought us out to rich fulfillment.'

"I know many of you feel tested right now for various reasons—relationship issues, job situations, health scares—and I know it hurts. I want to encourage you to keep the faith that you are being cared for in the fire. Trust that He hasn't left you, that He won't take His eyes off you. And you will come out of it shining."

Closing his Bible, Pastor Ben dropped his gaze and appeared deep in thought for a long moment. "Sadly, three days after the estate sale, that wonderful, wise woman went home to be with her Refiner. I might have been the pastor, but that day she ministered to me, and I pray that through my words she ministered to you today."

Motioning to the organist who softly played the first notes of a hauntingly beautiful tune, he lifted up the candlestick. "Now, friends, let your light so shine before men that they may see your good works and glorify your Father in heaven."

After a minute, Ian recognized the tune of "This Little Light of Mine." He'd sung it at the vacation Bible school his grandma made him attend over the summer many moons ago. He'd always thought the song was talking about a candle. Now he understood that it referred to the light that should be inside him, a light that only ever flickered and had long since been extinguished.

Maybe that's something I can change. He looked down the pew at his boys. Samuel swung his legs and wiggled his body to the beat of the song. Bradley had opened the pew Bible and was rereading the verse in the Psalms Pastor Ben had mentioned.

Ian lips curved upward in satisfaction. *I get it now. The light inside me is left over from the Refiner's fire. All this hurt, all this heat . . . Maybe the process has already begun, and maybe I will come out of it shining.*

Lying perfectly still in her bed, covers up to her chin and barely breathing, Jane waited until she heard the faint click of the door and the hum of the garage door. Then she bolted to the bathroom.

Ian had said church was an hour long, and she didn't want to be there when he got back. Taking a quick shower, she wrapped her hair in a towel, slipped into her terrycloth robe, and hurried down the hallway to the girls' bedroom. Tapping lightly on the door, she opened it a crack and peeked inside.

"Girls, rise and shine." She tiptoed to the window and cranked open the blinds.

Emma and Jessica both moaned and pulled the covers over their heads.

Jane walked back to the door. "Come on, girls. Up and at 'em. I have a fun day of shopping planned."

"Shopping? But what time is it?" Emma mumbled.

Jane took the towel off her head and patted her short hair. "A little after eight o'clock, I think."

Pulling the blankets down to her chin, Emma gave her mom a puzzled look. "Why do we have to get up now, Mom? Stores won't open for another couple hours."

"I know." Standing in the doorway, Jane thought fast. "It gives us plenty of time to go out for breakfast. Be downstairs in forty-five minutes."

Back in her room, Jane checked her phone, smiled, and replied to a message. She searched her closet for a casual but flattering outfit, finally settling on a pair of Capri jeans and a coral-colored, short-sleeved sweater with a boat neck. She took a few extra minutes with her hair and make-up, and spritzed on her favorite fragrance.

Stepping into a pair of sandals, she gave herself a once over in her full-length mirror, and liked what she saw. For the first time in as long as she could remember, she felt pretty. Walking a little taller, she grabbed her phone and hurried downstairs, where the girls were waiting for her.

"Wow, Mom. You look nice." Jessica sniffed. "And you smell good too."

Grinning, Jane wrapped her arm around Jessica's shoulders and kissed the top of her head. "Thanks, Muffin."

Emma crossed her arms. "What's going on here? You haven't called her Muffin since she was, like, three. What's with all the make-up and perfume? And why are you acting so . . . happy?"

Slinging her purse onto her shoulder, Jane planted her hands on her hips. "Would you rather I act miserable and grouchy? Because I can do that if that's what you want."

"No!" the girls emphatically said in unison.

Jane chuckled. "Come on. I hear a stack of hot cakes calling my name."

Fifteen minutes later, they pulled into the half-full parking lot of the Pancake Palace in nearby Cresthaven.

Everyone must still be at church. The niggling guilt at dismissing Ian's sweet offer to attend church together as a family dissipated as she found a parking spot close to the door. *This is going to be a good day.* They went inside, were shown to a booth, and opened their menus.

A minute later, a young woman with a friendly smile appeared at their table. "My name is Brea, and I'll be your server today. Can I start you off with something to drink?"

"Coffee, please. With cream and sweetener." Jane remembered her favorite coffee cup still sitting where Ian had left it on her bedside table. Untouched. Her bright smile faded a bit when she considered his kind gesture.

I would have given anything for him to treat me like that long ago, like I mattered. But how can I forget years of complete disregard because of one nice morning?

The girls ordered juice and the waitress hurried away. Perking up, Jane said, "So, what store are we attacking first?"

Emma shrugged. "You were the one who wanted to come shopping."

Jane exhaled slowly. "What about you, Je—"

"Jessica?" a man's voice said.

Glancing up, Jane saw Zach approaching their table. Whether her reaction was joy or panic remained the burning question in her brain.

"Hi, Mr. Andrews." Jessica's smile stretched from ear to ear. "What are you doing here?"

"Same thing as you, I bet. This is my favorite place for Sunday morning breakfast."

"Mine too." Jessica's cheeks turned rosy.

Watching the exchange ignited a fire deep inside Jane's soul.

"Well, I'm going to go see if I can get a table." Zach rested a hand on his flat stomach, just above the waistband of his perfectly fitting jeans. "Those hotcakes are calling my name."

Jessica practically jumped out of her seat. "Wait. You're all alone?"

Zach chuckled. "Yep. Just me."

"We've got room." Jessica turned her pleading gaze to her mom. "Can Mr. Andrews join us for breakfast? Please?"

Jane glanced at Emma, who yawned and appeared annoyed at having to be anywhere before nine-thirty in the morning, then gave a nod. "Sure. Why not?"

She scooted over in the bench seat, and Zach sat down next to her, across from Jessica. Although Jane consciously kept a good six inches between them, it wasn't far enough to keep their magnetic connection from pulling on her, drawing her to him.

The waitress delivered their drinks and took their orders. Unable to think straight enough to make sense of the words, Jane just pointed at an item on the menu.

The waitress wrote it all down, exchanged a look with Zach, and hustled to the kitchen.

In between sips of coffee, Jane smiled at the girls. "Why don't you two go wash your hands in the bathroom before we eat?"

Emma opened her purse and pulled out a bottle of hand sanitizer. "I'm good."

Jane set her coffee cup down. "Hand sanitizer is not as good as soap and water. You know that. Now please do what I asked."

The girls scooted out of the booth and headed to the rest-room, Emma pouting and Jessica practically skipping.

As soon as the girls had vanished from sight and earshot, Jane turned to Zach. "What are you doing here?"

"What do you mean?" His blue-gray eyes sparkled with amusement like sunlight on the sea. "Didn't you hear me tell Jessica this is my favorite place for breakfast?"

"Just because I told you I was bringing the girls here, it was-n't an invitation."

"I don't see what the big deal is." He grinned. "Jessica is lov-ing it."

"Right. And she's going to go home and tell Ian you had breakfast with us, which will only make things worse for me. Is that what you want?"

His expression softened. "Of course not."

Blowing out an exasperated breath, she shoved her fingers through her stylishly unkempt hair. "Look, Zach, it's hard enough to hide this . . . whatever this is between us at school, but now you're making me do it in front of my kids."

"I'm sorry." Reaching up, he brushed a wisp of hair from her face. "I just had to see you."

His beautiful words serenaded her heart and sent her spirit dancing. For so long Ian hadn't seemed to care whether he saw her, leaving before the sun rose and coming home late. Some days she wondered if he noticed her at all. Now someone had to see her? She hadn't known until that moment how ferociously she craved being wanted.

"You see me everyday."

"Not like this."

His sultry voice sent a fireball of excitement racing up her spine and exploding in her cheeks. She had no idea what to do with this attention, but she liked it a lot more than she should.

With very little warning, the girls approached, snapping Jane out of her brief euphoria. She swatted Zach's hand away from her face.

"Pesky fly," She begged him with her eyes to play along. "Did you get it?"

"No, I missed." His gaze intensified. "But it'll be back."

All during the meal, Jane's emotions swung back and forth like a pendulum between joy and fear, excitement and panic. She thoroughly enjoyed sharing a meal with a man who just wanted to spend time with her. It warmed her heart to watch him interacting with her daughters. She even caught Emma stifling a smile once or twice.

But she knew that as much as she liked it, it wasn't right. She was married. Her marriage might not be perfect, but relationships seldom were, and her husband was finally trying to change. It just felt like it was too little too late and love had already withered up and died. She hadn't meant for that to happen.

Mom would be so disappointed in me. She loved dad even when he spent more time in the bar than with her.

Jane's gut twisted with shame just as she swallowed a forkful of pancakes, and for a moment she was afraid her breakfast would come back up. Trying to relax, she told herself they were just coworkers. It was no big deal. It'd be no different if she was having breakfast with Kate.

But Kate doesn't make my heart turn cartwheels. She downed her last, barely warm gulp of coffee. After she and Zach paid their separate bills, they all slid out of the booth.

"Have a good afternoon," the waitress called after them, smiling at Zach.

Arching her eyebrows, Jane lowered her voice as they pushed through the front doors and headed into the parking lot. "That waitress was acting kind of weird. Do you know her?"

Zach shook his head. "I thought she was talking to you." Slowing to a stop at Jane's Expedition, he ruffled Jessica's hair. "I'll see you tomorrow morning, bright and early with homework in hand, right?"

Nodding, Jessica climbed into the back seat.

He held up his hand to give Emma a high five, which she ignored. "Hey, try not to smile too much. Boys just hate smiling girls."

The teenager rolled her eyes. "Whatever." She turned to climb into her seat, but not before Jane caught a hint of a grin.

Opening her door, Jane faced Zach. "Well, it was nice running into you like this. Maybe I'll see you tomorrow."

"You can count on it." He stepped away from the SUV. "Have fun shopping."

Jane spent the rest of the day with her daughters, but her mind stayed in the parking lot of the Pancake Palace. As much as she hated to admit it, her heart already looked forward to the morning.

Emma flopped onto Bradley's bed. "I'm so tired of mom and dad not getting along. It's like the tension in the house is so thick sometimes I can't breathe."

Bradley threw a sock at her. "Being a little dramatic, don't you think?"

"I don't like it either, but this morning was nice," Jessica piped up. "Mom was happy again. She even called me Muffin."

"Oh shut up, Jessie," Emma hissed. "What do you know? She was happy because your weirdo teacher was flirting with her."

Jessica crossed her arms in a huff. "Nuh uh."

Wearing his Superman pajamas, Sam took a flying leap into his bed. "Dad was fun today too. I liked going to church with him. Didn't you, Brother?"

Bradley tousled Samuel's hair. "Sure, bud."

Jessica shrugged. "If they're both happy apart, maybe if they weren't together, it wouldn't be the worst thing in the world."

Emma slapped Jessica on the arm hard enough to make a red mark. "Of course it would be the worst thing. Do you really want to go back and forth between mom's house and dad's house? Maybe they'd even have to sell this house. Is that what you want?"

Jessica's bottom lip quivered. "No. I just want them to be happy again."

Bradley sat backwards in his desk chair and crossed his forearms on the top of the chair back. "That's right, Jessie. But Emma's correct too. Mom and Dad belong together. All we have to do is remind them how happy they once were, and I think I have a plan that will do just that."

"Will it work?" Emma asked, a flicker of hope dancing in her eyes.

Bradley set his jaw and gave a determined nod. "I got Mom to come home, didn't I?"

CHAPTER
Eleven

Arriving early at the Bayside Cafe, Ian found the booth he shared with Pastor Ben the week before empty, and he made a beeline to claim it. He opened the menu even though he already knew what he was going to order. Somehow it eased his anxious spirit to preoccupy his mind with all the different choices.

Before long Maggie approached his table. He ordered an egg, ham, and cheese croissant with coffee. As she hurried off, his cell phone buzzed, and his heart rate gathered speed, like it always did. He hoped that Jane had come to her senses and was finally ready to work out the kinks in their relationship. But when he hit the button on his phone to display the text message, disappointment reined in his galloping heart.

It wasn't Jane. Of course it wasn't Jane. The message was from Bradley.

Hey, Dad. I need your help. There aren't enough chaperons for homecoming. Can you do it?

Ian ran his hand over his goatee, pondering the odd request. But no matter how strange it seemed to receive that text from his son at nine-thirty on a Monday morning, Bradley was asking for his help, and Ian wouldn't let him down.

You can count on me, son. He hit send just as Pastor Ben walked up with the morning paper under his arm.

"Good morning." Pastor Ben slid into his seat across from Ian and motioned at Ian's phone. "Everything all right?"

Ian chuckled. "After twenty years, apparently I'm going back to high school. Bradley just asked me to chaperon the homecoming dance."

"Ah. Now I understand your puzzled expression. High school dances aren't for the faint of heart."

"You've got that right." Turning off the ringer, Ian set his phone aside. "Looks like I didn't give you time to read the news today. I was a little hungry so I was just going to grab some breakfast before we talked."

Pastor Ben smiled. "Great minds think alike."

Maggie brought Ian's coffee and took Pastor Ben's order. After she left he turned his attention to Ian.

"How was your week?"

Ian shoved his fingers through his hair. "It's been trying, to say the least. Jane came home, but we're still living apart."

"I saw you had your boys in church yesterday."

"Yep." Ian sipped his coffee with a smirk on his face. "I'm wearing the family down two at a time."

Pastor Ben laughed heartily as his coffee arrived.

"Seriously though, I'm working on being the best dad and husband I can be, but Jane doesn't seem to be buying any of it."

Adding some creamer to his steaming mug, Pastor Ben stirred and took a sip. "What is your motive?"

"What do you mean? I'm making the list like you suggested. I'm taking the kids to school. I'm bringing Jane coffee in her favorite mug. I'm still working hard to provide for them like I always have, but now I'm trying to go above and beyond, to be extra patient, more generous, exceedingly thoughtful. I'm just trying to be better, and it's frustrating because she doesn't even seem to notice."

Pastor Ben folded his hands on the table. "I understand that, but you said Jane's not buying it. Are you really trying to improve yourself? Or are you just doing what you have to in order to sell yourself to your wife?"

Ian drummed his fingers on the table as he considered the question. He thought about the Labor Day picnic he'd planned for her and how mad he'd gotten when she had other plans. He could see Pastor Ben's point.

"I suppose a little of both. I like the changes I'm making, but I'd do just about anything to get my wife back."

"I get what you're saying, but she does too. If I had to guess, I'd say that she's noticed the difference, but she's afraid it's just temporary."

"So how do I make her believe it's not?"

Pastor Ben took a long careful drink. "Just keep doing what you're doing. When you feel like giving up, don't. Keep finding ways to be a little bit better than you were the day before for no other reason than you want to improve yourself. Any kind of change is hard, like refining silver. But if your motives are pure, you'll always come out of the fire shining. Understand?"

Ian nodded.

"Above all else, pray. It's amazing to see how God can move in a relationship when you pray in earnest for your spouse. Pray for Jane, for your marriage, and for your family. Spend some time everyday in the Scriptures. Do you have a Bible?"

Swallowing his gulp of coffee hard, Ian shook his head. "Probably somewhere, but I really don't know."

"If you're interested, after breakfast, swing by my office. I'll loan you one and a reading plan so you're not too overwhelmed."

Too late. Ian cast his gaze to one lonely, tiny, insignificant crumb on the table in front of him, just waiting to be swept away into oblivion. It annoyed him that he recognized the resemblance to his life.

Maggie delivered their food and refilled their coffee cups, and for several minutes they ate in silence. Pastor Ben washed down a bite and wiped his mouth.

"You're a sports guy, right?"

Ian perked up. "Of course."

"What would you say about Vince Lombardi?"

"He's arguably one of the greatest coaches in football history."

"Agreed. What do you think made him so great?"

Ian took a bite of his breakfast sandwich and pondered the question while he chewed, and then swallowed. "Well, he was knowledgeable about the game. He earned the respect of the team by proving his credibility as a coach and motivating his team to achieve success."

"He inspired many people, not just his team, because he understood that the principles of football could be applied to a person's life. Once he was quoted as saying, 'If you'll not settle for anything less than your best, you will be amazed at what you can accomplish in your lives.' He also said that it's easy to have faith and determination when you're winning. The key is to maintain that same attitude when you're losing."

Taking a bite, Pastor Ben chewed while Ian chewed on his words. "At this point, you may feel like you're losing. You may be tired of trying, but you can't settle for anything less than your best, not for the sole benefit of another player, but because you will be a stronger and better player regardless of the outcome. Then you'll find that the whole team will improve because of your leadership."

"I understand."

Ian knew his life meant more than just a football game, and his marriage far more than a series of plays to execute. But he could choose to approach his relationship with the same determination as a well-trained athlete. Whether his teammate was able to give it her all or not, he would bring his best to the line of scrimmage over and over again.

For the first time in weeks something about his life made complete sense to Ian.

Grading papers during her planning period, Jane drew big smiley faces on her students' perfect work with Mr. Sketch scented markers. Oddly the strong cinnamon scent of the brown marker transported her back to her graduation from Bowling Green State University. With her bachelor's degree in her hand; her teaching certificate applied for; her mom, her dad, and Ian all snapping photos of her big day, and all she really wanted to commemorate the event was her very own set of Mr. Sketch scented markers. All her favorite teachers in grade school had them, and she remembered sniffing her freshly graded papers until the color came off on the tip of her nose.

After she shed her cap and gown and they had dinner with her parents, Ian had taken her to the Creative Teacher, where he bought her a pack.

"Now it's official. You're a teacher," he had said with a proud smile, handing her the plastic bag containing the goods.

To anyone else it might seem like an insult to get a pack of markers for a graduation gift, so inexpensive and practical, but in twenty years of marriage it remained her favorite gift from him. It spoke to her as an artist as well as a teacher, and the rainbow of colors still made her happy, especially on difficult days, which had been on the rise lately.

She glanced at her silenced cell phone, and noticed that she had missed a text message. Her heartbeat picked up the pace a little. She wasn't sure if she hoped it was from Ian or Zach. She just knew she wanted to be wanted.

When she opened the message, she was only slightly disappointed. Her lips curved upward slightly as she read the text her son had sent her.

Hey, Mom. Been thinking. I'll ask Alison to homecoming, if you will chaperon. Deal?

Jane rubbed the creases out of her forehead as she pondered the odd request. A plan formed in her mind. What if Zach just happened to get invited to chaperon too? With him being a teacher, no one would think anything of it. It was the perfect scenario to spend time with him outside of school.

Deal. She hit send and set off down the hallway to fill Zach in on her brilliant plan before her break ended. Thankfully she knew from talking to Jessica that their breaks overlapped on Mondays. If he was in his room, he would be alone. Her pulse picked up speed at the thought.

Nearing his room, she heard his voice through the door, and she slowed her steps. Hearing no other voices, she deduced he must be on the phone and continued through the doorway. He stood near the windows, watching the sunny day outside as he talked.

"I told you, I don't know yet . . . Yes, I promise as soon as I find out I'll let you know . . . I can't wait eith—" He turned and his gaze landed on Jane. He froze. "Listen, I've got to go. I'll talk to you later."

Ending the call, he grinned sweetly at Jane, and quickly closed the gap between them. "To what do I owe this surprise."

"You're teaching my kid. It shouldn't be a surprise that I stop in your room every now and then." She shifted her weight to one hip and crossed her arms. "Who were you talking to?"

"I'm sorry?" He took a step back. "I didn't know I had to clear my phone calls with you."

Jane's demeanor softened. "Well, it sounded pretty serious. I just want to be sure your situation won't affect Jess's education."

Snickering, Zach moved to sit on the corner of his desk. "Come on, Jane. Don't be so serious all the time. Cut loose. Have fun."

Jane couldn't help but notice how well his black pants fit him and how the sleeves of his polo shirt encircled the well-defined muscles in his arms. It took her a moment to find her voice.

"Easy for you to say. You're not married with four kids."

"True." He lowered his voice and spoke tenderly. "But that doesn't mean I don't want to be. And it also doesn't mean I can't be happy where I'm at right now."

The roller coaster of emotions inside her made her head spin. "I've got to go. I came down here because Bradley asked me to chaperon the homecoming dance and I wanted to extend the invitation, but I can see that was a mistake."

Jumping off the desk, he rushed after her. "Why? Because I challenge you? Have you been a doormat for Ian for so long that you can't see that part of a healthy relationship is challenging each other to be better?"

She spun around, eyes narrowed, and jabbed her finger at him. "You don't know anything about my marriage. And let me get this straight. You are thirty-four years old, never married, no kids, and as far as I know this is the closest thing you have to a relationship—sneaking around, texting late at night—yet you want to talk to me about a healthy relationship? Do yourself a favor and grow up first."

Whole body trembling, Jane stormed out of the room, a difficult task on wobbly knees. Her spirit was in such turmoil she thought she might be sick. In such a short amount of time Zach had knocked down walls she'd spent years building and reinforcing. With just his words and tenderness he reminded her of her importance and value. With just his gaze he made her feel desired and beautiful.

Her mind soon cleared, though, and she sighed in relief that the heavy burden of participating in inappropriate behavior had lifted. No more sneaking around, hiding text messages, or wallowing in her guilt. Although she already missed the attention, she didn't miss the shame that came with it.

But ending whatever she had with Zach didn't fix the problems with her marriage. Zach had been a Band-Aid. Now that she'd removed it, the cut was still there and it still hurt.

Lined up in the hall outside the art room, her twenty-two wiggly five- and six-year-olds blurred behind her misty eyes. How could she have so much and still feel so empty? As Jane led her class back to their classroom, she thought about the pack of Mr. Sketch scented markers and wondered if she could ever try as hard as Ian had been lately. She'd given it her all for twenty years, and she was tired of trying. Her whole situation seemed completely and utterly hopeless.

"Mrs. Garner?"

Jane flipped on the lights and looked down into the chocolaty eyes of one of her sweetest boys, William Hickson. "Yes, Superman?"

William glanced at the superhero emblem on his blue shirt and gave Jane a smile that lit up his whole face. Jane had told him on the first day of school that was his super power. A few of William's good buddies, including Destiny, heard Jane's response and giggled. Winking at the little girl with the dark, curly pigtails, Jane made it her mission to make Destiny laugh at least once everyday so she would know that whatever Destiny went home to, she'd had a moment of joy.

"What do you need, William?"

"Mrs. Goodwin asked me to give this to you." He handed her a folded piece of paper from the art teacher.

"Thank you." Taking the paper, she directed her students to sit down and practice writing the letter and number of the day. Once they were settled down and engaged in the assignment, she opened the paper.

It was a flier for Stampede of Dreams, a therapeutic horseback riding program for adults and children with special needs located in the neighboring town where the art teacher lived. They were looking for volunteers to help out with some evening classes.

Mrs. Goodwin had written a note in the top corner. "Jane, I don't know why, but I thought of you when I saw this. Best, Brandi."

Initially, Jane dismissed the idea, tossing the flier on her desk to throw away later. But by the end of the day, after her students had gone home and the emptiness returned, it occurred to her that it might just be what she needed to restore her sense of purpose. She picked up the flier and reread the description.

She knew next to nothing about horses and had minimal experience with special needs, but she was well trained in helping people, and the flier made it sound like experience wasn't necessary. Finding the contact name, Sandy Lovato, followed by an email address, Jane opened her gmail tab on the computer and typed a short inquiry.

Hitting send, she felt the stress of the day weigh on her. She considered talking to Zach. She also considered going for a run instead, but just the thought of both options drained her further. With what little strength she had left, she gathered her belongings and went to get Jessica and Samuel. More than anything at that moment she wanted to get lost in a painting.

CHAPTER
Twelve

Jane thought she couldn't possibly feel more despair than she had over the past several months. Surely, she had hit rock bottom.

She was wrong.

That evening she checked her phone every fifteen minutes, give or take a few, her heart sagging each time she found no new messages from Zach. Rereading the thread of old messages only made her feel lonelier.

How can he say all these beautiful things to me, and then let me go so easily? Am I that unlovable?

She typed out a message: *I miss talking to you.* Before she hit send, however, she erased it.

She had meant what she told him in his classroom. He had no right telling her how to be happy when he knew nothing about her life. She knew happiness. Her four children made her smile on a regular basis. She enjoyed her students and felt confident in her ability as a teacher.

Her level of happiness didn't have anything to do with her tank sitting on E, stalling out whenever she attempted to move past this road block. Happiness was different than joy. She didn't know if she'd ever experienced true joy. She knew it wouldn't come by begging for Zach's attention, but she did miss seeing his pretty words pop up on her phone. Knowing that someone thought of her and considered her to be amazing and beautiful and talented served as a powerful drug to which she had become addicted. As wrong as it was, she craved Zach's attention.

She considered talking to Ian, accepting just a portion of the olive branch he had been extending. She considered leaving her paints and brushes and going to him, trying to connect with him. Lying in her big lonely bed, she longed to be close to him, not like they'd been before when she was left feeling unfulfilled, but in a new way.

Ian had been trying so hard with the picnic and the coffee and helping out with the kids. She appreciated that, but she also resented the fact that she had tried to be everything he wanted and needed and more for years to no avail. He still looked right through her, took her for granted. The notion that the only reason he even tried at all was because he finally saw what he stood to lose, infuriated her, and the tug-of-war going on inside of her, stretching her heart, pulling her mind, left her exhausted.

The disappointing bottom line was that an almost forty-year-old man was set in his ways. Ian would never change for good. He'd make little changes until he got what he wanted, then everything would go back the way it had been. And in the end Jane would be even emptier than before.

She tossed and turned all night. In the morning when she dressed, she cinched the belt that held up her baggy slacks to the tightest notch and it was still too big. She noticed an extra amount of hair left in her brush after she styled it, and no amount of make up seemed to completely cover the dark circles under her eyes.

She sighed. Lack of sleep and appetite was negatively affecting not only her health, but also her appearance. Something had to change. She needed peace, but she had no idea where to look for it.

The sun peeked over the horizon bright and cheerful, coloring the sky various shades of pink, orange, red, and lavender. Any other morning the artist in her would stop and marvel at the masterpiece. Today as she drove to school, however, it served as a sharp contrast to her depressed mood.

It would take all her energy to avoid Zach, to resist showing up in his classroom and telling him she missed their conversations. How would she maintain the enthusiasm needed to manage twenty-two five and six-year-olds?

She walked to her classroom, her pumps clicking on the floor and echoing down the dark, eerie hallway. Arriving at work so early had helped her be more prepared, but she had to admit that the big, dark, empty school spooked her every morning. When she reached the safety of her classroom, she exhaled her relief, flipped on the lights, and gasped.

Right in the middle of her desk sat a large glass vase exploding with the most beautiful flowers. Jane could smell the fragrant bouquet from the doorway. A smile spread across her face as she rushed in to examine this surprise more closely. She counted four huge bright pink lilies, six perfectly red roses, several orange carnations, and a few daisies with greenery and baby's breath filling in the few gaps. It reminded Jane of the sky that morning, a stunning sunrise.

Then she noticed the card nestled in between two pink petals, and it dawned on her that she had no idea who'd sent her this beautiful arrangement. Ian had never bought her anything so extravagant before, not even for their twentieth anniversary, but he was changing. Zach wouldn't openly give her something so personal, something that was totally inappropriate and that she couldn't honestly enjoy, would he?

Her heart thumped as she plucked the small envelope out of the bouquet. She opened it, and with just one glance her soaring spirits tumbled to her toes.

She didn't recognize the handwriting.

Somewhere deep inside her heart, where she held onto the magic of first love and the meaning of vows, she had wished to find Ian's chicken scratch that she knew by heart on the card. But once again she was let down.

What was I thinking? she scoffed at herself. *Of course, he wouldn't buy me flowers unless they were the five-dollar bouquets wrapped in cellophane from the Pit Stop.*

She stared at this foreign handwriting, the words blurred behind tears of disappointment. Blinking the moisture away, she read the note.

Jane, I'm sorry I upset you. The truth is I'm falling for you, and it scares me to death because I know how this will end. But it's no excuse for my behavior. Please forgive me. Zach

"Pretty flowers."

Jane nearly jumped out of her skin. She spun around, keeping the card behind her back, and slipped it safely into the back pocket of her slacks. "Kate! You're here early."

"Just trying to stay on top of things." Kate joined her at the desk to admire the bouquet. "Wow. Ian's really outdone himself."

Jane's gut twisted. How should she respond? She had to think quickly, but her emotions fogged up her brain. She despised lying. Never before could she bring herself to tell a lie, but she couldn't tell the whole truth either. Not even to her best friend.

Forcing a grin, she checked her back pocket to make sure the card was concealed. "He's definitely been trying to change lately."

Kate brightened. "So things are better between you two?"

Jane shrugged. "We have a long way to go."

Kate pulled Jane into a warm embrace. "Adam and I have been praying for you two. When he came home yesterday and said you both were signed up to chaperon the homecoming dance, I just knew that was an answer to our prayers."

"Wait." Jane felt the blood drain from her face. Stars floated in and out of her vision. "What did you say?"

"That we prayed for you? Or that you're both signed up to chaperon?" Kate clapped her hands together. "Hey! We should double date. It'll be just like old times."

How did this happen? She'd agreed to patrol the dance, but not to recreate old memories. Slowly, the fog lifted and picture became very clear.

"Bradley." His name escaped her lips in a breath.

"Jane?" Kate's brow knit together in concern. "Are you okay?"

"I think I'm going to be sick." Covering her mouth, she bolted to the small bathroom shared by the two kindergarten classes, and lost the contents of her stomach into the toilet. Turning on the sink, she dampened a paper towel and pressed it to her forehead. She leaned back against the cool cinderblock wall, resisting the urge to kick herself.

Of course, Bradley set us up. It would seem like the perfect plan to any teenager: Ian and me back where it all began. But things are complicated now. She envisioned the flowers on her desk and the card in her back pocket. *Very complicated.*

A soft tap on the door preceded Kate's voice from the other side. "Hey, Jane, why don't you go home and rest? I'll call you in a sub."

The thought tempted Jane, but she opened the door and shook her head. "Thanks, but I've already missed too many days taking care of Dad."

Kate crossed her arms. "And you've neglected yourself in the process. Now you're run down. These kids don't need a sick teacher. They need you well and energetic and . . . fun." Compassion flooded Kate's eyes. "They need the Jane I know and love but haven't seen for a while."

Jane's shoulders fell. She wanted to argue, to say she hadn't changed, but she knew it would be another lie. Her usual enthusiastic, upbeat, and slightly sarcastic self had taken an extended vacation to some happy place, and this negative, angry, cynical version who even she didn't recognize served as a bad replacement.

No, she definitely wasn't herself. Physically, she was dwindling. Spiritually, she was dying. And she had no idea how to save herself.

She still loved Ian. She'd been married to him for twenty years. He was the father of her children, including the one they lost way too soon. He'd been trying lately, but she wanted more than that. After twenty years, she wanted him to fight for her. She wanted to mean that much to him. Of course she still loved him, but she hadn't liked him for many months.

On the other hand, she did like Zach. A lot. He talked to her as if she was precious to him. He seemed to believe in her like no one else ever had, encouraging her creativity, calling

her talented and an amazing artist though he'd only seen the
snapshots of her work that she texted him. His attention
made her feel wanted. The time he spent with her made her
feel valued. And now the beautiful bouquet sitting on her
desk made her feel adored.

The problem was that she was not available to be wanted,
valued, or adored by another man. If he was, in fact, falling
for her as he stated in his card, then she'd let this escapade go
on way too long. Still, as wrong as it was to continue, she did-
n't want to lose this connection.

She cast her gaze to the floor. "You're right. I am different.
I don't like it, but I don't know what to do about it."

Kate slipped her arm across Jane's shoulders and gently
squeezed. "Go home and get some rest. Come back tomorrow
refreshed. That's at least a start."

"You'll call in a sub for me?"

"I'll take care of everything. I'll let Mrs. Zeller know and
get a sub in here." Kate helped gather up her belongings
including the vase of flowers and guided her into the hallway.
And don't worry about Jessie or Sammy. I'll bring them home
with me, and Ian can pick them up after work."

"Thanks, Kate. I'll call you later."

Jane pushed through the heavy doors and stepped out into
the cool morning air. Inhaling the refreshing air, she opted
out of climbing into her Expedition and strolled along the
sidewalk. She didn't want to go home, but her dad's house was
just a few blocks away. She would surely find respite there.

Lost in thought on the familiar streets of Harvest Bay, she
never noticed the brand new Mercedes Benz parked at the
side of the road or the dark-skinned man watching her from
behind the tinted windows.

"I'm running out of ideas on how to win her back. You've got to help me. Please."

Ian hadn't planned on visiting his father-in-law so early in the morning, but after another sleepless night, desperation had won out. He felt like he was playing unfairly, trying to gain pointers from the other team's coach, but he couldn't stand to lose this game.

Shaun Flanders sat in his La-Z-Boy, wearing his pajamas, his thin, white hair ruffled from the night's sleep. He stirred his coffee, set the spoon on a folded napkin, and took a careful sip.

"Ah, lad, in all my years, I've learned that I still have a lot to learn about women. They are complicated creatures, aren't they?"

Ian adjusted his glasses and rubbed his forehead. "Boy, you've got that right."

"But aren't they the loveliest things you've ever seen?"

"Jane's the most beautiful woman I've ever met. But I feel like I barely know her anymore.

"Indeed, ladies are a puzzle, but I can tell you one thing I've figured out. Women are stronger than any man. Just think of all they take care of throughout the day. And yet women are more delicate than a rose in a wind storm. I know Janey's mum never needed me as much as she wanted me. And my job was simple: to shelter her from the storms of life." The old man's eyes grew misty. "I tried my best, but I couldn't protect her from the worst storm of her life."

"I'm sorry." Sitting on the edge of the sofa, Ian clasped his hands in his lap. "But how do I do that when Jane won't let me near her?"

Shaun sipped his coffee. "My lil' lassie is a stubborn one. You've got your work cut out for you, that's for sure."

"That's why I'm here. I want my wife back. I want my family back. There isn't a price I wouldn't pay. Please, help me, I'm begging you."

"Janey is stubborn, but she's still a lady. Be there for her. Listen to her. Hold her. Even when she doesn't think she wants you to, hold her. I don't understand it, but there's somethin' 'bout a fella's arms can give a lady peace like nothin' else." Shaun made a fist and curled his left arm toward his shoulder. "Believe it or not, these arms could work magic on Janey's mum."

Ian chuckled. "I believe it."

"I'm sorry I can't help you more, lad. If I had the answers, I'd give 'em to you, but this is something you'll have to figure out on your own. Just don't quit. The moment you're ready to give up is usually right before a miracle happens."

Ian took a deep breath.

Shaun set his mug on the end table and leaned forward, propping his elbows on his bony knees. "Think of it this way. That rose in the windstorm I was talking 'bout, you can do one of two things with it. You can pluck it so you can enjoy it on your terms, knowing it will soon die. Or you can put in a little extra effort to water and fertilize it, keep the weeds away from it, build fences to protect it from storms and animals that might hurt it, knowing that you are helping it grow stronger and more beautiful for everyone to enjoy for an entire season."

Ian stared at the floor. "I picked Jane, didn't I?"

Sitting back in his recliner, Shaun returned to his coffee. "That's not for me to decide."

"What are you doing here?"

Ian jerked around, and his gaze landed on Jane. The bag that hung from her shoulder weighed her down as though it had bricks in it, and she looked so pale and fragile that his heart rate picked up speed.

He sprang to his feet. "What's wrong? Why aren't you at school? Are you okay?"

"I'm was perfectly fine until a minute ago when I saw your truck in the driveway. What are you doing here?"

Ian sank back onto the sofa, glanced at his father-in-law, and then at the floor.

"Simmer down, lassie. Ian just came over to have a cup o' joe with me and talk sports, isn't that right? Those Buckeyes sure are somethin' else, aren't they?"

"Yeah, they sure are." Ian turned to Jane with relief. "So what are *you* doing here? And who are the flowers from?"

Shrugging, Jane set down her bag, put the heavy vase on the coffee table, and dropped onto the sofa on the opposite end from Ian. "I'm just not feeling well. No big deal."

"And the flowers?"

She wouldn't meet his gaze. "A gift from a parent. Some people actually appreciate what I do, you know." She paused. "Aren't you supposed to be taking Jessie and Sammy to school about right now?"

"Bradley said he would take them this morning so I could have coffee with your dad." Ian returned to his feet. "But since you're here now, I guess I can go." He strode over to Shaun and shook his hand. "Take care."

Shaun nodded. "Sure will. And you make sure to water that rose bush."

As Ian left the house and climbed into his truck, he tried to make himself believe the story Jane had told him. But something didn't feel right.

That was an awful big bouquet for a parent to give a teacher.

He pondered Shaun's analogy about the rose bush. As he turned onto the road that led to the greenhouse he did frequent business with, he muttered to himself, "It doesn't matter who gave it to her. Those flowers will die, but I'm going to water mine."

Curling her legs up under her, Jane leaned against the arm of the couch, resting her head on the throw pillow and waiting for her dad to start asking questions. Instead he sat silently sipping his coffee until it was gone. Then he just tipped his head back against his recliner and closed his eyes.

Finally Jane couldn't take it anymore. "Dad?"

He cracked his eyelids slightly. "Hmm?"

"Aren't you going to ask me why I'm here or about the flowers or anything?"

"Your husband already did, and you answered him. Why should I think you'd tell me any different?"

The emotional levy in her soul broke, and she wept hard like she hadn't wept since her mother's funeral. "Because I lied, okay?" she said between sobs. "It is a big deal. I'm lost and lonely and these flowers aren't from a parent. They're from a coworker whom I've developed a relationship with.

"I didn't mean it. I swear I didn't. It started innocently, but it got out of control so quickly. Nothing has happened, but I'd be lying if I said I hadn't thought about it. Ian and I have been so disconnected for so long—not just different pages but in completely different books. With Zach I've felt alive again. I know it's not right, but I don't want to stop feeling important to someone. I'm sorry, Dad."

"Ah, my lil' lassie. I wish I could fix this for you, but I can't. I can tell you I understand." He paused for a moment. "Did I tell you I was watchin' a show the other day on National Geographic?"

Jane wiped the tears from her face. "No, but what does that have to do with this?"

Jane's dad nodded. "It was a program on birds. It showed how an eagle will work hard for his dinner, hunting it down, sometimes even putting himself in danger to get it. On the other hand a buzzard waits until an animal is killed, and then moves in to have his dinner, feasting on another creature's leftovers."

Jane stared at her dad. "You didn't really see a show on birds, did you?"

"My point is that there are two types of men in this world: the eagles and the buzzards. Unfortunately, I've been both kinds."

"You're not a buzzard."

"Not after I met your mum. Before her, I wasn't a man to be proud of. And I know for a fact that a man with the moral compass of a buzzard, who will make advances on a vulnerable married woman, will move on as soon as he finds another snack on the side of the road. A man with the values of an eagle, well, he might let you down a time or two—Lord, knows I let down your dear, sweet mum more times than I care to admit—but he won't ever quit trying."

"I understand what you're trying to say, Dad, but you don't know Zach. He's not like that. And even if he was, how do you revive feelings that are dead? Ian and I have been only slightly more than roommates for longer than I care to admit. I don't know whose fault it is, but I don't want to be in a marriage that just exists."

"There's a lot about relationships that I never figured out, but I know that it never helps to lay blame. You both are responsible for making it or breaking it. Relationships take communication and commitment. You have to be deliberate, tell him what you want and listen to what he wants. Respect him for who he is and he'll love you for who you are. There's a great big learning curve that shifts as you change individually and as a couple. And every relationship ebbs and flows. Sometimes the dry periods last a long time. During that time you just have to hold on and trust that the rain is coming."

Shaun studied Jane with gentle eyes. "Open your heart to Ian. Just try a lil' bit harder. The moment you're ready to give up is usually right before a miracle happens. You don't want to miss out on a miracle, do ya now?"

Jane shook her head. "No."

She didn't have it in her to disappoint her dad further by telling him that she didn't believe in miracles anymore. She got to her feet and went to kiss him on the cheek.

"I'm going to go check my email, and then lie down for a while. After lunch do you want to take those flowers up to Mom's grave?"

Grinning, Jane's dad patted her hand. "I think that's a grand idea."

Jane yawned, curled up on her bed, and pulled out her laptop. By now Zach should have figured out that she wasn't at school, and since her phone remained silent, she hoped to find an email waiting for her. Although she realized it wouldn't be wise to talk to him in the emotional state she was in, she wanted to know she was missed, even if it was wrong.

Out of the seventeen new messages in her inbox, the most recent one was from Sandy Lovato with the therapeutic horseback riding program. There was nothing from Zach.

It's just as well. Sighing, she opened Sandy's email, and started to read.

Good morning! Thank you for your email and interest in Stampede of Dreams. I understand the need to be involved with something that matters, and I think when you see how our riders respond to the horses despite their special needs and limited abilities, you'll agree this program provides a service that is invaluable. We are always looking for volunteers. No experience is necessary. We'll teach you everything you need to know.

We have classes tonight, tomorrow, and Thursday. Why don't you come for a visit? If you like what you see, we'll talk about setting up a training session.

Thank you,
Sandy

Sounds good, Jane responded. *I'll see you tonight.*

Hitting send, she shut down her computer. She had no idea what to expect, and the thought of adding one more thing to her plate exhausted her further. But as she drifted off to sleep, she hoped that by helping someone else she'd eventually find her own way too.

ane and her dad spent over a half hour at the cemetery, remembering her mom, talking and laughing about things she said and did. It should have been healing but it only added to Jane's loneliness. It had been a long seventeen years without her mom, and Jane needed her now more than ever.

At five o'clock on the dot they arranged the flowers on the grave, climbed back into Jane's Expedition, and followed the GPS directions out of town. She turned onto a back road with corn fields on both sides. The tall, golden stalks would soon be harvested, leaving the field empty and lonely, but they always had the hope of another spring, another planting season. Jane wondered how much longer she'd have to wait for her planting season.

Taking a few more country roads, Jane soon found the small farm that housed the Stampede of Dreams. She parked, got out, and was met by a middle-aged woman wearing a green Stampede of Dreams T-shirt, glasses, and a happy smile.

The woman stretched out her hand. "You must be Jane."

Jane accepted the gesture with a timid smile. "I am, and this is my dad, Shaun Flanders. Are you Sandy?"

A neat, chin-length bob the color of her name bounced as she nodded her head. "Yep, that's me. And this is the Stampede of Dreams. Come on. I'll show you both around."

As they walked toward a smaller red barn, Jane slipped her hands into her back pockets, her fingers brushing over the card she'd forgotten to throw away. Her cheeks burned as she remembered what it said. A small part of her couldn't part with it yet, longing to hold onto being wanted for just a little while longer. But more than anything else, she needed peace, needed whatever it took to heal her broken heart and wounded spirit.

Sandy began filling in details about the program. "Stampede of Dreams got its start in 2009 and is affiliated with PATH International."

Listening carefully as they walked, Jane kept one concerned eye on her dad fearful that he was growing tired. "Path?"

Sandy slowed to a stop at the entrance of the building. "Professional Association of Therapeutic Horsemanship. Basically, our purpose is to use the therapeutic benefit of horses and the compassion and dedication of our volunteers to provide individuals with special abilities the opportunity to experience their own personal healing and to reach their fullest potential."

Personal healing. That sounds nice.

They stopped at a table near the door. "This is where our students check in. At the first lesson a parent or guardian fills out a simple waiver that releases us of responsibility in the unlikely event of an accident." Sandy addressed several ladies standing there waiting for the students to arrive. "Everyone, this is Jane, a teacher at the elementary school. She's thinking about becoming a volunteer."

After receiving a friendly welcome, Jane uncertainly followed Sandy further into the building.

Smiling proudly, Sandy patted what appeared to be some sort of a primitive rocking horse with a long neck. "Then we move our students to our Equicizer to warm them up and stretch them out."

The expression on Jane's face as she examined the contraption must have communicated what she was thinking because Sandy's wholesome laugh echoed through the barn.

"This is Brownie. Hop on. I'll show you how it works."

Glancing over her shoulder at her dad, Jane hesitated.

Sandy stroked the wooden head of the pretend horse. "Come on. He won't bite. I promise."

Jane chuckled, already appreciating this woman's sense of humor. She inched closer to the contraption. "Just so you know, I'm not very coordinated."

"We'll see about that." Sandy pointed to the stirrup and firmly but gently instructed, "Put your foot here, then swing your leg over, and slip your other foot into the stirrup on the other side. Grab hold of the reins and move the horse, keeping your upper body tall and using your hips."

Feeling silly to be climbing onto a big rocking horse, Jane followed the directions. Once she was atop the contraption, her eyes widened.

"Wow. This feels like a real horse."

Sandy's smile reached her eyes. "My husband is a retired jockey. He designed the Equicizer after he'd been injured to rehabilitate himself so he could get back on the horses. It's been a huge benefit to our program because it helps special needs kids with core strength and balance. It also assists in reviewing a lesson or skill with a student before we mount them on a real horse." Sandy smoothed Brownie's mane. "And above all else, it's just fun."

Jane shifted her attention to her dad, who watched her with amusement dancing in his eyes. She laughed in spite of herself.

"You're next, Dad."

Putting his hands up, palms out, Shaun shook his head. "I don't think so, lassie. You get your dear ol' dad up there and I'm afraid you won't be getting him down."

Jane swung her leg over the Equicizer and dismounted. "You're right. That was fun."

Sandy motioned for Jane and Shaun to follow as she exited the barn and headed toward a bigger building. "After our students are warmed up and ready for their lesson, the volunteers walk with him or her over to the arena. We typically keep a ratio of two volunteers to one student."

As she neared the gate, Sandy called out to the three horses standing in the arena with their guide holding them by a lead. They each lifted their beautiful heads, perked up their ears, and pawed at the ground. Sandy crossed her forearms on the top bar, a satisfied expression on her face. It was easy to see that this work fulfilled her.

Jane marveled at how these magnificent creatures went from standing quietly to alive and ready to work at just the sound of Sandy's voice. She seemed to have that effect on her team too. Everyone appeared excited to be a part of Stampede of Dreams, and Jane's eagerness to be a small part of the program increased as well.

Sandy pointed to a ramp off to the right. "Our students mount their horses from that ramp. It's just easier to climb onto a horse from an elevated location."

That made perfect sense to Jane. She honestly didn't know if she, a relatively fit woman, would be able to mount such a mammoth animal without a boost. As luck would have it, a student had just arrived. As she prepared to take her place on her assigned horse, Jane was able to watch the process as Sandy continued to explain.

"There are three adults with the horse and rider at all times—a guide to lead the horse and a volunteer on either side of the student keeping a hand on her constantly. Then she directs the horse to complete small obstacles in the arena, all while maintaining proper posture and balance based on her special need."

"That's amazing!"

"What's amazing is how the horses heal the heart." For the briefest moment, deep sadness blanketed Sandy's cheerful disposition. "I understand needing to be a part of something that matters. When you watch a person who struggles with simple everyday activities climb onto one of these animals and suddenly it's okay that their two legs don't work right because they have four strong legs, that matters. It's okay that their speech isn't clear or that they have no filter for socially unacceptable things to say because somehow the horses understand.

"When my students come here, feeling like less of a person because of their disability, and are transformed into a king or queen sitting on top of their horse . . . " Sandy shrugged. "I just can't think of anything more worthwhile than that. And at the end of the day, you find you take a little bit of that transformation with you. Little by little. Day by day. Until one day you realize you're whole again."

"That's a nice thought." Jane had no idea what Sandy had experienced in her life, but she found it difficult to believe she would ever be complete again. "I'll be happy with just a little peace in my life."

Laying a hand on Jane's shoulder, Sandy gave a gentle squeeze. "There's a line in my favorite Beatles song that says something like the love we take ends up being equal to the love we make. If you want love, you have to give love. If you want peace, you have to give peace. If you want healing, you have to be a part of the healing process. Stampede of Dreams is about all of that."

Sandy's warmth thawed Jane's heart. "I'm in. Sign me up."

"All right." Clapping her hands together, Sandy moved away from the gate. "Let's go look at the calendar and see when we can get you in for some training."

Jane grinned. "Thanks for taking the time to show Dad and me around. I'm not sure why, but I already feel better."

"We all have down days. You just can't let it keep you down. My family, especially my little granddaughter, keeps me going. My horses keep me positive." Jane took a calendar off the wall, her joyful smile lighting up the small barn. "And the Beatles keep me singing."

The sun sat heavy just above the treetops, splashing the sky with vibrant shades of red, pink, and orange, but Ian was so agitated he didn't notice the beautiful sight out his window. He only honed in on the empty driveway. Jane had been gone all day without any indication of where she was and when she might be home. It annoyed him to no end.

I've been trying. Yes, it's late in coming, and, yes, I'm still screwing up, but Lord knows I'm trying. I don't expect any credit, but it'd be nice to get just a little bit of respect.

He tried praying but couldn't focus on anything except his anger. Storming to his office, which currently doubled as his bedroom, he flopped down on the lumpy futon and rubbed his forehead.

How could she do this to me? I've spent over half of my life loving her, and she's going to throw it all away? How could she?

Sitting up, he moved to the computer chair. It was almost more comfortable than the thin, uneven futon mattress, and he momentarily wondered if he could sleep sitting up. He also wondered if he was ever going to get to return to the bed he once shared with his wife.

That thought caused a tidal wave of loneliness to sweep him away. He missed lying next to Jane, his arm draped across her slender waist, her curves fitting so perfectly with his. He missed the smell of her skin and the rhythm of her breathing as she drifted off to sleep. He missed the way he felt like more of a man beside her.

As he booted up his computer, his conscience kicked into overdrive. He knew it was wrong, but he'd deal with the guilt later. For the time being he needed to feel like a man.

He quickly found the website and went directly to his favorite temptress's chat box. He likely wasn't the only man vying for her attention. As fake as common sense told him this was, Felicity had definitely earned her degree in boosting a man's ego.

Welcome back, Ian. What fantasy can I fulfill for you today?

His heart took off like a thoroughbred out of the starting gate when the message popped up on his screen. He swallowed hard, burning with desire, placed his fingers over the keys . . . and heard the front door slam.

Ian hastily closed out of the website, shut the computer down, and raced out to the living room. Somewhere along the way, his fresh desire converted back into irritation. Finding Jane in the dining room unloading her school bag and purse onto a chair, he leaned against the wall and crossed his arms.

"Where have you been?"

She stared at him, disbelief dulling her jade eyes. "Excuse me?"

"No, I'm not going to excuse you. It's late, and I don't get so much as a text message from you all day?"

Planting her hands on her hips, she narrowed her eyes. "You saw me this morning. You know I was with my dad."

Disappointment squelched the anger in his voice. "Yes, and I saw Kate, too, when I picked up Jessie and Sammy. She praised me up one side and down the other for the beautiful bouquet I got you."

Jane's pale complexion lightened a few more shades. "You didn't tell Kate the truth, did you?"

"Don't worry. I kept your secret safe."

"I'm sure you enjoyed her compliments."

The temperature under his collar rose to boiling. "No. No, I didn't because all I could think was that my wife lied right to my face and apparently to her best friend. That's not a good feeling. Not at all because there are a limited number of reasons why a wife would feel compelled to lie to her husband." His voice wavered. "So which reason was it? Who were the flowers from?"

Jane cast her gaze to the floor. "A coworker. He was just being nice. He knew I had a lot going on with Dad and with . . . " Her voice trailed off.

"Us. You've been talking to some strange guy about what's going on between us?"

"No. Well, not really." She exhaled a frustrated breath. "Oh, Ian, please. The whole town knows we're going through a rough patch."

Hope lit up his heart. "Is that all this is? A rough patch?"

She stared at him with eyes so unsearchable, Ian had no idea what she was thinking or feeling. "I don't know."

"Please, come and sit down with me. Let's talk about this a little more."

Jane turned away. "I'm tired. I don't want to talk anymore."

"Please. I'm trying very hard to learn how to be a better husband and father, a better man in general. I know I haven't been there for you like I should have been all these years. I'm working on that. All I'm asking in return is just a few minutes of your time. Please."

A soft sigh escaped Jane's lips, but she followed him into the living room. She perched on the edge of the sofa, hands on her knees, as if ready to bolt at any second.

Ian sat on the ottoman across from her. "I don't want to lose you, and I'll keep trying until my dying day to prove that to you." He paused, unsure if he could put a voice to his next thought. "But I can't keep going on like this. It's not fair to either one of us or the kids."

Jane folded her hands in her lap. "I agree."

"Believe it or not, I've only ever wanted your happiness. From the moment back in high school when you said you'd go out with me, making you happy was my number one priority." His voice cracked around the lump of emotion in his throat. "Since then, other things have tested that, mostly work and the kids, but at the end of the day, nothing about my life is right if you aren't happy."

Tears streamed down Jane's face. "I've tried to be happy, but I'm not."

"I know." Ian hung his head. "Do you really think you'd be happy with flower guy?"

Jane swiped at her tears. "What makes you think I have any interest in anyone else? Is it that hard for you to believe that someone would find me attractive and likable on his own without me making a pass first? Did you even notice I didn't bring the flowers home?"

"I'm sorry. All I could think about was seeing you holding that vase full of flowers and then hearing the lie you told Kate." Ian moved to the couch, close, but not touching her. "If you don't like the guy, why couldn't you tell the truth?"

Several moments passed. Jane sniffled, tears dropping from her lashes onto her folded hands. Finally, she lifted her watery gaze to meet his.

"Because I do like him. He's been a good friend to me, and he's been there for me more in a month than you have in years. But no matter how much I like him, I love you more."

His father-in-law's words from earlier that day rushed back to him. *"Hold her. Even when she doesn't think she wants you to, hold her. I don't understand it, but there's somethin' 'bout a fella's arms can give a lady peace like nothin' else."*

Summoning every ounce of his courage, knowing he might be pushed far away, Ian scooted closer to her and wrapped his arms around her tense body. At first she tried to resist the embrace, but he held on as his father-in-law had instructed, and something almost magical happened. She very gradually melted into him and let him comfort her.

He kissed her forehead. "I'm sorry I haven't been there for you, baby. I'm so sorry. Please give me a second chance."

She sat up, eyes wide. "What did you just call me?"

Creases of bewilderment formed on his brow as he searched his brain. "Umm . . . baby? It just came out. I didn't mean it in a bad way."

"I liked it." She returned her head to his shoulder. "You barely even call me by my name anymore. Sometimes I feel as if you look right through me."

Ian's heart broke at this revelation. "I'm sure I took you for granted, but I never meant to. I think people in general just get so busy with making a living they forget about all the important aspects of making a life."

"You mean aspects like this? I've needed you to hold me like this for so long."

He kissed her forehead again, wishing it could have been her lips. "I promise to try to be more sensitive and pay more careful attention to your needs if you'll let me."

"One step at a time. We still have a long way to go. This doesn't fix anything, but it's a pretty good start.

Ian remained silent, relishing the moment and the feel of his wife close to him again.

"So apparently our sneaky children have attempted to set us up. Bradley asked you to chaperon the homecoming dance?"

Ian glanced down at her. "Yeah. He asked you too?"

Jane nodded against his shoulder.

"How convenient." Ian slipped off the couch and onto one knee. "Yes, this is cheesy, but I'm going out on a limb." He took her hand. "Jane Flanders, will you go to the homecoming dance with me?"

Jane actually gave him a genuine smile. "I don't see that I have any other choice."

He chuckled. "I'll accept that answer." He stood and helped Jane to her feet. "You must be exhausted. Shall we go up to bed?"

Jane immediately bristled and stepped back. "I'm not ready for that, Ian. Too much has come between us. We can't just hop back into bed together."

Ian quickly covered his disappointment and offered her his arm. "Well, then, m'lady, will you allow me the honor of walking you to your door?"

To his relief, Jane laughed and played along, looping her arm through his. "Okay, but you should know I don't kiss on the first date."

"What? Since when?" They both laughed as they ascended the staircase.

Outside their bedroom door, she turned to him. "Well, here we are."

"Have sweet dreams."

"You too." She reached up on her tiptoes, kissed him on the cheek, and slipped into their bedroom, closing the door behind her.

He floated all the way back down the steps and into his office. But he returned to earth after stretching out on his uncomfortable futon.

Who is flower guy? Is he texting her now? How has he been there for her? Has he kissed her? That thought sickened him. No matter how much she loves me, as long as she likes him, he's a threat to my family. But I don't know how to protect my marriage from this.

He squeezed his eyes shut tight. "Oh, God, you've got to help me. And hurry!"

Bradley dashed up to his bedroom where Emma, Jessica, and Samuel waited for a report.

"Shhhh." Closing the door with a soft click, he leaned against it. "They're coming upstairs. Act casual."

Samuel tipped his head to the side and scrunched up his brow. "What does casual mean?"

"Never mind." Bradley grabbed two action figures off the floor and tossed one to his brother. "Let's play good guys and bad guys with your G. I. Joes."

"Okay, but I'm the good guy."

Emma opened her book, and Jessica put in her ear buds, but both girls joined Bradley in listening for clues about what was happening between their parents. They heard voices, but couldn't make out any words. Then they heard a door shut and footsteps fading down the stairs.

Tossing her book onto Bradley's bed, Emma crossed her arms. "I thought you said they were making up. It sounded to me like Mom went into her bedroom and Dad went back downstairs."

Bradley kept his voice low. "Trust me. They're making up. I saw them on the couch together. He had his arms around her. They talked about a lot of stuff. I mean a lot of stuff, including the fact that I asked them both to chaperon for homecoming."

"They figured out your plan?"

"Yeah, but it's okay because then he got down on one knee and asked her to go to the dance with him." With a soft whoop, Bradley threw his G. I. Joe into the air. "My plan worked."

Jessica gave a delighted gasp. "Mom and Dad are happy again."

Silent tears streamed down Emma's face. Bradley sat on the twin bed, wrapped one arm gently around Samuel's neck, and rubbed his knuckles on his little brother's head, while Samuel squirmed and wiggled to get out of his grasp.

Bradley released his prisoner and turned to Emma, easily warding off Samuel, who tried to return the headlock to no avail. "Em, what's wrong? I thought you'd be happy. Things aren't perfect yet, but they're getting better."

"I know. I don't know why I'm crying." Emma sniffled. "I remember listening to all the fighting, but sometimes the silence was scarier. I was so afraid of losing everything I love." Watching Samuel climb onto Bradley, trying his best to take their strapping big brother down, Emma laughed. "I was afraid of losing this."

Bradley picked up Samuel, body slammed him on the bed, and then pinned him, while Jessica counted to twenty. Bradley lifted his arms in victory as Samuel jumped onto his back.

"Never forget, Emma, that we are Garners. We might get knocked down for a while, but we always get back up." With his little brother hanging on his back like a monkey, Bradley scooped his two sisters into a warm bear hug. "And nobody will ever tear us apart, not mom or dad or the whole United States military. You three have my word on that."

CHAPTER
Fourteen

Jane lay awake in the bed she'd once shared with Ian, thoughts and feelings swirling around in her mind until her brain hurt.

Did that really just happen? Did Ian really hold me? Did we really just talk like husbands and wives are supposed to?

Now, separated from him again, it all felt like a dream.

All the rest of that last week in September, Jane tried to make heads or tails of their moment in the living room. Ian's actions seemed genuine, but that didn't mean he'd changed for good. After all, he hadn't tried to hug her again or call her a pretty name in the days that followed. They talked more than before, but never about what took place on the sofa. They also ate breakfast together a couple mornings, but there was still a vast distance between them without a bridge anywhere in sight.

It was probably all just an act. He's never done that before, take me in his arms and hold me when he knew I would try to push him away . . . Or maybe he is changing, not perfect but learning, and he's hurt because I lied. He has every right to be angry. Truthfully, I'm mad at myself too . . . Or maybe he's hurt that I admitted to him that I liked someone else, but I also told him I love him and he never said it back.

That stung her a little, but Jane thought about how she would feel if the shoe was on the other foot, and he told her he was interested in someone else. She would be devastated and probably mad with jealousy.

She had no idea what was going on between them, but she knew that he had been trying for several weeks, while she turned a cold shoulder to every kind gesture. Maybe the time had come for her to pick up a hammer and nails and figure out how to build a bridge.

There was a nip in the air Friday night, but as Jane and Ian climbed into the stands of the football field along with half the town to cheer for Bradley and the rest of their boys in green and blue, no one noticed the chill. Excitement sparked like high voltage wires under the lights. The smell of popcorn from the concessions mixed with the scent of autumn. The trees surrounding them made a beautiful backdrop with their leaves just beginning to change. Jane hoped a lot of things were just beginning to change.

They sat with Kate and several members of Adam's family while Emma, Jessica, and Samuel walked around with Madeline and Chloe, promising to check in periodically. The homecoming attendants rode around the track on the backs of convertibles, looking stunning, and transporting Jane back in time to her senior year. She and Kate had both been attendants. Neither had been crowned the queen, but it was a fun moment to share with her best friend, wearing her sash and watching from the stands as her boyfriend fought for a victory on that very field.

I'll bet I still have that sash in a box somewhere in the basement.

Ian stood and clapped, bringing Jane back to the present, as the senior boys, followed closely by Bradley and the rest of the team, ran onto the field through a tunnel of fans, busting through the banner the cheerleaders held.

She leaned closer to Ian. "Twenty-one years ago that was us. Do you ever think about it?"

He continued to clap, but she could tell by the far-off look in his eyes that he was somewhere else. "Every day."

Adam and the assistant coaches trotted out after the boys. Everyone removed their hat and covered their heart as the band struck up "The Star Spangled Banner," and the crowd cheered as the band dramatically drew out the last note. Then, playing Harvest Bay High's fight song, they marched off the field, and Harvest Bay prepared to receive the kick off.

Sitting shoulder to shoulder with Ian on the crowded bleachers, Jane slipped her fingers over to rest on his knee.

His eyes never leaving the game in progress, he curled his strong, calloused hand over hers.

It seemed like such a simple gesture, but it caused Jane's heart to grow wings. It had been months, maybe even years since he held her hand in public. For the entire first half, he only let her hand go to clap for a first down and for both of their touchdowns.

As the band entered the field for the halftime performance, Ian stood and stretched. "I'm going to the concession stand. Do you want anything?"

"No, thanks. I'm good." Jane smiled as she watched him go.

Scooting closer, Kate kept her voice low. "Things between you two just keep getting better, I see."

Jane shrugged. "Better than yesterday, I guess."

Kate nudged Jane's shoulder with her own. "Well, this is much closer to the best friend I know and love. The day off earlier this week must have helped."

Just then Jane's cell phone chimed. "It did help. Thanks for covering for me." She fished her phone out of her purse, tapped on her text messages, and felt the blood drain from her face.

Now I see why you've been avoiding me. Not even a thank you for the flowers. Too bad he won't ever treat you as well as I could. Oh, well. You made your choice. It's my loss.

Jane searched the stands but couldn't find Zach in the sea of faces. Her stomach turned as she tapped on his contact information and deleted all two hundred messages in their thread. All of his beautiful messages vanished before her eyes. She wanted to cry, to mourn her loss. Severing the connection she felt with Zach wouldn't be as easy, but she was supposed to be building a bridge. Zach's messages would only confuse and distract her, keep her wondering about the possibilities of what could be between them.

Searching the crowd again, she found him one section over and three rows up. She offered a weak, apologetic grin, her eyes welling with sadness, just as Ian returned with two bottles of water and a bag of popcorn.

"Everything okay? You look like you've seen a ghost."

"Of course. Just reminiscing, I guess."

He sat down beside her, loosened the cap on her water before handing it to her, and then offered her some of his salty, buttery snack. "Some days it seems like yesterday, and others it seems like forever ago."

Jane glanced over her shoulder. "You can say that again."

By the fourth quarter, the game was tied, but Jane felt pressure from a different source. She forced herself not to turn around again, although she could feel Zach boring a hole in her back with his stare. She focused all her energy on Bradley playing the game of his life as a starting sophomore. That was an incredible achievement, and he deserved it. He'd worked so hard to be the starting quarterback. Jane beamed with pride for her son, and she was happy to be sharing this moment with Ian, together the way they were supposed to be, Bradley's parents, husband and wife.

For tonight, she wouldn't dwell on the times Ian wasn't there for her, but instead concentrate on all the Biddy Football seasons he'd coached or helped coach their son. She refused to recall how he'd banished her dreams to their dark, dismal basement, but instead would celebrate how he'd helped Bradley reach for his dreams.

She would keep building this bridge and keep repairing their relationship one board at a time because it was the right thing to do. She believed she could ward off any sweet-talking, dark-haired, blue-gray-eyed temptation that came along. After her evening with Ian on the sofa, she was strong enough. Or possibly guilty enough after confessing to him the truth about her feelings.

Either way, it'll all be okay. She gasped inwardly. *Those are the exact words Zach said to me before I moved back home, when I spilled my guts to him about my dying marriage, and he promised he would still be there for me. He didn't have the right to be there for me. That was Ian's job, but Ian never made it his priority.*

One moment earlier her mind was crystal clear, and now it was a muddled mess. She'd never wanted to hurt anybody. She only wanted to find value in herself again, but somehow Ian and Zach had both been wounded by her carelessness.

Zach should have known better. I am married, for goodness sake, and we work together. He's Jessie's teacher. We have to put this crazy infatuation to rest and be professional. If nothing else, he at least deserves a thank you for his kindness, and an explanation as to why

I've been avoiding him, but I'll be lucky now if he gives me a second of his time.

She was saddened by the thought, and the urge to meet Zach's gaze got the best of her. But just as she turned, the crowd shot to their feet with a roar.

"Did you see that? Bradley just threw a thirty-yard touchdown pass. Harvest Bay won!"

"Of course, I saw it." Jane clapped with the fans, but her heart sank. *I missed my son's touchdown because I was more concerned about Zach's feelings—and I lied again.*

As the stands emptied onto the field, she hung back.

Ian reached the bottom on the stands before he realized Jane hadn't followed him. "You coming?"

"No . . . actually I'm not feeling very well."

That was not a lie. Her chest ached. Her head hurt. The emotional roller coaster had brought on a fierce bout of nausea.

"You go ahead. I'll meet you at the car."

"You sure?"

Forcing a weak smile, Jane nodded, and Ian flowed with the current of bodies out to the middle of the field. When it was safe, Jane glanced toward where Zach had been sitting, but he was gone. Although she scanned the crowd, she couldn't find him.

It's just as well. Forcing her train of thought back on the right track, Jane watched her son and the rest of the team celebrate on the field . Her heart swelled with pride, easing her heart's ache.

Groaning, she headed to the parking lot and climbed into the Expedition. *If only I could turn back time.*

She wondered how far she'd rewind her life. Just far enough to see Bradley's touchdown? Or to the faculty Labor Day party when the sparks between her and Zach started flying? Would she go all the way back to that August day when she went through with marrying her high school sweetheart, while secretly grieving the loss of her pregnancy? Would she do it over, do it differently, or not do it at all? She couldn't imagine not having the four beautiful children of her marriage, but she also couldn't imagine spending the next twenty years the way she'd spent the last twenty.

When they pulled into the driveway thirty minutes later, Jane had an atrocious headache. Emma, Jessica, and Samuel all dragged themselves up to their rooms, rubbing their eyes and yawning, and Jane was ready to follow right behind them. But Ian caught her by the arm.

"Are you okay? You were quiet all the way home."

"Of course. I just don't feel well right now. It's been a long day, and I'm tired so I think I'm going to go up to bed."

Ian released her and stuffed his hands in his pockets. "All right, but before you go, I had an idea I wanted to run by you. How about if tomorrow after we take pictures of Bradley and his date and send them off to the dance, you get ready at your dad's, and I pick you up there? It'll be just like high school but better because this time when I ask you to come home with me you won't be able to say no."

Chuckling, Jane nodded. "That sounds like fun."

Without another word, she plodded up the staircase. Dressing in her lounge pants and T-shirt, she crawled under her blankets, holding onto her phone like a favorite teddy bear, hoping for one more text message as she dozed off.

CHAPTER
Fifteen

Jane awoke several times throughout the night and checked the screen.

No new messages.

At seven o'clock the next morning, she checked again, but still nothing waited for her on her phone, so she reached for the next best thing: the card that came with her flowers. She kept it in the drawer of her bedside table. She reread it at least a dozen times. She held it close to her nose, inhaling the faint scent of flowers.

She mattered to him earlier that week, not the way she mattered to the people in her house. He had nothing to gain in valuing her. She wouldn't do his laundry or dishes. She wouldn't cook his meals or take care of anything that belonged to him. And yet she felt as if he'd set her up on a pedestal to be admired and adored.

She had never sought attention from anyone, but she liked his. She would learn to live without it, but she still liked it.

Returning the card to its safe place, she wrapped her terrycloth robe around her, stepped into her slippers, and shuffled downstairs, already feeling like she needed a nap. In the kitchen, she perked up when she saw that her coffee had already been poured. The steam was still rising from it. Ian must have fixed it just moments ago. Bringing the mug to her face, she smelled her favorite rich, chocolaty, salty aroma. She cautiously sipped it and closed her eyes.

Salted Caramel Mocha. Simply divine. She took another sip, and then carried her cup into the living room to enjoy her coffee curled up on the sofa.

A small gasp escaped her lips. A box about the size of the couch cushion, but not quite as thick and tied up with a big red bow, claimed the very spot where she was going to sit. Her name was written on the envelope tucked inside the ribbon in Ian's familiar chicken scratch. Delight and nervousness overtook her at the same time. It wasn't her birthday, their anniversary had passed, and Christmas was still months away.

I don't know if I'm more nervous about what's in the box or why Ian surprised me like this.

Setting her coffee cup on the end table, she slipped the card out and opened it. The simple note card had a couple holding hands on the front. She opened it and tearfully read Ian's words.

Jane,

Tuesday evening on the couch when you said you loved me more, that's all I needed to hear. I will fight to my grave for us. I have to because I'm no good without you. I'll prove to you we belong together forever . . . even if I have to take you back in time. Can't wait for tonight, my beautiful girl.

All my love,

Ian

Jane read the card three times. A tear plopped onto it and she quickly wiped it off. In twenty years she'd never gotten anything like this from Ian, and she didn't know what to think.

"Well? Are you expecting the box to open itself?"

Jane spun around to find Ian standing in the doorway holding a matching coffee cup in his dirty hand. Dirt caked the knees of his old jeans, which Jane noticed sagged on him a little. Had he been losing weight too? His unbuttoned flannel shirt revealed a plain white T-shirt streaked with mud here and there.

"What have you been doing? Playing in the dirt?" Jane wiped the remaining dampness from her cheeks.

"Maybe." He dragged the word out, but then his patience got the best of him. "Oh, just open the box, will you?"

Giggling, Jane sat on the sofa and pulled the box onto her lap, shaking it a little. It was light and didn't make any kind of clue-giving noise. As she slipped the ribbon over the corner, she glanced up at him.

"What is this for?"

Ian shrugged. "Didn't you read the card?"

"Well, yeah, but you've never done anything like this before." She finished slipping off the ribbon and lifted off the lid.

"I'm not the same man I was before."

She fished through the thin layer of tissue paper and pulled out a beautiful, long, dark-green evening gown. Her voice floated out on her breath. "I don't know what to say."

He set his coffee cup on a nearby table and stepped further into the living room. "Do you like it?"

"Like it?" Glancing up at him, Jane felt a stab of guilt for her part in all they'd been through together recently. "I love it."

"That's the same color dress you wore to our first homecoming together."

Her mouth fell open. "I don't remember that."

He closed the gap between and reached into his back pocket. "I do. I keep a picture from that night in my wallet." He flipped his wallet open and showed her the picture, the edges fading with age.

Jane stared at it in disbelief. "How long have you kept that picture in your wallet?"

Ian's gaze intensified. "Since Mom got them back from wherever she had them developed. It was the one night that shaped the rest of my life because that's when you finally agreed to be my girlfriend." He folded his wallet back up and returned it to his pocket. "So, yeah, I keep it close by."

Tears pooled beneath her lashes as she smoothed the soft chiffon on her lap. "I . . . I never knew that."

Ian shrugged. "You don't have to know everything," he said, his voice gentle. "You just have to trust. I might not have done a great job of showing you how much you mean to me all these years, but that doesn't mean you haven't always been my whole world and everything in it."

Silent tears fell onto the fabric and Jane quickly wiped them off.

"Well, I just came in to get another cup of coffee." He retreated to the table where his coffee cup waited for him. "Then I need to head back outside.

"Wait." Carefully setting the dress aside, Jane hopped to her feet and followed him. "I'll get it for you. I'll top mine off, too, and join you on the front porch."

"Okay." Smiling, Ian stepped outside into the sunshine and closed the door behind him.

For a long moment, she stood in stunned silence, not knowing whether to laugh or cry.

Why did it have to take over twenty years and us nearly splitting up for him to let me know he keeps a photo from our first dance in his wallet? Trust is based on a person's actions. If I'm left alone, playing second fiddle to work and kids, yeah, I might start to question my value.

A tiny bubble of anger tried to rise at that thought, but she no sooner reread the card than it popped. Sighing, she picked up his coffee cup and carried it into the kitchen. *It doesn't matter. It's in the past. All we can try to do now is move forward, and this is a good start.*

Jane spent all morning and most of the early afternoon on the porch. She and Ian talked some, but he was busy with some landscaping project. Eventually, the kids woke up and joined them. Bradley helped Ian until it was time for him to get ready to pick up Alison. Samuel ran around playing pirates in the yard, while Emma and Jessica hung out on the porch with Jane.

She easily could have pretended that nothing was ever wrong between them, that they were the model family. And maybe someday they'd get to that point, but she knew that first there was a lot of healing that needed to take place.

Watching Ian work in the earth, planting a small bush and mulching around it, Jane began to see him in a different light. Instead of viewing him as uncaring and self-centered, she began to wonder whether Ian was too caring and selfless.

He typically worked from dawn until dusk six days a week and made up for shortened days on the seventh. Jane had always thought success was his motivator, but watching him with Bradley and stopping a few times to be the bad pirate and chase Samuel around the yard, Jane realized that he wanted his family to have the best life, to be more than just comfortable, to have everything he never had growing up. He had great intentions, but even they had consequences because feelings died if they weren't nurtured.

Jane had tried for so long to take care of her feelings herself, but it was like trying to paddle a boat with one oar. She often felt like she was going in circles. Every day she felt more and more like a machine rather than an important part of her own household.

She'd grown weary, frustrated, and lonely. Her love for Ian had slowly faded over the course of many months, and it couldn't be revived with just a few meaningful words and a beautiful dress; for all she knew this was a one shot deal, and soon he'd go right back to his old ways. But something familiar inside her heart had begun to stir as if waking up from a deep sleep.

Later that afternoon, Bradley went in to shower and change and stepped out onto the porch a half an hour later more handsome than Jane was prepared for in a charcoal suit and lavender shirt. Clearing her throat of the emotion that had tightened it most of the day, she grinned.

"Where's my baby boy?"

Bradley heaved an exaggerated sigh. "Go ahead and say whatever you want now. Get it out of your system. I don't want you embarrassing me when I bring Alison back for pictures."

Emma and Jessica both jumped up and raised their voices an octave, while batting their eyelashes. "Oooooh, Bradley. Oooooh." When they added kissy noises, he swatted at them and chased them off the porch, while Jane and Ian watched in amusement.

Shaking his head, Bradley teased, "Remind me again why you couldn't have just stopped with me." He slid into his car and backing out of the driveway, never seeing Jane's smile falter.

You weren't supposed to be the oldest, Son.

By the time he returned with his date, the gloomy little cloud had lifted from Jane's heart. Alison looked beautiful in her purple dress, with her hair done up and her make-up applied perfectly. Jane could easily see what Bradley saw in this girl. Alison's smile was as bright as the afternoon sun, and her good manners impressed Jane. Bradley slipped a pretty corsage on Alison's wrist, and she pinned a matching boutonniere on his jacket, while Jane snapped one picture after another.

Finally, when Jane was satisfied with the number of photos she'd taken, Bradley kissed her on the cheek, shook Ian's hand, and escorted Alison to his car. Like a gentleman, he opened the door and assisted her inside. It warmed Jane's heart to watch their son treat his date like a lady.

She couldn't help wondering where he learned it since Ian never opened her car door anymore, but she decided it wasn't important. With a wave, Bradley backed out of the driveway and the teens were off to their first dinner and dance together.

Jane glanced up at Ian. "I wonder if twenty years from now he'll still be carrying a photo from tonight in his wallet."

Stuffing his hands in the pockets of his dirty jeans, Ian shrugged. "It takes a pretty special couple to make it that far."

Jane wondered whether he was insinuating that they were a special couple, or that they weren't going to make it. But she decided not to make a big deal of it and gathered up her stuff for the dance.

"I'm going to Dad's. I'll see you in a couple hours."

Ian only nodded.

His reaction puzzled Jane. All the way to her dad's she wondered how Ian could be such a changed man as he appeared to be that morning, so thoughtful, caring, and sweet, and then by the afternoon be cool to her. He didn't even offer her a smile as she left with the dress he'd bought her. It confused her to no end. Was he going to step up and be the kind of man she'd been practically begging him to be for years or not? Had he learned to value her, to really see her? Or was she still a convenience to him to be taken for granted? Exhaling in a huff that rustled her unkempt bangs, she parked in her dad's driveway and hauled her dress and cosmetics into the house.

Her dad sat at the small kitchen table playing solitaire. Looking up, he brightened. "That's my Lassie."

"Hi, Dad."

Setting his cards aside, he swiveled in his chair toward her. "Come now. Why the long face?"

Jane sighed heavily. "I don't know, Dad. All this with Ian is so confusing. One minute he acts like a changed man, but the next he doesn't seem to want to even look at me."

"Well, now, just exactly how much do you expect him to change? And how fast?"

Jane stuck her chin out. "I don't expect him to change at all."

"If you two are going to stay together, you do. I guarantee that, as a man, Ian's thinking, 'Either I change completely or I lose my wife.' And, as a man, I can also tell you it's not an easy choice because he's been hurt in this situation too."

She plopped down in a chair next to him, gathering her armful of stuff into her lap. "Wait just a minute. What is happening here? You're my dad and you're taking his side?"

Chuckling, he leaned over and patted her arm. "Of course not, Lassie. Just trying to help my stubborn girl see things in a different perspective."

"Tell me what else I should think. We had a few wonderful, almost magical minutes this morning, and then it was like I wasn't even there. He spent the rest of the day planting some bush and landscaping around it."

Her dad's eyes twinkled behind his glasses. "Tuesday morning when he was here, he wanted my advice on how to be a better husband for you. I helped him to see when you like a flower, you pick it, but when you love a flower you plant it, water, and fertilize it, weed it, and watch it bloom. I bet you never took the time to find out what he was planting or why he was planting it, did you?"

Jane shook her head, her heart plummeting to the pit of her stomach.

"See? Perspective." He returned to his cards. "And just like that plant will never be anything other than that type of plant, you can't expect Ian to be anything other than who he is. Oh, he can grow and bloom, but sometimes he might need some pruning. You just might need some, too, Lassie. We all do from time to time. Just be careful how much you ask him to change. Understand?"

Nodding, she stood. "Thanks, Dad. I'm going to go shower and get ready for the dance."

In the safety of the hot, steamy shower, Jane cried. She had been so selfish. Ian hadn't been the thoughtless one. She had.

How could she have not asked him about the sudden landscaping job in their front yard? He probably felt like she was the one who didn't care, wasn't trying, needed to change. And he would have been right.

She sank to her knees, tears of shame mixing with the cleansing water. She needed to change. She had to try harder. Silently she vowed to do everything in her power to make things right.

CHAPTER
Sixteen

Jane glanced at the grandfather clock, her mother's favorite antique. Most of the time she coped well with losing her mother before even becoming a mother herself, before she really even knew what life was all about. But though her dad went the extra mile to make up for the void, her heart still longed for that missing piece of her life. And now, in her dad's bedroom, looking through her mother's jewelry box that he still kept out on the dresser, Jane felt her presence all around her.

Mom, how did you know Dad was the one?

The twenty-plus-year-old memory enfolded her like the embrace of an old friend. It was right after her and Ian's first homecoming dance. . . Still wearing her gown, Jane sat cross-legged on her mother's bed while her mother sat behind her, removing all the bobby pins from her hair and brushing it out.

Hmm . . . let's see . . .

Jane teared up at the memory of her mother's voice.

I always knew I loved your dad. He and I were more than lovers. We were buddies. We had so much fun together. But I don't think I knew he was my one and only until after we'd been married a few years. We saw some deep valleys I didn't think we'd make it through, but instead of calling it quits, your dad, the stubborn Irish man that

he is, insisted that we sit down together and work out our differences.
You see, it's easy to be in a relationship when you're on the mountain
top, my sweet Jane, but to find someone who'll walk with you through
the valleys, that's pretty special.

Her mother was right. She and Ian had some work to do to
rebuild their relationship and make it better than before, but she
believed that together they could come out on the other side of
this valley.

The doorbell rang, and it felt as though her heart turned a
somersault inside her chest. She took one last long look in her
mother's full-length mirror. The elegant dress softly flowed
around her ankles with each step. The modest v-neckline
pointed to a gathered waist that accentuated her petite figure,
and the sheer material floated around her arms in an almost
angelic type of short sleeve. Jane had been surprised by how well
it fit her. After having lost some weight, she didn't even know
what size she wore.

She'd styled her hair carefully around a rhinestone-embel-
lished headband. Her make-up covered the tired circles under
her eyes well and accentuated their jade color. The last thing
she did was paint her lips a bright berry and add some gloss on
top.

Even she, her toughest critic, thought she'd cleaned up
pretty well. Sucking in a deep breath, she walked down the hallway and met Ian in the living room.

"Wow," he breathed, staring at her. "You are stunning."

Jane smiled. "The dress is beautiful and it's a perfect fit. How
did you know what size to buy?"

It seemed to take him a few minutes to find his voice. "I-I
asked Kate to help me. She checked the size of a dress you wore
earlier this week and suggested I try a size smaller."

Jane remembered Kate telling her that the tag on her dress was sticking out and tucking it back in for her. She laughed.

"Very sneaky, Garner. Very, very sneaky."

Fumbling with a small box, Ian finally got it open and lifted out a delicate corsage. "This might be cheesy, but I found a picture of the flowers mom ordered for our first homecoming, and I took it in to Not Just A Pretty Vase. This corsage isn't exact, but it's close."

Gazing into Ian's eyes, Jane held out her wrist. "I think it's perfect."

As Ian awkwardly slipped his arm around Jane's waist so her dad could snap a couple pictures, she felt as though they had taken a step toward healing, and she marveled at how easy it was with an open heart.

Ian opened the door of his truck and helped her inside, just as they'd watched Bradley do earlier. They drove the short distance to the school in silence. Ian parked in the lot, cut off the engine, and turned to Jane.

"You know, I hate to admit it but I'm as nervous tonight as I was that night twenty-something years ago."

"You shouldn't be nervous now, and you shouldn't have been back then either. It's just me."

"That's what you've never understood. There's no such thing as 'just you' because you've always been everything. You're strong. Sometimes I think you're stronger than me. I know you've been through a lot more than I have. You're confident, not just in yourself but in the ability of others too. You make people believe they can do things they never imagined they could. That's why you're such an amazing teacher. And that's the only reason I even tried to start my own business. You're creative and funny and kind and generous. And good heavens," he breathed, "you're so beautiful."

Jane frantically dabbed a tissue under her lashes. "Thank you. I've been needing to hear that for a long time." Her voice cracked. She sniffled and fanned herself. "But maybe it would have been better if you waited until the end of the night to tell me. I worked really hard on my make-up."

They both laughed. Ian climbed out of the truck and circled around to open the door and help Jane step out of the truck.

She looped her flower adorned wrist through his arm. As they walked into the high school together, a river of memories flooded over her. Once again she felt like she was being transported to a simpler place and time.

They were early, beating the teenagers and the majority of the chaperons there. The old gym was decorated in streamers and lights. A disc jockey claimed a corner near the refreshment table with speakers that were almost as tall as Jane, and he was busy checking the sound levels. The photographer had set up his equipment on the stage, complete with a fairytale garden backdrop.

Jane took it all in. The music had changed some in twenty years, styles had changed more, but some things always remained the same about high school dances, like the opportunity for new beginnings, the chance to fall in love.

"Hey," the photographer called from the stage. "Can I use you two to test my equipment?"

Ian glanced at Jane and shrugged. "Sure." He took her hand and led her up the few steps to the designated photo area.

Positioning them in front of the backdrop, the photographer snapped a few pictures, readjusting his camera in between shots. "All right. I think we're set. Thanks for your help." He handed them a ticket. "Just in case you want to look at your photos, here's the website and this is your number."

Ian returned Jane's hand to his arm and covered her fingers with his own. "Happy to help." They strolled over to the refreshment table, and Ian poured them both a cup of punch. "Better get some now before it's spiked."

"You're right." Returning his teasing grin, she lifted her cup. "Here's to coming home."

They tapped their plastic cups together and took a long swig. Jane marveled at how this moment felt so different than any other in her life. She'd been married to Ian for twenty years, dated him several years before that, had been classmates since kindergarten, and yet she didn't know this man.

This relationship they were embarking on felt brand new. The way he treated her, the way he looked at her and talked to her, he seemed more like a boyfriend, still falling in love with her, than her husband, whose feelings had grown stagnant. It made her heart race and swell and turn cartwheels. It was beautiful.

Her grumbling stomach reminded her she hadn't eaten, and she grabbed a small plate and a handful of chips. "So you haven't told me much about your meetings with Pastor Ben." She popped a chip into her mouth. "Is it top secret or something?"

Ian took a swallow of his punch. "No, not at all. What do you want to know?"

Jane shrugged. "You seem to have changed a lot in just a few short weeks. I'm just wondering if he's some sort of hypnotist on the side. Or maybe he has a potion and he slipped it into your drink."

Ian's grin faltered, and the sparkle in his eyes faded a bit. "You don't believe I can change on my own?"

She set her plate down and touched his arm. "Come on, Ian. I was joking. Of course, I believe you can change or do anything you want to do. I'm truly interested in how it's going."

Downing the last of his punch, he refilled his cup. "It's going well. He helps me see things in a different perspective and pinpoint the areas where I need to improve."

Looking down at her cup, she traced the rim with her fingertip. "Do you ever talk about me?"

"Some, but mostly we talk about me."

He stole a chip from her plate, and Jane playfully slapped his hand. "Classic move, Garner."

Ian grinned. "You know, if you're so curious, the offer still stands for you to come with me to counseling and to church. The boys loved it."

"I'll think about it." She paused. She couldn't hold it in any longer; she had to know. "Why didn't you tell me earlier why you were planting that bush in our yard?"

He swallowed his punch, almost choking. "What do you mean?"

"I thought it was just another one of your projects until Dad told me what you two talked about."

"Don't take this the wrong way, but I didn't plant it for you. I planted it for me, so that I always remember to take care of you like a husband should and not just pluck you for my own benefit."

Impulsively she grabbed his free hand and laced their fingers together. "Maybe we can take care of it together. What kind of plant is it?"

"It's a rose bush I had special ordered from one of the nurseries I use quite a bit."

"What's so special about it?"

"They're Sweet Jane roses. They'll bloom a pretty yellow copper color." He shrugged. "I couldn't plant anything else."

"Sweet Jane," she breathed. "That's what Mom used to call me. Now I know why." A tear dropped from her lashes onto their entwined fingers, and Ian pulled her to him in a fierce hug.

"Hey, you two. Keep it G-rated."

Turning their attention toward the familiar voice, Jane and Ian smiled. Ian shook Adam's hand, while Jane embraced Kate.

"It's about time you got here. I was getting ready to put a big dent in that bag of potato chips."

Kate laughed. "Yep, just like old times. Hey, does the DJ have karaoke? Maybe you two can sing 'I Got You, Babe' again."

Jane and Ian groaned simultaneously, then Ian chuckled. "Not if we want our son to speak to us ever again."

They all laughed and visited with each other as students began to trickle in. Jane tried to play it cool when Bradley walked in with Alison and a group of their friends, but inside she was tickled to watch her son experiencing a romantic relationship for the very first time. It was definitely shaping up to be a magical night all the way around.

Within an hour the night was in full swing. The girls danced in the middle of the crowded gym floor to every song the DJ played, while most of the guys hung around the perimeter talking with each other and watching their dates.

Ian leaned in close so Jane could hear him, his breath against her neck causing chills up and down her spine. "Not much has changed in twenty years, has it? The fellas still own the walls."

Jane laughed, her cheeks suddenly ablaze. "It was a shame back then that you were too cool for dancing. You could actually move."

"What do you mean back then? I can still move."

Jane could feel the sparkle inside her chest escaping through her eyes. "Prove it."

Ian held his hand out to her. "Right this way."

He led her to a less crowded area of the floor, closer to the exit leading to the hallway and farther away from the enormous speakers. With his right arm around her petite waist, he used his left hand to hold her hand close to his heart as they rocked to the rhythm of the music. He twirled her so that her back was pressed against his front, and he wrapped both of his arms around her waist, still swaying to the beat.

His mouth was right beside her ear, his voice low, his breath felt like butterfly wings on her neck, mimicking the butterflies inside her chest. "We haven't danced like this since our wedding."

Jane opened her mouth to respond, but then snapped it shut as her gaze fell on Zach standing in the doorway, watching her intently.

Ian spun Jane back around to face him, continuing to sway to the music. When the song ended, Jane glanced over her shoulder, but Zach was gone.

He still wasn't texting her. He hadn't stopped by to see her at school. Wondering if she'd hallucinated seeing him at the game and just then, she came up with a fast excuse.

"I need to go to the ladies room." She chuckled to hide her nervousness. "That punch is going right through me."

Clutching her purse, Kate stepped in line with Jane. "I'll come too."

"No." Even Jane could tell her response was just a little too sharp. Softening, she smiled sweetly. "I mean, unless you have to go. I don't want you to miss all the fun. I'll be right back."

Turning, she hightailed it out of the gymnasium. Once in the hallway, however, her steps were slow and deliberate.

Where would Zach have gone? There really isn't anywhere to go, except home.

At the thought she picked up her pace again and pushed through the heavy double doors into the cool late September night breeze. She shivered, unsure whether it was caused by the temperature or guilt.

"Zach?" Squinting, she searched the dark. "Zach, are you out here?"

"Yeah, but why are you? You seemed awfully cozy inside." He sat on a bench along the walkway that led to the street, staring into the darkness, his arms crossed.

Descending the steps, Jane went to perch on the edge of the bench, her body angled slightly toward him. "Zach, I'm sorry."

"I believed you when you said you didn't want to live with him because he doesn't treat you as well as I do. 'He doesn't listen to me or make time for me or compliment me,' you said."

"I know. He didn't, but he's changing."

"You honestly believe that? I told you the first day we talked in your classroom that people don't really change."

"I'm so sorry I let you develop feelings for me. It shouldn't have gone so far. Maybe things would have worked out between us in a different time and place, but Ian is my husband and he is trying." Jane took a deep breath, ignoring the ache in her heart. "So I have to try too."

"We had something real, Jane. Don't try to deny it. We had a connection from the moment our eyes met, and you're telling me you're going to throw it away for someone who didn't start trying for twenty years? He didn't care until he saw what he stood to lose."

Raw emotion—anger, sorrow, disappointment, shame—pooled beneath her lashes. "I have to try. I made a commitment to him."

Zach bolted upright and grabbed Jane firmly but gently by the shoulders. "And what about his vows, Jane? Is he honoring and cherishing you?" By the faint glow from the street light, Jane could see the muscles in his jaw flex. "I should shake you, but all I want to do is hold you."

"Get your hands off my wife."

Jane bolted to her feet. She couldn't meet Ian's gaze, and it took a long minute to find her voice in the flood of tears.

"Ian, I can explain. This is all a misunderstanding." She wrapped her arms around her middle, trying to ease the pain.

Ian glared at her. "You mean just like you explained the flowers?"

"Jane?" Kate stepped to Ian's side, frowning. "I thought you told me Ian got you those flowers." On her other side, Adam wrapped a protective arm around her shoulders.

"No, that's what you assumed," Jane said in a low voice, hanging her head. "I just didn't correct you."

"You lied to me? Back then and just a minute ago." Kate pointed a finger at her. "I honestly did have to go to the bathroom. When I didn't see you, I got worried."

"I'm so sorry."

Zach rose and stretched his arms out. "Stop. All of you. Just stop. It might not be my place to say anything, but I don't want to see Jane hurt anymore. She isn't the one to blame here." He rounded on Ian. "If this is anyone's fault, it's yours. What kind of a man can't take his amazing and beautiful wife out on their twentieth anniversary?" He turned to smile at Jane. "If you were with me, every day would be our anniversary."

As Zach returned his attention to Ian, Ian's fist made contact with his nose. He fell backward, cracking his head on the concrete walkway.

"Ian! What have you done?" Jane knelt beside Zach and pressed the hem of her dress against his bleeding nose.

Zach looked up at her with pain and regret in his eyes.

Ian shook his head, shoulders slumped. "He crossed the line, and now you have too." He sucked in a deep, shaky breath. "Kate, take her to her dad's. I don't want her staying at my house. Then call my sister Ava. Let her know I'm going to be home later than expected, possibly not until morning, and ask her to please stay with the kids until I get there. Adam, call your brother at the fire station. Ask him to come and check out this guy's face. I'm going to find Bradley." Ian spun on his heel.

As Kate helped Jane to her feet, she wailed, "Ian, please! Listen to me!"

He only put his hand up as he strode away, not looking back.

CHAPTER
Seventeen

October blew in cold and dreary. Unfriendly. Lonely. It was an appropriate representation of Ian's spirit. As he tried to stay preoccupied, the thought that he was in the autumn season of his marriage continually crept into his mind, wreaking havoc on his heart. He could feel his life with Jane dangling like the leaves about to fall from the trees.

He wasn't exactly sure why they were both still holding on at this point. If he ripped the Band-Aid off quickly, it would hurt a lot less, at least in theory. But that didn't take into account the amount of him that would be ripped off with it.

Anger came and went in powerful waves. Every time he pictured Jane kneeling beside "flower guy", mopping up his blood with the hem of the dress Ian had bought her, his blood pressure rose to dangerous levels. It had been at least a decade and a half since he last decked someone, possibly breaking his nose. He wasn't proud of it, but he hadn't been able to stop himself.

Now a different part of him wished he could take it all back, especially the ugly words he said in front of Jane about not wanting her in his house. Of course he wanted her there with him and the kids. Together. This family wasn't complete without her, but he didn't know where to begin to mend what had been broken in their marriage. He was hoping Pastor Ben had some answers.

Pulling up in front of the Bayside Cafe at the usual Monday morning time, Ian filled his lungs with air and his spirit with courage. He headed inside, ready to receive a heaping helping of inspiration. Heaven knew he needed it.

The little bell above the door announced his arrival, but their usual booth sat empty. He hadn't felt up to leaving the house for church the day before, and it dawned on him that he should have confirmed their meeting.

He gave a heavy sigh and ambled toward the table. *Oh, well. While I'm here I might as well get breakfast.* He slid into the seat and reached for the menu tucked between the wall and the napkin dispenser. When someone approached, he didn't look up, assuming it was Maggie.

"Just bring me a coffee for now."

A soft, baritone chuckle startled him, and he looked up to see Pastor Ben slide into the booth. "I'd get it for you, but I'm not too sure the staff would appreciate a customer going behind the counter."

Ian shook his head and shoved his fingers through his hair. "Sorry. I thought you were Maggie."

Pastor Ben waved his apology away. "I get that all the time."

Ian laughed. After the past two days it felt good.

"I didn't know if you'd be here since I wasn't in church yesterday."

Pastor Ben shrugged off his blazer and opened the other menu. "I thought I'd take my chances. Worst case scenario, I'd get some coffee and breakfast and go back to work."

Ian grinned. "Exactly."

Maggie came to the table, and they both ordered coffee. After she hurried off, Pastor Ben said, "So how was your week?"

Ian adjusted his glasses. "Good. Great. Progressing better than I expected . . . until Saturday night."

"What happened?"

Ian related the sordid details of the dance. "And then when he started running his mouth about how this wasn't Jane's fault, I couldn't help it. I hit him."

Pastor Ben's eyebrows arched as his eyes widened. "You hit him?"

Maggie arrived with two steaming mugs and a small bowl of creamers. "Are you ready to order?"

Pastor Ben smiled. "Not quite yet. *Gracias*, Maggie."

"*De nada*. I'll check back in a bit." She bustled away.

Ian added creamer and sugar to his cup and took a careful sip. "Yep. I decked him. I might have broken his nose."

"What happened then? I mean, is he okay?"

Ian shrugged. "I don't know. I guess. Adam called Owen over at the fire station, and he brought the rescue squad. But the guy had already left under his own power. I'm willing to bet he doesn't want it getting out for the exact opposite reason that I don't want it getting out."

Pastor Ben sat his cup down and folded his hands. "And what reason would that be?"

"Well, it seems to me that he was acting inappropriately with a married woman. I certainly wouldn't want the town to be talking about that if it were me."

"True. So what is your reason?"

"I'm just trying to protect my family."

Pastor Ben seemed to carefully consider Ian's answer. "I've seen you with your boys in church. I hear the way you talk about your wife. I believe one hundred percent that you want to protect your family. But are you sure your reaction isn't slightly self-imposed?"

Ian narrowed his eyes. "This isn't about me at all. I've been doing everything I know to do to be the husband and father my family deserves."

"I understand that, and you've made some remarkable changes. But I also know that if a man's wife is unhappy, he sees it as a direct reflection on him. Are you sure you don't want Jane's unhappiness in the gossip mill because you believe people will think you failed?"

The words hit Ian with as much force as his blow had struck flower guy. "I suppose there is some merit to that statement."

"There's a saying I heard once that goes something like: 'What others think of you is none of your business.'"

Ian snorted. "Tell that to my mom and dad."

Pastor Ben rubbed his chin. "Why? What's the story with your mom and dad? You've mentioned your sister Ava but never your parents."

"Because I hoped the topic wouldn't come up." Ian took a deep breath. "Dad is into politics. I don't know if you remember the name David Garner?"

Pastor Ben shook his head.

"Anyway, he was town mayor for several years back when I was little, and he did a great job. People really respected him, and I did too. After so long, though, he gained enough support to move up the political ladder. He became involved in state government, and now he's a senator in Washington D.C."

"Wow. That's great."

"You might think so, except when he went into state politics, his image began to matter more. He and Mom disapproved of Jane and me getting married so quickly out of high school, but when I refused to enter the political arena with him and started my own construction company instead, he had a big problem with it. 'Garner men were made for greatness, not construction work,' is the way he put it. 'We were meant to build up the nation, not a subdivision.'

"I tried explaining to him that my mind didn't work like his. I struggled all the way through school and didn't want any part of post-secondary education, but he insisted that no son of his was going to be satisfied being a blue collar worker, barely making ends meet and living paycheck to paycheck." Ian hung his head. "So I told him that I guessed I was no son of his. We haven't spoken since. They've never met Jessie or Sammy, and the last time they saw Bradley, Emma was just a baby. That's the way we've left it."

"Oh, man. That's tough."

Ian returned to his coffee cup. "I've spent all of these years trying to prove him wrong, that a construction worker can be as happy and successful as someone sitting high and mighty on Capitol Hill. Some days I believe it, some days I don't, but I still wake up every morning with it on my mind, and I work my tail off every day just to prove that I'm worthy of being his son."

"Do you understand that success is a relative term? It means something different to everyone. Ian, the cold reality is that you may never fit your dad's definition of success, and you have to be okay with that."

"Have you ever stopped trying to make your dad proud?"

"My dad was an alcoholic and left when I was just a baby, so even though I spent some time curious about who he was, I never tried to make him proud. Mom, on the other hand, worked two jobs to support all us kids, while my oldest sister basically raised us. I always wanted to make them proud of me.

But shortly after I was ordained I realized that, sure, it'd be nice to make my mom and siblings proud, but it was more important that I make my Father in heaven proud. If I worked to do right by Him, I found that everything else fell into place, and the small amount that was left over didn't really matter."

Maggie returned to the table to refill their cups and take their orders. After she headed back to the kitchen Pastor Ben said, "You've been working really hard at bettering yourself. Now you need to ask yourself, what are your motives? Are you trying to change because you want to be better? Or is it to prove something to your parents?"

Ian pondered the question. "Maybe a little of both. And also because I'm trying to make Jane happy. I don't see what's wrong with that."

"Nothing is wrong with it, per se, but in the long run if you aren't making changes for you and only you, you're wasting your time right now. Nothing you do to become better is going to stick if you don't do it for you."

Ian nodded. "I think I understand."

"Good. Have you forgiven your dad and Jane?"

Creases of confusion formed in Ian's brow. "They haven't apologized."

"Sometimes you'll never get an apology, but that isn't what gives you peace anyway. Forgiveness is not for the person who wronged you. Forgiveness is for you. And it doesn't mean you accept what happened. It simply means that you acknowledge it, recognize you are still okay despite the hurt it caused, make peace with it, and move on. Your dad hurt you, understandably so. You don't have to accept his words and his lack of communication since then. Simply acknowledge that it happened and that you are still doing just fine, and let it go. See how it works?"

Ian set his coffee cup down. "I don't know if I can let something like that go. My dad deserted me because I didn't want to be like him. I wanted to be my own person, and he rejected that."

"Your heavenly Father would never desert you—"

"See, that right there is where this faith train leaves the station without me. I'm sorry, but I can't understand how to rely on a Father I can't see or hear or feel. I can't talk to Him like I'm talking to you. It means nothing to me for you to say a God I'm not one hundred percent sure exists would never leave me."

"That was actually the very same question I had before I became a Christian and dedicated my life to the Lord. Kate's Grandpa Clayton mentored me and got me started on my faith journey. When I confessed to him that I didn't know how to believe in someone I couldn't see or hear or feel, he told me something that stuck with me all these years.

"He said that there are a lot of things in this world he could see, hear, and feel, but that didn't make it real. Something becomes real when you make the conscious choice to push your doubt aside and let it in your heart. God won't become real to you until you open your heart to him and choose to accept him. I like the quote by C.S. Lewis, 'I believe in Christianity as I believe the sun has risen: not only because I see it, but because by it I see everything else.' "

Taking his glasses off, Ian cleaned the lenses on his shirt, hoping maybe it would help him see the situation in a different light.

"It takes time, but you'll get there. In the meantime, just know the Bible promises us over and over that He is always with you, through the best and worst times. Trust that, even if you don't understand it quite yet. Lean on it when you're weak, and recognize that your dad is only human. He makes mistakes, and chances are he's regretting his words as much as you are. Jane is human. She's going to make mistakes, but she's going to get a lot of things right too. Did you stop to ask her side of the story?"

Ian frowned, remembering Jane screaming for him to listen to her. "No. I haven't said a word to her since Saturday."

"Maybe what you thought you saw isn't exactly what happened. Maybe it is. Either way the real tragedy occurs when people jump to conclusions instead of seeking the truth." Pastor Ben spoke gently but firmly. "And often the hardest person to forgive is yourself."

Just then Maggie arrived, carrying a plate in each hand. Setting the meals in front of them, she smiled.

"Can I get you anything else?"

I'll never forgive myself. Never.

Ian stared at the huge burger and heaping portion of fries, doubting he could get a bite past the lump in his throat. "Yeah, a To-Go box, please."

CHAPTER
Eighteen

J ane kept one goal in mind: Just get through the day. Every time she thought about Ian's angry eyes and hurt expression she hated herself. When she remembered Zach's bloody nose, she despised herself even more. And to think all of this could have been prevented had she just chosen to not allow her feelings to dictate her behavior.

She painfully waited until Monday morning to send Zach a message. *I'm so worried. I wouldn't blame you if you didn't want to talk to me, but please let me know you're okay.*

He responded right away. *I don't regret it. I'd do it all over again for you.*

Her heart raced. *I wouldn't let you. We have to stop this now.*

We should, yes, but we won't because we both want this.

Inside her head, Jane screamed that they were both going to wind up hurt in the end, and broken hearts never healed as well as broken noses. Worse yet, her kids would be devastated if they ever found out what had happened.

Bradley hadn't talked to her since the incident, and it made her sick to think she had let her son down. She didn't know if the other three knew anything about it, but they certainly knew she wasn't at home and something once again wasn't right with their family.

Everything about continuing to communicate with Zach was so wrong in every way, but the notion that he believed she was worth fighting for swept her away. He stood up for her knowing the odds weren't in his favor, knowing that since she was married he had nothing to gain, and he still chose her.

Relief resonated through her as her heels clicked softly on the tile floor and echoed down the empty hallway on the way to her classroom. Zach had taken a few days off to heal. She could avoid dealing with her sin a little while longer.

Turning the corner, Jane noticed the light on in Kate's fourth-grade room and slowed. Should she stop? If she did, what could she say that would begin to convey her shame and embarrassment? Somehow sorry just didn't seem to be enough. Adjusting the shoulder strap of her purse, she rushed past, keeping up the pace until she reached the safety of her own classroom.

As she flipped on the lights, she put Kate, Ian, and, most of all, Zach out of her mind and busied herself with her normal morning routine: setting out morning work, correlating phonics sheets, cuing up a short Sesame Street video on the number twenty on her smart board, and finally punching in her code on her classroom extension to check her messages. Many mornings her voice mailbox sat empty, but today she had two messages waiting for her.

Destiny Shoals's mother informed her that Destiny was not feeling well and would hopefully be back tomorrow. Jane's brow creased with concern. Something wasn't right. She hit the replay button and listened more closely. It could have been her overactive imagination, but the mother's voice sound strained, as if she had been crying or screaming moments before the message.

Fear knotted Jane's stomach. She checked the caller ID, but it read "unavailable". She quickly searched in her record book for Destiny's contact number. When she dialed it, an automated voice quickly picked up.

"This number has been disconnected or is no longer in service."

Frustrated, she slammed the receiver down.

"What did that phone ever do to you?"

She swung toward the voice and froze as her gaze met Kate's. "Oh, hey. Sorry. I got a message from Destiny's mom saying she's not going to be here, but something about the message seemed a little off. So I called back but her number has been disconnected."

Kate walked over to the desk. "Let me listen."

As she replayed the message, the hairs on the back of Jane's neck rose. In all her years of teaching, she'd never had a situation that worried her quite so much.

"I see what you mean. That mom seems upset." Crossing her arms, Kate leaned against the edge of the desk. "So what are you going to do?"

"I plan on talking with Mrs. Zeller about it first thing this morning. I don't know what else I can do."

"No. I meant about whatever is going on with you and Zach."

Jane's shoulders fell, and she blew out and exasperated breath. "Nothing is going on between Zach and me. If Ian would only have listened to me before everything got out of control, I could have explained it."

Kate narrowed her eyes.

"It's the truth! Zach and I had been texting. It started out as friendly coworkers chatting about our day, and he usually had something to say about Jessie. I admit some feelings gradually developed. I continued talking with him simply because he had become a good friend, but I told him I was married with four children and that wouldn't change. Saturday night, I knew Ian wouldn't understand me leaving the dance to go talk to Zach so I lied and said I was going to the bathroom just so I could tell him again that I am committed to my marriage."

"I see. What was he even doing at the dance?"

Averting her guilty gaze, Jane shrugged. "I don't know. He must have been asked to chaperon."

"That's strange. Adam didn't see his name on the list." Standing, Kate closed the gap between them. "Listen, I know things haven't been great between you and Ian. No marriage is perfect, and I don't know what will happen between you two. But you've been my best friend since high school. You were there for me when Ryan died and after I moved back to Harvest Bay. You were there for me when I was scared to start dating again. I'll always be here for you, but don't lie to me anymore. No one deserves that."

"I know. I'm sorry." Jane's vision blurred. "So you aren't mad at me?"

"Of course, I'm mad at you." Giving her a quick hug, Kate strolled toward the door. "But you are my best friend. I love you and I'll forgive you." With a small grin, she disappeared into the hallway.

Jane swiped the tears from her cheeks, her heart swelling. She wished she could be more like Kate, so quick to forgive and let go of past hurts, trusting God for justice.

But sometimes life just isn't fair and justice never comes, her mind protested. Sighing, she hit the play button, and returned to her voice mail.

"Hi, Jane. This is Sandy Lovato from Stampede of Dreams. Sorry to bother you at school, but this was the only contact I had for you besides your email. Anyway, I just wanted to remind you about the volunteer training session we scheduled for this evening. If I don't hear from you, I'll assume I'll see you at five o'clock."

It had been almost a week since she spent time with Sandy at the Stampede of Dreams. The day she got the beautiful bouquet from Zach. The first time she lied to her best friend and her husband.

Those beautiful moments working with the gentle horses and challenged individuals had helped her escape her own problems for a while. Yes, she needed this opportunity more now than ever before. She'd be there.

She looked up at the big round clock on the wall as the first of her students trickled in. How was it already time to start her day? She already felt weary.

Before taking time to unload his backpack, William approached her desk, his chocolaty eyes troubled.

Jane squatted down to his eye level. "What's up, Superman?"

At the nickname his lips turned up slightly, but then fell again. "Destiny wasn't on the bus this morning."

"Don't worry." Jane tousled his dark hair. "Her mommy called and said she wasn't feeling well. But she sure is a lucky little girl to have such a good friend who cares about her. Would it make you feel better if you colored her a get well card this morning?"

As William sped off to put his belongings away and start on a construction paper card, Jane hoped beyond all hope that the intuitive little boy was just being overly sensitive.

Jane saw only one other car parked near the barn when she drove up the long gravel driveway later that evening. Had she heard the time wrong on the voicemail? she wondered.

She parked her Expedition beside the gray Hyundai, hopped out, and wandered toward the smaller barn that housed the ingenious Equicizer where the students checked in each week.

"Hello?" she called out. "Sandy?"

"Over here!" The faint voice came from the arena.

Jane hurried to the bigger barn. At the metal gate, she found Sandy holding onto the lead of a beautiful mahogany horse, stroking his strong neck.

"This is Logan." As Sandy spoke, the horse bobbed his head, seeming to greet Jane. "The first part of your training is to gain perspective from the student's point of view. Come on over to the ramp, and I'll help you on."

Jane hesitantly followed Sandy's instructions. She'd been around horses at the Sullivans' farm but had never ridden one. She was out of her element and quite intimidated.

Once she was situated on Logan, Sandy talked her through how to give basic directions to the horse. "If you want to go to the right, pull the reins in your right hand to your pocket. Do the same thing but with the left hand if you want to go left. If you want to stop, pull back gently and say, 'Whoa.' "

Jane's confidence grew as she completed the tasks, and she began to understand why this therapy worked so well for students with special needs. So much in her life had spun out of her control, and she imagined that kids with significant challenges felt this even more. Suddenly feeling in control of something big and powerful gave her deflated self worth a much-needed boost.

"When the student gets the hang of those directions, we then add some obstacles, such as to lead Logan over here to this football, grab it, and then toss it in the net."

Holding onto the saddle horn with one hand, reaching for the ball with the other, and then tossing it into a net all while maintaining her balance on Logan was more difficult than it seemed, but Jane accomplished the goal. She then guided Logan through a short series of obstacles before she dismounted.

Back on her feet, she patted Logan's shoulder. "I can definitely see how this program would be so beneficial to people with challenges."

"These horses meet all needs—physical, mental, emotional, spiritual. Somehow they sense where you're weak, and they're strong for you." Moving around Logan, Sandy stood beside Jane and showed her how the saddle and bridle fit on the horse. "As a volunteer, you'd walk beside the students, keeping a hand on their leg at all times to ensure their safety. If you notice something wrong, it's your job to tell the guide, and together you'll correct the situation immediately."

Jane nodded. "I understand."

"Good." Smiling, Sandy pushed her glasses higher up the bridge of her nose and motioned for Jane to come alongside her as she walked Logan back to his stall. "So now that we've covered the technical stuff, tell me a little about yourself. I know you're a teacher so you must have a recent background check on file."

"I do. I can get you a copy."

"That'd be great." Sandy got Logan fresh water and a treat of alfalfa. "Do you have any children?"

Jane leaned against the stall's wooden gate. "Yes. Bradley is sixteen, Emma is fourteen, Jessie is twelve, and Sammy is nine."

Sandy's eyes widened. "Four kids." She gave a long, low whistle. "And you don't already feel like you're a part of something that matters? Being a parent is the most important job there is. Nothing matters more than that."

Jane straightened. "I agree, and my kids are everything to me. But parenting can be a lonely and emotionally draining job when you don't see eye-to-eye with their father."

"I see."

"Life with Ian has been nothing short of a roller coaster for the past several months," Jane blurted out, feeling a sudden need to confide in this woman she barely knew. "Amusement park rides make me sick, so you can imagine it's been trying, to say the least. One minute he'll act as if I don't even exist—up with the sun and not coming home until after dark. Anything intimate between us seems to be the last thing on his mind. Then he bought me a beautiful dress and planted a Sweet Jane rose bush in the yard. He talked to me as if he valued me, and he actually held me like I'm precious to him, only to become distant again a few hours later." Jane shook her head. "I just don't understand."

Closing and locking the stall gate, Sandy motioned toward a bale of hay. The two of them sat down side by side.

"What don't you understand?"

"The ups and downs. The way he seems to keep reeling me in just to push me away again." Jane jerked a piece of hay from the bale and twirled it between her fingers. "We've been together for over twenty years. Somewhere along the way, while trying to be everything he wanted and taking care of the kids' every need, I lost myself. I'm not sure if it happened gradually or suddenly, but one day I woke up and realized this wasn't what I'd dreamed of when I was a little girl."

"What would you change if you could?"

Jane pondered the question, at the same time wondering why she felt so comfortable talking about this to someone who was practically a stranger. "I guess I would make more time for my painting. For as long as I can remember, it was my passion. I just loved making the colors work together to tell a whole story in one picture. I could completely lose myself in a painting." She dropped her gaze. "It got me through some really difficult times. But with each baby we had Ian worked more and more, and I painted less and less."

"Do you think you resent Ian for that?"

Jane glanced up to see Sandy watching her with friendly compassion in her eyes. There was no judgment, no disappointment, but Jane guessed that would change if she told Sandy about Zach.

No one would understand how a married woman like me could develop feelings for another man.

"I'm sorry. That's none of my business. You don't have to answer that if you don't want to."

"I don't mind. It's nice to have an unbiased person to talk to." Jane shrugged. "I don't think I resent Ian for me falling away from my painting. I resent him for leaving me alone. The daily grind of raising our children—the homework, the discipline, the fighting and crying and laughing with them, the doctors appointments and sports practices—it has all rested on my shoulders. For years I worked all day, then came home and worked harder tending to our home. And it only got worse as time went on. I never got a break. I couldn't even take a bath without someone needing something. I'm beyond burned out now, and I have no idea how to rekindle my passion for life. I appreciate that he works hard for our family, but at what cost?

So that's why I need to be a part of something that matters, that makes a difference in the world."

Pushing to her feet, Sandy smiled. "Well, you've come to the right place. And when the day is done, I think you'll find that Stampede of Dreams makes the biggest difference in your own little world. At least, that's how I feel every evening when I go home."

Jane stood and they strolled together to where their cars were parked. "As far as experiencing peace in any relationship, I practice the Four Agreements."

Creases formed in Jane's brow. "I'm not familiar with that."

"We'll work on it together. When you're a part of Stampede of Dreams you're never alone. Okay?"

Jane nodded and climbed into her Expedition before Sandy could see the moisture in her eyes. It wasn't the words Sandy had said but the genuine way she said them that had Jane believing for the first time in months that she really wasn't alone.

CHAPTER
Nineteen

The days turned into weeks. For most of it, Jane functioned on autopilot. Settling into her room at her dad's, she enjoyed spending the extra time with him and chose to see this separation from her home as a gift, instead of a punishment.

Most days Jessie and Sammy stayed with her. They'd staked their claim to the third bedroom. Bradley drove Emma home at night so they could both sleep in their own beds, but Jane saw all of them every day. She ran with Kate almost every afternoon, except for Tuesdays when she volunteered at Stampede of Dreams, painted every night after the kids and her dad were in bed, and spoke to Ian only when she had to. It wasn't the ideal situation, but she told herself she could survive living in this numb state as long as she had to.

In eight more years, Sammy would be a senior. Jane didn't know if her overactive boy would pursue college or a trade, but either way, he'd be ready to spread his wings. With her nest empty she could feel free to spread her own wings. Hopefully by then they would still carry her.

Regardless, that was the plan for now. It only seemed unmanageable every single second she thought about Zach.

After he returned to school, Jane tried to keep her distance, but just like that proverbial moth would surely end up flying around the porch light, the electricity between them drew her in. The episode at homecoming had clued Kate in that something was going on between them, however, and now they had to be even more careful than before.

Not that anything had ever or would ever happen. She just loved being connected to him, talking and texting a lot, flirting a little, and always experiencing a charge of energy in their communication. She'd never in her life felt so listened to or, for that matter, so spoken to.

They talked about everything: all their hopes and dreams, fears and failures, revolutionary ideas and mundane daily lives. Jane had enough common sense left to understand that more than that might lead to crossing that forbidden line, which would certainly then lead to devastating consequences. Zach disagreed but said he was willing to wait on a physical relationship.

I'd wait forever just to spend a moment with you. Most of his text messages she deleted, but she'd found a way to save that one, and she reread it often.

With Halloween falling on a Saturday, classroom parties would be held on Friday afternoon. This year she actually looked forward to the holiday when everyone was supposed to wear masks and pretend to be someone they weren't. Unfortunately that felt like every day to Jane.

Arriving at her usual early hour, she began to organize for a day of managed chaos. Scribbling notes in her lesson plan book, she shook her head at everything she had planned for that day.

"If I can get in just one phonics and math page, I'll probably be doing good."

"Lofty goals."

Lifting her gaze toward the voice, she saw Mrs. Zeller and sighed. "Yeah, well, in all my years teaching kindergarten, the one thing I've learned is that not much mind shaping happens when candy's on the brain."

Chuckling, Mrs. Zeller came further into the classroom and lowered her voice. "It sounds like you have enough to worry about. I thought I'd give you one less thing. Overnight, Damien Shoals was arrested again on drug trafficking charges. We can all rest a little easier with that threat removed."

Jane slumped back in her chair. "I hate to say that I'm glad Destiny's father is out of the picture, but it does put me at ease to know she's not in danger."

"I understand." Mrs. Zeller returned to the door and paused. "It's never ideal, but sometimes it's better for a family to be apart."

Yeah, sometimes it is better.

"Well, relax and enjoy your kiddos today. After the past two months, you deserve it." Mrs. Zeller punctuated the friendly order with the clack of her heels echoing down the hallway.

In the silence of her classroom, Jane let her guard down and a few tears fell with it. The fear she struggled with everyday as she put Destiny on the bus, not knowing what kind of environment she went home to, melted into a certain measure of peace.

She glanced at her phone, wanting to share this good news, but there was no one to share it with. Ian didn't even know there had been a threat to begin with. After not saying more than a few words to him for weeks, she certainly wasn't going to celebrate with him. She'd most likely tell Zach later. After all, the threat had affected him and his students too. He'd understand her elation better than anyone else, besides Kate.

Her students arrived with their costumes in their backpacks, and she taught the scheduled phonics and math lessons with outward enthusiasm. After lunch and recess, the students came back to their classroom to find Elsa from the movie Frozen as their teacher, and the excitement was uncontainable. Jane giggled inwardly as the girls eyed her long braided wig.

"Boys and girls, it's time to change into our costumes and start our Halloween fun. The other classes are waiting to watch our parade. If you need to use the bathroom to change, make one line by the door. The rest of you may get your costumes out of your backpacks and put them on over your clothes."

Thankfully William's mom had come in early to help with the party preparations. She took the handful of students at the door to the bigger bathrooms at the end of the hall to change, while Jane had her hands full with those trying to put their costumes on over their clothes. Destiny came over to her with a perplexed expression on her corkscrew-framed cherub face.

Jane bent down, smiling. "What can I help you with?"

Destiny lifted up her hands full of red and blue material.

"Use your words, please. What can I help you with?"

"I don't know how this goes." Jane was pleased that the child's tiny, unsure voice grew a little stronger every day.

"I see." Jane took the pieces of the costume from her. "Let's see if we can figure it out together."

Within a few minutes Destiny had been transformed into a miniature Wonder Woman. Jane thought no costume could have been more fitting.

"Where did Destiny go? I only see Wonder Woman." Jane pretended to look around while Destiny giggled. At that moment, William ran up wearing his Superman costume. "What? Now there are two superheroes. Are you two teaming up to take on the world?"

Destiny stuck her arms out as if she was going to take flight, while William struck a Superman pose with his fists on his hips.

His mom snapped a couple photos of the pair and promised to send a copy to Jane.

"All right. If everyone is in their costumes, it's time to line up so we can start our parade."

Like lively little mice, the children scurried to get in line, and Jane led them down the hall in and out of every classroom. The Harvest Bay Elementary tradition took on a new meaning when she reached Zach's room. Slowing her pace, she wove her students around the desks, taking a few extra minutes, waving at Jessica and catching Zach's admiring gaze multiple times. She hated that she so loved the way he looked at her.

By the time they arrived back in their classroom ready for games and crafts, Jane already had a text message waiting for her.

Some people are worth melting for. Zach quoted a line from *Frozen* that completely melted the cold, hard core of her being.

"You must have just gotten some good news. You're practically glowing," William's mom commented as she oversaw a game.

Hastily Jane masked her emotions. "Just a nice message. No big deal." Tapping the screen, she saved the message, put on a smile and joined in the classroom fun.

But she was thinking, *Eight years is too long. Something needs to happen now.*

Saturday morning Ian poured a strong cup of coffee and plodded back into his den. Even with Jane being gone for a month, he couldn't bring himself to sleep in that big empty bed that still smelled like her. He'd grown accustomed to the hard, lumpy futon and the companionship of his computer. He was learning how to manage on his own, and each passing week felt a little less torturous.

He'd quit meeting with Pastor Ben, and without the pressure to change, to work on being a better man his heavy load lifted. It was ridiculous for Pastor Ben to suggest that Jane wasn't at fault for their marriage's demise. As far as Ian was concerned their separation was all her doing.

He had done his best to be better for her, but finding her sitting with another man had been a very painful slap in his face that he didn't know if he could ever recover from. Just like he couldn't recover from his father's rejection or from the secret that he could never forgive himself for. He'd survive Jane's betrayal the same way he survived everything else: He'd work the pain away.

At his job sites he felt respected and honored. He felt appreciated and useful. He was confident in his ability to run a construction company, not in his ability to run a home. But he shouldn't have to run his home. He should be able to just enjoy the home he worked so hard for.

When he was growing up, his mother always took care of buying the groceries with money his father gave her. She made a hearty meal, had it hot on the table by the time his dad got home, and afterward cleaned up all the dishes. She took care of the cleaning and laundry. She made sure he and Ava were at school, sports practices, and doctor appointments on time.

Women everywhere for all generations had done this without complaint. He couldn't believe Jane had it any worse. Instead he chose to believe that she was just ungrateful for all he did for her.

He woke his computer to the invoices he'd been attempting to complete, but quickly became distracted by thoughts of the raven-haired beauty waiting for him on another website. It was early in the morning for delving into such fantasies, but that hadn't stopped him lately.

His excitement mounting, he'd just opened the page and found Felicity when he heard the front door open and slam shut. Bradley and Emma were still asleep upstairs, and Jane hadn't set foot inside the front door since homecoming. But who else could it be?

He closed the sensual web page and headed toward the living room. Jessica and Samuel ran past him on the way.

"Hi, Daddy! Bye, Daddy!" Their voices blended together to make one strange noise.

"Hey, what are you two doing here?"

They bounded up the stairs as though they hadn't heard him. He continued into the living room and found Jane standing by the door, her hand on the knob, looking as if she was ready to bolt.

Ian's heart leaped, and then sank in his chest. The sight of her stole all the air from his lungs. He'd spent so much time blaming her and feeling sorry for himself that he'd forgotten how much he missed the only woman he'd ever really loved.

He'd forgotten how beautiful it was to share that intimate moment with her on the sofa more than a month earlier after she'd chose to come back home. He'd forgotten how it warmed his soul to watch her face light up after receiving his card and the dress . . .

The same dress she'd wiped up flower guy's blood with.

They stood silently staring at each other, arms crossed, neither one budging for a solid minute. Finally Jane narrowed those mesmerizing jade eyes.

"I see you ripped out your new rose bush. That's real nice."

Ian planted his hands on his hips. "No, what's real nice is you making a fool out of me in front of our friends. I can never forgive you for that."

Jane snorted and threw her hands up. "That's fine. I don't need or want your forgiveness, but I didn't make a fool out of you. You did that on your own. What were you thinking punching someone before you knew the facts? I should have known the changes you were making to become a 'better man' wouldn't last. Your hot head hasn't changed one bit since high school."

"I had all the facts I needed. My wife lied to go spend time with another man."

"Yes, to tell him I'm committed to my marriage. I said I was going to the bathroom because I knew you wouldn't understand me talking to him, and I was right."

Ian shook his head. "Did you hear how that guy talked to me? He had it coming."

"Did you hear how *you* talked to me? You. My husband. Not wanting me in *your* house? You don't do that to your wife, the one who has made this house a home for years. Just because you built it doesn't make it yours."

Clenching his fists, Ian could feel the veins bulging in his neck. "This is my house and so is that dress that you used to mop up your boyfriend's blood."

"You've got to be kidding me. The dress?" Jane stared at Ian. "It was all I had to help another human being. I would have done the same thing if it happened to you or Kate or anyone."

Ian's anger grew with every word she spoke. He just wasn't exactly sure who he was angry at.

"So are you still going to counseling?"

"Yeah. So what?" He forced the lie out of his mouth for the sake of his pride.

"Because you and I have a choice to make. We either need to go to counseling together or we need to file for divorce because we can't go on like this any longer. It's not fair to us. It's not fair to the kids."

His heart stopped. A bubble of panic rose up in him.

"Divorce?"

"If that's what we both feel is best, yes." She cocked her head. "Oh, come on. You've thought about it too. You said you didn't want me here. You pulled the rose bush up. What else does that mean?"

"It means I'm angry."

"Two people can't live like we have the last several months and not consider it. This isn't a marriage. It's not even a friendship."

"Every relationship goes through a rocky period. Just because we're traveling down a bumpy road you mean to tell me you're going to bail out?"

"Don't put words in my mouth. I didn't say I'm bailing at all. I'm saying that we're at a crossroads and need to decide which way to go from here. And this isn't just a rocky road. It's not a rough patch or a dry spell. This . . . " She waved her arm in the space between them, "is nothing. It's an empty void where there used to be something special a long time ago, but it's been gone for months and months. Maybe even years. We either need to find it again somehow . . . or we need to be over."

She opened the door and stepped out onto the porch. "I'm picking the kids up at four o'clock for Kate's Halloween party and then Trick-or-Treating. Think about what I said. I can't go on like this anymore." She turned and left, without looking back.

Divorce? It was so final, so permanent, and it petrified him. *"We either need to find it again somehow . . . or we need to be over."*

He'd loved this one woman all his life, and now she suggested ending their marriage? How dare she hand him that ultimatum! She couldn't tell him what to do! Fear turned to boiling hot anger. He slammed the door shut and stalked off to his den.

"Now where was I?" With just a couple clicks of the mouse, he pulled up the website where he would find Felicity. He desperately needed something, anything, to dull this sharp pain.

Samuel burst into their bedroom, his hands over his ears, waking Bradley from a dead sleep. Bradley moaned and squinted at him.

"What's up, buddy? I didn't know you were coming home today."

Samuel uncovered one ear to point toward the floor. "Mommy and Daddy are fighting."

Cocking his head, Bradley made out the muffled voices of his parents downstairs, raised in anger. He blew out an exasperated breath and threw off his covers.

"Come on. Let's go talk to the girls."

They didn't wait for permission before pushing the door of the girls' room open. Emma was sitting up in her bed, hugging her knees to her chest, a deep scowl on her face, while Jessica sat on the edge of her bed, swinging her legs and softly crying.

"I thought you said your plan was going to work," Emma hissed.

Bradley's shoulders fell. "I know. I thought it would. I'm sorry."

Emma exploded off her bed, stomped to her desk, and picked up her diary. "Why should you be sorry? This is all Mom's fault. If she wasn't so busy making goo-goo eyes at Jessica's weirdo teacher, she'd see that Daddy works hard for us."

"Whoa, whoa, whoa. Wait just a minute." He grabbed the diary out of her hands. "I don't think it's that cut and dried, and I really don't think it's for us to decide who's to blame. They're our parents. It's our job to honor them and learn from them."

"Where'd you learn that from? Church? Or your goodie goodie girlfriend? All I've learned from Mom and Dad is that love isn't real and relationships don't last." Emma snatched the book back. "I have news for you, big brother, you can't fix Mom and Dad, you can't stop us from losing this house, and you can't keep us four together because I'm never going to live with her!" She shouted the words at his face.

Wrapping Emma up in a fierce hug, he stroked her tangled hair. "I know you're scared and confused. We all are. But we have to stick together."

Emma shoved hard against his chest. "Leave me alone! I hate you! I hate all of you! I just want to be alone!"

Bradley sighed. "Come on, Jessie. Let's go back to my room. You, Sammy, and I can play a game."

"Oh, can we play Uno?" Samuel piped up. "That's my favorite."

"Sure, buddy."

Following Jessica and Samuel out of the room, Bradley closed the door to a crack, stood by it, and listened to the sobs coming from his little sister. He was the oldest. It was his job to protect his siblings, but he couldn't save them. And he couldn't hold them together if they didn't want to be held.

The Indian summer sun streamed through the kitchen window. Pouring both her and her dad a cup of coffee, Jane carried them to the round table. She added milk, stirred, and took a sip.

"It's beautiful weather for Trick-or-Treating. The kids will be able to wear their costumes without getting cold."

Splashing a bit of Irish cream into his mug, her dad nodded.

She reached across the table and patted his hand. "Don't worry. You know your house is the first stop on the route."

"Is Ian going with you and Kate?"

Her smile fell. "No, probably not. He's never gone any other year." She stared at the steaming, light brown liquid. "Everything is up in the air right now. I love being here with you, but not while I'm still married. It's just not right."

"I understand that, Lassie."

"I told Ian this morning that we either need to go to counseling and work things out or we need to split up permanently."

His hand trembled as he brought the mug to his lips. He took a careful sip and eyed her suspiciously.

"You didn't hesitate when you mentioned breaking up."

She tipped her head. "I'm sorry?"

"In all my years I learned that when someone doesn't want to leave a relationship, they can't bring themselves to mention it, but you didn't hesitate. You already have your mind made up, don't you?"

She shouldn't have been so surprised that he was so intuitive. Sometimes she thought Shaun Flanders was a better detective than the FBI.

"I don't know, Dad. Our relationship was improving a month ago, but now it's worse than before. *He's* worse than before."

"Are you sure you aren't the one who's changed?"

"What do you mean? I haven't changed at all." Jane thought of Zach's words the afternoon of her anniversary. "I heard once that people don't really change at all. They may grow and fulfill different roles in life, but the essence of a person always stays the same."

"Whoever told you that is full of malarkey. I'm living proof that a person can change. I was a completely different person before I met your mum. I made all kinds of bad choices, choices I never would've made if I was even half the man I am today." He glared at her over his coffee cup. "Don't tell me a person can't change."

Jane's eyes grew wide. "I'm sorry. I just don't see how I'm that different. Because I realize I can survive apart from my husband?"

Sticking his bottom lip out a bit, he nodded thoughtfully. "That might be part of it. You've never been on your own. You went right from our house to making a home with Ian. I think as you've matured over the last twenty years you've realized your strength and independence. That's definitely a change."

"In my opinion that's a good change. But Ian's become cynical and angry and confrontational." She turned her nose up. "He also needed a shower. Bad."

Her dad held up his hand. "Hold up there, Lassie. That doesn't have to do with your relationship. His pride is hurtin'. With your new independence, he doesn't feel needed. He was humiliated in front of his friends so, sure, he's going to have a pretty low opinion of himself right now, but that shouldn't be a factor in your relationship."

"Don't you have to be able to take care of yourself before you can take care of someone else?"

Her dad rubbed the stubble on his chin. "I see your point, but don't let it be the straw that broke the camel's back. The poor ol' fella is going through a grief process. Your relationship the way he knew it is changed. It's not as simple as it once was. He has to work through that, and it takes a hard-headed fella some time. Trust me. I know."

"I just can't keep living like this. I don't know how he can either."

Her dad nodded. "You've made up your mind then?"

Jane silently stared at her coffee for a long time. When she finally answered her father, she barely recognized her own voice.

"Yeah, Dad, I think so."

CHAPTER
Twenty

The first week in November crawled by. Ian missed church again as well as his Monday morning counseling session with Pastor Ben. He just didn't see the point.

Only work made his days worthwhile. Homes were going up fast in the subdivision his company was contracted to work in, hopefully homes where happy families, unlike his, would live and grow and make memories. He established a routine of leaving before the sun came up and working for a couple hours. Then he'd take a break to pick up Jessica and Samuel from his father-in-law's and drive them to school. After that, he'd return to the job site and work until the sun went down.

Saturday morning gray clouds rolled in and a cool breeze picked up. Inspired to work harder and faster, Ian thought, *Winter is coming. I have to work while I can. Besides, what good would it do to stay in a house empty of love and laughter with only haunting memories for company?*

As he nailed shingles onto the roof of a modest ranch-style home, Ian glanced up to see a familiar black truck pull to a stop in front. Adam climbed out and started up the ladder.

"What are you doing here? Shouldn't you be watching game film and lifting weights with the boys?"

"Nah, not today. Losing last night, knocked us out of the running for the playoffs. With our season over, there's no big rush to watch game film. I did see Bradley, though. He said you were working." Adam held up his own nail gun. "I thought you could use a hand."

Ian stretched his aching back. "Thanks."

The pair drove nails into shingles in silence for over an hour. Finally Adam said, "Why don't we take a break and go get some lunch at Bayside Cafe? Then we'll come back and finish this roof. What do you say?"

Ian's stomach grumbled. "Okay. Let's go."

They arrived at Bayside Cafe during the lull between the breakfast and lunch crowds, and sat at the same booth Ian had shared with Pastor Ben. Oddly, it comforted and at the same time annoyed Ian.

Maggie came to the table to take their drink orders. Adam ordered water, and when she turned to him, Ian said, "I'll have my usual."

As she hurried away, Adam arched his eyebrows. "Your usual?"

Shrugging, Ian glanced over the menu. "For several weeks I met Pastor Ben here on Monday mornings. We had breakfast and talked."

"For several weeks?" Adam set the menu aside. "So you're done now?"

"I guess, for the most part. I just figured what's the point, you know? I was working on making myself better for what?"

"For you, dude. What else? You make yourself better because you want to be better."

Shaking his head, Ian stared blankly at the menu. "I like myself the way I am. I was trying to become better for Jane, and we see how well that worked. After I found her with that guy she actually gave me an ultimatum." Ian snorted. "Can you believe her nerve? I'm the one who deserves to be handing out ultimatums."

Maggie brought their drinks to the table and pulled out her notebook. "What can I get for you to eat?"

Her thick Spanish accent made such a simple, ordinary sentence beautiful. At one time Jane had that ability, too, because everything she said was coated in love and adoration. When exactly did that change?

After she took their orders and left, Adam leaned toward Ian. "So what was her ultimatum?"

"She said we either need to go to counseling together or we need to get a divorce."

"Whoa." Adam sank back against his seat. "So when do you start counseling?"

Ian cocked his head. "Who said we're going to counseling?"

Perplexed creases formed in Adam's brow. "Please don't tell me you're choosing divorce over counseling. Have you not learned anything from what I've been through?"

Ian couldn't meet Adam's gaze. "No, I'm not choosing divorce. I'm not choosing either one. Not right now. I need time to sort it all out in my head."

"No, you're not sorting anything out. What you're doing is avoiding the issue altogether and hoping it just fixes itself. You used to do the same thing in high school, and you did the same thing with your dad. Tell me, how'd that work out for you?"

"Leave my dad out of this!"

"You have a wife who is willing to work with you on your marriage. Do you know how long I begged Alexandra to go to counseling with me?" Adam paused, but Ian remained silent. "A long time, but she didn't want to try. She just wanted out of the marriage that was holding her back from her dreams of being a big-shot reporter. Whether you choose to recognize it or not, you've been given a gift. Now you can choose to waste it or swallow that ridiculous ego of yours and accept it."

Bolting out of his seat, Ian jabbed a finger at Adam. "Before you start condemning me for my pride, get all your facts straight. I did try. For weeks, I was doing everything I knew to do to be the husband she wanted, and it wasn't enough. *I* wasn't enough. So forgive me if I'm not jumping for joy at the thought of going to counseling with her. The truth is some days, like this one, divorce just sounds better all the way around."

He got out his wallet, threw a couple five dollar bills on the table, and stalked out. At that moment, he needed to be at the only place where he could find solace, and that was on a roof driving nails into shingles. But Adam's words hung in his mind like the thick, late autumn clouds.

Jane yawned and stretched. She loved waking up whenever her eyelids opened on Saturday mornings, no alarms going off and nothing planned all day. Not quite ready to leave her comfy cocoon, she rolled over and wrapped the covers around her tighter.

If she stayed right there long enough, she wondered, would she turn into a butterfly? Like her dad had said a week earlier, she felt some things changing, growing stronger. She'd discovered a new confidence inside her spirit that grew exponentially as her passion for painting was rekindled. Her dad had already hung the pieces she completed around the house, and Jane smiled every time she walked by one, which was often. She had a painting on her easel waiting for her, beckoning from her bed.

"Five more minutes." She mumbled the same three words she used to tell her mother when it was time to get up for school. As if in response, her phone chimed, notifying her of a text message. As she opened it, a smile spread across her face.

Good morning, beautiful. How did you sleep?

She tapped the screen. *I slept well, but I told you not to call me that.*

Laying the phone on her pillow, she closed her eyes and imagined a different life with a faceless man, not Ian or Zach, but someone who loved and cherished her the way every woman should be. This rock and hard place she was trapped between hurt more than she let on. As she'd suspected, Ian hadn't changed at all. He'd gone right back to showing no feelings for her whatsoever, while another man she had no business communicating with as long as she remained married showered her with beautiful compliments. It simply wasn't fair.

Her phone chimed again and she reached for it.

Hey, I'm just an honest guy. And this is me honestly wishing you were waking up beside me . . .

Another message popped up. It was a selfie of Zach, apparently still in bed himself. His dark hair was rumpled against his white pillow cases, and he was signing "I love you" with his free hand against his bare chest.

She stared at the picture for a long moment, the core of her being warming up. Finally she tapped out a reply.

I've told you I can't set the example for my kids that anything like this is ok.

She got a reply almost immediately. *So it's ok for them to see you being treated like an option instead of worshiped like a priority? That's not right either.*

Her skin prickled and her heart squeezed. "Maybe he's right." She could only whisper such immoral thoughts. "Maybe I'm doing my kids a disservice to stay in a miserable marriage. If, down the road, any of them are in my shoes what would I tell them to do? I'd tell them to do whatever they had to in order to be happy again."

It was too early in the morning to be faced with such a dilemma. She turned off her phone, crawled out of bed, checked on Jessica and Samuel, and went to a therapy session with her easel. She completely lost herself and all her troubles in her painting, missing breakfast and lunch completely.

At half past four, Samuel barged into her room, snapping her out of her euphoric state and scaring the living daylights out of her. She jumped, her brush smearing green on the canvas where it didn't belong.

"Sorry, Mom."

"Come here."

Timidly, Samuel shuffled to her, and she kissed him on top of the head. "It's okay. I'll wait until it dries and paint over it."

How she wished life could be so easy! Make a mistake, wait for it to dry, and just paint over it as if it had never been there.

"Now, what do you need, son?"

"Oh, right." He raced back to the door. "Daddy's here."

"Wait. What?"

But Samuel had already bolted. Glancing down, Jane groaned inwardly. She was still in her pajamas. She hadn't brushed her teeth or washed her face or attempted to do anything with her hair. Changing into a pair of jeans and a hoodie, she slipped two doors down the hall into the bathroom to at least rinse out her mouth with Listerine. Then she trudged out to the living room to see what Ian wanted.

She found him standing by the door, the kids nowhere in sight. He straightened when she came into the room and looked her up and down disapprovingly.

Crossing her arms, Jane narrowed her eyes. "I've been painting all day. What's your excuse?"

He opened his mouth, snapped it shut again with pursed lips, and rubbed the back of his neck. "Look, I don't want to fight with you—"

"That's a change."

He briefly closed his eyes, apparently working hard to maintain his composure. "I tried calling a couple times before I came over, but it just went straight to voice mail."

"I had my phone turned off. I just told you I was painting."

He nodded. "Right. The ultimatum you gave me last week . . . I've been thinking about it some this afternoon. I think I want to try counseling."

"Oh." Suddenly, Jane was on the verge of bawling like a baby. "You think?"

"I talked to Pastor Ben a few minutes ago. We can start tomorrow after the late service if you don't have plans."

Swallowing a thick lump of emotions, she forced a weak smile. "I don't have plans. Tomorrow is fine."

"Good. I'll pick you and the kids up around ten o'clock. Adam and Kate said they'd take the kids home with them while we meet with Pastor Ben."

"You talked to them about us going to counseling before you even talked to me? And you still don't know what is wrong with us?"

Adrenaline pumped through her veins. An angry tear slipped out of the corner of her eye but she brushed it away before it could slide down her cheek. She wanted to scream, to punch something, to do anything to release the rapidly building raw emotion.

Opening the door, he stepped one foot onto the front porch. "I'll just see you tomorrow."

By the time he reached the bottom porch step, Jane crossed the room and slammed the door shut so hard the windows shuddered. Stalking back to her room, she paced the floor for a moment, knowing she should go for a run. Instead she crumpled into a heap on the bed.

She reached for her phone and turned it on. Immediately it buzzed wildly with notifications, and through her tears she smiled.

CHAPTER

Twenty-one

I an half-heartedly walked through the heavy wooden doors at Harvest Bay Community Church the next morning. Jane trailed a few yards behind him, and between them all four of their children maintained various levels of enthusiasm.

At the low end, Emma scowled with her arms crossed as if coming to church was unfair punishment. Samuel occupied the opposite side of the spectrum, exuberantly skipping along beside Ian. Bradley and Jessica were some where in the middle, Bradley searching the crowd for Alison, and Jessica just happy to be somewhere together as a family.

Ian wished he could be happy that all six of them were there together. A couple months earlier he would have given his right arm to have them with him in church. Now, however, he felt like a fraud.

None of them was really happy. They weren't a family anymore, living in different houses, having different agendas and priorities. Surely this was apparent to everyone at church, like a billboard stretched out above their heads announcing, "This family is dysfunctional." It humiliated him.

Ducking into the first empty pew he came to in the back of the sanctuary, he tried to keep a low profile. But Harvest Bay was a small town, and Jane was a popular teacher. Remaining unnoticed proved to be impossible. By the time the small band of this contemporary service struck up the prelude and people filed in to find their seats, his cheeks hurt from the fake smile he kept pasted on his face.

He gave a mere nod of greeting as Adam, Kate, Chloe, and Madeline claimed the pew in front of them. He had swallowed enough of his pride to call Adam after their dispute and ask him for the favor of watching their kids, but too much of his male ego remained to extend a warm handshake.

Adam just didn't get it. He was a teacher and a coach. He had no idea how much pressure came along with owning one's own business. Adam had a great relationship with his parents, and even though his first marriage had ended, he had a great marriage now with Kate. He'd never understand Ian's point of view. Truthfully, Ian doubted the counseling session today would help at all, and he dreaded going just to rehash everything that was wrong in his marriage.

Finally Pastor Ben made his way to the pulpit, carrying a metal coffee can in one hand and his Bible in the other. "Grace and peace to you from God our Father." He set the can on the flat lip of the podium and stepped into the aisle. "With Thanksgiving just a few weeks away and Christmas just a few weeks after that—"

A groan rose from the congregation.

"Ah, yes. You're welcome for the reminder that shopping and baking is in your very near future."

The groan was replaced by a chuckle from seemingly everyone except Ian. *All I can see is loneliness for my holidays. Merry Christmas to me.*

"Anyway, I thought this would be an appropriate time to tell you a story about a poor orphan girl named Maria. One day

Maria was walking to the market and sat down by the roadside to have a short break."

Ian glanced around. So far he wasn't getting into the story, but everyone else already appeared enthralled. Many sat listening with their heads tipped slightly to the side or they leaned forward slightly.

"Maria glanced down and saw this pitiful, little bird lying there all dirty and with a broken wing. So she scooped it up and carried it to the market with her. She spent what little money she had on everything she would need to nurse to this hurt creature back to health. Day by day she watched the little bird grow stronger, which was great, but there was a problem."

Ian found himself inching forward, wondering what kind of problem a child could possibly have and betting his troubles were worse.

"Christmas was quickly approaching. The church was all decked out in lights and decorations, and it was a tradition in Maria's town to bring an offering to lay by the manger in the nativity. The people brought all kinds of fancy, expensive gifts, but Maria had nothing except for that little ragamuffin bird with the broken wing. She was embarrassed to even consider giving a baby king such an unworthy offering, so she waited until almost everyone had left the church. Looking at all the beautiful gifts there, she glanced at her bird and started to cry. She couldn't bear to leave something so pathetic."

Ian shifted his gaze down the pew and noticed moisture collecting in Jane's eyes. Jessica swiped at a few tears sliding down her pink cheeks, and Jane slipped her arm around her, while Emma crossed her arms and scowled at them. How could she be so cold toward him and so tenderhearted toward their children?

"Then the Lord spoke to Maria. He said, 'If the bird is your gift, open the door so I can see it.' She was afraid to because she was afraid what she offered wouldn't be good enough. Have you ever felt like that?" Pastor Ben paused for the congregation to consider his question.

Ian wondered if Pastor Ben had read his mind.

"I know I have. No matter how hard I tried or how much I put into the gift or relationship or career or sport or whatever the case may be, it wasn't enough. And there isn't a whole lot more hurtful to a human spirit than to think that you just didn't quite measure up. But here's the good news: That is not the truth. It's what we humans tell each other. It's what we tell ourselves, but God has never said we are not good enough."

He pulled his Bible out from under his arm. "If you have your Bibles with you, open them to the first chapter in Genesis. In verse twenty-seven it says, 'So God created man in His own image; in the image of God He created him; male and female He created them.' Now skip down to verse thirty-one. 'Then God saw everything that He had made, and indeed it was very good.' It was very good. Nowhere in these scriptures does it say that Ben Andrews just doesn't measure up. It says I am very good. And so are you. And so was Maria. She opened the door to the cage, and that little dirty bird that she so tenderly nursed back to health, giving everything she had for it, flew to the rafters, singing a song more beautiful than anything she'd ever heard before."

A knot of emotion rose up from Ian's gut and lodged in his throat. *If I'm good enough for Jane and my family, why do I feel so cast aside? What does the Bible say about that?*

"That story comes from a contemporary Christmas song titled 'The Gift,' " Pastor Ben continued. "But there's another story I want to tell you about that comes from the Gospel of Luke in the twenty-first chapter. Once again, people were giving their gifts. The rich people were making quite a show dropping their coins into the treasury outside the temple. You can imagine the sound."

Picking up the coffee can, Pastor Ben shook it. A metallic clanking noise filled the sanctuary . He chuckled.

"It reminds me of *A Charlie Brown Christmas* when Lucy is offering her advice for five cents, and she says, 'Boy, what a sound! That beautiful sound of plinking nickels.' "

Snickers and murmurs came from the congregation.

"I believe the rich were probably thinking the same as Lucy when they deposited their offerings. They liked making a show out of how much they gave. And it was good that they gave, but they had an abundance and not a care in the world about their livelihood.

And then along came this poor widow. Her offering was meager compared to what the rich folk contributed, but it was all she had. She didn't have a cushion to fall back on. She had no emergency fund, no savings, no 401K. She tried to be inconspicuous about it so no one would notice how little she put in, but Jesus saw it all, and He said, 'Truly I say to you that this poor widow has put in more than all; for all these out of their abundance have put in offerings for God, but she out of her poverty put in all the livelihood that she had.' She had no abundance, but what little she gave was worth more than the rich men because she gave it all. And Jesus Himself said it was good enough."

Pastor Ben came further up the aisle into the congregation. "Wrapping this sermon up, I want you to walk away from this service today understanding that these stories were about much more than giving. Yes, it is important to give, but it's more important to surrender. What is the difference? You give a thing, but you surrender yourself.

"God doesn't need a bird or coins or anything at all, but God wants you. Give yourself to God. Surrender everything that makes you who you are, and trust like the widow did that He will take care of you. Trust like Maria did that He will accept and love you, quirks and all. Hey, He made you that way and He made you in His image, right? Empty yourself. It's the only way you can be filled with the Holy Spirit. Trust that He will supply all your needs according to His will, and then let it all go.

"When you're used to relying on yourself, it's a very frightening concept. I understand. I've been there. But ask yourself this: Would you rather hold on and trust the one who causes you to second guess if you're good enough? Or surrender it all and trust the One who has already given His life for you because He knows you are most definitely very good."

Pastor Ben paused, scanning his congregation, and for a brief second his gaze locked with Ian's. "Amen."

Jane thought for sure she was having an out-of-body experience after the service as she followed Pastor Ben out of the sanctuary and toward his office with Ian two steps ahead of her, like always. It would have been appropriate as often as she felt dead inside.

She could see herself trudging down the maze of hallways as if heading to the trial of "who is at fault for the demise of this marriage," where she would surely be found guilty. Pastor Ben and Ian had bonded over coffee at Bayside Cafe. They were on the same team. The sentence would most likely be life without the possibility of parole in the same prison she'd been surviving in for years.

Glancing inside what she assumed was a string of Sunday school rooms, she smiled at the Christian- themed artwork on the walls. These days she only felt remotely alive inside when she was painting or communicating with Zach. When she lay awake in bed and pondered why this was the case, it dawned on her that maybe it was because neither her paintings nor Zach ever expected anything from her, never demanded that she be something she was not or accomplish more than she was capable of.

Instead they recognized and encouraged her gifts and the fact that, given the opportunity, she could contribute a lot to their community. She had so much to give. She really could make a difference in the lives of kids like Destiny or older adults like her dad or individuals with challenges like the ones she helped at Stampede of Dreams. Art spanned all ages and abilities.

Ian never understood that and never seemed to acknowledge that she could do anything more than take care of their home and her classroom. Living in an environment with such low expectations made her feel like a bird living in a cage when she should be soaring to the treetops.

She loved her children with every ounce of her being, and she gave them everything she had, but at the end of the day, she often went to bed feeling more depleted than fulfilled. Her students sapped her energy as well, and she couldn't help hoping this was only a short sentence, that someday, when her kids were grown and on their own, she would be set free to soar like she always dreamed of without anything holding her back.

It was the one hope she focused on as they turned down a short narrow hallway. *This will be over soon . . . My dreams are on*

*their way to coming true . . . One step closer to happiness . . . This is
just a hurdle, but I'll be over it soon . . .*

Pastor Ben stopped by the last door on the left and motioned
for them to go inside. Jane followed Ian through and sat at the
opposite end of the sofa in a cozy corner of the office. Walking
over to his desk, Pastor Ben grabbed a pad of paper and a pen
and made himself comfortable in an adjacent chair.

"I want to start by saying I'm glad you both are here. The
fact that you've chosen counseling is a hopeful sign for your relationship." Pastor Ben offered them both a warm smile and an
encouraging nod. "I must inform you, though, that I'm only here
to assist you in working through your differences. I can't promise
to save your marriage. That will be up to you, and it will take
hard work and dedication on both your parts. You'll need to
commit to being deliberate with your words and actions in the
days, weeks, and even months ahead. What I can promise you is
that I won't leave you in this process. I won't quit unless one or
both of you decides to quit. Okay?"

Resting his elbows on his knees, Ian rubbed his hands
together. "Okay. Thank you."

Jane only nodded in agreement.

Pastor Ben tapped his pen on the pad. "Jane, why don't you
start by telling me a little about your marriage from your perspective?"

Clearing her throat, Jane slid her gaze toward Ian. "Well,
what exactly do you want to know?"

"Just the facts right now—when, where, things like that."

Exhaling, Jane crossed her ankles and folded her hands in
her lap. "Well, we were married on August twenty-sixth at two-
thirty in the afternoon."

Pastor Ben scribbled a few notes. "How long ago?"

Jane couldn't stop another long sigh from escaping. "I thought Ian would have told you. Twenty years."

"That's a long time."

From where Ian sat on the couch, he snorted. "You're telling me."

Biting her tongue, Jane dropped her gaze to her lap.

"Jane, what do you remember most about that day?"

Silence enveloped her as she wondered for several heartbeats how open she should be. But she couldn't see why it really mattered now anyway. Their marriage was on a ventilator. There was no point in protecting it, and there simply wasn't much she could say or do to revive it. Maybe if she was completely honest, she'd do them both a favor by pulling the plug.

"I remember how I had to hide my sadness. In all the pictures, visiting with our families and friends, I had to smile like everything was all right, but it wasn't."

Ian threw his hands out as if begging for clarification. "How can you say all you remember is the sadness? It was the happiest day of our lives."

"Ian, Jane is entitled to her feelings. It's time for you to just listen." Laying his pen down, Pastor Ben leaned forward slightly and redirected his attention toward Jane. "Why wasn't it all right?"

Jane's voice wavered. "Because I miscarried our first baby a month before our wedding. I was about ten weeks along."

"That is what you were thinking of on our wedding day? Of all things, that was what your mind was on?"

Jane had never heard such a level of outrage in Ian's voice, and tears slid freely down her cheeks. "You will not make me feel ashamed for admitting that. I lost a part of me that day. I don't expect you to understand what it's like for a woman to miscarry her baby, but I do expect you to respect it, and you never have. Instead you just act like it never happened."

Pastor Ben picked up his pen and jotted a note, and then shifted his attention to Ian. "Did you really listen to what Jane just communicated to you?"

Ian gave a curt nod.

"Okay, it's your turn now, Ian." Pastor Ben sat with his pen ready. "What do you remember about your wedding day?"

"I remember the promises, not just to each other but for our future. Yes, we lost our first baby, but instead of dwelling on that one, I focused on the hope that we'd have more. We lived in a tiny apartment, but I knew I'd work hard to provide a big home for my family someday." He glanced at Jane, and then at his hands in his lap. "It wasn't that I didn't think about that baby. I just thought we could overcome it and anything else we were faced with."

"Overcoming doesn't mean forgetting about it and moving on," Jane said, her voice thick with emotion. "You never let me talk about it. You never let me grieve the child I never got to hold or rock or play peek-a-boo with."

Tears dropped onto Ian's hands. "That's because I was ashamed of myself," he muttered.

"Yeah, I know. We shouldn't have gone so far on prom night, but—"

"I'm not talking about that." He took a deep, slow breath. "After you told me about the baby, I actually wished it would end."

His words cut Jane so deeply that she sucked in a sharp breath.

"I don't expect you to forgive me," Ian continued quickly. "I've never forgiven myself, but I am sorry. We were just so young. I had no doubt you'd be a great mom. You were always a natural with kids. But the thought of having to be responsible for another life when I'd only just become an adult scared the living daylights out of me. We barely had enough room for the two of us in that one-bedroom apartment, and I had no idea how I was even going to provide for you let alone a baby too. I started adding up the cost of formula and diapers and uninsured trips to the doctor, and I became so overwhelmed I wished it was over." He hung his head. "I'm so sorry."

"You were the only person who could help me shoulder my grief. No one else knew about the baby. But you really weren't grieving, were you?"

"Jane, believe me. If I could take it back, I would."

"Ian, I'm glad you were honest about your feelings," Pastor Ben broke in. "Tell me more about why you married Jane. I mean, you've been married for twenty years, so I'm certain it wasn't just because she was pregnant."

"No, of course not. I knew I wanted to marry her before I even got home after our first date. Jane and I had been friends since the first day of kindergarten. I don't remember a day of my life that she wasn't in it. If I was Linus, she was my blanket. Just seeing her face put me at ease.

"But then when we started dating, she made me feel stronger, more confident in my own abilities. For a long time I felt like I was the puppet and she was the hand because she made me come alive and believe I could accomplish goals I never even would have tried without her." He motioned toward her. "I mean, just look at her. She's a beautiful person inside and out. I'd be crazy to not want to spend the rest of my life with her."

"You've never told me any of that." Jane swiped at her tears. "Why haven't you ever told me that? For so long I've felt so insignificant to you, taking a back seat to your career and the kids."

"What about you, Jane? Why did you want to marry Ian?"

Jane blew out an exasperated breath. "Well, for starters, we used to talk all the time for hours on end about everything, sometimes without words. We'd just look at each other and know what the other was thinking, we were that connected. And I loved how Ian could make me laugh. We truly were the best of friends. I used to find it hilarious that he would always act all macho around his buddies, but when we were alone together he was sweet and gentle and sensitive, like a big teddy bear. I always teased him that one day I would rat him out." She glanced at Ian and caught a hint of a far-away smile on his face. "I guess today's the day, huh?"

She turned back to Pastor Ben and cleared her throat. "I also appreciated how hard he worked, and I knew that he would always take care of his family." Dropping her gaze, she whispered, "I just didn't know what it would cost."

"I'm sure you both have a cost—what went wrong in the relationship. The fact of the matter is that it takes two to make a marriage and it typically takes two to break one." Pastor Ben tapped his pen on his pad. "Instead of focusing on the cost, today let's concentrate on the coupon, or what you both can do to try to save your marriage."

Slumping back on the sofa, Ian crossed his arms. "I've been trying. I started that list like you said. I made her coffee and bought her a dress, and I take the kids to school every morning."

Pastor Ben held up his hand. "Hold on, Ian. That list was supposed to be for you, not Jane. Have you been listening to her? Or just trying things you think will help the situation?"

Ian shrugged. "Maybe a little of both."

"Fair enough, but now it's time to listen. I want you both to turn so you're facing each other. I want you to take turns telling each other three things the other person could do to help mend your relationship. You're only allowed to name three things, and you are not allowed to speak while the other is talking. Just listen."

Jane hesitated but finally turned to Ian. A bubble of panic formed at her toes and rose to her chest. Facing him intimidated her as much as facing her biggest fear. She was so much better at avoiding confrontation or responding with sarcasm so she wouldn't have to feel pain or rejection. At this moment, her vulnerability overwhelmed her.

Several moments of silence passed before Pastor Ben said, "Jane, why don't you go first?"

"Okay." Sucking in a long breath, she closed her eyes for a second and blurted out, "Well, first, I guess I wish I had more of your time and attention. Going on special dates like we did for the homecoming dance or hanging out at home in our sweats with a movie. Just being together, talking, laughing, cuddling like we did in high school. I feel like as soon as you started Garner Construction our relationship became a second thought. And then when the economy tanked you worked so much we weren't much more than ships passing in the night. I never saw you long enough to have a conversation with you. And even when we were in the same room for more than a couple minutes, you were so distracted you weren't really there."

She paused waiting for him to argue. Instead he sat silently watching her with unexpected compassion in his eyes, so she plunged ahead. "Second, I wish I'd have more of your help at home. For sixteen of the twenty years we've been married, I've taught all day long, but then I feel like when I get home I'm still working. I'm the nanny, the disciplinarian, and the tutor for our kids. I'm the maid, the cook, and the chauffeur service. Most days I can handle it all, but some days it's overwhelming, and I feel like I'm already a single parent."

Ian's eyebrows arched high on his forehead. "What do you mean by already?"

"I mean, we're married but some days I feel like I'm in this all alone." When he didn't respond, she continued, "Last, I wish you'd compliment me every now and then. I know I'm a good mom, but it'd be nice to hear it. It'd also be nice to hear that you think I'm pretty and smart and talented. It'd be nice to know that you're proud to have me as your wife instead of me thinking you couldn't care less.

"Ian, I never knew all the reasons why you married me that you just told Pastor Ben. It seems like you quit flirting with me shortly after we were married, and you stopped even noticing me after the kids were born. That doesn't do much for a woman's confidence."

"What are you talking about? You're the most confident person I know."

Laying his pen down on the pad, Pastor Ben leaned forward. "Ian, this is your turn to listen. Jane is entitled to her feelings."

Ian knit his brow and clamped his lips shut.

"I am confident in certain abilities, yes, like teaching and painting. But a lot of good it does to be confident in my artistic ability when you shove my paints and easel into a dark and gloomy basement and never bother to keep your promise to build me a beautiful studio with big windows. Those lies added to all kinds of other insecurities have destroyed my self esteem. You have no idea. You don't look at me anymore. You never even say my name. Sometimes I feel like you look right through me, like I'm invisible, nonexistent." She shrugged. "I'm just saying a little recognition and affirmation would go a long way."

Glancing over his notes, Pastor Ben nodded. "Ian, what did you hear Jane say she wished was different?"

Ian rubbed his hand over his face. "I don't give her enough time and attention, I don't help out enough around the house, and I don't pay her enough compliments."

Jane narrowed her eyes at him. "That would be all you heard."

"Okay, Ian. Now it's your turn."

"Well, first of all, I really wish I would hear more about what I get right and less about what I get wrong. You're so critical of everything I do. Did you ever consider that we don't talk like we used to because every conversation turns into something I forgot to do or didn't do right? I'm sick and tired of it. In twenty years, yeah, I've gotten some things wrong, but I love you and our kids, and I work hard for you. That should count for something." Pausing, Ian eyed Jane as if expecting her to argue.

All kinds of objections swirled around in Jane's head, but she refused to give him the satisfaction. She stared at her hands in her lap, examining her nails and telling herself she needed a new coat of polish.

Sighing, Ian said heavily, "I wish you respected me as a man, a provider and the protector of our family."

"Provider? You might have built our house, but I work hard too. And protector?" Jane snorted. "How can you protect us when you aren't home? If you're our protector, why didn't you start with protecting us from this?"

Pastor Ben again lifted his hand. "This is your turn to listen." He nodded at Ian. "Tell Jane how you wish you were respected."

"I know you're smarter than me. It's no secret that school was never my thing, and part of the reason I fell in love with you was because you were the one person who never made me feel stupid . . . that is, until we were married. I feel so small when you correct me in front of the kids or, even worse, our friends. I feel like a fool every time you talk down to me, and I feel like an idiot when you completely ignore me like I'm not even here trying to talk to you. And then you wonder why we don't communicate anymore? It's because we can't open our mouths without being disrespectful.

"You wonder why I work so much? I enjoy knowing I'm doing something to make your life and the kids' lives better, but even more than that, at work I'm valued. People listen to my thoughts and ideas, and they actually take them into consideration. People recognize and appreciate my dedication to the company. They respect me." Pausing, Ian took two big breaths. When he spoke again his voice wavered. "And then recently when you lied to me, right to my face? I don't think there's anything more disrespectful than to be dishonest, and I'm not sure I'll ever be able to get over it."

Jane hung her head to hide her flowing tears, torn between feeling horrible about how she'd treated Ian and feeling justified because of the way she'd been treated.

"My last wish . . . I'm just going to be honest here. I need more physical attention from you. I remember a time when we couldn't go a couple days without being together. A week was torture. But it's been months since the last time. And months before that. And don't think I can't tell you're never into it, not even on our anniversary. I can't recall the last time you kissed me like you meant it. Lately you pull away from me when I try to touch you. You have no idea how demeaning it was while you were home to not even be welcome in my own bed."

Jane seethed. "That's because it's only physical to you. There's no emotion or romance or anything involved. You give me no reason to want to be physical with you."

The volume of Ian's voice cranked up a few notches. "You're my wife. Isn't that reason enough?"

"Not for me. Not when there's no intimacy between us. The connection we had when we made so much love together is gone."

"What do you mean it's gone? We have children. We have a home. Of course there's still a connection."

Jane lowered her voice. "Strangers can have children together. Our kids and our house have nothing to do with how close we are to each other."

"Jane is on to something. Let me explain."

Leaning forward, Pastor Ben laid the legal pad on the coffee table so Jane and Ian could both see it and drew a triangle. On the top point, he scribbled the word God. On one of the bottom points he wrote Jane's name and on the other one he wrote Ian's.

"Kids, work, life in general can pull couples apart, each one vying for the husband's or wife's attention. But every good marriage that I know of is, in fact, a love triangle. And look what happens." Pastor Ben placed one finger on Jane's name and another on Ian's. "As the couple individually draw closer to God . . . " he slid his fingers up the sides of the triangle toward the top point " . . . they ultimately draw closer together." He sat back. "Where do both of you stand on your faith journey?"

Jane looked down. She didn't have to consider it. She knew where she stood.

Ian rested one ankle on his other knee. "I've started back to church for the first time since Grandma took me. I've been meeting with you. I feel like I'm starting to make progress—slow, but progress."

Pastor Ben nodded and turned to Jane. "And what about you?"

"Where am I on my faith journey?" she snapped. "After some of the things I've been through, I might actually be going backwards or maybe in a circle. I don't really know."

"I appreciate your honesty. I can work with that if you have an open mind and a willing heart."

"Well, I'm here, aren't I?"

Pastor Ben grinned. "Noted." He placed the pad in his lap and folded his hands on top of it. "And faith is a journey—a marathon, not a sprint. The first step is to choose to believe even if you don't understand who Christ is or what it means to have faith in Him. You have to choose it over and over again. If you can do that and you gradually learn about God's love for you, you'll discover a new love and appreciation for each other, okay?"

Jane nodded skeptically.

"Just believe?" Ian snapped his fingers. "Just like that?"

"It's not rocket science, but it's a little more than that. Start by trying to see things, especially your marriage, with your heart. Not with worldly eyes, but with a loving and compassionate spirit. We'll go from there. I'll conclude our time together today with a word of prayer. You're welcome to join me."

In all honesty Jane just wanted to be done, but she bowed her head respectfully as Pastor Ben prayed for their marriage and for her and Ian individually. When he finished, Jane mumbled. "Amen," and heard Ian do the same. Swallowing back fresh tears, she was surprised by the emotion that stirred in her.

Maybe there is something to this faith thing after all.

Twenty-two

By Tuesday afternoon Jane had been digesting the counseling session for two days, and it still wasn't settling well. As classes at the Stampede of Dreams finished up, however, her spirits elevated slightly. It was hard to be anything but happy while in the presence of the gentle horses and the disabled students who loved them.

After the last student left, Jane stayed to help Sandy bed down the horses for the night. The smallest of small talk passed between them, but Jane waited for something more meaningful. She figured she should be an expert by now at waiting for something more meaningful—in her marriage, in her life. Sandy hadn't let her down yet, always offering a nugget of wisdom, so Jane continued with patience. Before she knew it, however, chores were done and Sandy headed toward her Elantra.

"Wait."

Putting on the breaks, Sandy turned to face her with a questioning look. "What's wrong?"

"Nothing . . . I mean, everything . . . I mean, I don't know." Jane exhaled heavily. "Ian and I went to counseling on Sunday. Now I'm more confused than before I went. You seem to have special insight in situations like this. I hoped you could help me sort through some of it."

Sandy pushed her glasses up further on her nose and chuck-led. "That isn't insight. That's called experience." She patted Jane on the shoulder and motioned toward a nearby picnic table. "I've lived lots of life, my dear. I've had some hard losses, but I've also experienced the best joys."

They sat on the same bench and rested their backs against the table top. "Why don't you tell me a little bit about what happened?"

Jane briefly recapped the events of Sunday afternoon. "Pastor Ben wants to see us again next Sunday, and between now and then Ian and I are supposed to make a date, spend some time together without the kids away from the house."

"That could be a good thing."

Jane shrugged. "Except for the fact that I've been so let down by him in the past. I pushed him as far away as I could and have no idea how to be close to him again. You know I've been stay-ing with my dad, but Sunday Ian asked me if I wanted to come back home."

"That's good, isn't it?"

"I don't know, and I have too much weighing on my mind to even try to make sense of it. I never wanted to hurt Ian, but I've been so hurt and disappointed and lonely that I'm just numb. When he was supposedly trying to be a better husband and father, I liked how he treated me, but truthfully I didn't believe it would last."

"You believe your marriage will last, don't you?"

Jane slipped her hands between her knees. "I don't know. I still love Ian, but I haven't been in love with him for a very long time. I miss that close connection, that intimacy. I'm not exactly sure we've ever had it, but I know I want it."

"But you love him?"

Jane's eyes became misty. "Since ninth grade."

"There's your answer." Smiling, Sandy patted Jane's knee. "It's nice to be in love, but those are just feelings, and feelings come and go. Love goes beyond feelings. It's an action. It's also a commitment. Love is a part of you. Love is helping and supporting each other. Love is wanting the best for each other."

"I feel like I do that for Ian, but I don't necessarily get it from him in return."

"That's tiring, I know, but love isn't selfish. If you do something out of love, it doesn't matter if you get anything in return. And a word of advice: Men show love differently than we ladies do. Ian may very well be showing you he loves you, and you just don't recognize it."

Sandy paused for a moment, and Jane soaked in her words.

"You see, good relationships aren't the ones where everything is wonderful all the time. Good relationships go through serious trials and survive because the individuals are committed to spending the great times together. That is love." Resting her arm across Jane's shoulders, Sandy gave a little squeeze. "Don't give up hope yet."

"I don't know how to hold onto something that's not there."

"It might be there, just buried under a whole bunch of life. Everything that has any value in this world is buried deep. Think about it. Diamonds, pearls, gold—none of them is easy to get to, but they are worth it. So is your marriage."

"So how do I start trying to uncover it?"

"Do you remember the day you came for training I mentioned the Four Agreements?"

Jane nodded.

"The first one is to be impeccable with your word. That's a good place to start."

"Impeccable?" Jane thought about the sarcastic tone she often used when saying everything on her mind, including words better left unsaid. "That's a pretty tall order."

Sandy's good-natured laugh echoed on the air. "It does take some practice at first." Tucking a wisp of her brown bob behind her ear, she explained, "Basically, you use your words to say only what you mean and know to be true. Let your words reflect your good moral standards."

Considering the feelings she'd allowed herself to develop for Zach and the words they'd exchanged in texts, Jane couldn't help questioning her own values.

"You have to learn not to speak negatively about yourself or gossip about others. There is power of the spoken word. Use it for truth and love, and you'll be surprised at all the blessings that will follow." Sliding her gaze to meet Jane's, Sandy gave her a wink. "A good time to practice would be on that date."

The late fall days were becoming shorter and colder, which annoyed Ian. He worked past dark most nights, using a spotlight as his guide on the structures that didn't have electricity installed. It tacked on a few extra hours to his work day, but it kept his projects on schedule.

As he untied his steel-toed work boots and kicked them off at the door, he wished he had some sort of a guide for his marriage. Two days had past since their counseling session, and he didn't see any progress in their relationship. No change at all. At this point he was at a loss as to what he should try next. Truthfully, he wasn't motivated to try anything after the way his efforts had been received before.

He grabbed a can of condensed soup, opened it, pulled a clean spoon from the dishwasher, and plodded into the living room. It seemed odd that Bradley's old Taurus sat in the driveway, but the house was silent.

"Anybody home?" His voice rang through the house as he shoveled a spoonful right from the can into his mouth.

"Just me."

Ian jumped and swallowed at the same time. Coughing and sputtering, he managed to get Jane's name out. "I wasn't expecting you."

She stood. "And I wasn't expecting to be here so late. I've got to get back to Dad's now."

"Why didn't you text or call?"

"What I needed to say should be said in person." She walked to the door and turned to face him. "I'm sorry. For everything I've done to disrespect you or make you feel like less of a man, I'm sorry."

Stunned, Ian wiped his chin and tried to find his voice. "Thank you. I'm sorry too."

Jane slipped into her shoes and coat. "Thanksgiving is right around the corner, and Christmas soon after that. Are you interested in completing our homework assignment this Saturday with dinner and some shopping?"

Trying his hardest to conceal the wild river of emotions that rushed through his body, he said, "That sounds like fun. Should I pick you up at around four-thirty or five o'clock?"

"Sure. See you then."

She opened the door and dashed out to Bradley's car sitting in its usual spot in the driveway. Hopping inside, she backed up and drove away.

Ian scratched his head. *Why did she bring Bradley's car over? I wonder if her Expedition is running okay.* He rubbed his chin. *I probably should just be happy she suggested a date, but I wonder what changed. Maybe the counseling really is helping. Or maybe she just wants to be able to say she tried.*

Leaving his can of soup on the counter, he headed to the bathroom for a hot shower. After dressing in a pair of sweatpants and a clean T-shirt, he retreated to his den to unwind.

He stared at his sleeping computer. Invoices called his name, but they weren't as tempting as the raven-haired beauty waiting for him on the other side of the screen. He stared at his reflection in the blank monitor and realized that Jane never caused him to feel as low and unworthy as he felt on his own after every visit to the scantily clad goddess's website.

He grabbed a pad of paper and a pen, turned from the computer, and reclined on his futon. If Jane could come over and suggest a date, he could try again too.

"What I Can Do to Be a Better Husband." He scribbled the words across the top, and then went down to the first line. "1. Stop lusting after photoshopped pictures of women I don't know, and start desiring my wife."

Closing his eyes, he tried to form a seductive vision of Jane in his mind, but before the mental picture materialized, he dozed off into a sound sleep.

The rest of the week seemed to resemble a rocket shooting across the sky. Saturday afternoon arrived before Jane fully prepared for it emotionally. Showering and dressing in a pair of jeans and a soft, burgundy sweater for her date with Ian, she reminded herself of the first agreement Sandy told her about.

"Say only what you mean . . . Use your words for truth and love . . . Say only what you mean . . ."

She groaned inwardly. At this point, running a marathon wouldn't be as big a challenge for her as this date might be.

She fixed her hair and applied just enough make-up to convey that she'd put forth an effort, but she made sure not to over do it. She didn't want him thinking this date was anything more than two people having dinner and Christmas shopping. She didn't expect it to be a cure-all magical event that would fix everything between them.

Her phone notified her of an incoming text message. When she tapped the screen, Zach's contact information greeted her, and she quickly retrieved the message.

Haven't heard from you. Are you painting?

No. Getting ready to go out.

Sounds fun. Why wasn't I invited?

Jane stared at his words, wondering if he was serious. *Because you aren't invited. I'm having dinner, and then Christmas shopping.*

With who?

The two harmless words annoyed her. Who did he think he was to question who she was spending the evening with? He had no right to be texting her, a married woman, at all. Still, she couldn't make her fingertips type Ian's name as a reply.

Excuse me?

Sorry. Just trying to make conversation. I haven't talked to you much this week, and I miss you.

With those three little words, her annoyance evaporated.

He messaged again before she could reply. *Have fun tonight. Text me if you think about me.*

If it were possible, the rock and the hard place she was trapped between felt even more uncomfortable. *Ok.*

A soft tap on the door jerked her gaze away from her phone. She exhaled and smiled when it landed on her dad.

"I remember when ya were still in high school getting ready for dates with Ian in this room. Brings back a lot of memories for this ol' man." Shuffling to the twin bed, he sat on the edge.

Jane perched beside him. "Me too. In some ways it doesn't seem like that long ago, but on the other hand it seems like a whole lifetime ago."

Chuckling, he patted her knee. "Oh, you're telling me, Lassie." His eyes danced and twinkled like sunrays on Lake Erie. "This is a good thing you're doing. I should have taken your mum on more dates. I didn't think it was important until it was too late."

She covered his calloused hand with hers. "I know, Dad, but you and Mom had a great relationship."

"No relationship is bulletproof. Just like anything else, it takes time and attention to help it grow strong and solid." His gaze softened. "Your mum was just a truly remarkable, patient woman."

"Yeah."

Jane's heart sagged in her chest. She wasn't half the woman her mom had been. She would never even consider accepting text messages from another man no matter how lonely she was in her marriage. Jane suddenly understood that she had let down her mom. It was one of the worst feelings in the world.

More than anything else, Jane missed her mom. She would have given anything for one more day, for one more heart-to-heart talk on that very bed with her. She had plenty to talk about, that was for sure.

"Maybe my goal should be to exemplify Mom in my marriage."

"She's a good one to model." Reaching up, he redirected a wild wisp of hair, tucking it behind her ear. "But if she was here, I think she'd tell ya to just be the lassie Ian fell in love with and look for the lad ya promised to love and cherish twenty years ago. People do grow and change, just like a flower, but that seed determines what they'll become, and there's always a hint of it left behind."

"I hear what you're saying, Dad." She leaned over and kissed his cheek. "I love you, but I better finish getting ready. Ian doesn't like to be kept waiting."

He pushed to his feet with a grunt and a groan and shuffled to the door. "That day when we visited your mum's grave, and then that horse program—do ya remember what I told you?"

Jane searched through her memory. So much had happened in just a couple months that it seemed like eons ago.

"Let me remind ya. I told you to be deliberate with your words and your actions. Use your voice and your ears well. Respect him for who he is and he'll love you for who you are. Keep trying and wait for a miracle."

Her shoulders drooped. "Ah, yes. The miracle."

He stepped into the hallway and pulled on the doorknob. "It'll happen, Lassie. Don't give up."

But I've been holding on for so long I don't know if I can anymore.

Finishing her mascara, Jane applied some lip gloss, and then pulled on her brown leather boots. After tying a scarf around her neck, she gave herself a glance in the mirror.

Eh. Not bad. I've looked better, but I've definitely looked worse too.

At that moment the doorbell rang. Glancing at the clock, she smirked. *Four-thirty. Right on time as usual.* She headed into the living room, wanting to enjoy herself but afraid to hope for anything other than a fight with Ian.

He stood just inside the doorway, wearing a pair of jeans and a button-down shirt she'd never seen before and holding a bouquet of roses. Her heart danced an unfamiliar jig as he grinned bash-fully and held the flowers out to her.

"They're not from The Pit Stop." He lifted his right hand in pledge fashion. "I promise."

Jane gave him a sideways glance. "Hey, that's not funny."

"I know." He cast his gaze to the floor. "I just didn't know what else to say."

"Well, thank you. I'll go put them in some water, and then I'll be ready to go."

She carried the bouquet to the kitchen in search of a vase and a quick minute alone. While the water filled the mason jar, she inhaled deeply.

Say what you mean . . . Use your words for truth and love . . . Believe in miracles . . .

She left the bouquet on the counter, grabbed her purse and returned to the living room.

Bending over, she kissed her dad on the cheek. "Emma and Jessie are at Kate and Adam's. Sammy is having a sleepover with another friend. Bradley is hanging out at Alison's, but he said he'd be happy to come over if you need anything. You have his number, right?"

He shooed her away. "I'll be fine, for goodness sake. Stop fussin' over me, Lassie, and go have a good time."

"Okay, okay." Jane chuckled. "I love ya, Dad."

"Right back at'cha, Janey."

Ian followed Jane out, closing the front door behind them. "Did you want to eat or shop first?"

Jane feigned disbelief, but even she could feel the sparkle in her eyes. "Do you not know me at all anymore? Eat, of course. I'm starved."

Chuckling, Ian opened his truck door for her. "Good. That's what I thought." He hurried around to the driver's side and climbed in. "How does Bella Notte sound? I made reservations for five o'clock."

My *favorite restaurant*. A genuine smile, spread across her face. "That sounds perfect."

With a satisfied look, Ian put the truck in gear and eased out of the driveway. "Is the Expedition running okay? On Tuesday you drove Bradley's car over so I was just wondering. I can take a look at it if it's not."

Instead of being quick to respond, Jane listened carefully not just to Ian's words, but to their meaning. It occurred to her that this was one way he expressed his love, by taking care of his family.

"It's running fine. Bradley just happened to be parked behind me." Her voice and heart softened. "But thank you."

A peaceful lull settled over them for the rest of the drive into Cresthaven. Jane marveled at how new this twenty-plus-year-old relationship felt. Pastor Ben's prayer from almost a week earlier came into her mind.

To restore something, by definition, you take something on the verge of falling apart and make it beautiful again. If God really is into restoring things, could that be what's going on here?

Sliding her gaze over to Ian, Jane noticed how his well-trimmed goatee framed his lips, how his dark eyes assessed the road and traffic ahead of them, how his strong hands controlled the steering wheel and skillfully maneuvered the truck. She swallowed hard against a rising bubble of excitement.

I guess there's only one way to find out.

CHAPTER
Twenty-three

Jan sensed Jane watching him, but managed to keep his eyes on the road. He worried about what was going through her mind. When she looked at him did she still see the physically fit boy she fell in love with long ago? Or did she see someone she didn't recognize? If he'd become as much of a stranger to her as he felt, would she want to get to know him again?

He didn't know that answer and, as he turned into the parking lot of Bella Notte, he wasn't sure he wanted to find out. The idea that she could live so easily without him scared the living daylights out of him. Sure, he'd survive on his own, he'd keep breathing, keep putting one foot in front of the other, but that wasn't his definition of living. He longed to laugh and talk, love and hope, fight a little bit and make up a lot again with his wife. *That* was really living.

He slid out of his seat and rushed around the truck to open her door. Pushing all negative thoughts to the back of his mind, he grinned up at her.

"Ready?"

Nodding emphatically, she climbed down. "I'm starving."

"Me too. Let's go."

Acting on impulse, he grabbed her hand. A surprised expression crossed her pretty face, but she didn't pull away, and that calmed his fears slightly.

Inside the restaurant, Ian gave the hostess their name and they were quickly shown to an intimate table for two. Studying the menus in silence, he inwardly offered the simplest of prayers. *Oh, God, be near.*

He took a deep breath. "What are you thinking about having?"

She chewed on her lip as she glanced over her choices. "The Portobello ravioli looks good. What looks good to you?"

Hesitating for only a second, he swallowed his fear. "What's sitting right in front of me."

A hint of rose brushed across Jane's cheeks, and the reaction bolstered Ian's confidence.

Just then, the waitress approached their table. "Can I take your drink order?"

Ian ordered a bottle of the restaurant's signature cabernet sauvignon. Then, glancing at Jane and receiving an approving nod, he added, "I think we're ready to order."

"Okay. What will you be having tonight?"

Jane ordered the ravioli dish, and Ian decided on the prosciutto and pasta with a rich cheese sauce.

"All right. I'll go put this order in, and it'll out in just a bit."

As the waitress hurried off, Ian reached past the lit candle to lace his fingers with Jane's. "I'm glad we're doing this. Thanks for suggesting it."

Shrugging, she stared at their connected hands. "It's no big deal. I'd just be sitting at Dad's painting, and we need to at least start thinking of Christmas. Not just presents, but arrangements."

"Arrangements? You mean like who gets the kids for Christmas Eve and who gets them Christmas Day? I want to make arrangements for you to come back home. Let's spend Christmas together like a family again."

"I'd like that, but I guess we should talk about what we discussed at counseling."

Ian's shoulders drooped slightly. "That's what the homework assignment is, but I don't want to argue. Why can't we just have a nice evening together?"

Pulling her hand back, Jane crossed her arms. "I don't want to fight either, but we can't move forward without resolving our issues. So maybe we need to figure out a new way to communicate."

Doubt returned to Ian's spirit, and he began to regret this date. "How are we supposed to resolve issues that have been twenty years in the making?"

"It won't happen overnight, but every journey begins with one step, right?" Dropping her hands to her lap, her gaze fell with them. "After twenty years together, aren't you willing to give it a try?"

Ian bit his tongue and resisted the urge to shout that he *had* been trying. How many cups of coffee had he made for her? And months ago he offered to take her on a picnic, but she had other plans. Or what about the dress that she used to mop up flower guy's blood and the Sweet Jane rose bush that he ended up ripping out? He had been trying, and it hadn't been enough.

But for the first time in months, maybe even years, Ian's heart melted a little. How long had he wanted to hear those words from her?

"Yes, I am."

The waitress returned then with the wine and two glasses. Opening the bottle, she poured them both a glass and set the bottle on the table.

"Your meals will be out shortly."

"Thank you." Ian took a sip and returned his attention to his wife. "Where do you want to start?"

"At the very beginning, with the baby we lost."

"Jane, I've thought about that baby every day. I wonder what he might be like, if he'd be strong and athletic like Bradley or more into academics like Emma. Would he be a peacemaker like Jessie or a handful like Sammy?"

Through a steady stream of tears, Jane chuckled. It was a beautiful sound to Ian's ears.

"No, at first I didn't want the baby. I just wasn't ready. I had no idea how to be a dad. Then when we lost him, I was heartbroken, too, but I didn't know how to comfort you when I felt like it was all my fault. I wanted to be there for you. I wanted to bawl my eyes out right with you, but my guilt was so heavy that it was easier for me to just try not to think about it." Reaching across the table, he offered her his hand again. "I'm so sorry. Can you believe me?"

She placed her hand in his. "I do, but I wish you would have told me this a long time ago. All these years I thought you just didn't care."

Ian gently rubbed the back of her hand with his thumb. "Nothing could be further from the truth."

"How did you know it was a boy?"

Ian's brow knit together in confusion. "What do you mean?"

"You said, 'when we lost him.' How did you know our baby was a boy?"

Blinking back threatening tears, Ian murmured, "Just a feeling, I guess."

Jane's perfect lips curved upward. "I had the same feeling."

"And I'm sorry you've felt like work is more important to me than you are . Nothing has ever been more important to me than you and the kids. I couldn't believe it when you finally agreed to go out with me back in high school. You could have dated anyone, and everyone knew you were way out of my league. I always felt like you deserved someone smarter and better looking, a doctor or a lawyer, or a CEO. In my own mind, I had to work extra hard to be a success and provide a comfortable living for you to prove myself worthy of such a remarkable woman. I can see now that I was wrong, but I've always had the best of intentions."

"I realize that, and believe it or not I do appreciate how hard you work for us. It can just be overwhelming for me to teach all day, and then come home to take care of four kids. With homework and practices and appointments, their schedules are maddening, and then add household chores on top of that. Without your help, it got to be lonely."

Studying him, she shook her head. "But whoever said I was out of your league was out of their mind. I'm sorry if I ever made you feel that way. You've done a lot of things right in twenty years. I should have told you that more often."

"I'm not a very eloquent writer, but do you remember what I said to you in that card I gave you the morning of homecoming?"

She nodded and took a small sip of wine, gazing at him over the rim of her glass. "I remember every word."

"I must admit I've had a hard time dealing with the picture of you sitting on that bench so close to another man because I have insecurities too. But I told you the truth in that card. I'm just no good without you. You give me purpose and direction. You give me the confidence I need to succeed. I realize I haven't done a very good job of letting you know that, but when I saw you with him, I lost it because that was the first time I really believed I might lose you. I was angry at you, yes, but I was also angry with myself for allowing us to drift so far apart without making more of an effort to keep you close to me."

His voice broke with emotion. "I promise things will change. I will do whatever I have to do to fix what's broken between us. But one thing won't change. I will still fight to my grave for us."

Sniffling, Jane swiped the fingertips of her free hand under her lashes. "I'm so sorry I disrespected you and lied to you that night. I never meant to hurt you, but I've been hurting, too." She squeezed his hand, smiling. "But you won't have to fight to your grave for us. It won't come to that. We'll figure this out."

He wanted to believe her. He hoped she wasn't just saying what he wanted to hear.

He didn't think it was going to be as easy as she made it sound, but they were moving in the right direction, and with one look into her eyes wet with emotion, he trusted her. Completely. He'd bet his life on her.

Over an hour later, Jane left the Bella Notte with Ian by her side, carrying a brown paper bag containing two Styrofoam containers of leftovers, satisfied in more ways than just her appetite. The time they spent together had been beautiful, and she wanted to believe everything Ian had said even though a small part of her remained skeptical. After all, he had started to change before, but soon things returned to the way they had been when she'd felt empty and disconnected in their marriage. This time seemed different, but her guard remained on alert.

Why hadn't they talked so openly before? Could one counseling session make that big of a difference? Even the few times just before homecoming hadn't been as honest and emotional as what they had shared inside her favorite restaurant. Still, she couldn't help being afraid he'd just told her what he knew she wanted to hear.

Ian opened the truck door and offered his hand to help her up.

Such little gestures warmed her frozen heart. Situating herself in the passenger seat, she watched Ian climb in behind the steering wheel, closer to her than he'd been in ages, and found herself melting toward her husband.

"Do you want to walk around the mall? I've got a few ideas for the kids for Christmas."

Ian offered her a mischievous grin as he put the truck in gear. "Sure, but not quite yet. It's still early, and I have an idea."

As they merged into traffic, Jane's cell chimed notifying her of an incoming text message. He glanced at her, and she couldn't tell if it was worry or annoyance she saw clouding his deep, chocolate-brown eyes.

"You gonna get that?"

Truthfully, she was afraid to. *What if it's Zach? What will I tell Ian?* "It's probably nothing important."

"What if it's the kids or your dad?"

What if it's not? "If it was important, they'd call. We're supposed to be on this date to talk about us, not the kids."

"Okay." Ian stared straight ahead.

After being married to him for twenty years, Jane could tell exactly what he was thinking. He doubted her commitment. He wanted the reassurance that another man wasn't sending her messages, trying to move in on his territory. She knew it. And she could understand his point of view.

Blowing out an exasperated breath, she reached for her phone and sent up a silent prayer. *Please, God, let it be one of the kids.* When she opened her messages, she rejoiced inwardly in secret relief.

"It's from Bradley. He and Alison are going to hang out at Dad's for a few hours. He just wanted to let us know where he was." She held her phone up for Ian to see Bradley's name and message for himself.

Nodding, Ian visibly relaxed. "Good."

"Hey." She placed her fingertips on his knee. "I told you I'm committed to our marriage, and I mean it, but you have to trust me."

"I know. I'm trying. I can't lose my insecurities overnight."

"Would it help if I blocked his number?" Her heart raced as she tapped her screen a few times, and, just like that, she could no longer receive messages from Zach. "There. Done. Better?"

She didn't know whether to laugh or cry. Those sweet, flirtatious messages that made her feel beautiful and wanted and cherished, gone with one tap of her screen, taking with them the heavy burden of sneaking around, covering her tracks, all the lying and deceit. She and Ian were facing desperate times. This drastic measure provided an instant detox for her addiction, and she already felt like a better person.

Ian covered her fingers with his strong hand. "Jane, you know I'd do anything for you."

"Just don't let me feel lonely anymore, okay?"

"I promise." Ian flipped on the turn signal and turned onto a country highway that led back into Harvest Bay.

Jane frowned. "I thought we were going shopping. This is the way home."

"Trust me. We have time for shopping. This can't wait."

After two more turns, Ian slowed down and guided his truck onto a dirt path that ran along the edge of the Sullivans' farm.

Jane's lips curved upward. "What made you think of this?"

Ian shrugged. "It just seemed right."

The path led back to a small grove of trees that lined a small, private meadow, where the land sloped gently to a pebbly beach that kissed the waters of Lake Erie. As teenagers, it had been their favorite hangout. Adam's parents had held post-football game bonfires back there. Jane remembered so many fun, peaceful times, watching the fire and listening to the waves, while laughing with their friends, singing songs, and just being alive.

Anna and Jacob Sullivan loved Ian like another son and had given him permission to enjoy that lovely little hidden gem whenever the mood hit. Right after high school, Ian and Jane used to steal quiet moments there almost every pretty weekend, including their wedding night. Laying blankets down in the bed of his old truck, they watched the sun sink into the lake as an ocean of stars appeared above them. They talked and laughed, fought a little bit and dreamed a lot about their future.

Aside from coming out to the annual Sullivans' Fourth of July gathering, Jane and Ian hadn't used their privilege for years. Now they were in a different truck and living a much more demanding life than they'd hoped for, but coming back now, just the two of them, resurrected passionate feelings for Ian that Jane had long since pronounced dead.

Ian parked where the grassy meadow blended into the pebbles and shells. The sun appeared to be lazily sitting right on top of the water, casting out vibrant red, pink, and orange colors for the clouds to catch.

"Looks like we're just in time."

Instead of taking in the sunset, Jane gazed at Ian. "I think we are just in time."

He brought her hand to his lips and kissed the back of it. "It's chilly, but I brought a blanket if you want to sit outside a while."

"I'd like that."

Finding a spot on the beach, they huddled close together, wrapping an old, thick, brown and white afghan around them. The moment was simple but beautifully intimate, exactly what Jane had been craving for years, and deep from within her soul sighed.

"Ian?"

"Yes?"

She rested her head against his strong shoulder. "Being here with you like this feels so good it scares me."

He wrapped his arm around her and held her close to his side. "I know what you mean. I'm fighting those feelings, too—almost like it's too good to be true."

"Right now, sitting here with you after talking over dinner, I feel closer to you than I think I've ever been. But it's because we're spending time together. And I know life is just busy for us with our work schedules and the kids' activities, but what happens to us tomorrow when it's back to reality? Will we start drifting apart again?"

He kissed her forehead. "I hope not." Sighing, he rested his cheek against her head. "I don't have the answers. I've learned the hard way that our relationship isn't something I can just fix on my own. We have to work together and get a little stronger every day."

The sun dipped into the frigid water that already reflected a hint of moonlight. Jane tried to memorize the stunning scene so that later she could paint the opposing forces working so well together. She thought she might name the painting "The Garners."

Shivering, she snuggled closer to Ian. "What if we starting fighting again?"

"We will fight because that's what couples do. We'll just have to trust that we'll resolve the issue instead of letting it grow to become the Goliath we were just up against."

The sky above them faded into a deep violet, while right at the water line a ribbon of magnificent magenta seemed to wrap the day up in a pretty bow. Jane's heart sagged. She didn't want to see this day end yet.

She tilted her face up to him. "Did we have enough rocks in our slingshot for this Goliath?"

He kissed the tip of her nose and smoothed her untamable hair. "We only need one."

"Why didn't we ever go to church before?"

"I don't know." Ian tipped his head from one side to the other. "I guess, speaking for me personally, I just never made it a priority. I thought it was more important that I work hard for my family."

Rising, he offered his hand to Jane, and they walked back to the truck together. "Truthfully, sometimes I watched Adam and Kate together or with their girls, and I envied their closeness. I just always thought it was the love they shared, but now I think it's more than that. I think there's something almost magical about sharing that time in church with your family." He opened the passenger door. "Now how about some shopping?"

On the drive back to Cresthaven, Jane pondered his words and actually found herself excited about starting this new weekly routine with her family, even after their counseling sessions were over. Maybe the time they spent together in church would provide her the assurance that they wouldn't drift apart again. Maybe it would be the miracle she and Ian needed to not just fix what was broken, but to strengthen and fortify their relationship.

After they finally found a parking spot in the crowded lot, they headed into the mall. Ian held Jane's hand as they walked down the busy corridor, peering through the store windows and pointing things out to one another that reminded them of the kids, her dad, or his sister.

The longer they window-shopped for their families, the more Jane realized something was missing and had been for quite some time. She made a beeline for a bench, pulling him with her.

"What are you doing?" He had his familiar perplexed expression on his face.

"I want to ask you a question, but I don't want you to get mad at me."

Ian crossed his arms. "Okay. I'll try."

"When are you going to make amends with your dad? The kids need their grandparents. I want to know my in-laws."

"Why do you want to know someone who'll just throw you out like yesterday's garbage?"

Prying his hand away from his body, she held it in both of hers. "I don't think that's what happened. I think there was a misunderstanding between the two of you. But Sandy from the Stampede of Dreams where I've been volunteering taught me that words are powerful if you use them in love and truth." With a finger on his chin, she turned his gaze to meet hers. "We were very broken, and by using our words some healing has occurred. We still have a long way to go, but we're on the right track. Why don't you give it try with your parents?"

He patted her hand and stood. "Did you say that Bradley wanted a new pair of Nikes and gloves for football? Let's go down to Footlocker and see what they have."

Jane heaved a sigh and allowed him to lead her into the store. They bought Bradley gear for the game he loved and found gifts for Samuel, Emma, and Jessica.

By then, it was nearly closing time. Disappointed by how fast the evening had gone, Jane said reluctantly, "I guess we should call it a night."

Ian held up the four large bags containing their purchases. "I'd say we got a pretty good start."

"We did." She stuffed her hands in the pockets of her coat as they walked out to the parking lot, feeling like a silly school girl. "I had such a nice time with you tonight, and I'm not ready for it to end."

"It doesn't have to." Ian opened the truck door, set the bags inside, and gave Jane a hand climbing up. "Let's take these gifts home, and then maybe we can pop some popcorn and watch a movie. Or brew a pot of coffee and talk some more." He hopped into his seat and started the engine. "Like you said earlier, we'll figure it out."

Driving home, they made some small talk, laughed a little, and sang a lot to the radio. Before she knew it, Ian pulled into their driveway, hit the button on the garage door opener, and eased into the garage. Disappointment gnawed at her when she glanced at the spot where her Expedition should be.

She climbed out of the truck and grabbed the bags behind the seat. *But things are improving.*

Ian took a couple of the bags from her, lightening her load. "Where do you want to keep these?"

"Wherever the kids won't look for them."

"Your closet?"

Nodding in agreement, Jane stepped through the doorway, feeling as if she stepped through a portal to another world. Yes, this was her home. But they were the same walls within which she'd felt her loneliest.

She remembered days when she was so overwhelmed with schedules and projects and to-do lists that she thought she might explode. Today, however, ascending the same stairs she'd climbed daily with dread and anxiety, she experienced peace and contentment. To be completely at ease and relaxed in her own home seemed a little like heaven on earth.

She paused at the closed bedroom door and tossed Ian a questioning glance.

"I haven't spent much time in here since you moved out. It was just easier to keep the door shut." Reaching around her, he turned the knob and pushed it open.

As she stepped into their bedroom, a shiver ran through Jane, and she wasn't sure if it was from the cool, closed off room or something more. She crossed to her walk-in closet and set the bags in the farthest corner behind her handful of special occasion dresses. Ian followed suit.

Straightening, he touched the sleeve of a beautiful periwinkle cocktail dress. "I remember when you wore this dress for Adam and Kate's wedding several years ago. You were stunning. I couldn't keep my eyes off you all night long."

"I loved wearing that dress." Gazing up at him, she swatted his arm. "But why didn't you tell me that then? Why has it taken us falling apart for me to know what I mean to you? That's not fair."

He caught her hand in both of his. "I know. I'm sorry. I'm a guy. I don't always understand my feelings, and on the rare occasion that I do, I'm not any good at expressing them."

Leading her out of the closet, he pulled her close to him, wrapped his arm around her petite waist, and laced the fingers of his left hand with her right hand. Slowly they started to sway back and forth.

"But even when I don't say it, you should know what you mean to me. You are my whole world. In kindergarten, I knew I'd always like you. In high school, I knew I'd always love you. After the first time we made love, I knew I'd always want you. And after almost losing you, I now know I'll always need you."

"Wow." It took her a minute to find any other words, then they came out on a breath. "I'd say you did a pretty good job expressing yourself."

His mouth curved into the boyishly cocky grin that used to turn her insides to goo. So many years later, it still had the same effect. Twirling and then dipping her, he slowly brought her back into his arms, closer than before. She inhaled his familiar cologne, the fuel that set a fire blazing in her cheeks.

His eyes danced along with their bodies as he began humming Sonny and Cher's "I Got You, Babe", their signature song since high school, when they'd sung it sitting around bonfires after football games. Softly she sang the first lines, and he responded with the next. They half sang, half laughed the chorus together.

Their rhythm slowed, their bodies so close she could feel his heart beat against hers. Lowering his face to the crook of her neck, his whisper against her skin caused shock waves through her body.

"I got you, babe?"

She lifted his face so their lips were a breath apart. "Yeah. I got you, babe."

In an instant, his mouth was on hers. Looping her arms around his neck, she leaned into him. His lips caressed hers, stirring up inside her a new passion for this man she'd known almost her whole life.

How many times had she longed for such a toe-curling embrace instead of just pat on the back in passing? How many times had she desired such a breath-stealing kiss instead of just a chicken peck? How many times had she imagined such a response to her touch?

As Ian swept her up into his arms and carried her to their bed, she understood for the first time the ultimate connection of two souls mingling. Wasn't this what marriage was supposed to be like? After twenty years, she was finally experiencing deep, true intimacy with the man she'd vowed to love all her life.

Her dad had been right. A miracle had occurred that night. God had taken a broken marriage and restored it to something more beautiful than she could ever have imagined.

CHAPTER

Twenty-four

For the first time in months, Jane slept soundly, and for a breath of a second, she couldn't remember where she was when her eyes cracked open the next morning. Then in wave after glorious wave, the events of the previous evening came back to her, flooding her heart all over again. When she rolled over to face her husband, to kiss him good morning, however, the flood waters quickly rose to her eyes.

His side of the bed was empty.

Last night was just a bunch of saying everything I wanted to hear. Nothing has changed.

In a huff, she flopped back on her pillows, crossed her arms, and stared at the ceiling as tears slid down into her ears. "I'm so stupid. I should have known."

"Known what? That I was going to go downstairs and make you a cup of coffee?"

She snapped her gaze to the bedroom door, where Ian entered, wearing a pair of lounge pants and carrying a steaming mug in each hand. Propping herself up while hugging the warm comforter to her chest, she quickly wiped the moisture from the sides of her face.

"I-I was just expecting you to be here."

"I am here." Crossing the room to her side of the bed, he handed her a cup and sat on the edge of the bed facing her. "You have to trust me. I understand where I went wrong before, and things are going to be different."

A smile spread across her face as she lifted the mug to her lips. "It'll take some time, but I think I can get used to it."

Scooting up next to her, he reclined against the pillow-softened headboard, and wrapped his free arm around her bare shoulders. He kissed her temple and then took a sip of his coffee.

"But the question is, are *you* going to be *here?*"

She rested her head against his shoulder, relishing the comfort and security of the moment. "I don't know. I haven't had much time to think about it. Dad is doing well enough for me to come back, but I don't want to confuse the kids or give them false hopes." She froze. "The kids! Does Bradley know anything happened last night?"

"Bradley spent the night with your dad. He texted late last night and I got it this morning." He set his coffee cup on the night stand. "But what do you mean 'give them false hopes'? If that's the case, then after last night I have false hopes too. Jane, you were the one who said we're going to get through this. Don't you believe it? Don't you feel that the worst is behind us, and we'll just move forward from here, getting better and stronger every day? Because I do."

She leaned forward and pressed her lips to his. "Of course, I do. I'm just trying to be cautious. I'll move back home if you feel it's best for everyone."

"Thank you." He held her for a long minute, his chin resting on the top of her head. "You know we should probably start getting ready for church."

"What time is it?"

"A quarter after nine."

She groaned. "I don't want to move. How late did we stay up talking?"

"Until about three o'clock, I think." Pushing to his feet, he gazed down at her. "Just think of how good a nap will feel later this afternoon."

She snuggled down into the covers and closed her eyes. "Five more minutes?"

"Come on, sleepy head. I'll go start the shower."

A minute later, she heard the spray of water come on followed by her husband's voice echoing off the tile walls as he sang their song slightly off key. A blissful smile spread across her face, and she kicked off the covers and headed into the master bathroom.

Ian walked a little taller that morning entering Harvest Bay Community Church with Jane by his side. His smile was more genuine as they greeted the friendly faces of the other congregants. They expected Bradley to join them soon, though Emma and Jessica had most likely gone to the early service with Adam and Kate, and Samuel was still with his friend's family. But even though they weren't worshiping as a family yet, walking into the sanctuary holding Jane's hand and sitting in a pew beside her might have been the most meaningful thing he'd experienced in months, possibly even years.

Ian was under no illusions. Last night was just one night, but they were finally on the right track. Where there had been doubt before in Ian's mind, now there was hope. They weren't fixed yet, but they were in the rebuilding stage, and for a guy whose livelihood revolved around construction, his confidence in his ability to make their marriage beautiful again hung somewhere near the clouds.

He dropped his gaze to Jane's soft, delicate hand nestled perfectly in his strong, calloused one, remembering once again how different they were, and yet they fit together perfectly, complimenting each other like no one else could. Where one of them was weak, the other was strong. He didn't know exactly where they'd gone wrong before, but he vowed not to let their perfect balance get so out of whack again.

God, I'm still learning about You and about who You want me to be, but I want You to help me every day to be the man Jane needs me to be.

The small band struck up an uplifting version of "How Great is Our God," filling the peaceful atmosphere and signaling the start of the service. Ian looked up, and immediately anger erupted into a blazing inferno. He glanced at Jane, temporarily relieved to see that she hadn't seemed to notice yet.

She met his concerned stare with a questioning expression. "What's wrong?"

Jerking his head in the general direction, he barely kept his voice to a whisper. "What's he doing here?"

She followed his gaze, and her eyes widened as they landed on flower guy. "I have no idea, Ian. I promise I don't." She reached into her purse and handed him her phone. "I blocked him, remember?"

Ian shifted uncomfortably in the pew.

Squeezing his hand, she leaned close to his ear and murmured, "Hey, I'm here with *you*. I'm holding *your* hand. Remember last night and this morning? That was with you. I can't control what he does or how he feels, but I've already told him I'm committed to *you*." She stared at him with pleading eyes.

He remained stone faced.

She pulled her hand free from his grasp and slid about three inches away, still close enough to whisper. "I see how it is. You expect me to trust you that things are going to be different now, but you can't trust me."

"It's a little bit different because trusting me doesn't involve my feelings for another person."

"You don't think I've spent time jealous of your work? Yes, you have had a mistress, and her name is Garner Construction."

"No, that's called providing for a family of six. Putting food on the table and clothes in the closets. Think about it, Jane."

"I have thought about it, and here's the thing: I work too. I pay bills too. I buy groceries too. But you're the only one who gets the credit. How exactly is that fair?"

Pastor Ben made his way to the pulpit. "Grace and peace to you from God our Father."

Grace and peace. It dawned on Ian that he'd played right into flower guy's hands. Jane was right, and after the past evening and morning he had every reason in the world to believe she was one-hundred percent committed to him. His insecurities caused irrational fears, and that was his problem, not hers.

Closing the three inches gap between them, Ian wrapped an arm around her shoulders and leaned close to her ear. "I'm sorry, my love. Please forgive me."

Her lips curved upward slightly. "Shh. You're going to get us in trouble if you don't be quiet and listen."

Smiling, Ian kissed her temple, and tried to concentrate on Pastor Ben's message. His attention deficit disorder kicked into high gear, however, and his mind wandered as he stared at the back of flower guy's head.

The service finally ended, and Jane exhaled in relief. She could-n't remember the last time she'd felt so uncomfortable. And, of course, Zach would have to sit in front of them. She had to force her gaze to stay on Pastor Ben. She didn't blame Ian for ques-tioning her even though she had done everything right this time by blocking his number from her phone and giving her all to her marriage. She truly had no idea what he was doing there.

She turned her attention to Ian. "I guess Bradley must have gone to the early service."

"It's okay. We'll all be together next week." Ian captured her hand in both of his. "Do you want to head down to Pastor Ben's office?"

As if right on cue, Pastor Ben approached them. "You're sit-ting a little closer than you did last week. That's promising."

Jane glanced at Ian and chuckled along with him.

"Are you ready to do a little more digging?"

Ian stood. "Give me a shovel."

At that moment, Zach strolled up to them. Jane's heart knotted when Ian bristled and clenched his fists, the muscles flexing along his jawline.

Pastor Ben stretched out his hand. "Zach, it was nice to see you in church today."

Accepting the gesture, Zach pumped Pastor Ben's hand twice, grinning. "Hello, Uncle Ben. I figured it was as good a time as any to come back. I need to make it a part of my week-end routine again."

Uncle? Jane resisted the strong urge to smack her forehead. Of course two men in such a small town who shared the same last name of Andrews would be related.

She peered at Zach through narrowed eyes. Every fiber of her being wanted to call him out in front of his uncle right there in the middle of the sanctuary. Did he think she was stupid? No, he didn't think it was a good time to come back, and he didn't want to make it a part of his routine. The only reason he showed up in church today was because she'd been becoming more distant, and since she'd blocked his number last night, he figured out she was with her husband. He obviously thought showing up in church today would throw her for a loop, but his dashing good looks and charming smile couldn't shake her. Not this time.

She clutched Ian's hand, laced their fingers together, and lifted her chin. "We're going to let you visit with your nephew and meet you in your office."

Pastor Ben gave her a nod. "I'll be right behind you."

She led Ian out of the pew and past Zach without giving him a second glance. Together they retraced their steps from the week before through the expansive building, down hallways of Sunday school rooms and offices. When they reached their destination, Ian leaned heavily against the wall beside the door and pulled her to his side.

He planted a kiss on her temple. "Thank you for getting us out of there."

She leaned her head against his shoulder. "It wasn't exactly the church experience you talked about last night, was it?"

"No, but we got through it together." He chuckled. "I figured we'd run into some challenges along the way. Every couple does. I just wasn't expecting this particular one so soon."

Jane's laugh carried down the hallway.

"What a difference a week can make." Pastor Ben's smile floated to them on his words as he approached. "Please, come in. Let's chat."

Jane preceded Ian into the office and walked over to the sofa, where just a week earlier they'd sat on opposites ends. Today they sat next to each other, Jane resting her hand on Ian's knee, while he wrapped his arm around her shoulders.

Grabbing his legal pad off his desk, Pastor Ben sat in his chair. "So tell me about your week."

"Well, I spent a lot of time thinking about what we discussed last week. And I talked some with a lady friend of mine and with my dad. Tuesday, Ian and I decided to go to dinner and do some Christmas shopping for the kids so we did our homework last night." Glancing at Ian, Jane grinned. "I think it went well."

"It sure seems like it did." Pastor Ben tapped the end of his pen on his pad. "Did you resolve your differences or just have a good time together?"

Shifting his gaze from Pastor Ben to Jane and back to Pastor Ben, Ian ventured, "I'd say a little of both. I think we did a pretty good job at talking about the three things we wished were different in our relationship and looking at it from the other's point of view."

Jane nodded in agreement.

"That's great. And what's even better is that I'm hearing that you both are all in with trying to fix what's broken in your marriage. Honestly, for most couples I've worked with one spouse was half-hearted about reconciling or, worse yet, had already emotionally left the relationship. Let's face it, it's hard work when both individuals are trying, let alone when just one is, but I don't think I've ever had a couple make such quick progress as you have."

Jane cringed to think that at one point she'd actually believed divorce was a reasonable solution to their broken marriage. What had changed so drastically in such a short amount of time? Maybe she'd discovered that working on renewing their marriage had definite advantages. It felt like a brand new relationship, but with the comfort level of having been with the other person for years. It was refreshing and exciting, yet at the same time calm and safe.

"That's not to say your work here is done. Being in a marriage is a never-ending teaching and learning experience. Jane, you have to teach Ian what you want and need from him as your husband, while at the same time learning from him what he wants and needs from you. And you need to do the same, Ian. That's ongoing for as long as two people are married. The moment one stops teaching and learning is about the time the spouse begins to feel unloved or unwanted. Does that make sense?"

Jane nodded and so did Ian.

"So last week we talked about three things you both wish were different in your relationship. Today I want to talk about love. I'm sure you both are familiar with the popular verses in First Corinthians 13. 'Love suffers long and is kind; love does not envy; love does not parade itself, is not puffed up; does not behave rudely, does not seek its own, is not provoked, thinks no evil; does not rejoice in iniquity, but rejoices in the truth; bears all things, believes all things, hopes all things, endures all things. Love never fails.'

"This passage gives us a guideline to strive for, and love gives us something to believe and hope in. Love helps us endure and bear all things. True love will never fail. That's why you both are here. I know you love each other. You know you love each other, but how do you show your love for each other? Everyone registers love and affection within themselves differently, and that's not a bad thing. Where it becomes a problem is when you show love the same way you receive love instead of the way your spouse receives it. You may have the best of intentions, but it may not register with your spouse as an act of love."

Pastor Ben leaned forward, looking from Jane to Ian. "For example, my wife feels loved most when I compliment her or praise her or recognize her hard work. But if I try to show her I love her by rubbing her back or holding her hand because that's how I feel loved, it doesn't register the same with her. She might appreciate the back rub, but it doesn't speak to her the same as if I told her how beautiful she is while she's sweeping the floor."

Jane couldn't help chuckling, and Ian joined her ruefully.

"So my question to you is, what can your spouse do for you to express love and affection?"

Jane considered the question for a long moment, and then answered confidently. "Spend time with me." She turned to Ian. "When you spend time with me, even if we aren't really doing anything, it tells me I must be pretty important and worth your while for you to want to hang out with me. It means the world to me when you choose me over work or anything else."

Ian squeezed her to him. "I'd choose you one hundred times over anything else. I'm sorry that I've gotten so caught up with making a living I've forgotten about making a life with you."

Pastor Ben turned his attention to Ian. "What about you? How can Jane show you she loves you?"

"I think I'm like your wife. I grew up in a house where my parents had really high expectations of my sister and me. She lived up to them. I didn't, so I was constantly being told how I needed to be better, smarter, more motivated, more organized, you name it. I'm sure it's part of the reason I work so much. When I'm at a job site, I hear positive comments about something I did right, how I'm ahead of schedule, how well built the structure is, how the individual will recommend my company for another project. All of that boosts my self worth." Ian turned to Jane. "Compliment me on the things I do well. Your praise and approval registers as love to me."

"I didn't realize that." Jane patted his knee. "You do a lot of things right. You're a great dad, and I really appreciate the relationship you have with my dad. And you take care of me. It may not always be the way I need you to, but you've always tried. You've never given up on us. And I love you for that."

Seeing Ian's face beam made Jane's eyes moisten even more. How could she have been married to this man for twenty years and never seen before how a tiny bit of praise completely changed his demeanor and made him come alive.

Pastor Ben set the pad on the coffee table between them. "Are you ready for your homework assignment?"

"Already?" Hearing Ian echo her surprised comment, Jane looked over at him with a grin.

Pastor Ben chuckled. "See what happens when you make such progress? This week I want you to remember that your love for each other is not perfect because neither of you is perfect. There was only one perfect love and that's Jesus'. Even the happiest couples who have been married for fifty years or more have experienced struggles along the way. Every couple has their share of arguments. They've let each other down. They've been in ruts and often on different pages, or maybe even on different planets."

Jane joined in Ian's laughter.

"The difference between couples who make it through and couples who break apart is that they know how to see each other through the valleys. I want you to come up with a plan, both individually and together, for how you will handle the setbacks that will arise." Pastor Ben held his hands out. "For example, maybe you both agree on a cooling off period when you both spend a given amount of time alone individually, praying and sorting through your own feelings. Then, when the time is up, you come back together," he brought his hands together and intertwined his fingers, "and calmly discuss your feelings regarding the situation. Does that make sense?"

"So, you mean, kind of like what happened this past week?" Ian asked. "Time apart, and then time together?"

"If that's how you and Jane want to deal with any challenges that come up, sure. Just be careful not to let too much time go by before you come back together to resolve the issue or you'll just move on around it. If that happens, it'll just crouch in a dusty corner of your mind, only to bite you when some other issue drags it back out again." He propped his hands on his knees. "Let's pray, and then I'll see you back here next week. Okay?"

Ian enfolded Jane's hand in his. "Sounds great."

Just then Adam appeared in the office doorway, a troubled expression on his face. Jane bolted to her feet, followed by Ian and Pastor Ben.

"Emma? Jessie?"

Adam shook his head. "Emma and Jessie are fine. It's your dad, Jane. Bradley has been trying to reach you all morning."

Jane frantically fished in her purse for her cell phone. "We both had our ringers turned off for church, and I never turned mine back on." Pulling her phone out, she found six missed calls and twelve unread text messages. "W-what's wrong with dad?"

"I don't know any details except that Bradley found him in his recliner this morning. The left side of his face was drooping. His speech slurred when he tried to tell Bradley he had a headache."

Jane's voice choked. "A stroke. Just like Grandpa Clayton."

"Bradley called the rescue squad, and when he couldn't reach you, he called me. I already called Nathan, and he's on his way to the hospital."

Jane flashed a frightened look at Pastor Ben.

He reached in his blazer pocket and pulled out his car keys. "I'm right behind you, and I'll be praying on the way."

I should have been with him last night, not Bradley, Jane agonized as they rushed out to the parking lot together. *What if Bradley hadn't decided to stay and Dad was all alone?*

As she and Ian sped down the country roads between Harvest Bay and Cresthaven, Jane stared ahead out the windshield, wondering how she'd ever deal with her dad suffering a stroke, while she and Ian had spent a lovely evening together. Yes, her husband needed her attention, but last night her dad had needed her more.

She'd thought facing Zach and putting her feelings for him in the past would be their biggest challenge. But as this new mountain rose up in front of them with no plan in place on how to conquer it, her hopes plummeted.

CHAPTER
Twenty-five

When Ian pulled up to the hospital's emergency entrance, Jane jumped out of the truck before he'd even come to a complete stop. The doors opened with a *whoosh,* and she dashed inside.

"Mom!" Bradley rushed toward her.

"I'm here, Bradley. I'm here." She wrapped her strong, strapping almost sixteen-year-old son in as tight a hug as she could manage, "Where's your grandad? Can we see him?"

"They took him in right away to do a CT scan of his head. That was a little while ago, and I haven't heard anything since."

With Bradley at her heels, Jane rushed to the window and asked for information about her father. As the nurse stepped away to check for an update, Ian appeared at Jane's side, flanked by Adam and Pastor Ben.

"Any news?" Worry clouded Ian's eyes.

"Not yet. The nurse is going to check."

Ian put his arm a round her shoulders, and she leaned heavily against him, thankful that this time that he was there for her, not just physically but emotionally as well.

At last the nurse returned. "He's still in radiology. I'll show you to a consultation room where you can wait for the doctor."

Jane followed the nurse down a long, sterile hallway on autopilot, her emotions too wild to corral. This hospital had been the setting for her highest highs when each of her babies was born, and the lowest of lows when she accompanied her mother for the chemo treatments that left her lifeless and sick. Jane had sat in this hospital a handful of years ago, while Kate said her final good-bye to her Grandpa Clayton.

This hospital had been a starting point and a finish line on the circle of life for so many people. But Jane wasn't ready for her dad to cross the finish line yet.

The nurse ushered them into the same room where Jane had waited for news about her dad just three months earlier. "The doctor should be in shortly."

Ian nodded. "Thank you."

Jane felt her body moving to the sofa, but she didn't remember telling her feet to walk or her body to sit. Bradley began pacing, and although Jane knew he was anxious, he was stirring up tension in the constrictive atmosphere and making her dizzy in the process.

She held her hand out to him. "Come here and sit by me."

He obeyed and dropped his head to her shoulder.

Adam went to the door. "Come on, Ian. Let's go to the cafeteria and get some water for everyone."

Ian glanced from Adam to Jane and back to Adam, appearing torn.

Needing to gather her thoughts and emotions, Jane said, "It's okay. Bradley will take good care of me, and Pastor Ben is here." She forced her lips into a hint of an upward curve. "I could really use something cold to drink."

"Okay. I'll be right back." He kissed the top of her head, then followed Adam down the hall.

Jane became aware of moisture seeping through the fabric of her blouse and looked down at Bradley. "Hey, now. Your grand-dad would have none of that."

Bradley sniffled. "I know. I'm just scared. You should have seen him sitting there, Mom, so helpless, knowing something was wrong, but not able to do anything about it."

"I'm sorry you had to experience that, son." Jane smoothed his short sandy brown hair, guilt knotting her stomach. "I should have been there."

"I'm glad you were with Dad, and I'm glad I was with Granddad. I just wish I could have done more to help him."

"You did the best you could. It's all any of us could do. The rest we have to leave up to God." She paused, not knowing if she truly believed her words. This God she barely knew had worked a miracle in her marriage, so couldn't He also perform one for her dad? "Right, Pastor Ben?"

Standing quietly in the corner of the room, Pastor Ben nod-ded. "Your mom's right, Bradley." He moved over to join them on the sofa. "Do you like to go to Cedar Point?"

Bradley perked up. "Of course. It's fun."

"What's your favorite roller coaster?"

Bradley considered the question. "Probably the Mean Streak. I think it's cool that it's one of the tallest wooden roller coasters in the world."

"Life is a roller coaster. It can be exciting and thrilling one minute and terrifying the next. But it wouldn't do you any good to try to control it, would it?"

Bradley shook his head.

"All we can do is hold on tight and try to enjoy the ride for as long as we can. Your granddad is on the not-so-fun part of the roller coaster right now. But he's not alone. He wasn't alone when you found him, on the ambulance ride over here, or even right now when the doctors and specialists are trying to diagnose the cause of his pain."

Pulling a small Bible out of the breast pocket of his blazer, Pastor Ben turned to a marked page. "The verse I always turn to for comfort at a time like this is Isaiah 41:10: 'Fear not, for I am with you; Be not dismayed, for I am your God. I will strengthen you, yes, I will help you, I will uphold you with My righteous right hand.' We can't control this roller coaster, but we can trust the One who is controlling it."

Jane swallowed a thick lump of rising emotion. "Can you read that verse again?"

"Sure." As Pastor Ben reread it, Jane experienced a surge of peace and comfort, and the corners of her mouth lifted. "Thank you."

At that moment Ian and Adam walked through the door, each carrying two bottles of water. Jane was just about to tell them they were missing a bottle when Dr. Nathan Sterling walked in carrying two more.

Jane's heart rate accelerated as she tried to read his face. Fighting back tears, she quipped, "Nathan, we've got to stop meeting here like this."

Chuckling, Nathan handed a bottle of water to Pastor Ben and cracked the second one open. "I agree. Whole heartedly."

"W-what's going on with Dad? Is it a-a stroke like Grandpa Clayton?"

He sat on the arm of the sofa. "Based on the results of the CT scan and an MRI that Dr. Khalilah ordered to confirm her suspicions, it appears your dad didn't have a stroke." He took a swallow of water and capped the bottle. "It's also highly likely that the TIA three months ago was misdiagnosed."

A wave of relief washed over Jane, but delight quickly dimmed. "So, then, what's wrong?"

"Preliminary tests indicate that your dad had what's called a hemangioblastoma."

"A what?"

"Basically a benign tumor that occurs in the blood vessels of the brain."

Jane's voice climbed an octave and a few decibels. "A what?"

Nathan moved from the arm of the couch to the seat beside her. "I know it sounds scary, but the good thing is that we're not dealing with cancer."

"My dad has a brain t—" She couldn't finish the word. Her chest rose and fell, panic threatening to smother her. "H-how did this happen?"

"There are no known causes for hemangioblastomas. What we do know about them is they're relatively slow growing and, as is your dad's case, often affect the cerebellum. That's the area of the brain responsible for movement, balance, equilibrium, and muscle tone, so the symptoms may mimic that of a TIA or a stroke."

Jane rubbed her forehead. "Umm . . . how do we treat it?"

"That'll be the difficult part of this journey. It'll most likely have to be surgically removed, the sooner the better, and brain surgery isn't easy on anyone, let alone someone your dad's age. But since these tumors involve blood vessels, they do pose a threat of rupturing, causing bleeding into the brain."

Nathan reached across Jane and patted Bradley's knee. "And that is why you may have saved your granddad's life with your quick actions. Good job!"

He turned his attention back to Jane. "Dr. Khalilah will talk with you later to confirm her diagnosis and discuss treatment options. And you know I'll be right here through the whole process. Your dad isn't going through this alone, and neither are you. Okay?"

Jane nodded, silent tears finally letting go to slip down her cheeks.

"But for now I do have to go check on a couple other patients." Nathan rose and crossed the room to the door. "I'll be back in a little bit. In the meantime, if you need anything, send me a message or have me paged." Giving them a parting nod, he slipped out the door, closing it behind him.

Jane stared after him, trying her best to process the information she'd been given. *My dad has a brain t—*

Her mind went to the verse in Isaiah that Pastor Ben had just read: *"Fear not, for I am with you."* She repeated those few words over and over, but it didn't help. She was still terrified. Maybe she was doing it wrong.

"Pastor Ben, could you please read that verse again?"

He pulled the Bible from his breast pocket once again. As he read, she curled up into a tight ball in the corner of the couch and wept from the depths of her soul.

The day passed in a blur. After Jane's dad was moved into a room, Nathan and Dr. Khalilah confirmed the diagnosis and explained the treatment procedure and outcome to him. Surgery was scheduled for the following afternoon and, he was told that, given his age, he'd likely spend the rest of the week recovering in the hospital.

Jane listened from the doorway still disbelieving this was happening. Her dad, her rock, had a brain tumor. Just thinking that ugly word made her want to throw up, but she had no choice but to accept it and keep moving forward.

Ava, Ian's sister, was happy to stay at their home and take care of the kids when Ian was working or with Jane at the hospital. which would be easiest on the children. At least they would have the stability of their own home. Jane also made out a long grocery list of regular weekly items as well as her family's favorite Thanksgiving dishes and handed Ava enough cash to cover the bill. With the holiday only a week and a half away, and given the amount of time she would be spending at the hospital, she wouldn't be able to get all the ingredients, but she was determined to give her children a decent Thanksgiving. Since the holiday was the time to count one's blessings, Jane counted her sister-in-law twice.

Kate pitched in by taking care of everything in Jane's classroom. She called in a sub for the week and pulled plenty of worksheets and activities that would review the skills Jane had taught them over the first three months. She also offered to keep the kids if Ava had plans or needed a break. True friends were hard to come by, Jane reflected, and Kate was by far the best.

Running home and to Shaun's house, Ian packed Jane a bag of all of her essentials. He even stopped at the store and bought her an adult therapeutic coloring book and a pack of colored pencils. Attaching a Post-It note to the cover, he wrote, "I couldn't pack your easel and paints. I figured this would be the next best thing,"

Pastor Ben sat with her and her dad in his room for a long time, not really talking about anything in particular, just being a source of support. It meant more to Jane than she could ever put into words.

Finally, at eight o'clock, Pastor Ben stood and stretched. "Well, I'm going to let you get some rest. You have a big day tomorrow. Do you mind if I pray for you before I go?"

Jane's dad grabbed her hand and gave the pastor a weary smile. "That'd be just fine. Thank ya."

Standing at the foot of the hospital bed, Pastor Ben bowed his head and prayed earnestly for Shaun, Jane, and the doctors and nurses. "We thank you for every day You give us on this earth," he concluded, "and we humbly ask you to teach us to count our days and to make our days count. I ask all this in Jesus' name. Amen." Tapping the foot board, he said, "Get some rest, Shaun. I'll see you in the morning."

When he slipped into the hallway, Jane dashed out the door. "Pastor Ben, wait."

He turned. "What is it?"

"I just want to thank you. I mean—Ian and I—we aren't members of your church, but you agreed to work with us, to help us try to get back on track. You spent your entire day here away from your family. I don't know why you did it, but thank you."

Smiling warmly, he motioned for her to sit with him on a nearby bench. "Why do you think I did it?"

Jane shrugged. "I don't know. Because you're a good guy and you like to help out?"

"Thank you, I think." Pastor Ben chuckled. "Jesus once said, 'Those who are well have no need of a physician.' My wife and my congregation are taken care of, but you and Ian needed a physician."

"That's why you helped, but why did you stay?"

"I've been in your shoes a time or two. My wife lost our first baby. Did I tell you that?"

Jane's eyes widened. She shook her head.

"We've also lost both of our parents. A few other things have happened along the way, and there's one thing I noticed each time. A lot of people wanted to be there for us, and they thought they had to do something to help. But what I remember the most are the people who just sat with us. They didn't say much, didn't do much, but they were there. I learned something from those people."

"Then you understand how much it means to me."

"I do." Pushing to his feet, he hit the elevator button. "I've also been where you are in your faith journey. You want to believe, but you've been so hurt and disappointed by life you don't think it could possibly be that easy." The elevator doors opened, and he stepped inside. "But it is."

Jane watched the elevator doors close, and then stared blankly at them for several moments, thinking about his words, arguing with them inside her own mind. *It's not a light switch. You can't all of a sudden decide you believe, just like I couldn't turn my feelings for Ian back on with a snap of my fingers.*

Creases formed in her brow. *But it did kind of happen that way. Something magical happened last night. Maybe I never really lost my love for Ian. It was just buried deep under so much hurt and disappointment.* She thought about how comforting it felt to have him at the hospital this time, a stark contrast from three months ago.

It had also soothed her anxious spirit when Pastor Ben read that verse in Isaiah. She couldn't remember the numbers or all the words, but she knew it said, "I am with you." She couldn't see or hear God, but after Pastor Ben read that passage she felt something warm and calming. It was the same sensation that came over her when he'd prayed a week earlier at their first counseling session. She had no idea what it all meant, and, given everything her dad was getting ready to go through, she didn't have time to figure it out.

Maybe when Dad is safely out of the woods, I'll try to make sense of it all.

As she turned to head back to her dad's room, the elevator doors opened. A gasp escaped Jane's lips and her pale complexion lightened a few shades as Zach stepped into the hallway, carrying a cheery bouquet.

"What are you doing here?"

"Mrs. Zeller sent out an email about your dad. I just wanted to show my support."

Planting her hands on her hips, she glared at him. "You mean, it's not enough for you to show up at church? You have to come here, too, where you know I'm going to be upset and vulnerable? Listen to me, I don't want your support."

Zach stepped so close that only the small bouquet separated them. "I think you do. Come on, Jane. Just admit it. We both felt that connection between us."

She glanced up and down the busy hall, then grabbed his sleeve and pulled him into a vacant sitting area tucked away at the end of the corridor. "There was a definite mutual attraction between us, yes, but you have to understand that I'm married, and I'm trying to do the right thing. I can't leave my husband and tear my family apart because I have feelings for another man."

"Feelings? They weren't just feelings, Jane. I've fallen in love with you, and I know you love me too."

Jane dropped her gaze, her cheeks heating. "There are many different kinds of love, Zach." Grasping his hand, she willed him to understand. "We work together. We support each other professionally. You teach my child, and you've made quite an impact on her. But Ian and I have a history, and I can't throw that away."

"It's not a reason to stay either." He released her hand and brushed his fingertips across her cheek. "You deserve to be happy the way I know I can make you happy. You deserve to be appreciated and cherished from the start, not after twenty years. It shouldn't take almost losing you for him to tell you how beautiful and talented you are. I know you know that I'm right. I know you're in love with me, and I'll be waiting right here when you're finally ready to admit it to yourself."

Her insides churning, she pulled away from his touch. "Ian ran home to make sure the kids are settling in with his sister, but he'll be back soon. You have to go."

He pressed the bouquet into her hands, leaned in, and before she realized what was happening, his lips were on hers.

Jane pulled back and wiped her mouth with her sleeve hoping it would remove the tingling sensation his kiss left behind. A whisper was all she could muster.

"Please leave."

Rising, Zach retraced his steps to the elevator, a satisfied expression on his face.

She stood in stunned silence for several moments. With the roller coaster of emotions over the past twenty-four hours, she wondered whether she was hallucinating. She touched her flaming cheek, still feeling the soft caress of his lips.

This was the last thing she'd wanted or expected to happen. She had to focus all her energy and strength on her dad, not on Ian or Zach or even Jesus. Her dad needed her, but she needed him more.

Leaving the flower arrangement on the end table, she threw away the card and hurried back to her dad's room.

He brightened when she entered. "There's my lil lassie. I wondered where you took off to."

Her tears spilled. "I'm sorry, Dad."

"Oh, come now." He patted the bed beside him. "Tell your dear ol' dad all about it."

She wedged her body onto the edge of the small bed beside him, laid her head on his chest, and listened to his strong heart. At that moment, it was all that mattered to her.

"I'm just scared."

He smoothed her hair. "Don't worry, sweet Janey. It'll all be okay."

It was the same promise Zach had made her more than a month ago. This time, though, she found it hard to believe.

CHAPTER
Twenty-six

The projected six hour surgery lasted eight agonizing hours. By the time Dr. Khalilah entered the waiting area to give a report, Jane felt as though she'd paced a groove into the floor.

"The surgery was a success. Your dad's heading to recovery. You can see him in a bit."

Just when Jane thought she was all cried out, tears of sweet relief poured down her face as she thanked the doctor.

It hurt to see her dad, the fighter who had overcome so many adversities, looking so weak, with bandages wrapped around his head and medicine dripping through a tube into his arm. *At least he's still here,* she kept telling herself, wiping away moisture from her eyes. *And day by day he'll get stronger. It'll all be okay.*

There was that promise again. It kept turning up, reminding her that it really wasn't okay yet, filling her spirit with dark doubts.

A couple of minor setbacks lengthened Jane's dad's hospital stay from five days to ten. It probably would have been a few days longer, but he wanted to be at home for Thanksgiving, and Nathan promised Dr. Kahlilah he'd make daily house calls in addition to the home health care that was already in place.

Tuesday afternoon, two days before Thanksgiving, Jane brought her dad home. Though she and Ian were still working out their issues, Ian agreed that her dad needed her more. Other than going home to sleep, he would spend all his non-working hours at her dad's house.

That evening they spent time together as a family, playing Uno around the coffee table, laughing, talking, and snacking, while her dad rested on the sofa, the designated cheerleader of sorts. Before Ian left to return home with the kids, he kissed Jane good-bye.

That night, lying alone in her childhood bed so far past the point of exhaustion that sleep eluded her, Jane wondered if everything would really be okay. Worries and fears about the future threatened to suffocate her. That her dad was recovering from brain surgery was traumatic enough, but having Zach show up at the hospital and kiss her just about put her over the edge.

Zach's number remained blocked, and she hadn't been in school to see him, but he emailed her regularly, the sweetest, most tender love notes she'd ever received. Every word made her heart flutter as he eloquently described what she meant to him. Although she forced herself not to respond, secretly she looked forward to receiving them.

Wednesday morning she awoke to the sound of rain gently tapping against the window. The rhythmic sound almost lulled her back to sleep until she glanced at her digital alarm clock. The glowing red numbers read, "10:30."

Not even fully awake yet, she was already behind. She had casseroles to put together for quick warm up on Thursday and a turkey to marinate. They had so much to be thankful for this holiday season, and she was determined to make it a wonderful celebration with her family and friends.

Groaning, she threw her covers off, crawled out of bed, and plodded to the kitchen to start a pot of coffee before checking on her dad. When she reached the kitchen her eyes opened a little wider as she inhaled the rich, warm, and inviting scent of freshly brewed coffee. But who made it? She hoped her dad hadn't gotten up on his own.

A small red envelope waited for her propped against the coffee pot. Opening it, she smiled.

I thought you could use a pot of coffee this morning. Just wanted you to know I'm always thinking of you.

Forever yours,

Ian

"See? What did I tell ya? He's an eagle, that one."

She glanced into the living room to see her dad reclining in his La-Z-Boy and rushed to his side. "Dad, what are you doing up? You're not supposed to be getting out of bed yet on your own."

"I didn't. When Mr. Eagle stopped to make the coffee, he helped me out of bed, to the bathroom, and then got me comfortable out here in my favorite chair so you could sleep a little bit longer."

Jane decided that if her heart swelled any more, there might not be room in her chest for her lungs. She squeezed her dad's hand.

"They say a woman tends to pick men who remind her of her father, and I have to say it just might be true. Ian comes real close to measuring up to you, Dad."

"Now I wouldn't go that far. He's not that good."

Jane laughed. "Well, funny man, I'm going to have a cup of coffee. Are you ready for breakfast?"

"Breakfast? It's almost time for lunch."

"Oh, I want breakfast," Samuel piped up from his place in front of the TV.

"Yeah, me too," Jessica added. She and Emma were curled up on the sofa, each with their nose in a book.

Jane chuckled and with a shake of her head returned to the kitchen. "Well then we'll make it brunch."

She glanced out the window at the dreary drizzle. *Maybe Ian will be home from work early today.* That thought caused other thoughts to float across her mind.

She grabbed her cell phone. There were two missed calls, but no messages left on her voice mail. She shrugged and opened her text messages, tapping Ian's thread.

Thanks for the coffee this morning. I'll have to think of a way to repay you. Adding a winky face and a kissy face, she hit send, then busied herself with fixing brunch.

As the eggs sizzled in the pan and the bread cooked in the toaster, she gathered up her recipes for their feast. It didn't dawn on her that she hadn't gotten a reply from Ian until after she washed the dishes from brunch and the two casseroles she'd made.

Drying her hands on a dish towel, she picked up her phone. It seemed to be working fine. She had a text message from Bradley saying he was on his way over with his sisters and brother, a handful of emails, and two missed calls, again from the same number.

Against her better judgment, she opened her email and found three junk messages waiting for her, one bank statement, and an email from Zach. The subject line read, "Good morning, beautiful." Her heart fluttered at the three pretty words, an involuntary response that she had no control over. She glanced over her shoulder at the coffeepot, not getting quite the same surge of emotions from Ian's thoughtful gesture.

Why can't I experience the same reaction with Ian that I do with Zach?

Because Zach had nothing to gain by chasing her, and Ian had everything to lose.

Without opening the email, she deleted it. It stung a little to know that beautiful, poetic words were being thrown away before she even read them, but she had to purge Zach from her personal life once and for all. Her sanity as well as her marriage depended on it.

Jane closed out her email as Bradley strolled in with his siblings close behind.

"Hey, Mom." Bradley kissed her cheek on his way to the living room. "Hey, Granddad. Looking good all kicked back in your recliner. How are you feeling?"

"Ah, thar's my favorite grandson. Never felt better."

"Hey, I heard that." Samuel broke away from his favorite cartoon long enough to scowl at his granddad.

"I'm just jokin' with ya, lad. What kind of a cartoon is this anyway? Who ever heard of a talking sponge? Back when I was a wee lad we didn't even have a TV . . ."

Tuning out the antics of her son and father, Jane returned to the task of prepping food for their dinner. But suddenly something seemed off, almost like when a cold front moved through. Nothing appeared different at first, but then the skies darkened and there was a chill in the air.

Maybe it was because she was still on edge from her dad's surgery and the days spent in the hospital. Even after sleeping in as late as she had, the exhaustion reached her marrow. But she couldn't shake her fear that something bad was going to happen.

Okay, God. If you're really up there listening, I need you to bring me peace. At least enough to get me through Thanksgiving, and then I can fall apart until Christmas. I guess that's it for now, so amen.

Bradley strolled back into the kitchen. "Need help, Mom?"

"Sure. Do you want to get the turkey out of its packaging so I can start marinating it?"

"I can do that." Grabbing a pair of kitchen shears, Bradley got to work.

Watching him out of the corner of her eye, Jane inwardly beamed with pride. This boy of hers had grown into a kind-hearted and responsible young man.

She mixed a package of green beans with a can of cream of mushroom soup. "So how are things going for you and Alison?"

"Pretty good. She's planning on stopping over tomorrow for a little while."

Bradley heaved the turkey into a large container in the sink and reached inside to remove the giblets. He gave the bird a good bath and patted it dry with a paper towel before depositing it in the roasting pan. As he scrubbed his hands with soap and water, he gave her a sideways glance.

"The better question is how are things going with you and Dad? You must have had a nice time together on your date, but then Granddad went into the hospital, and the last time that happened it wasn't good for your relationship."

Jane mixed garlic and spices with olive oil and began to massage it into the turkey. "Yeah, but this time is different. Your dad and I have reached a deeper level of understanding. We both did and said things that hurt each other, but up until about a week ago neither of us could see the situation from the other's point of view."

Jane put the lid on the pan and put it in the fridge. "But that's just part of being in a relationship, son. There are good times and bad times. There are times you want to quit, but you keep holding on because you believe it'll be worth it in the end. Just as an example, this morning your dad stopped over, helped granddad get up so I could sleep a little longer, and brewed a pot of coffee so it would be waiting for me when I got up, all before going to work because that's what you do when you love each other. When one is weak, the other is strong."

"This morning?" Leaning against the counter, Bradley crossed his arms. "Mom, it's raining. Dad's been home all morning. He left just before I did to make a trip to one of his suppliers, but he hasn't been at a job site."

"He hasn't?" Jane leaned shoulder to shoulder with Bradley against the counter. "I wonder why he's not here then? Why would he come over to make a pot of coffee, help dad, and then just go back home?"

Bradley pushed off the cabinets. "Who knows?"

He swiped an apple from a care basket of fruit someone from the church dropped off and took a big bite. Going into the living room, he plopped on the floor next to Samuel.

If he didn't go to work, why isn't he here with me? We could be talking and working on these darn casseroles together. Annoyance nibbled away at her spirit. *He must have a good reason, but if he's been home, why hasn't he at least texted me back?*

Just then her phone filled the kitchen with an old Irish song, the ringtone indicating an unknown caller. If it was Ian, she'd hear Sonny and Cher. Disappointed, she answered the call.

"Mrs. Garner, this is George from Gordon Lumber's corporate office. There's a problem with your account."

Garner Construction's number one supplier. Tensing, Jane asked, "What do you mean? What kind of a problem?"

George cleared his throat. "It's delinquent by two months."

Two months? It dawned on Jane that was shortly after her dad's first trip to the hospital, and she hadn't been there to help with the books.

"I'm sorry. We've had some personal business to take care of at home recently and I'm sure it just got over looked. I'll go take care of it right now. Thank you so much for bringing this to my attention. Have a happy Thanksgiving."

She hung up and snatched her keys and purse off the table. After explaining where she was going, she dashed out the door to her Expedition.

She tried to push away the thought that this was somehow her fault, that Ian would be so angry if he knew this account was delinquent. Garner Construction would fold without his suppliers, and especially Gordon Lumber. It had never been any trouble for her to help him with the books. It just required basic accounting skills, and their software had taken the hard number crunching out of it. But because of her selfish behavior, she'd neglected the books as she'd neglected Ian.

When she reached the house, she ignored the shoes and backpacks that littered the living room and made a beeline for Ian's den. She pushed open the door and was hit by a potent mixture that she guessed was made up of two parts rotten food and one part sweaty socks. She glanced around at the unmade futon and overflowing trash can and made a mental note to invest in a HAZMAT suit if he wanted her help tidying up.

Maneuvering her way to the desk, she booted up the computer. She opened the bookkeeping software and found the Gordon Lumber account.

Something seemed different. It was as if someone had worked on the books, but it appeared that nothing had been paid.

That's odd. If Ian opened this program, he should have paid these accounts, but it looks like he just moved the accounts around.

She clicked to select an amount that would bring the Gordon Lumber account current, but before she could submit it, a box she'd never seen before popped up on the screen. Befuddled, she leaned closer to read the message.

"Hello, Ian. Back so soon?"

What in the world? Clicking on the small chat box, she read a long, very descriptive, quite provocative thread between her husband and this Felicity person that dated back to the beginning of September. Her blood ran colder with each word, turning to ice and freezing her heart.

Their last exchange happened at ten o'clock that morning. *No wonder he wasn't at Dad's with me. He was talking dirty to this girl.*

She clicked on the browser's history. Their bookkeeping program popped up repeatedly, paired with some dollhouse website. She clicked on that link. Her eyes widening, she pressed her hand to her mouth to stifle a gasp as pictures of scantily clad, erotically posed women filled the monitor.

"My husband's addicted to porn." The words came out in a whisper.

She closed out the website, opened the company's bank account, and glanced quickly through the transactions. It appeared most of them were legitimate. Plenty remained in the account to pay the bills, and she believed he'd intended to take care of them. But he'd become distracted by sexy pictures of these women.

Then she noticed one withdrawal for ninety dollars in September to a company with "dolls" in the name.

It's the same as those old nine hundred numbers, but instead of a charge being added to your phone bill for phone sex, he paid money straight to this website to chat with this girl. Money he supposedly made to provide for his family.

In an instant, the temperature of her blood spiked from frigid to boiling. As she dropped her gaze, it landed on a note-book lying open on the desk in front of the monitor. Recognizing Ian's handwriting, she began to read.

What I Can Do to Be a Better Husband
1. Stop lusting after photoshopped pictures of women I don't know, and start desiring my wife.

It was one thing to read a typed letter, but to see her hus-band's very familiar handwriting—the same handwriting on the note he'd given her a month and a half earlier saying how he'd fight to his death for their marriage—now spell out that her hus-band didn't desire her was beyond a crushing blow. it undid everything they'd just worked so hard to fix. She was disap-pointed and disgusted and devastated.

Oddly enough, at that moment she thought of the home-work Pastor Ben had assigned. They hadn't yet developed a plan on how to handle any differences that arose between them. But as she slipped off her wedding band and laid it on the pad of paper, she didn't really care.

This mountain was impossible.

Ian pulled into his father-in-law's driveway and immediately noticed that Jane's Expedition wasn't there. Concern instantly filled him.

What if something happened and her dad was rushed back to the hospital?

But that morning when Ian helped Shaun out of bed, he'd seemed to be doing well, considering his skull had been cut open a week earlier. Ian bounded up the front steps and through the front door.

"Jane?" The sight that met him was such a relief that he laughed out loud. All four of his children were playing Twister, while Jane's dad, kicked back in his La-Z-Boy, called the hand or foot and color. "Having fun?"

"No!" Emma closely resembled a pretzel.

"I am." Samuel was quite obviously stretching the rules more than his body.

Ian chuckled. "Do any of you know where your mom is?"

"She said she had to run home. That was about forty-five minutes ago."

"She must have left about the same time I did then," Ian said. "I had to stop and get gas."

His strong arms trembling, Bradley grunted. "Hurry, Granddad. Spin it."

Shaun flicked the arrow on the spinner and waited for it to come to a rest. "Right foot, blue."

At sight of the four kids twisting, Ian laughed, then turned and retraced his steps to his truck. The rain had stopped falling, but the atmosphere remained damp and gloomy.

The perfect weather to spend curled up on the couch with my wife.

As he neared home, his pulse quickened the thought that they would be alone. *Or we could curl up somewhere else.*

He barely had his truck in park before he jumped out. Scurrying up the front steps, he threw the front door open.

"Jane?" His voice echoed through the house.

"I'm right here."

He found her around the corner, sitting like a statue at the dining room table, her emotionless expression matching the flatness of her voice.

His bright smile faded a couple notches. "What's wrong?"

"I got a call today from Gordon Lumber. Your account with them was two months past due."

"Oh." Ian's spirits picked back up. "With everything that's gone on between us and with your dad over the past few months, I completely forgot. I'll go pay it right now."

"Too late. Somehow I thought it was my fault that the account was delinquent, so I rushed over here to bring the books and all the accounts up to date."

Ian felt the color seep from his face. "Y-you did?"

"Yes, Ian, and I saw why those accounts weren't paid. While you shamed me for talking to another man, you were looking at pictures of naked women and spending money to talk dirty to one of them. Tell me, how is that even remotely okay?"

He stuffed his hands in his pockets. "They're just pictures."

Jane snorted. "Just pictures? Now who's lying? In your mind you were doing things with that Felicity person you've never done with me. I read all about it. I've never been so hurt by anyone before."

Rising, she strode toward him, stopped, and turned, her hands on her hips. "You know, I might have understood if this happened a month ago or maybe even a year ago. But this morning,

Ian? After counseling and our date? After that night and morning together? You came over, helped dad, made me a pot of coffee, and left me a sweet note—which I know now was nothing but lies—and then you came back here to look at naked pictures of a girl you've never met? Telling her how you could imagine running your hands through her hair. How could you do such a thing?"

She threw her hands in the air. "I haven't been perfect, but I was committed to you even when someone else showed interest in me. Even when *you* were the one who left *me* lonely, I was committed to you. But now it's your turn to be lonely. Let me know how well she, in all her photoshopped beauty, keeps you warm at night."

Ian could hardly breathe. "What is that supposed to mean?"

"It means I'm done, Ian. I quit. We'll get through the holidays and then decide where to go from there, but I can tell you I'm not going to compete with a perfect pretend girl. I shouldn't have to. That's not a marriage. And I'm not going to spend the rest of my life with a hypocrite, condemning me for something you were doing all along."

She moved to the door, swung it open, and looked back. "You'll find my rings on the notebook right under the list you started on how to be a better husband. And here's a clue: There are all kinds of goals you could write down, but desiring your wife shouldn't have to be one of them." Stepping through the threshold, she slammed the door shut behind her.

And she was gone.

Ian trudged to his den, turned on the light, and stared at the glint of gold on top of the stark white paper.

This time she was really gone. And he didn't blame her. He recognized his own hypocrisy and it made him sick inside. But the emptiness the sight of those two rings caused felt as though it would destroy him.

He dropped to his knees, choking on sobs. "What have I done? Oh, God, what have I done?"

His hand trembling, he pulled out his cell phone, found the number in his contacts, and tapped the keys. "I need help. Please help me."

CHAPTER
Twenty-seven

B y the time Pastor Ben arrived late that afternoon, Ian hadn't moved from where he collapsed in the hallway at the door of his office. He couldn't find the strength to answer the front door when the bell rang.

"Hello? Ian?" Pastor Ben called out. "I got your message and came as fast as I could." He wandered cautiously through the house until he found Ian slumped over in the hallway, and rushed to his side. "Ian! What's wrong? Are you hurt? Do you need an ambulance?"

Ian blinked away the gritty residue from his tears. "She's gone for good. I lost her."

"Oh, no. You were doing so well too. Your relationship seemed to be heading in the right direction anyway." Sinking to the floor beside Ian, Pastor Ben leaned against the wall. "Why don't you tell me what happened?"

Ian confessed his recent obsession. "It happened completely by accident. I was searching for plans to build a dollhouse, and this site came up. I should have clicked out of it right then and there, but I took a peek and got hooked. From that day on, whenever I came into my office to settle accounts with suppliers or finalize invoices, I'd remember the images and go back. I didn't think it was hurting anything—they were just pictures—

until I started chatting with one of the women. Even so, I don't know these people. We were just making each other feel good. It wasn't like I was ever going to act on anything I said to her."

Pastor Ben tipped his head back against the wall. "Let me guess. Jane found these messages."

Ian nodded. "I was so afraid of her developing feelings for the guy I saw her with at homecoming—who happens to be your nephew, by the way—but what I was doing was worse, wasn't it?"

"Sin is sin, Ian. It's all the same in God's eyes. Having helped couples through this type of thing before, I think it's safe to say that knowing you were behaving inappropriately just amplified your insecurities about Jane."

"Do you think she'll ever forgive me?"

"With time, probably. But first you have to ask God to forgive you, and, even more difficult, you have to forgive yourself. You had a void inside your heart you thought you could fill with lustful images and fantasies. That didn't get you very far. But when you fill that empty space with the Lord, He'll give you the power to overcome temptation and live in a way that's pleasing to Him."

"I'm a good guy for the most part, and I believe in God. What more do I have to do?"

"Even the devil believes in God. But when you dedicate your life to Jesus, you establish a relationship with Him and make a conscious effort every day to exemplify Him in your thoughts, words, and deeds through the power He gives you." Pastor Ben held his hands out matter-of-factly. "Look, you're at a very low point right now. The way I see it, you can either stay there and hope to be strong enough to climb out on your own someday. Or you can call out for help and accept rescue. The choice is yours."

"It's not going to be easy, is it?"

"Not always, no. If Jesus is going to be the Lord of your life, you have to die to yourself everyday, make yourself—your own wants and desires—less so He can be more. I'll be the first to admit that some days are a lot harder than others, but nothing worth having is easy all the time. It takes hard work and discipline."

Ian shook his head. "I can't imagine God would want me on His team with the choices I've made and the pain I've caused the ones I love the most."

"It says in the Bible that all have sinned. Every single one of us. You aren't the first one to mess up, you won't be the last, and God still wants you on His team."

"If I know I'm going to screw up, what's the point in even trying?"

"Because Jesus died for us while we were still sinners and He isn't going to give up on us now. He wants to make us better. If He waited for us to make ourselves good, then none of us would have any hope. Through Jesus, God freely gives us the gift of eternal life and the power to become a new person."

Ian swallowed a lump of emotion that suddenly formed in his throat. "But I don't deserve that."

"Is there anything you wouldn't do to save Bradley, Emma, Jessica, or Samuel? God loves you even more than you love your kids. I won't lie. Even I am faced with doubt at times, but the commitment I made to trust God's promise covers me every time."

Ian took a deep breath. "I want to be rescued. I want Jesus to help me live my life right and teach me how to be the man Jane deserves whether she's with me or not. But how?"

Pastor Ben placed a firm hand on Ian's shoulder. "Admit and accept that you're a sinner. Believe that Jesus is God's Son and that He died to save you. Then tell Him you'll follow Him, love Him, and serve Him. He's waiting to accept you with open arms."

Sitting side by side on the floor, Pastor Ben and Ian prayed together, and Ian felt his life change forever as he committed to trusting God's promises. He saw his relationships and experiences through new eyes and the traces of God's love in each instance. A peace and hope filled his heart that he had never before experienced. Although he knew he would face trials and temptations, he no longer had to face them alone.

They visited a few minutes longer before rising from their place on the floor. Then Pastor Ben shook Ian's hand.

"Ian, you're a new creation in Christ. That's the first and most important step. Let's resume meeting on Monday mornings to study the Bible together so you can begin to grow in Him. In the meantime, start praying for your wife, not out of your desire to be with her, but God's desire to be with her. Understand?"

Ian nodded and walked Pastor Ben to the front door, feeling stronger and yet weaker at the same time. "I don't know how to begin to thank you."

Patting him on the back, Pastor Ben stepped out onto the porch. "You already did." He paused, then added, "Oh, and for the record, Jane would be wise to stay far away from Zach. He's my nephew and I love him, but my father's family was known more for their poor choices and bad decisions than for their good moral standards."

With a parting wave, he strolled down the steps, leaving Ian alone with a brand new faith and a friendly word of caution. One brought him peace. The other threatened to take it.

Sitting in the driveway of her dad's house, Jane was truly lost. She didn't know where to go, not just at the moment, but permanently. As much as she loved her dad, his house just wasn't big enough for her and four children to move in, but she couldn't stay in the home she'd made with Ian either. Not now. Not after the whiplash she'd received from feeling so loved to feeling so undesired in a matter of a few minutes.

She'd never realized how damaging betrayal could be until all the hope she'd had for her marriage dissipated like dew on a hot summer day. Gone, just like that. Now she didn't want to be married to that man a minute longer than she had to. She wasn't sure she'd ever be able to erase those nasty, degrading pictures from her mind. Seeing Ian's passionate words to another girl had felt like a switchblade to the gut. She'd survive, but she'd never be the same.

As she watched the wipers clear the fine mist off the windshield, she made a tentative plan: She'd try to enjoy the holiday with her kids, then call a lawyer first thing on Monday morning.

She grabbed her phone and sent Bradley a message. *Is everything okay?*

Almost instantaneously, she received a thumbs-up emoji as a reply.

I have a couple errands to run. I'll be back soon.

Again a thumbs-up arrived in her inbox.

She turned the key and headed out of town in search of some peace. There was only one place where she had even a remote chance of finding it.

Pulling up the long gravel driveway of Stampede of Dreams, she was disappointed to see that the place was deserted. She wasn't really expecting Sandy to be there the day before Thanksgiving, but just being on the property, smelling the fresh, damp country air, thinking about the horses and eager students brought some calm to her spirit.

She parked in her usual spot and strolled aimlessly across the wet grass toward the quiet arena. Propping her elbows on the gate, she crossed her arms and rested her chin on them. The dimly lit, vacant arena seemed to reflect her future. Empty. Where it had once been so full of joy, now there were only bittersweet memories.

Her marriage may not have been perfect or passionate or fulfilling, but she had experienced happiness and hope. And she'd had a home.

"Now what do I do?" Her voice echoed through the big barn.

"Well, you can start by helping me bed down these animals."

Startled, Jane squinted against the darkness. "Sandy? Is that you?" She climbed through the wide bars in the gate and crossed the expansive sawdust-covered ground to the stable, where she found Sandy hard at work in Logan's stall. "I didn't know anyone else was here. I didn't see any cars."

"Frankie dropped me off, and then went to run some last-minute errands." Sandy glanced up at Jane, concern clouding her eyes. "How's your dad?"

"He's good." Jane hesitated. "Well, as good as to be expected after such a tough surgery. He's home recovering now."

Sandy nodded, her light brown hair swinging back and forth. Straightening, she pushed her glasses a little further up her nose and studied at Jane. "So what are you doing here on the day before Thanksgiving?"

Jane stroked Logan's mane. "Just trying to clear my mind, I guess."

"And how's that going for you?"

"I just got here, and there's a lot to sort through."

"I see." Sandy returned her attention to her task. "Well, let me know if you want some help."

"I don't really know where to start." Jane found a seat on a bale of hay. "After I thought Ian and I were moving in the right direction, I found porn on his computer and he'd been chatting with one of the girls from the website. It's been going on for months, and he did it again this morning. The really twisted thing about it is I actually had the thought that I'm partly to blame since I haven't been very affectionate. But that's not fair to me. There were days when he didn't even acknowledge my existence, but I didn't go looking at naked pictures of other men." She blew out an exasperated breath. "I was so sure we were on our way to enjoying the best years of our marriage."

"And so why aren't you? Because he made a mistake?"

Jane snorted. "He's made a lot of mistakes. We both have, and I forgave him every last one. But he was talking to another woman in a way that he should have saved for me, his wife. I can't just forgive that."

Setting the feed scoop down, Sandy joined Jane on the bale. "I understand that you're hurt. I don't know what your beliefs are, but I believe that if God's willing to forgive me for all my mistakes, I should at least try to do the same for others."

Jane's thoughts drifted to the texts she'd exchanged with Zach. They hadn't been blatantly sexual, and there were no naked pictures involved, but it was inappropriate, and she did like it. She'd never invited that kiss at the hospital, but occasionally, when her mind wandered, she could still feel the tingle on her lips.

"I think it's time we talk about the last three agreements."

"If you think it'll help me come to terms with this situation. But I can tell you right now I won't forgive Ian. You didn't read what he said to some woman he doesn't even know. You didn't see his desire for someone else spelled out on the computer screen. I can't forgive him."

Sandy held her hands up. "Hey, I'm not saying you have to. I'm simply trying to give you a different way to look at your situation."

Jane jerked a piece of hay from the bale and twirled it between her fingers. "Okay. I'm listening."

"You know the first agreement is to be impeccable with your words. The second is to not take anything personally. Nothing anyone says or does is because of you, but instead because of how they perceive things. That includes what happened with Ian. When you learn to become immune to the opinions and actions of others, you won't feel like a victim anymore."

"It's kind of hard not to take what Ian did personally."

"I never said it would necessarily be easy. That leads right to the third agreement: Don't make assumptions. Did you ask Ian how this came about?"

"I think it's pretty obvious."

"Maybe, maybe not. Communication is the key to any successful relationship, and misunderstandings are the underlying cause of every last one of them falling apart."

Jane sniffed. "He did a really good job of communicating with that girl."

"He was doing a good job of communicating with you too. You were on your way to the best years of your marriage. You can't get to that point without communication and understanding, right?"

Jane shrugged.

"The last agreement is to always do your best, and that definition will change from moment to moment. Your best today will be different than your best tomorrow, and it'll be different still next week. That bar is set high when you welcome your first child into the world and lowered considerably when you have to bury your parents and sister. At times like that just breathing might be the best you can do."

As she glanced at Jane, a heavy sadness flooded Sandy's eyes. "A lot of people claim to be doing the best they can. It's different for everybody, and it's not for anyone else to judge. But if you can honestly say you couldn't have possibly tried harder, done more, loved better, talked sweeter, you'll be able to rest easy at night."

"Nobody does their best one-hundred percent of the time. People screw up."

"You mean like Ian did?"

Jane dropped her gaze.

"And I'm willing to bet he won't be resting easy tonight."

"Are you a religious person, Sandy?"

Sandy turned the gold band on her left ring finger. "Overly religious, no. Spiritual . . .I'd say so."

Jane clenched her hands together. "Do you pray?"

Sandy nodded. "Faith can be like an ocean, ebbing and flowing. I've had moments when I was stronger, and there have been times when I was weak. But through it all, there's no question in my mind that prayer is one of the most important things you can do for a relationship, for people in general." Rising, she returned to Logan's stall to finish up. "Yep, the world would be a better place if we all did a little more praying. And spent a little more time with horses."

Logan bobbed his head up and down, and Jane chuckled. Her voice softening, she said, "I don't know what to believe anymore."

"You've been handed a lot to think about. Listen to your heart. You'll figure it out."

As Jane helped Sandy finish the stalls, they chatted about holiday plans. Finished, they wished each other a happy Thanksgiving, then Jane returned to her Expedition thinking about their conversation and repeating all the agreements in her head.

Be impeccable with your words. Don't take things personally. Don't make assumptions. Always do your best.

She imagined they would be good rules for her kindergarten classroom. *My students would probably do better than me at keeping these agreements. Heaven knows they're much quicker to forgive than I am.*

As she drove back down the driveway and turned onto the quiet county road, she vowed to do her best to make it through the holidays. That alone would surely test the limits of her physical and mental strength.

CHAPTER
Twenty-eight

At noon the next day, all of Jane's family and friends made their way past the roaster, a heaping bowl of mashed potatoes, and several casseroles sitting on the counter buffet style, loading their plates, and then claiming a spot in the small house to eat and visit. Jane filled a plate for her dad first and, serving herself last, returned to the living room to eat beside him.

She enjoyed reminiscing with him about past Thanksgivings and how her mom always had a knack of making each one special. Truthfully, this year Jane was just glad her dad was still with them to celebrate. That was where she tried to keep her thoughts. She visited when approached, but for the majority of the afternoon she hung close to her dad and avoided Ian.

Jane spoke fewer than ten words to him the entire afternoon and tried not to even look at him if she could help it. She knew her words wouldn't be impeccable so she did her very best to just not say anything, which was struggle enough.

At one point, she did spot him at the kitchen table having what appeared to be a pretty deep discussion with Adam, which ended in a brief embrace. Later, from across the room, she noticed Ian and Ava seriously talking about something, then Ava brightened and threw her arms around her brother.

Watching that infuriated Jane. Didn't Adam and Ava know what Ian had done? Standing up in a huff, she stormed into the kitchen, poured a cup of coffee, and carried it out to the small back patio.

She marveled at the beautiful scene in front of her. She'd caught the very moment in the early evening when the sun bent down and kissed the earth, making the whole sky blush. It felt a little like she was an intruder on an intimate moment, and her cheeks heated up as she remembered that moment at the hospital when Zack had kissed her.

The sun and the earth don't belong together either. The sun would destroy the earth, but he still paints her a dazzling sky every morning and every evening. Zack would hang the moon for me if he could, and he wouldn't let me down like Ian did.

Shivering, she raised the steaming mug to her chin to breathe in the heat. Just then someone laid a thick parka across her shoulders. Jerking her head around, she came face-to-face with Ian.

"The food was really delicious. You outdid yourself." His voice was so tentative, the compliment almost came out as a question.

She turned away and sipped the coffee cradled in her hands. "Thanks."

He moved into her line of sight. "Can we talk? Please?"

"Go ahead." She looked past him and lifted her chin. "I don't have anything to say."

"Fair enough." He took a deep breath. "I hired Ava as a part-time assistant to take care of the finances."

She arched one eyebrow. "Why would you do that?"

"I removed the computer from our house. I don't want anything to do with it. So I needed someone who was technologically savvy to help with the bookkeeping. Ava was happy to help. I'm done with everything that dishonored you, Jane. The websites, the pictures, the chat boxes—"

"That list in your own handwriting."

"Everything. It's all gone. After you left, Pastor Ben came over. I accepted Jesus as my Savior and committed to following Him." He stuffed his hands in his pockets. "I want to get right with you too. I don't expect you to forgive me, but I will never stop being truly sorry for what I've done."

Shrugging away from his touch, she hissed, "I'll never forgive you. Never. And I don't believe you. Do you really think moving your computer will keep you from looking at that trash? If you take a smoker's cigarettes or an alcoholic's liquor, are they going to quit smoking or drinking? Sex is everywhere—on the TV, in movies and magazines. You can't even go to the mall without seeing a life-sized poster of a Victoria Secret model wearing nothing but her underwear in the window of their store. You'd have to pluck your eyeballs out of your head not to look at it."

"You're right. And before last night I probably would have taken every opportunity to look, but today I promise you the only woman I want to look at is my wife."

"Well, congratulations. I'm so happy that you've found Jesus and have become a changed man. Again." She felt a twinge of guilt for mocking him, but she was also shamefully satisfied. "But Monday I'm calling Matt Johnson to get the preliminary paperwork started."

Ian staggered back a step. "Is that what you really want after all we've been through together? A divorce?"

Tears stung her eyes and blurred the beautiful sunset. "I want to be married to someone who already desires me, not someone who has to add it to a to-do list. I want to be with someone who will cherish me for *me*, not just because he realizes after twenty years that he could lose his marriage."

A tear slid down Ian's cheek and he swiped it away. "You're right. I haven't cherished you like I should have all these years. And I don't want to lose you, but I'll do whatever it takes to make you happy."

Jane stared at him, trying to understand his motives.

"I'm going to head home. Are any of the kids coming with me tonight?"

"No. They're staying here."

He backed up to the door. "Okay. I'll just talk to you later then. Happy Thanksgiving, Jane." Turning on his heel, he yanked the door open, stepped through, slid it shut, and was gone.

Jane didn't go inside until she was sure Ian was at least halfway home. She grabbed an afghan, curled up on the couch near where her dad reclined in his chair, and watched *A Charlie Brown Thanksgiving* with her children. Samuel cozied up next to her, while Jessica used her hip as a pillow. Bradley and Emma both sprawled on the floor, half watching the classic cartoon and half engaged in a heated game of Rummy.

It should have been the perfect way to unwind and clear her mind after the events of the previous two days. On top of preparing all the food and entertaining their guests, the confrontation with Ian had drained the last of her of her already low energy level, though, and her eyelids grew heavier than the weight sitting on her shoulders.

"Don't stay up too late. Sleeping bags are in the closet. You can camp out here or stay in the spare room."

"Okay, Mom. Good night." The children's unique voices melded into one.

She kissed them all, told them good night, and as soon as she made sure her dad was comfortable in his bedroom, she retired to hers. After changing she collapsed into her bed and pulled the warm comforter up to her chin. Thinking about her conversation with Ian, she quickly grew wearier. Did he think telling her he'd become a Christian magically fixed everything? This was one thing he couldn't fix.

Jesus Himself couldn't fix this.

She grabbed her phone, unblocked Zach's number, and laid it on the pillow beside her. Then she drifted off into a sound sleep.

At eleven o'clock, assuming his brother and sisters had fallen asleep, Bradley changed the channel to ESPN.

"Hey, turn it back. I was watching that."

Bradley remained focused on the sports channel. "Really, Emma? You were watching the news? Stop acting like Dad, just trying to be difficult."

Glaring at him, she sat up on the sofa. "Mom's been flirting with Jessie's teacher. While we were at the hospital one day after school, I caught a glimpse of her email and saw, like, five emails from him in her inbox. She and Daddy went on their date and everything seemed better, and now she won't even look at him. She's tearing our family apart while Daddy has changed and is trying to keep us together."

Bradley popped the footstool down on the recliner, leaned forward, and pointed his finger at his sister. "You need to do a little more investigating, Nancy Drew, because you only got half of your facts straight. Mom won't look at Dad because she found porn on his computer. She accidentally hit the dial button on her phone and called me yesterday when she went over there. I heard their entire conversation. Mom hasn't been perfect, but you can't put this all on her."

Tears slid down Emma's cheeks. "What? That can't be true."

"I'm sorry, Sis, but the fact of the matter is that Mom and Dad are both human, and all we can do is love them. No matter what happens."

"What is going to happen?"

Samuel sleepwalked onto Bradley's lap, curled up into his side, and dozed right back off.

Yawning and stretching, Jessica propped herself up on her elbow. "What are you two yelling about?"

"Nothing important, Jessie." Emma stroked her sister's rumpled hair. "Go back to sleep." She gave Bradley a questioning stare.

"I don't know, Emma," he said, keeping his voice low and hugging Samuel a little tighter to his side. "Mom and Dad have to make their own decisions and we have to let them. But I promised you that nobody will ever tear us four apart, and I keep my promises."

CHAPTER
Twenty-nine

Monday morning Jane headed back to school. After so much time off, her nerves fired up as if it was the first day of a new academic year. The above-average temps added to the first day feeling, and she made the impromptu decision to bundle up a little and walk the few blocks to school, hoping the fresh air might clear her mind and invigorate her spirit. Since she hadn't been on a run for a couple weeks, the exercise would be an added bonus.

Confident that the home healthcare nurse would take excellent care of her dad and Ian would take care of the children, she got ready early and headed down the sidewalk toward Harvest Bay Elementary. The sun was just barely peeking its nose over the horizon, and the cool, quiet morning soothed her battered soul.

As she neared the school building, she spotted a dark-colored Mercedes Benz with tinted windows parked along side the road, and she slowed her steps. A car like that wasn't typical in a small farming town like Harvest Bay.

She squinted against the early morning dimness, but the tinted windows blocked the figure behind the wheel. Her heart rate rocketed as she clutched her purse closer to her body and dashed to the front entrance. Pulling the door open, she glanced over her shoulder just in time to see the unfamiliar car roll away.

Beyond spooked, she used her key in the second set of doors, which always remained locked, and hurried down the dark, echoing hallway to her classroom. She closed the door behind her and leaned up against it. When her racing heart calmed, she fished her phone out of her purse and dialed the town police department.

"Harvest Bay PD, Sergeant Rusty Wilcox speaking."

"Hi, Sergeant Wilcox. It's Jane Garner, kindergarten teacher here in town. I want to report a strange car in front of the school this morning. It took off when I went into the building, but it just sits uneasy with me. Can you patrol the area around the school extra closely today?"

"Did you get a look at the driver?"

"No. The windows were tinted, but I did notice that the car was a dark color Mercedes Benz."

"A Benz, huh? No one in Harvest Bay that I know of owns a car that fancy."

"That's what I thought. I'm sure it's nothing, probably just someone passing through, but you can't be too careful when you're dealing with children."

"Copy that. I'll keep an eye out. Thanks, Jane."

Feeling a little more at ease, she ended the call and started preparing for her day. Her substitute had done a great job, but there was still a stack of papers to grade and lessons to plan. When her students began arriving, she quickly put aside the work that remained to be done, however. She hadn't realized how much she missed these sweet, energetic five- and six-year-olds. As they embraced her tightly, their bright, shining faces smiling up at her, she was thankful that she had been missed as well. Destiny, William, and several others showered her with construction paper cards that meant more to her than she could express.

With her students eager to please their newly returned teacher, Jane surprisingly accomplished a lot of teaching during the first half of the day, but by lunchtime, she was ready for a break. She walked the children to the cafeteria, helped them get settled, and then left them in the care of the lunch monitors, while she returned to her classroom. Dropping into her chair, she heaved a sigh, picked up her phone, and dialed the law firm's number.

The attorney was in court that day, and as the receptionist transferred Jane to his voice mail, she swallowed the thick lump in her throat, wondering whether she should wait until after Christmas. But starting preliminary paperwork would make the process less painful.

It was hard to believe this was actually happening to her, but she had been pushed to her limit. There had been so much hurt that a lifetime couldn't heal her broken heart. A divorce would let them both just move on.

At the beep she left a message and her number, then ended her call. She honestly didn't know whether to laugh or cry. She didn't know how to feel, but she knew she would no longer be let down by the one person who should be lifting her up.

"I just took the first step toward ending my marriage." Her whisper filled the quiet room, turning her intentions into reality, giving her power and scaring the daylights out of her.

"Well, now. Why the sudden change of heart?"

Jane jumped out of her chair, her heart picking up speed as she faced Zach. Smiling, he stepped into the classroom and closed the door.

"Just a couple weeks ago you insisted you were going to make your marriage work."

"Yeah, well, things change." Shrugging, Jane walked on wobbly knees to the giant pocket chart stand and slipped each activity of the afternoon into the see-through pockets. "Don't worry. It doesn't have anything to do with you. I'm not interested in pursuing a relationship with someone who's interested in married women."

He strode up behind her, turned her around in his arms, and backed her up against the dry erase board. "That's good news because I'm not into married women. I only want you." He leaned in so close his cologne filled her senses. "And I'm willing to bet you want me too. If I had to guess, I'd say you haven't stopped thinking about that kiss. I know I haven't."

"You haven't?" she breathed.

Shaking his head, he ran his fingers down her jawline, his thumb gently brushing over her lips. "It's the first thing I think of every morning and the last thing I think of at night. And I want to do it again right now."

"Right now? But I-I can't. Not while we're at school." She hated the fact that his charm and good looks kept sucking her in. But the truth was that she was addicted to being so desired after months of loneliness.

"It's okay." His low voice sent sparks up her spine, and set the core of her being on fire. "No one will know." He leaned closer and softly caressed her lips with his.

In her head she knew this was a very bad choice and there would be consequences to pay, but her heart exploded with excitement and a passion she'd never known. She pressed her body closer to his.

"If no one will know, then do it again."

His grin matched hers as he kissed her a second time.

The moment was fleeting, here and gone in a heartbeat, but, like the first time in the hospital waiting room, it lingered in her memory long after the school day ended and added fuel to the fire that already burned brightly between them.

Later that evening, as Jane helped her dad get comfortable in his bed, he chuckled. "Ya know, it doesn't seem like that long ago that I tucked my lil' lassie into bed. Isn't it funny how ya start out in life needing help and end up the exact same way?"

She kissed his cheek. "I'm happy to help you, Dad. I wouldn't have it any other way."

His tender gaze met hers as he reached for her hand. "And what about your marriage? Are ya happy to help it too? I might have had brain surgery, but I'm not blind. These old eyes see what's happening between ya and Ian."

"I know, Dad. My marriage is ending soon." She hung her head. "I called the lawyer's office and left a message for Matt Johnson today. Ian has done some things that we just aren't going to be able to work through."

"I see." Nodding, he pulled the covers over him. "You can't forgive him, but ya expect him to forgive you."

She crossed her arms. "No, I don't. And whether he forgives me or not is his business, not mine."

"Do ya still love him, Lassie?"

"I love *you*, Dad, but I'm tired and I'm going to bed." She stalked to the bedroom door. "Good night."

"If ya still love him, ya gotta fight for him." He managed to get the last word out as she closed the door.

The weight on her shoulders expanded as she climbed into bed and sank heavily against the pillows. Just then her phone chimed. She smiled as she retrieved Zach's message.

Are you thinking about those secret kisses? Because I am.

She tapped out, *Maybe.*

Are you thinking about more than those kisses? Because I am.

It felt as though an earthquake shook her body. *Like what?*

We could be so good together, Jane, in every way, and you know it.

Her hand trembled as she typed, *Yes, we could.* But before she could hit send, a chimed announced the arrival of another text.

Ian's contact information and picture popped up next to his very simple, yet complicated message: *I love you.*

CHAPTER

Thirty

December arrived later that week bringing with it the gift of a peaceful snowfall. Lining up at the windows, Jane's students pressed their noses against the glass to watch the fluffy flakes. Even Jane became mesmerized and decided there wouldn't be any harm in taking her students out for a few minutes to catch snowflakes on their tongues.

She clapped out a catchy rhythm to grab her students' attention. "Everybody get your coats, hats, and gloves on. We're going outside to do an experiment."

"What kind of 'speriment?" William looked up at her with warm chocolate eyes that melted her heart every time and a cute cowlick on his left side that always made her smile.

"We are going to find out what snowflakes taste like."

A happy cheer filled the classroom as the five and six-year-olds scurried to get dressed in their winter gear.

Pulling on her thick knitted hat, Destiny leaned closer to William. "I bet they taste like chicken," Jane heard her whisper. "Mama says everything tastes like chicken."

Laughing, Jane corralled her class into one straight line and led them to the fenced playground behind the school that ran along a small portion of West Street. The children dispersed like dandelion fluff on a summer breeze, heads tipped back, tongues sticking out, squealing with delight when they actually caught a flake. Jane watched in amusement, and by the time she lined them back up, her side ached from laughing so much.

Whenever her students came out to play, Jane made a habit of being aware of her surroundings and the location of all the children. Now as she waited for the last few stragglers to join the line, she scanned the playground's fenced perimeter one last time. When her gaze reached the far left side, she froze.

A dark gray car with tinted windows rolled slowly down West Street.

A shiver trickled down her spine. "Come on, boys and girls. Let's hurry back inside and thaw out."

Once everyone was safe inside their classroom, Jane got her students started on a worksheet. Figuring they'd be busy for a few minutes, she stepped over to the room phone in the semi-private corner behind her desk and dialed Mrs. Zeller's extension.

The principal picked up on the second ring. "Hi, Jane. Everything okay?"

"I think so." She hesitated. "Has Damien Shoals' status changed?"

"Not that I'm aware of. Why?"

"Monday morning when I walked to school I noticed a dark-colored Mercedes Benz parked in front of the building. It took off as soon as I came inside, but it just didn't feel right so I filed a report with Sergeant Wilcox. I didn't think too much more of it until just a few minutes ago. I took my class out to catch snowflakes, and I noticed what had to be the same car driving very slowly down West Street. I've never seen this car any where in Harvest Bay before Monday."

"I'll look into it right away and let you know what I find out. Good job staying alert and aware."

After hanging up, Jane returned her attention to her students. She tried to shake the nagging sense of apprehension that hung over her, a difficult task between her disintegrating marriage, her developing relationship with Zach, and her dad's health issues.

A knock on her classroom door almost sent her through the roof. But when she snapped her gaze to the door, her heart dove to the pit of her stomach.

Ian stood just outside, holding a vase full of flowers, smiling uncertainly.

"Boys and girls, it's almost time for lunch. Please start cleaning up your supplies. The red table is the first group to wash their hands today."

She hastily stepped out into the hall, leaving the door ajar. "What are you doing here?"

"Sammy is having career day. I thought he told you. He asked me to come talk about construction work." With his other hand he gripped a stack of plastic hard hats.

Jane felt the corners of her mouth turn up. "The boys and probably half the girls will love those hats. Congratulations. You'll earn hero status today."

His smile faltered. "How do I earn hero status with you?"

Jane's gaze shifted past Ian's shoulder just as Zach came around the corner at the other end of the hall. He put on the breaks and met Jane's gaze, holding it for a breath of a second before silently retreating.

Exhaling heavily, Jane accepted the roses. "Thank you for these. They're beautiful, but it's too late for us. We'll never be the same again."

"You said you didn't want it the same. I don't either, but we can be better."

She poked her head into the classroom and instructed the blue table to wash their hands and get ready for lunch.

"I can't discuss this now. I'm working."

"I realize that. There never seems to be a good time. I just want you to be happy, Jane, but I'm not giving up on us." Holding the stack of hard hats against his hip, he stuffed his other hand in his pocket. "Can we discuss it later then? Maybe Sunday after church?"

"Yeah, maybe. We'll see." She swung the door open and stepped back into the classroom. "You're taking the kids for the weekend, right?"

"Yeah. We're leaving right after school today and driving to Pittsburgh."

"You mentioned that. I'm not so sure I feel comfortable with you taking the kids out of state."

"Ava will be with us, and it's just for the night. We'll be back tomorrow evening." He dropped his gaze to the tile floor, and then lifted it to meet hers. "I thought Pittsburgh would be better than taking them all the way to Washington D.C."

Jane arched her eyebrows. "You called your parents?"

Ian nodded. "I was thinking about what you said in the mall. It's just for lunch tomorrow, but it's a baby step in the right direction." He reached out to her. "I'd love for you to come with us."

She shrank back out of his reach and shook her head. "I don't think so. It'll be good for you and Ava to get reacquainted with them and for the kids to get to know their grandparents." She gave him a parting wave. "Thanks for the flowers. Sammy's probably waiting for you. I'll talk to you sometime later."

She slowly closed the door to her classroom, feeling as though she closed the door to their marriage as well. And a hollow, empty feeling settled in her heart.

Sitting with her dad in the living room, Jane stared out the window that faced the street. About an hour earlier the sun had called it a day, while the street lamps and the thumbnail of a moon took over the night shift.

Ian, Ava, and the kids are probably almost to their hotel by now.

Jane wasn't sure how she felt. This was what she had wanted. She didn't wish to spend the majority of the weekend in close quarters with Ian. When she looked at him now, all she could see were those erotic words he'd written to someone he didn't even know.

She wanted to hold on to that grudge. It hurt her too much to just forgive him and let it go, especially after all they'd shared the night of their date and the morning afterward. But instead of celebrating having a weekend mostly to herself, she felt strangely left out. She'd had no idea that this arrangement she thought she wanted would leave her feeling so lost and alone.

She enjoyed spending time with her dad and focusing on his needs, but he seemed more easily agitated since his surgery. The doctors had cautioned her that this might happen, especially if there was any swelling in the areas of the brain that affected his personality, but that didn't make it any easier to cope with. It only magnified the intense feeling of loneliness.

Her thoughts drifted to Zach. She wondered if he was thinking about her too. As their relationship grew closer, Jane felt even more emotional turmoil. Nothing about what they were doing was right, but the few moments they found each day to sneak a quick embrace and the flirtatious texts they sent back and forth boosted her confidence. And during the evening Zach's messages became longer and more descriptive, often leaving her with rosy cheeks and a racing pulse.

It felt so good to be desired.

She checked her phone again. It had been a couple hours since she'd heard from him, and she was craving his attention.

She pushed off the couch, went to her room, and changed into a few layers of running apparel. She wasn't going to sit around feeling sorry for herself, and watching one more minute of *Wheel of Fortune* would make her go insane.

Before leaving, she kissed her dad on the cheek. "I'm going for a run. I won't be long. You have your Life Alert button around your neck and my number on speed dial in case you need anything, okay?"

"Go on, Lassie. I'll be fine." He waved her away, and then shouted the answer to the puzzle. "Good things come to those who wait!"

Chuckling, Jane headed out the front door and down the sidewalk, slushy with snow. She adjusted her headphones under her ear warmers and pulled her scarf up on her neck, then took off on a slow but steady pace. Consciously staying on well lit roads, she focused on her destination—of this run and of her life. What did she really want?

She wanted to find something to ease the ache in her heart and clear the loneliness deep in her soul. She wanted someone she could run to, who would be there for her. And after pounding the pavement for fifteen minutes, she'd almost reached him.

She had never been to Zach's apartment, but they'd texted about it enough to know right where it was. She often drove by, imagining what it was like inside. Now reaching his street, she slowed to a walk, each step more hesitant than the last.

What am I doing? And what exactly do I expect to happen when I get there?

Jane checked her phone. He still hadn't messaged her.

Maybe he's not home. Maybe I should just turn around right now.

Despite her reservations she kept putting one foot in front of the other. Her phone chimed, and she quickly opened her messages. Her smile faded, however, when she saw that the text was from Ian.

We're here. Wish you were too.

She let out a small groan. *How can he think it's even remotely reasonable for me to just forgive him and take him back like nothing ever happened?*

The message filled her with new resolve. She was moving on with her life, starting right now.

As she approached Zach's apartment, she saw lights on inside and someone's shadow pass by the window. Her heart leaped, and her knees wobbled.

Ian had been her one and only for over twenty years. It annoyed her that they'd gotten so comfortable with each other that neither one of them found it necessary to close the bathroom door any more. Yet the idea of starting over again terrified her.

It won't be so scary anymore after tonight.

The pep talk propelled her forward. Taking a deep breath, she stepped up onto the small stoop and knocked.

After a moment the door opened a body's width, revealing Zach, shirtless with the top button of his jeans undone and his thick hair rumpled, He stared at her with a perplexed expression.

He was so handsome he looked like a model on the cover of a magazine. Self-conscious of her own appearance, she ripped her ear warmers off and ran her fingers through her short hair, damp with sweat.

"What are you doing here?"

She'd imagined all kinds of greetings on the run over, but this wasn't one of them. "Umm . . . well . . . I was just out for a run and thought I'd stop by. Is this a bad time?"

"Yeah . . . kind of." He scratched his head. "You ran all the way over here? With snow on the ground?"

"The sidewalks are just wet, and I'm dressed for it. But I'm getting chilled now. Can I come in?"

"Uh—"

A voice from the other side of the door cut him off. "Zach, sweetie, is that our pizza?"

Jane stared hard at him. Suddenly the dense fog surrounding the situation lifted, and everything became crystal clear. She felt like an idiot for not recognizing it sooner.

"That's the waitress from Pancake Palace, isn't it? And that phone call I walked in on when I was going to invite you to homecoming—it wasn't your mom, was it? It was her. Or maybe another girl?"

Acting on impulse, Jane shoved the door out of Zach's grip, revealing the young woman from the restaurant. Her long hair was damp, and she only wore a towel wrapped around her unnaturally tanned and toned body.

"You might want to tell her she's not dressed for pizza." Feeling the sting of angry tears, Jane took a step back, putting distance between them. "And while you're at it, tell her how you sneaked kisses from me and sent me dozens of texts and emails declaring your love for me, elaborately describing how good we could be together."

As she turned away, Zach caught her arm. "Jane, wait. Brea and I aren't exclusive. She knows I see other people."

"Good for you and Brea. But I didn't know that."

"Of course you did. You see someone else every time you go home at night. You can't expect me to be dedicated to you when you're dedicated to someone else."

"Because I'm married." Hot, angry tears streamed down her face, cooling fast in the freezing air. "I never wanted this, but you and all your pretty words sucked me in and made me think there was something right about something so wrong. Now it's all very clear to me. I am stupid and gullible, and you are a manipulative liar. If I never see you again, it'll be too soon." She took off down the sidewalk, forcing herself not to look back.

His voice trailed after her. "I am not a liar!"

On the long run home, all the beautiful things he'd said to her and all the flattering messages he'd sent came flowing out with her tears. *Lies. They were all lies. When he told me I was beautiful and talented, making me feel like he actually saw me as special, they were just lines. He was saying the same thing to other women. When he told me I deserved to be cherished from day one instead of after twenty years, he didn't mean it. He just wanted to win. I compromised my morals and jeopardized my professional reputation for someone just playing a game of chase.*

The thought made her sick. And as she stopped and heaved the contents of her stomach onto the ground, she was thankful she hadn't eaten much for supper.

She knew exactly where she was physically. She knew all these streets by heart and could probably make it back to her dad's blindfolded. But she had never been more spiritually lost.

A wedge had started separating her from the Lord with the loss of her first pregnancy. Her mother's death and her failing marriage had driven it further. After discovering her husband had been lusting after other women, she'd turned her back on God.

But now, after she'd indulged in some crazy fantasy that made her feel good, and worse, after she'd made up her mind to engage in an affair, surely God had turned his back on her. No amount of faith could bridge the divide between her and her Creator now. She had acted so despicably that she couldn't believe she was worth the attempt to cross the gap. Not after today. She wasn't worth saving.

She burst through the front door of the home she'd grown up in, where she often found comfort and solace, and raced to her bedroom. Slamming the door shut, she fell onto her bed and wailed.

There was no comfort to be found today. She ached from her head to her toes. Her chest hurt from the cold air and her broken heart. Her head throbbed at the thought of her poor choices and stupid decisions.

I can't believe I was so naive to actually fall for his sweet talk. Even after Dad tried to warn me.

Hugging her knees to her chest, she wept from the depths of her soul. *Mom, where are you? I need you so much. I feel so alone. I've been selfish and made mistakes because they made me feel good for a moment. Oh, Mom, I'm so lost. I don't know how to feel whole again with you gone. I just want peace.*

The brief, irrational thought floated into her mind that whatever afterlife there was didn't sound so bad if her mom was there. Remembering that her dad kept a box of her mom's belongings on the top shelf in his closet, she bolted to his room on the off chance that she might find something to numb her pain. Seventeen-year-old medicines couldn't possibly be as potent as when they'd initially been prescribed, but maybe there would be something to help her block out her tormenting thoughts so she could get some rest.

Heaving the box down, she lugged it to her room. Her dad had fallen asleep watching *Jeopardy,* but she shut and locked her door to ensure her privacy. When she lifted the lid off the box, the familiar scent that wafted out of it caused a tidal wave of emotion.

She pulled out one of her mom's favorite scarves, buried her face in it, then draped it across her shoulders. She found some jewelry, including her mom's wedding band, and tried each piece on. There were no prescription bottles, and truthfully she didn't expect there to be any. She just wanted to find something, anything, to take away the heartache.

Moving two photo albums aside to look at when she felt stronger, she gazed at what she'd uncovered. Her mother's Bible.

Fresh tears blurred her vision as she gently lifted it out of the box. She'd seen it lying on her mom's bedside table, but she'd never opened it or looked through it. Her mom had often said it was her most valuable possession. Jane had never understood how a book could be worth more than her mom's diamond engagement ring or antique china, but she respected her mother's words. Now, as she opened the burgundy leather cover, she felt as if she was on the verge of uncovering a secret treasure.

The first few pages listed a family tree and significant dates—births, marriages, and deaths. Jane touched the familiar perfect cursive, wishing she could feel her mother through the pen strokes. She found her name under births, and again with Ian's name under marriages. She hadn't realized how much she missed seeing her name in her mother's handwriting.

She glanced under deaths and her breath caught in her throat as she read the words, "Baby Garner—July 17, 1996."

She knew? Mom knew about my baby. All this time I thought I was so alone, grieving in private, but Mom was grieving with me.

New tears surfaced, tears of relief that a heavy burden had been lifted off her shoulders, and a small measure of peace came with the knowledge that her shameful secret hadn't been a secret from her mom.

Throughout the Bible, Jane noticed Post-It Notes and pieces of lined notebook paper sticking out. Curious, she flipped to the first one. Psalm 27:14 had been highlighted, and Jane read it out loud, hoping to hear her mother in her own voice.

"Wait on the Lord; Be of good courage, And He shall strengthen your heart; Wait, I say, on the Lord!"

Her hand trembling, she opened the folded piece of note-book paper, and began to read her mother's words.

"Father in Heaven, I am trying so hard to be patient, but it's hard when it seems my husband would rather spend time at work or in the bar than with me. Give me the strength it takes to love him well. Give me the courage to do what's best for both of us. You are a good and merciful Father. I pray you forgive me in advance for the break I must take from Shaun to renew my own spirit. Guide and direct my steps, and help me every day to wait on You, Precious Savior. I pray these things in Jesus' holy name. Amen."

Jane choked on a sob. "Oh, Mom. You knew. All this time you knew exactly what I was going through with Ian."

It eased her spirit to share her marital struggles with her mother in this unconventional way, and somehow in the quiet room, Jane felt her presence. Closing her eyes she basked in that comfort for a moment and released her anger, frustration, disap-pointment, and rejection. Once the tears subsided, she took a breath and turned to the next marked page.

Still in Psalms, Jane read the highlighted verse in chapter thirty-four. "The Lord is near to those who have a broken heart, And saves such as have a contrite spirit."

Unfolding the piece of paper, she read. "Gracious and loving God, You give and take away, and through it all I will praise Your name. Be near to my daughter Jane right now. She needs You more than ever as she is grieving a baby that she was trying to keep secret. Give me the strength to respect her privacy even when I know her pain all too well. After losing two babies before conceiving her, I know it's something you never get over. Your heart never completely heals. I'm begging You, Jesus, fill that emptiness in her life with Your love. Be near to her. Wrap Your arms around my baby girl. Comfort her. Bring her peace. Please, God. Bring my daughter peace. Amen."

Overwhelmed, Jane had no words to express her emotions, only a river of tears. Clutching the Bible to her chest, she rocked back and forth. It seemed as if the motion caused a heavy weight to fall off her shoulders, and a soothing sensation wrapped around her, like a warm, fleece blanket on a cold winter day, easing her troubled spirit. Peace.

When she'd regained strength and the desire to see what else her mom had prayed, she skipped a few Post-It Notes, turned to the next page marked with a piece of notebook paper, and read 1 Corinthians 10:13.

"No temptation has overtaken you except such as is common to man; but God is faithful, who will not allow you to be tempted beyond what you are able, but with the temptation will also make the way of escape, that you may be able to bear it."

Eagerly she unfolded the paper to read her mother's words. "Oh, God, my God, You know my heart. You know I am dedicated to my husband. But I know You see how I enjoy the attention I've been receiving from Jim. Help me to crave Your attention more than anything else, I pray. Help me to love you more than anyone else. Help me to set my sights on things above, not things of this world. And when I am tempted, Lord, make a way of escape. I plead this in Jesus' name. Amen."

Jane stared at the words in shock, then, stifling a gasp, reread the beautiful handwriting. "Mom understood that temptation too!"

She wondered if her dad knew about her mom's feelings. She could easily imagine how heartbroken he would have been if he'd found out.

Guilt gnawed at her spirit as she thought of how she had treated Ian. Remembering how she'd expected her evening to go as opposed to how it turned out, Jane began to see it in a new light. As hurtful as it was to find Zach with another woman, it was a way of escape. After she was certain God had turned His back on her, He had provided her a way out before she made her mistake even bigger.

Inundated with a flood of emotions, Jane decided to only read one more scripture and prayer for now. She turned to 2 Corinthians 12:8-10.

"Concerning this thing I pleaded with the Lord three times that it might depart from me. And He said to me, 'My grace is sufficient for you, for My strength is made perfect in weakness.' Therefore most gladly I will rather boast in my infirmities, that the power of Christ may rest upon me. Therefore I take pleasure in infirmities, in reproaches, in needs, in persecutions, in distresses, for Christ's sake. For when I am weak, then I am strong."

As she unfolded the paper, she caught a whiff of her mom's favorite perfume, and the tears fell before she could even read the words. "The diagnosis came in, God. Stage four cancer. I begged You to please let it not be cancer, and if it was, let it be early enough that a simple procedure could heal me from it. But Your thoughts are not my thoughts, and my ways are not Yours. I will choose to trust You, Lord. I trust that when I'm no longer here you will take care of my daughter. There will be times when she will need her mother. Help her to search inside herself and find me there. You are a God of amazing grace. You have given me a life so much better than I deserve. And as my earthly body weakens, my faith will stay strong. I will praise Your name as long as my heart beats, with every breath I breathe. Amen."

"Thank you, Mom," Jane whispered. "When I was little you held my hand and walked with me to and from school so I wouldn't get lost. You were always there when I needed you. And now you reached out from heaven and helped me find my way." Smiling through her tears, she dropped her gaze to her hand resting in her lap. "I can almost feel you holding my hand, leading me toward my next step."

Closing the Bible, she hugged it to her chest. Finally she picked up her phone and tapped a number on her speed dial. After the fourth, ring it was answered.

"Hi, Kate." Jane's voice trembled. "I'm sorry. I know it's late, but can you come over? I really need your help."

"Give me fifteen minutes," Kate responded.

CHAPTER
Thirty-one

The next morning, after the most restful sleep she'd had in months, Jane rose with the sun, refreshed. She couldn't help smiling at the precious memory of sitting on her bed the night before, gripping her mother's Bible in one hand and Kate's hand in her other as she poured her heart and soul out to God, admitting her sins, pleading for His forgiveness, and asking Him to be the Lord of her life.

It was the most beautiful, magical moment Jane had ever experienced. A peace she couldn't explain wrapped around her and a sweet joy she'd never known rained down on her. She could actually feel her spirit radiate from within her.

She dressed and went to the early service with Kate and Adam, but she wasn't ready to share this experience with Ian yet. She wanted to spend some time focused on finding her worth in Christ first. She agreed with Kate that, after falling into such a dark place, she should pursue regular counseling sessions with Pastor Ben. She had so many buried emotions to dig up and sort out once and for all, but she finally had some peace. She knew the difference between happiness and joy, and now she had both. Best of all, she had hope.

That hope intensified every day closer to Christmas. Having her students come to school so excited renewed the childlike wonder in her spirit. On the last day before break she decided she would share her news with Ian that evening after the school Christmas program. She truly hoped he would forgive her and allow her to move back home to stay.

When her class arrived back in their room after spending the majority of the morning practicing for the program, Jane allowed her students to relax on the large carpeted area. She put *A Charlie Brown Christmas* on the smart board for them to watch during the fifteen minutes before lunch. Returning to her desk where a short stack of papers waited for her, she reached for her phone in her back pocket as the school's P. A. system came alive with static feedback, followed by Mrs. Zeller's urgent voice.

"Attentions teachers! This is a code red lockdown. I repeat a code red lockdown. Lock your doors immediately and go to your place of safety. This is not a drill."

Code red is imminent and major danger to school safety. Jane bolted out of her chair, her heart racing as she rushed to the door. She glanced over her shoulder at the frightened faces and found Destiny's among them.

"It's all right, boys and girls. Mrs. Zeller is just keeping us all extra safe. Don't worry. Everything will be fine."

She had no idea if that was true. In all of her years of teaching at Harvest Bay Elementary, she'd never heard such desperation in Mrs. Zeller's voice.

She grabbed the handle, exhaling a small sigh of relief as she pulled the door closed. An instant before it could click shut, however, the handle was yanked out of her grasp as the dor jerked open.

Jane looked up in horror into the grim face of Damien Shoals and stumbled several paces back. Stepping into the classroom, he shut the door behind him and pulled out a gun.

Behind her she heard several children start to cry. But what broke her heart most of all was Destiny's anguished scream.

"No, Daddy, don't!"

Jane rushed to corral her students into a tight group, keeping them behind her, with Destiny in their midst. Clearing her throat, she turned back to Damien, sucked in a breath and, voice trembling, said, "Good morning, Mr. Shoals. Every parent is welcome in my classroom, but not with a gun. Please put the weapon down and we can talk."

That seemed to infuriate him, and he lifted the gun, aiming it at her head. "I didn't come here to talk. I want my daughter! Seems the courts think I ain't fit to see her. I'm gonna take her and leave town so they won't be able to stop me."

"Mr. Shoals, I understand. I have four children of my own, and I'd hate to not be able to see them." Her voice cracked at the realization that she might never see her children again. Suddenly understanding his desperation, she gathered her courage. "But this isn't the way to do it. I assure you the police will find you. Unless . . ." She hesitated.

"Unless what?"

She cringed at the rage in his voice. The sway in his step, his unfocused eyes, and the edginess of his demeanor indicated that he was high on something. A plan began to form in her mind.

He jabbed the gun in the air. "Unless what, woman?"

She took a careful step toward him and lowered her voice. "Unless we devise a plan to get you and Destiny out of the country."

She held her breath. *Please, God, please have him take the bait and play along.*

She heard a rustling outside in the hallway. Mrs. Zeller was evacuating the other students. Thankfully, Damien was too busy thinking about Jane's suggestion to notice.

Without warning, he closed the gap between them and struck her across the face with such force it knocked her to her knees. Her students began to wail.

William ran forward to help her, and as she looked up at him with tears welling in her eyes from the pain, she managed a small smile. "I'm okay, Superman. Go back with the others and stay with Destiny."

"You think I'm stupid?" Damien screamed the words. "Why'd you help me?"

She pressed her hand against her stinging cheek and stumbled to her feet. "We all need help every now and then."

"Give me one good reason to trust you!"

Jane forced herself to remain calm. "The way I see it, you don't have a choice. By now the local police are probably here and have put a call in to the State's Special Response Team. This situation will be resolved one way or another, and you'll be removed from this building either in handcuffs or a body bag."

"I ain't afraid to die."

The coldness of his tone shook her, but she refused to let him see it. "It doesn't have to come to that. I know a way out of this building that the police won't think to check." She eyed him to gauge whether or not he was buying her lie.

Damien's eyes narrowed as he looked from her to Destiny, who shrank back out of his sight. "And what happens after Destiny and me gets out?"

"We can't discuss that right now." She motioned toward the children cowering in fear. "Little ears. They'll hear everything and blow our cover. You have to let them go."

"What?" Reaching out, he grabbed a handful of her hair, pulled her to him, and snarled, "I ain't lettin' any of the little brats go, you hear me? It's the only way to get what I want."

Jane fought to keep her composure. "You're wrong. You have options, and these children are only going to slow you down."

He shoved her away from him, and she stumbled backward. Increasingly agitated, sweat beading his face, he strode over to the window.

"Half the town's out there already."

"Then you better decide fast. What's it going to be?"

He waved the gun around, while pacing back and forth, muttering to himself. Abruptly, he stopped and pointed the gun at her. "Okay. Get those kids out'a here, and then get me and Destiny out. Hurry up!"

She could hear Destiny's sobs, but she blocked out the sound. "Boys and girls, line up at the door, please. Quickly."

Damien returned to the window to watch the activity outside, a scowl contorting his face. She kept a wary eye on him over her shoulder as she edged over to her desk and grabbed a pad of paper and a pen. Hastily she scribbled a note, tore it off the pad, and folded it in half.

Dear God, just get these babies out of here safely.

Positioning Destiny in front of her to shield the terrified child from her father's line of vision, Jane said, "William?" When he stepped forward, she stooped and whispered, "It's time for you to really be a superhero. Think you can do that?"

He stood up straight and gave her a firm nod. "Yes, ma'am."

"Good. I want you to lead your classmates straight out the front doors. Don't stop until you see Mrs. Zeller. There'll be police officers there, too, but don't be frightened. They're there to help you. Do you understand?"

The boy nodded.

Jane glanced over her shoulder to find Damien still preoccupied with the crowd and muttering to himself. She turned back to William and handed him the piece of folded paper.

"Two more things, Superman. These are very important so listen carefully. I need you to give that to Mrs. Zeller and tell her it's for Mr. Garner." Her voice wavered.

There was so much more she wanted to tell Ian, so much more life she wanted to live with him. But there was no time to think of that now.

She moved her class to the door. "All right boys and girls. William will lead you outside just like we're going to the buses. Stay in a line and walk quickly."

William looked at her quizzically. "Wait. What's the second thing, Mrs. Garner?"

Jane darted a quick glance over her shoulder one last time, took a deep breath, and put Destiny's hand in his. "Hold onto her. Don't let go until you reach Mrs. Zeller."

She could see the questions and fear in eyes at leaving her alone with this man, and she straightened, waving the children off. "Now go. Hurry. No dawdling. Go!"

While the children obediently filed out of the classroom, she quickly devised another plan, hoping this one would be equally successful. Acting fast, she pulled her cell phone out of her back pocket, hit the call log, and found the police station still near the top of the list. She knew that if no one was at the station, the call would be forwarded to Sergeant Wilcox's cell phone, giving the authorities an ear into her classroom. She hit dial, locked the screen, and slipped it back into her pocket as her last student made it through the doorway.

Oh, dear God, please be near. Taking a deep breath, she shut the door and leaned against it.

The click echoed in the near empty classroom and captured Damien's attention. He shifted his narrowed gaze from the commotion outside to the cheerful room and to the only other person left in it.

Ian lifted his hammer to drive in a nail just as his phone rang. It was Adam.

"Hey, Adam. What's u—"

"Ian, get down to the school. We're on lockdown over here, and all I know is an intruder with a gun is inside the building. I haven't heard from Kate. Man, that's our wives and kids over there!"

Ian reached his truck and had his key in the ignition before Adam finished talking. "On my way."

He ended the call and tore across town to where his whole world hung in the balance, uttering the only prayer he could think of: *God, keep them safe! Keep them all safe!*

Screeching to a stop in front of the school, he cut the engine, jumped out, and raced across the snowy school yard. Classes were pouring out of the doors and heading across the street to the football stadium, the designated safe zone where the students could be reunited with their parents. He immediately headed there. When he found Samuel and Jessica he pulled them both out of line and enveloped them in a fierce, tearful hug.

"Thank God! Oh, thank God!" He kissed the tops of their heads, and then searched the river of people for Jane's class. "Where's your mom?"

"I don't know, Daddy, but I'm scared." Tears plopped from Jessica's long eyelashes.

Samuel nodded. "Me too."

"Okay. It's okay." Looking up, Ian saw Mrs. Zeller descending the school's the front steps as Sergeant Wilcox intercepted her.

"There's your principal. Let's see if she can tell us anything."

When they approached, Mrs. Zeller met his gaze with a worried expression. A knot formed in Ian's stomach.

"I don't mean to bother you. We're just looking for Jane."

The principal exhaled heavily. "She's still inside."

Ian could feel his heart thudding inside his chest. "She couldn't evacuate?"

She shook her head. "The intruder is in her room."

Panic like he'd never known flooded his body. "Let me get this straight. My wife's locked in a room with a man with a gun, and we're all just standing out here?" He handed his phone to Jessica. "Call Adam, Aunt Ava, and Pastor Ben. Let them know what's going on. I'm going in there to get her."

Sergeant Wilcox held his hand up and said forcefully, "Hold on, Ian. I can't imagine how you must be feeling, but you can't just rush in there and break them out. You'll not only be putting Jane in more danger, but also all of her students." He rested his hand on Ian's shoulder. "Trust me. Let me do my job. We have all our officers scoping out the building, and the State Highway Patrol Special Response Team has been dispatched. We'll get her out."

"How did this happen?" Ian's voice shook.

"Sergeant Wilcox and I are still trying to put the pieces together, but it seems the intruder broke out of jail early this morning," Mrs. Zeller explained. "We're not sure how or where he went between then and now, but Jane did report a strange car around the area over the past few weeks. Just before lunch our secretary buzzed in a parent who was coming to eat with her child, and she unknowingly held the door open for him. The secretary didn't catch it until he was past the office and halfway to Jane's classroom."

At that moment the school's front door opened and a line of small children walked down the steps toward Mrs. Zeller.

Her eyes widened and she covered her moth with her hand. "That's her class, and the intruder's daughter is with them." She squatted down to talk to the line leader. "William, what's going on here? Where's Mrs. Garner?"

William's bottom lip quivered. "She's still in there with that mean man. She told me to bring Destiny and the rest of the class straight to you and to give you this. It's for Mr. Garner."

"You did a good job, William. Thank you for being brave and doing exactly as Mrs. Garner told you." Mrs. Zeller rose and motioned toward Ian. "This is Mr. Garner. You may give the note to him, and then we'll go see if Mrs. Goodwin can walk you to our safe area and stay with you until Mrs. Garner can join you."

His face creased with worry, William handed Ian the folded piece of paper, then followed his friends as Mrs. Zeller led the class away. Ian unfolded the paper. He could barely read Jane's handwriting, and he tried not to imagine what had been going on in the classroom while she wrote the note.

Dear Ian,

I love you. I've always loved you and I'll love you forever. Just wanted you to know.

Jane.

Clutching the paper to his chest, Ian sank to his knees in

the muddy snow. "God, please help her. I can't fix this. She's in Your hands. Please let me see her again."

"Hey, Margaret." Sergeant Wilcox waved Mrs. Zeller over. "Listen to this." He put his cell on speaker phone. There was so much racket it was hard to make out any voices.

Mrs. Zeller knit her brow together. "What is it?"

"Jane must have called the station, and it was forwarded to my cell. She's giving us an ear into what's happening in that room. That'll help us figure out the right time to go in and get her." He turned to Ian. "You sure do have one brilliant wife."

Ian managed a shaky grin. "You haven't seen anything yet."

Using her arms as a shield, Jane cowered in a corner, while Damien continued his rampage, throwing chairs and throwing over tables. "You lied!" He tipped over her book shelf with a thunderous crash.

"My job is to keep Destiny and all of my students safe."

"Well, you were stupid to have stayed because now I hafta kill you. You screwed up my plans!" Damien bellowed in seemingly complete and utter frustration.

"Look, I understand you want to see Destiny, but kidnapping her isn't the way to do it."

"What do you know? You don't know nothin' 'bout me."

"I know you made some bad choices, but I also know it's not too late to change. I made some mistakes that could have cost me my family, too, but with Jesus' help I changed."

"Jesus? What can Jesus do for me?" Damien snorted in disgust. "Man, you just don't get it. When you grow up like I do, there is no change. Everybody in my neighborhood either sold drugs or did 'em. Or both. I wanted a different life, but you just can't break the cycle."

"Mr. Shoals, Jesus can save you, just like He saved me. He can give you a new life, better than you ever imagined, and a future in heaven for all eternity." She took two cautious steps toward him. "There are programs that can help you get and stay clean. The Department of Job and Family Services can help you find a job so you earn an honest living instead of living a life of crime. You can break the cycle."

Damien glared at her. "You lied to me before, and you're lying again." His hand trembled as he raised the gun. "I can't go back to prison."

"Mr. Shoals, you're young. You can serve your time, right your wrongs, and get out in plenty of time to enjoy life with your daughter. But if you kill me, you'll waste your future and spend the rest of your life behind bars."

"You gave me no choice! You screwed up my plans, and I said I'm not going back!" His voice echoed through the room. As his finger tightened on the trigger, there was a loud crash, followed by two gunshots.

And everything went black.

To Ian's relief, Pastor Ben and Ava arrived at the school just after the Special Response Team. One of Kate's team teachers was watching her remaining students, while she stayed with Ian, Mrs. Zeller, and the officers on the school lawn. Only Adam was missing. The high school remained locked down, but Ian knew Adam had his phone with him while keeping his students safe and calm.

They stood huddled around Sergeant Wilcox's cell phone listening to the escalating situation inside Jane's classroom. "She's doing a good job trying to talk him down," one of the special response team members commented.

Ian blew out a breath. "So when can you go in and get her out?"

"Soon. I have officers entering the building now."

"Mr. Shoals, Jesus can save you, just like He saved me. He can give you a new life, better than you ever imagined, and a future in heaven for all eternity." Jane's words came through the speaker loud and clear.

"She's saved?" Ian blinked back tears as he shifted his gaze to Kate. "When did that happen?"

Kate's eyes shone with moisture. "When you were in Pittsburgh. She wanted to focus on discovering who she was in Christ before she told you. I hope you're not upset."

He shook his head and swallowed a lump of emotion, unable to speak. Tears slid down his cheeks.

She knows no matter what happens, she'll be all right. And I do too.

"Okay, folks. My officers just radioed. They're in position. It's time to get her out," the special response team leader informed the group.

The knot in Ian's gut tightened. Fear like he'd never known gripped his heart.

"You gave me no choice! You screwed up my plans, and I said I'm not going back!" The intruder's booming voice was punctuated by a loud crash and two gun shots. A second later the call ended.

"What happened?" A bubble of panic settled in Ian's brain. "Why did the call drop? Is my wife okay? Please tell me my wife's okay."

"I don't know why I lost the call, but those officers are very good at their job," Sergeant Wilcox said reassuringly. "I'm sure—"

An unfamiliar voice came over the special response team leader's radio. "I need an ambulance on the scene ASAP. Gunshot wounds to the shoulder and chest."

"Jane!"

Ian sprinted across the lawn toward the building. When he reached the steps he stopped short, his eyes widening as an officer pushed through the door with Jane leaning on his arm.

Waves of joyous relief washed over Ian. He half ran, half stumbled up the steps, and swept her up into his arms. Burying his face in her hair, he wept.

"Thank God you're safe. I was so afraid . . . " The thought of how close he'd come to losing her choked the words in his throat. Pulling back, he held her at an arms length, anxiously taking in the purpling lump on her forehead. "Are you okay? Did he hurt you?"

Jane swiped her own tears away. "I passed out when the officers burst through the door, and I hit my head. Other than that, I'm fine."

The wail of a siren cut off her words as an ambulance pulled up in front of the school. Two paramedics emerged and bolted up the steps and into the building.

Ian stretched his hand out to the officer. "Thank you for rescuing her."

He gave Ian's hand a firm shake. "Your wife did all the hard work, and the intruder took himself out. We didn't have to fire a shot." The officer started down the steps. "You might want to get your wife's head checked though. She's got a pretty good goose egg."

"All right. And thank you again."

Jane looked up at Ian, her chin quivering. "There's so much I want to tell you."

"Shhh." He pulled her tight against his chest and held her there, memorizing the feel of her in his arms, the scent of her hair. "We've got time for that. Right now all that matters is that you're free."

They both were finally free.

Epilogue

Jane awoke with a start, gasping for air, her heart racing. Even after all this time she still had nightmares about that terrifying ordeal.

As always before, Ian's arm tightened around her. For a breath of a second she couldn't remember where she was. But once her eyes adjusted to the silver moonlight pouring through the open window and the mosquito netting that enveloped their bed, she exhaled and relaxed against his bare chest.

"You all right?"

She nodded and allowed herself to drift back to that beautiful moment when the officer had led her out through the school doors and into the sunlight. She hadn't seen anyone on that snowy lawn except for Ian, flanked by Jessica and Samuel, half her whole world. She remembered being engulfed in Ian's embrace, the second sweetest feeling in her life next to that moment when she committed her future to Christ. And when Bradley and Emma arrived, the six of them stood there for some time just holding one another.

"I ought to be over this by now," she murmured.

"Hey, babe, you went through a really traumatic experience. It's only been six months. Your counselor said it could take years to work through all of it."

"I know." She tipped her head to look up at him. "But God has brought some good things out of it, hasn't He?"

She could see his smile in the moonlight. "Us. Together again. But better. So much better."

She let out a contented sigh. "And Damien too. I wouldn't have believed it was possible before the Lord changed me."

He bent to look into her eyes. "If the Lord can change a man like me, He can change anybody."

She grinned at his dry tone. After a moment she mused, "It seems strange to say it, but going back to prison may be the best thing that's happened to Damien. It's going to be a long time before he gets out, but that prison ministry is making such a difference. So far he's staying clean of the drugs, and he's hoping for a better future. The change in him the last time I visited was amazing. I'm just praying that Destiny and her mother can forgive him."

"You have," Ian reminded her.

"I have," she agreed. "God can use all things for good for those who love Him." She twisted around to face him. "Like this trip. Who ever thought we'd go on a mission trip together?"

They both laughed.

"When Pastor Ben announced he planned to take a team to Malawi for two weeks, and I said we ought to volunteer to go as our second honeymoon, I didn't expect you to agree so fast," Ian teased. "You didn't even bat an eye."

A smile spread across Jane's face. "It just sounded like the kind of adventure we needed."

And it has been the greatest adventure, she thought.

Ian was using his God-given talents to make much-needed repairs to houses in the town. Jane had packed some of her art supplies, and every day she painted and played with the children after serving them their one meal for the day. And both of them felt that they received so much more from these desperately poor people than they could ever give.

Through it all they felt their hearts growing, blossoming, opening further to the Lord and to each other. And when they collapsed into their bed each night, side by side, almost falling asleep before their heads hit the pillows, it didn't seem like a honeymoon at all.

It meant so much more.

Only a few days remained before they had to leave Malawi. Suddenly she was eager to get back home, back to their children so she could tell them about the people they'd been given the privilege of serving. Maybe next time they could go as a family.

She became aware that Ian was studying her intently. "Thinking about the kids?"

She nodded. "It's hard to believe they're a half a world away."

"Not when you have to sleep on a bed like this, it isn't," he said, giving a bounce that caused the ancient bed springs to squeak. He wiped the sweat from his face with the edge of the sheet. "And I don't know about you, but I could sure use some air conditioning. And probably a shower."

She giggled, then slowly sobered. "Seeing how grateful these dear souls are for the little they have makes me feel like we have more blessings than we deserve."

"I think we're going to be a lot more thankful from now on," he agreed. He ran his fingers up and down her bare arm and kissed her shoulder. "Once we get home, you can get back to that nice studio I built for you—"

She grinned at his teasing tone and hushed his words with a kiss. "Thank you. I love it! Those big windows bring in so much natural light that painting is a joy. And all those shelves for my paints and supplies—"

It was his turn to interrupt her with a kiss. "It was your design. The thing I love the best is that we worked on it together."

"And I adore my Sweet Jane roses. I'm so glad you planted them where I can see them from the windows."

"They sure are thriving, aren't they?"

"That's 'cause we both give that bush a lot of attention," she said, arching her brow.

She loved how often that broad grin covered his handsome face nowadays. Knowing she was the source of it warmed her to her toes.

Ian often sat in her studio with her on Saturday mornings while she painted, drinking a cup of coffee and reading the news instead of rushing off to work. He'd stopped working on Sundays altogether, and his business had never been better. It seemed as if they couldn't spend enough time together, and Jane was determined to make sure that never changed.

Having her dad move in with them had also changed a lot of things for the better. It eased the burden of his care for Jane, while Bradley, Emma, Jessica, and Samuel couldn't be happier to have their granddad close. Ian delighted in spending time with him too.

Every couple of months they made a trip to Pittsburgh to visit Ian's parents, and later in the summer, they would take a family vacation to Washington D.C. And together she and Ian had decided that she would return to school in the fall to study art therapy. Their future couldn't have looked more beautiful.

She felt Ian nuzzle her neck, and his breath tickled her skin. "I got you, babe," he whispered as he drew her to him.

Joy tingling through her veins, she lifted her face to his kiss. "And, baby . . . I got you."

Discussion Questions

Jane Garner

1. In what ways can you identify with Jane? Discuss her strengths and weaknesses.

2. Jane's major conflict throughout this book is feeling valued and important instead of unappreciated and taken for granted. Have you ever experienced such a conflict? Who or what helped you through that time?

3. Initially, Jane's struggle is intensified with the attention and affection of a coworker. But eventually, the Lord reveals the error of her ways and a better plan for her life. Have you ever experienced a time when the Lord turned a struggle into a blessing? Tell about that experience.

4. Read 2 Corinthians 12:8-10. How could this verse be used as a theme Jane's faith journey? How could you apply it to your own personal faith journey?

Ian Garner

1. In what ways can you identify with Ian? Discuss his strengths and weaknesses.

2. Ian's major conflict throughout this book is feeling a lack of respect in his home and searching for it in inappropriate ways. Have you ever struggled with this? How did you overcome it?

3. Ian eventually puts his trust in Adam and takes him up on the offer to attend a church service. Think about someone in your life who never gave up on you. Tell about that individual and what he/she means to you.

4. Read Psalm 66:10-12. How could this verse be used as a theme for Ian's faith journey? How could you apply this verse to your own personal faith journey?

JANE & IAN

1. Two broken individuals, initially at odds with one another, finally really listen to the other's feelings and begin to understand each other's point of view. And through this process, healing occurs for them both in amazing and miraculous ways. Have you ever experienced a relationship that became rocky, but eventually, with prayer and patience, blossomed into something beautiful? Tell about that experience.

2. Read Romans 8:28. How could this verse be used as a theme for their marriage? How could you apply this verse to relationships and/or situations in your own life?

Congratulations to Alice-Lyle Hickson who won the "What a Difference You've Made in My Life" contest. Alice-Lyle nominated her son, William Hickson, a brave boy who changed the life of everyone who knew him. It gives me great pleasure to introduce you to . . .

William Hickson

Born on August 17, 2006, William entered this world like a superhero, capturing the heart of everyone who got to cuddle and kiss him. For many months it seemed to be the perfect family: a devoted mother, a hardworking father, a protective big brother, a nurturing big sister, and a beautiful baby boy.

Gradually, however, several things—reflux, slow development, seizures—led William's family to seek answers from a neurologist. The results from a muscle biopsy confirmed their worst fear. At eighteen months old, William was diagnosed with Mitochondrial disease, a chronic illness that causes debilitating physical, developmental, and cognitive disabilities. It's a progressive disease for which there is currently no cure.

His remarkable family chose not to allow his disability to define his life as a tragedy but to cherish him as the blessing he was. If he couldn't take on the world, his family would make every attempt to share as much of the world with him as they could. His adventures included being kissed by a princess in Disney World, crossing the finish line of a 5-K race with his mom and dad, trick-or-treating with his brother and sister, and hitting the surf on the Carolina beaches.

Along the way, William touched the hearts and forever changed the lives of his family and friends, his compassionate caregivers, and skilled medical professionals with his sweet disposition and laid-back attitude. You could regularly see him bright-eyed, with a smile on his face and wearing one of his many fun T-shirts displaying the best messages, including: "My cape is in the wash" and "I'm always on vacation."

On March 9, 2015, five months before his ninth birthday, William's long-lashed, chocolaty eyes fluttered closed for the last time as he breathed his last breath. Many may say that Mitochondrial disease prevented William from really living, but in reality he lived better than most. He never told a lie or became impatient or did even one hurtful thing. William Hickson was a real-life superhero.

In *The Heart's Hostage* we meet William's character in Jane's kindergarten classroom, where he is a healthy, active boy, an engaged student, and a caring friend. I pray that who reads *The Heart's Hostage* will be inspired by William—the brave little boy with a superhero's heart.

> *Congratulations also go to Bridgette Firestone, our second winner in the contest. Bridgette nominated her dear friend, Sandy Lovato, a wonderful, wise and compassionate lady who made a difference in many lives as you will soon see through her character in this book. It gives me great pleasure to introduce you to . . .*

Sandy Lovato

Born on December 15, 1959, Sandy (Sweet) Lovato became passionate about animals, specifically horses at an early age. She got her first pony when she was just 5 years old and showed horses throughout her childhood. Shortly after she graduated from high school, she moved to Hialiyah to work with a horse trainer. There she met the love of her life, jockey Frankie Lovato, Jr, who was working with a horse in the same barn as Sandy's, and the two were eventually married. In 1979, they moved to New York where they settled down and raised their three children.

Sandy loved to be involved with programs that helped people. She served as PTA president, where she received numerous service awards for her dedication and time. She also served as President of the Wooden Horse Corporation, a family-owned company that produces the Equicizer, a mechanical horse that simulates riding to improve overall fitness and practice skills, while exercising specific areas of the body and muscles needed for riding horses.

In 2006, Sandy and her husband returned to her hometown. She became a caregiver to her older sister who had polio, making her final years on this earth as comfortable as possible. Through that experience, as well as witnessing the benefits of the Equicizer, Sandy became inspired to begin a therapeutic riding program for children with disabilities. Her dream began coming true in 2009 when she founded Stampede of Dreams in Norwalk, Ohio. SOD is a 501c3 non-profit program offering Equine Assisted Horseback Riding lessons that provide therapeutic benefits for children and adults with special needs.

In 2010 Sandy became a PATH International Certified Therapeutic Riding Instructor. The difference she made in the lives of individuals with disabilities was profound. She also made a difference in the life of her granddaughter, Allie, to whom she passed her love of horses.

On September 3, 2014, Sandy tragically lost her life in a car accident. But the impact she left on the hearts of her family, friends, and those involved with Stampede of Dreams continues.

In *The Heart's Hostage*, Sandy's character is the gentle, wise, compassionate director of Stampede of Dreams where Jane becomes a volunteer in order to be involved in something that matters. Sandy helps Jane through her struggles with her marriage by encouraging her to pray and introducing her to the Four Agreements. I pray that through this story Sandy's memory is honored in the utmost way: that everyone who reads *The Heart's Hostage* will be inspired by Sandy to see the best in a situation and always use the power of words for truth and love.

Acknowledgements

Everything happens in His timing. I truly believe that, and *The Heart's Hostage* has proven to be no exception. During this long writing process, I've only become more aware and appreciative of the people in my life who helped make this book possible.

First, and above all else, Father God, I'm eternally grateful for Your grace and mercy. Thank You, my Savior, for loving me with a love far greater than any human being has ever known. Thank You, my King, for forgiving me and for choosing to see my potential instead of my failures. Thank You, sweet Jesus, for sacrificing everything so I can have the hope of a brighter tomorrow. I pray my stories bring glory and honor to You, my Rock and my Redeemer.

Alison, I'm so thankful God chose me to be your mother. You have a wonderful sense of humor, just like your Pepaw. I love your compassionate spirit, and your brilliant creativity keeps me inspired. Olivia, my world became sweeter the day you were born. I'm so proud of your independence and perseverance, and I love your gentle spirit. Soon, both of you girls are going to spread your wings and soar, but no matter where you go in this great big world or what you do, you'll always be close to me in my thoughts, prayers, and always in my heart. Nothing will ever compare to the joy of being your mother. I love you so much, Ali and Livi . . . all the way to heaven and back.

Brian, you found me when I was at my lowest, and you were a true friend. Now you are not only my best friend but my true love. You are my teammate and my fellow adventurer in life. You believe in me—as an author, a teacher, a mother—and you believe in us. Because of you, I know a happiness I've never experienced before. Because of you, I look forward to every tomorrow knowing you'll be by my side. You're the answer to my prayers, my real-life hero, and I'll always be thankful you chose me. I love you.

To Chris and Cassidie, thank you for accepting me into your life. You didn't grow in my womb, but you've grown in my heart, and I will always be here for you. Always.

To Joan Shoup and Sheaf House Publishers, thank you so much for believing in me yet again. You've given me the creative freedom I needed to bring this story to life, and you've placed my childhood dreams in my hands not once, not twice, but three times. How can you thank someone for that? I don't know, but I hope I've made you proud.

Marisa Jackson, once again you designed the perfect (pink!) cover for this book. It's beautiful! Thank you. Jim Brown of Jim Brown Illustrations, I just have to thank you again for bringing Harvest Bay to life. The map is stunning and, after all these years, I still find new little details that I love about it. I'm also grateful to Alice Wisler, Shayla Eaton, Kinda Wilson, and Amber Stockton, who took the time to read this book, and then write such lovely endorsements for it. Your words of encouragement were an incredible blessing to me.

To my step-parents, Shirley Dominick LaVoie and Tom Otto, I never truly appreciated you until I became a step-parent. For as long as I can remember you've been there, and though I know I didn't always make it easy, I want to thank you both for loving my parents enough to accept the responsibility of helping to raise someone else's child. As a result, you played a role in making me exactly who I am today, and I'm grateful for it.

Daddy, I miss you! Not a day goes by that I don't wish you were here, but I take comfort in knowing that you are a big part of everything I am today. Thank you for teaching me about living and dying, laughing and crying, for introducing me to a boy named Henry, and instilling in me a love of storytelling. I love you!

To Bonnie Fellows, Julie Roeder, and Karen Pantaleo, my best childhood memories involve you. You're not only my sisters, but you were my first friends and continue to be three of the biggest blessings of my life. Also, to my brothers-in-law, nieces, and nephews, you complete our family, and I love you all.

To my grandparents, Granny and Grandpa Moltz and Grandma Dominick, thank you for giving me the roots I needed to be confident in who I am today. I'm so proud to be your granddaughter.

To my church family at TLC, especially Pastor Amy Little, you accepted and enveloped my girls and me from the very beginning. My family is so blessed to worship with you and I'm deeply grateful for the encouragement and support you have always given me.

To my coworkers and sisters-in-Christ, Molly, Melinda, Tonya, Ranae, Ellyn, Heather, Mikki, and Erika, I'm beyond blessed by your friendship, and so privileged to be a part of what you are doing at Trinity Christian Academy. Thank you for your support in my teaching, my writing, and in my faith journey.

To Farrah, every girl should be so lucky to have a friend like you. You've stuck by me at my worst and celebrated with me at my best. I love you like a sister!

Last, but certainly not least, I thank you, my reader, for picking up another Jen Stephens book. I pray this story captivates your heart long after the final page is turned.